MAGGIE
NEEDS AN
ALIBI

*Also by Kasey Michaels
in Large Print:*

Bachelor on the Prowl
Marrying Maddy
Someone to Love
Raffling Ryan
Jessie's Expecting
Indiscreet
Too Good to Be True
Waiting for You

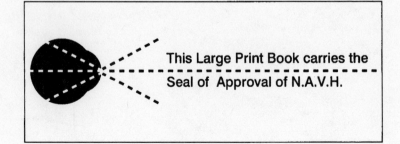

This Large Print Book carries the
Seal of Approval of N.A.V.H.

MAGGIE NEEDS AN ALIBI

Kasey Michaels

Thorndike Press • Waterville, Maine

Published in 2002 by arrangement with Kensington Books, an imprint of Kensington Publishing Corp.

Thorndike Press Large Print Americana Series.

The tree indicium is a trademark of Thorndike Press.

The text of this Large Print edition is unabridged.
Other aspects of the book may vary from the original edition.

Set in 16 pt. Plantin by Minnie B. Raven.

Printed in the United States on permanent paper.

Library of Congress Cataloging-in-Publication Data

Michaels, Kasey.
    Maggie needs an alibi / Kasey Michaels.
      p. cm.
    ISBN 0-7862-4765-7 (lg. print : hc : alk. paper)
    1. Detective and mystery stories — Authorship — Fiction.
2. Women novelists — Fiction. 3. New York (N.Y.) —
Fiction. 4. Large type books. I. Title.
    PS3563.I2725 M28 2002
    813´.54—dc21   2002028911

For Megan and Joe.
Here's to a long, healthy,
and happy life together.

To know is nothing at all; to imagine is everything.

— Anatole France

One never knows, do one?

— Thomas "Fats" Waller

PROLOGUE

It all began innocently enough. A desire to explore a larger world, that's what he said. A chance to step out, expand our horizons, spread our wings, and all of that.

I gave my approval, not that the man had applied for it, and came along because . . . well, that's what I do. Besides, I will have to confess to some curiosity of my own, most especially about the food. The food really interested me.

So we were off, or out, or whatever the vernacular. He thought it would be informative. He said it would be educational.

I supposed it might be fun, a bit of a lark.

Nobody had mentioned murder. . . .

CHAPTER 1

Rock music blared from the speakers on either side of the U-shaped work station, aimed straight at Maggie Kelly's desk chair.

M&Ms were lined up neatly to the right of the computer keyboard, color-coded and ready to eat. Maggie was up to the reds, with the blues always saved for last.

A half-eaten cinnamon-and-sugar Pop Tart topped off the full trash basket shoved under the desktop. An open bag of marshmallows spilled over dozens of scribbled 5 x 8 file cards to Maggie's far left. The bag of individually wrapped diet candies, more a fond hope than a brave supermarket aisle life-changing epiphany, hadn't been opened.

Towers of research books littered the floor like literary Pisas. Others lay open around the base of her chair, scattered about like fallen birds, their spines cracked and broken.

A Mark Twain quote scribbled on a Post-It note was stuck to the edge of the huge, hutch-top desk: "*Classic:* A book which people praise and don't read."

There were two ashtrays on the desk

(sugar fixes always to the right, nicotine fixes to the left, as a person had to have *some* order in her life). One ashtray was usually reserved for the cigarette that was burning, another for the butts. One fire in the waste can had been enough for Maggie to set up this, to her, quite logical system. Today, however, both ashtrays overflowed with butts, while a used nicotine patch was stuck to the larger ashtray.

The entire room, from noise to clutter to smoky haze, advertised the fact that Maggie Kelly was wrapping up the manuscript for her latest Saint Just Mystery.

And, sure enough, in the middle of the mess, dressed in an old pair of plaid shorts, a threadbare T-shirt with *F-U University* printed on it, topped by a navy blue full-length bathrobe that should have hit the hamper a week ago, sat Maggie Kelly herself.

Thirty-one years old. Short, curly, coppery hair with really great, wincingly expensive dark-blond highlights. Irish green eyes; huge, round horn-rimmed glasses falling halfway down her rather pert nose. Unlit cigarette dangling from a full, wide mouth just now curved into an unholy grin. An all-American, cheerleader type . . . with an attitude problem.

9

That was a quick snapshot of Maggie Kelly, the quintessential "successful writer at home." Five feet, six inches, one hundred sixteen pounds of *New York Times* best-selling author.

If she stood outside her Manhattan apartment with her empty teacup in her hand, she'd probably snag a quick five bucks from pitying strangers in ten minutes, tops.

Two Persian cats lay at her feet, snoring. A black one, Wellington, and a grey and white monster named Napoleon. Napoleon was a girl, but that knowledge had arrived after the inspiration for her name, so Napper was stuck with it.

Maggie dragged on the cigarette, frowned when she realized she hadn't lit it, and rummaged on the desktop for her pink Mini-Bic. She bought only throwaway lighters, one at a time, always swearing she would quit smoking and wouldn't need another one. She was beginning to think she was the one faithful consumer standing between Bic's lighter manufacturing division and Chapter Eleven.

She lit the cigarette, squinted as smoke invaded her left eye, and collected her thoughts. After a few moments, her fingers punched at the keys once more as she hunched forward, eyes shut tight as she concentrated.

Maggie was on a roll. She could creep for chapters, that damn "sagging middle" she slaved over, but the end always came to her in a rush. The faster she wrote, the harder she hit the keys. She began chair-dancing, moving to the rhythm of Aerosmith at its most raucous, and the keyboard practically winced.

Saint Just, *she pounded out,* damnable, damned sexy quizzing glass stuck to one dazlzing blue eye, pivoted slowly to face the earl. "One of the people present in this room knows precisely what happened here the night Quigley was murdered. Actually, not to be im-modest, two of us do," he drawled in his maddeningly arrogant way that melted the innocent (at least the fe-males) and inspired dread in the guilty.

Pause. Open eyes. Hit Save. Read. Cor-rect the spelling of dazzling. Eat two red M&Ms. What the hell, eat the whole row. Smile as the next song begins. Keep to the tune, keep to the rhythm.

Maggie tapped both bare-footed heels against the plastic rug-saver beneath her

11

swivel chair while doing her best to "Walk This Way" while sitting down. She could do that today. She could do anything. She was Maggie Kelly, writer. And, hot-diggity-damn, by midnight, she'd be Maggie Kelly, a writer having written.

"For the remainder of our assembled company, my good friend here, Mr. Balder, will help demonstrate as I explain. Sterling, if you please?"

"Again? I'm always the corpse. Don't see why, but all right," Sterling said, walking toward the fireplace to join his friend.

"Ah, very good. Now, if everyone will refresh their memories of the evening poor Quigley met his Maker? Just here, I believe. Sterling?"

Sterling Balder sighed, split his coat-tails, and lay down on the floor, crossing his arms over his ample belly.

"So there he is, poor Quigley, his life-blood draining away. Sterling, please try not to look so robustly healthy if you can manage it. Be more desperate, if you can, knowing death is imminent but wanting to tell everyone who did the dastardly deed. Ah, wonderful. And now we need someone to play the murderer. My lord? If you would please be so kind as to take up a position providing a clear shot at Sterling? Pretend he's still upright, as he's looking quite comfortable down there, and we don't want to disturb him."

"Me? Why me? Surely you don't believe . . . you don't think . . . what utter nonsense!" Shiveley backed up a pace, trying to straighten his spine, and failing miserably. He cast his panicked gaze around the crowded drawing room, looking for allies, seeing only unsmiling faces. Condemning eyes. "What are you all looking at? I would never do such a thing. He was my very closest, *dearest* friend."

"Really? And who would say otherwise? But to get back to the murderer. Fortunately for us, your *dearest friend* had time, as he lay dying, to employ his own blood to tell us all who killed him. That's it, Sterling, pretend to write on the marble hearth. I commend you, you're really getting into the spirt of the thing. Shiveley? Now come, come. Be a good fellow and pretend you're the one who fired the fatal shot."

"Oh, very well, but I'm doing this under protest. You're an ass, Saint Just.

Always poking about, pretending to be a Bow Street Runner. As if the word *flowers* means anything to anybody."

Saint Just watched as Shiveley walked to precisely the spot he had concluded the murderer had stood that fatal night. How very helpful of the man, for Saint Just had come into this gathering tonight still unsure of Shiveley's guilt. It was so pleasant when one's hypothesis was proved correct.

"Yes, Shiveley, *flowers*," Saint Just said, shooting his cuffs, careful to contain his glee that Shiveley was behaving just as he'd hoped. He winked at Lady Caroline, wordlessly assuring her that there would be ample time for their assignation later that evening. Wouldn't do to ever disappoint a lady. Especially one of Lady Caroline's talents, who had just lost a bet.

"Excuse me. Where was I? Oh, yes. No one knows what it means. At least, not until one expands their imagination to include sources of flowers. Sources such as the markets in Covent Garden. Flowers. So much easier to spell out in blood than Covent Garden, I suppose, although dying utterances — or, in this case, scribblings — have this nasty way of being unnecessarily cryptic, don't they? Difficult to believe a man known best for his mediocrity could rise to such heights just as he was about to expire, but perhaps approaching mortality concentrates the mind. Still, I digress. Flowers, and Covent Garden. One word, to mean both place and person. Do you know, Shiveley, what I learned when I mentioned Quigley's name in the theatre at Covent Garden? Perhaps if I were to say the name Rose? Does that jog your

Aerosmith's Steven Tyler opened his larger-than-life mouth and screamed.

Maggie screamed with him. Some jackass was leaning on her doorbell. She hit Save — damn near snapping the keys in half — swiveled in her chair, glared at the door. "Go away. She's not home. She broke her leg and we had to shoot her."

Wellie and Napper, who could sleep through Aerosmith at top volume and squared, woke at the sound of Maggie's voice and trotted toward the kitchen, believing it to be time for their afternoon snack, no doubt.

"Eat the dry stuff in the dish," she called after them, "and I'll open a can later."

Damn it. The doorbell. Cats. Was it too much to ask to be left alone? She was just getting to the best part. So was Tyler: "Dream on, dream on . . ." She reached over to the portable stereo system sitting on the shelf of the desk unit and cranked up the volume.

"Had to shoot her? Maggie? Maggie, I know you're in there. Come on, sweetheart, open the door. Can you even hear me?"

Maggie's shoulders slumped. "Kirk," she mumbled as she turned the volume down a notch, angrily ground out her cigarette in the ashtray, and threw her computer glasses on the desk. On a scale of one to ten, ten being the highest, if anyone were to ask who she wanted in her apartment at the moment, she'd give Kirk Toland a One and killer bees a Six, with a bullet. "Go away, Kirk. You know I'm writing."

"I know, sweetheart, and I apologize. Maggie, this is embarrassing. I can't grovel out here in the hall. Let me in, please."

Kirk Toland, groveling? Not a pretty mental picture. Besides, he wasn't supposed to be groveling. He was supposed to be moving on to greener pastures, and the blondes lying in the clover, waving condom packets at him. She pushed herself to her feet, aimed herself at the door, undid the three dead bolts and the security chain, and pulled it open.

"Kirk," she said shortly, then turned her back on him and headed for one of the overstuffed couches in the center of the large living room.

He followed her, like an eager puppy coming to heel, hoping for a treat. "Maggie," he said, his carefully cultivated Harvard accent evident in that single word — which was a neat trick if you could do it. Kirk Toland could.

Kirk Toland could do a lot of things. Tall, as trim as his personal trainer could get him, distinguished looking at forty-seven with his just-going-silver hair and smoke-grey eyes, Kirk was handsome, twice divorced, richer than God, and pretty decent in bed. But not great, which was one of the reasons Maggie had tossed him out of hers. That, plus the fact that she didn't like threesomes, and Kirk's ego was always between the sheets with them. Kirk Toland, Maggie had decided two months ago, had been a prize, a rite of passage. And a complete mistake.

Unfortunately, Kirk Toland was also something else. He was the publisher of Toland Books, Maggie's publishing house.

Which pretty much made it a little sticky to flat out tell him to take a hike.

Maggie had been tossed out of Toland Books once, and didn't much long for an encore. Six years ago she had been Alicia Tate Evans, historical romance author (three names are always so impressive on a book cover). She'd also been a historical romance author cut loose by Nelson "The Trigger" Trigg when Toland Books had brought the bean counter on board and he'd blown away more than three dozen midlist authors with one shot of his smoking red pen.

Alicia/Maggie had bummed for about a week. Her checkbook balance hadn't allowed for more of a pity party. And then she'd gone to work on reinventing herself. She turned her back on the genre that had turned its back on her and entered the mystery market. All she kept was her usual early-nineteenth-century English historical settings as she created Alexandre Blake, Viscount Saint Just, amateur sleuth, hero extraordinaire, world-class lover.

And, damn, the switch had worked. Her editor had slipped her new pen name, Cleo Dooley (Maggie had decided that Os looked good on a book cover), past The Trigger, smack back to a spot on the list at

Toland Books (See? Even Toland Books agreed on the Os). The tongue-in-cheek Saint Just Mysteries had started strong and grown rapidly, so that her house had just asked for two books a year, and had put her in hardcover. The third installment made the extended *NYT* list; the fourth had climbed to number seven, stayed in the top fifteen for three weeks, and had gone *NYT* again in paperback. Her Alica Tate Evans romances had been reissued, and this time hit the charts.

Maggie Kelly didn't need Kirk Toland. She didn't need Toland Books. But she felt loyal to her editor and good friend, Bernice Toland-James. Bernie liked Maggie's work and was a brilliant, insightful editor. And the topper — Bernie had been Toland Wife Number One and knew what a pain in the ass Kirk could be. You couldn't buy that kind of empathy in the open market.

Pulling the edges of her robe around her, Maggie flopped down on the couch and let the pillows envelop her. She watched, biting her bottom lip, as Kirk seated himself on the facing couch, careful not to lean back into the cabbage-rose jaws of life that regularly ate her guests.

"I really am writing, Kirk," she said, waving one arm toward the U-shaped desk and her very new, definitely unprofessional-looking computer, the one with the flowers on its cover. (Yes, and that had given her the idea for using "flowers" as the cryptic message — never look too deeply for the "why" of a writer; the answers often aren't that esoteric.)

The Aerosmith gang was still in good voice, still shouting and screaming, and obviously annoying the hell out of Kirk. God love them all.

"Writing? Yes, I can *hear* that. Could you possibly turn it down?" Kirk asked, inclining his head toward the portable stereo.

"Nope," Maggie said, feeling her mood brighten. "It's my muse, you know."

Kirk reached up one manicured hand and adjusted the knot in his tie. "Is that what you call it? I guess you know better than to call it muse-*ic*." And then he grinned, as if he'd just told a fantastic joke, and Maggie remembered another reason she'd broken it off with Kirk. The blue-blooded man's attempts at humor were so jarring and out of character, they were embarrassing — rather like being tied down and forced to watch George Dubya try to be coherent without cue cards.

"Very funny, Kirk. You crack me up, really.

Did Socks let you in?" she asked, referring to her doorman, Argyle Jackson. Poor guy. He blamed his unfortunate yet inevitable nickname on his mother, whom he believed should have known better. "I've asked him not to do that. What did you tip him? Had to be worth at least a twenty to you."

"I could have had him for twenty? Damn. I did buzz, Maggie, not that you could have heard it over this noise," Kirk told her, shooting his French cuffs with the gold Gucci links. The man was forever fussing with his clothing, as if he couldn't get enough of touching himself, congratulating himself for being so perfect. What *had* she seen in him? "Anyway, you're right. When you didn't answer, Argyle was kind enough to let me in. Pleasant boy, Argyle, even if he is one of those light-in-the-loafers types."

Maggie winced again. What was that? Strike seventeen? There was so much she couldn't stand about Kirk Toland, mostly that she had been vulnerable enough, flattered enough, stupid enough, to have let him talk her into bed six months ago. "Socks is a nice guy, period. Try to get that straight in your very straight head, Kirk, okay? I mean, does Socks go around saying

21

that we're pleasant types, even if we are heterosexual?"

"As I've explained to you before, Maggie, you make too much money now to remain a damned liberal Democrat. There's no profit in it." Kirk stood up, began to pace the oriental carpet Maggie had indulged in after the sale of her third Saint Just mystery. "But let's not argue, all right? That's not why I came here."

"It isn't?" Maggie uncurled herself from the couch, stood up, and turned toward the hallway leading to her bedroom. "Have you come for the rest of your clothes? I'll get them for you."

And that was her second mistake. The first had been letting Kirk into the apartment. The second was turning her back on him. She'd taken only three steps when she felt his hands come down on her shoulders. He turned her around, stepped closer to her, pelvis first, spreading his legs slightly as he planted his feet and smiled.

Nothing. She felt nothing. The strings of her heart did not go *zing*. She was free. Really free.

"You've *got* to be kidding," Maggie said, trying to peel his fingers from her shoulders. "One, are you blind? I look like I've been mauled by bears and then left beside the trail. Two, I probably smell like a bear. Three, we've been here before, Kirk, and we're not going here again. Got that?"

Kirk had great caps, and liked showing them off. He did so now, his smile part indulgent, part determinedly sexual. "Maggie, you don't mean that."

She pushed herself away from him, delighting in the knowledge that Kirk Toland meant nothing to her, less than nothing to her libido. "What is it, Kirk? You can't lose? You can't be the one who gets his walking papers? Do I have to take you back so that you can drop me, tell everybody you dropped me? What? Work with me, Kirk. Give me a hint here, okay?"

The caps disappeared as Kirk turned angry. "It's my reputation, isn't it? It's Bernice, and the rest of them. Damn it, Maggie, don't listen to them. I love you, don't you understand that?"

Aerosmith was really on the ball, as "Same Old Song and Dance" began blaring out of the speakers.

Maggie wrinkled her nose. "Actually, Kirk, no. No, I don't understand that you *love* me. I don't know why. Maybe it was the picture in yesterday's *Daily News*, showing some blonde with a really horrific glandular problem leaning her boobs all over you. Maybe it's the fact that we were together for four months and you cheated on me for three of them. Maybe I'm afraid you haven't had all your shots. No matter what, it's over, has been over for two months, never should have started in the first place."

For a Harvard man, Kirk Toland could be as thick as a Gallagher's filet mignon. He took another step toward her; she backed up two, amazed that she didn't feel trapped, panicked. "It's my age," he said, nodding. "Sixteen years, Maggie. That's not so much. And I'm certainly not lacking for stamina, right?"

"You're a fricking god in bed, Kirk," Maggie lied sincerely. "Never had better. I'm a hollow shell without you. There, happy now?" She neatly sidestepped him, headed for the front door of her apartment. His clothes could rot in her closet.

He tagged along behind her, amusing her. She was beginning to warm to the doggy analogy. Here, boy. Wanna go outside?

"Then we'll have dinner tonight?"

Correction. He could be as thick as a McDonald's milkshake, and twice as full of empty air. "No, Kirk, we will not have dinner tonight. I told you, I'm wrapping up my book. A three-alarm fire wouldn't get me out of this apartment tonight, or for the rest of the week, while I reread, print out the pages. You know the routine, right?"

"Friday, then? Saturday? We could fly to one of those islands, maybe one with a casino? Anything you want, Maggie. Anything."

"Really? How about this. I want you to leave, Kirk," she said, opening the door. Then she caved. She always caved, damn it. Big mouth, no follow-through. "Tell you what — I'll see you at the party I'm giving next Saturday night to celebrate getting this book out of here. Not this Saturday, Kirk, *next* Saturday. Can you remember that? Is that a deal?"

She watched, amazed, as Kirk digested this information, thought about it. A party? He liked parties. Sit up, boy, give me your paw and I'll give you a treat.

And, once everyone went home, he could have a party of his own, with just he and Maggie. She could nearly read the words as they crossed his forehead, like a ticker tape of lascivious thoughts.

"Kirk? This isn't a test. Just answer yes or no."

"Deal." He leaned down, his handsome

face slapably smug, and aimed a kiss at her mouth. She turned aside, so that the kiss landed on her cheek. "I'll get you back, Maggie. Believe me when I say that. I don't lose."

"Uh-huh. Sure. See ya," she said, quickly closing the door behind him, then glaring at it as she threw the deadbolts, shot home the chain. "Creep."

"A first-rate suggestion, my dear, if Mr. Toland in fact heard you. Quite an insupportable person. He definitely should be crawling away on his hands and knees, preferably over shards of broken glass."

"Not that kind of creep. I meant —" Maggie's hand stilled on the security chain. *"Who said that?"*

"And now an excellent question, and so much more commendable than a maidenly scream. Please accept my compliments, Miss Kelly, but then, I already know you've got bottom. As for who I am, if you were perhaps to turn around, I do believe all your questions would be answered quite at once."

She was hearing voices? This was good. Not. How could she be hearing, talking to, voices? Who was in her apartment? How did he get in? Maggie froze, her back to the room. *Don't wanna look, don't wanna.*

Stupid fingers, stop shaking. Turn the locks, turn the damn locks. Get me the hell out of here.

"I reiterate, Miss Kelly," the fairly deep, highly cultured, damned sexy, and scarily familiar male voice continued in a remarkably pure British accent, "if you were to turn around? Mr. Balder is poking about in your kitchen, impervious to my suggestion that he behave. Therefore, we won't wait on the man, if that's all right with you. So, if you will simply turn around, allow me to introduce myself? Formally, that is. As it is, we've been rather intimately acquainted for several years."

The deadbolts were open. The chain was off. Maggie's hand was on the doorknob. The man wasn't coming after her, grabbing her; he didn't seem to be threatening her, unless he was planning to talk her to death. She could be out of the apartment in three seconds, four if she stumbled. If her damn feet would even move.

And then it hit her. The voice had said "Balder." It had, hadn't it? Still with her back to the room, and doing a pretty good mental imitation of an ostrich pretending that lion lying in the tall grass didn't exist, Maggie croaked: "Balder? As in Sterling Balder? *My* Sterling Balder?"

"I do believe my dear friend prefers to consider himself his own man, Miss Kelly, but you're quite correct, *your* Sterling Balder. Ah, how pleasant. It appears I've found the correct knob on my first attempt. I should be complimenting myself. I've come to harbor a certain appreciation for Mr. Aerosmith, thanks to you, but that particular composition is rather jarring. Frankly, I much prefer selections from *The Scarlet Pimpernel*. And *Phantom of the Opera* has a certain panache, don't you agree? I notice you prefer that music when you're orchestrating my romantic seductions."

It took Maggie a moment to realize that the stereo speakers had indeed gone silent. Which was rather unfortunate, as now she could clearly hear the beating of her pounding heart, on top of the amused male voice that showed no signs of falling silent anytime soon.

Swallowing hard, and feeling herself caught between episodes of *America's Most Wanted* and some of the screwier *X-Files*, she turned toward her desk. Slowly. Tentatively. Keeping her gaze on the parquet floor as long as she could before raising her eyes an inch at a time . . . until she saw the pair of shiny, black, knee-high boots.

"Oh boy," she breathed, pressing her back against the door, her hand still on the doorknob. *X-Files*. Definitely *X-Files*.

The boots were attached to legs. The legs were encased in form-fitting tan breeches.

"No. This isn't happening. I'm working too hard. Or maybe it's nicotine poisoning from smoking too much. Am I drooling?" She wiped at her chin. "You drool with nicotine poisoning, right? I don't know about hallucinations, but I could buy it if you're selling. Because this is *not* happening."

She dared herself to look higher. There was a white-on-white waistcoat beneath a dark blue superfine jacket. A gold-rimmed quizzing glass hanging to the waist from a black riband. A fall of lace at the throat, repeated at the wrists.

There were *hands* at the end of the lace cuffs.

Maggie closed her eyes, took a deep breath, lifted her head — and stared straight at the man standing beside her desk.

And there he was, in all his glory. Alexandre Blake, Viscount Saint Just. All six feet, two inches, one hundred and eighty-five pounds of the well-built hunk of her imagination, come to life. She recognized him at once. After all, she had created him.

Hair as black as midnight, casually rumpled in its windswept style, à la Beau Brummell. Eyes as blue as a cloudless summer sky, as mesmerizingly blue as Paul Newman's. Those winglike brows, the left one currently raised in wry amusement, rather like a refined Jim Carrey. Her creation did wry amusement well. He also excelled at sarcastic, insulting, inquiring and, most of all, sexy.

His head was well shaped, his face longish, with a strong, slightly squared jaw, his skin lightly tanned. Full lips patterned closely on Val Kilmer's sensuous pout. Slashes in his cheeks and fascinating crinkles beside his eyes when he smiled, both copied from a younger Clint Eastwood, when old Clint was knocking all the women dead in his spaghetti Westerns (put a thin cheroot between this guy's teeth, have him crinkle up his eyes, and the entire female population of Manhattan would melt into a puddle). Peter O'Toole's aristocratic nose. Sean Connery's familiar, and only slightly more British, bedroom voice. A composite for her readers to fantasize about as their husbands or boyfriends watched television in their boxer shorts and scratched their butts.

"No. It's not possible."

"I beg to disagree, Miss Kelly. It is very possible. I fear I shock you, and make no doubt that you are experiencing some difficulty in believing the evidence of your own eyes. But please do try to come to grips with the obvious. I am Saint Just. *Your* Saint Just, if that makes any of this easier."

She took a single step forward. Blinked.

He was still there. Worse, his smile crinkled the skin around his eyes, serving to produce those sexy cheek slashes. The man was a god. No, scratch that. The figment of her imagination was a god.

She'd been working too hard. She'd been under way too much pressure. Smoking too much, eating and sleeping too little. Because this couldn't happen. It just couldn't.

"Ah, we're alone now that odious man is gone. Good. The fellow's pushy and revolting, and all of that."

Maggie's head snapped around to see yet another Regency-era dandy advancing on her from the kitchen. Again, recognition was simple. This could only be Sterling Balder, Saint Just's good friend and compatriot. She'd invented Sterling Balder because every hero needs a sidekick, a foil, someone to talk to so he isn't talking to himself. Preferably, a hero needed a slightly bumbling friend, as bumbling, adorable sidekicks made for the best theater. So Maggie had made Sterling short, plump, balding (Balding, Balder. Get it?), and rather delightfully dim-witted. Her readers loved him; he even had his own fan club.

But he shouldn't be in her living room, damn it, holding the KFC chicken leg she'd been saving for her lunch.

"Delighted and all of that, Miss Kelly," Balder was saying as Maggie tried to hear him through the sudden ringing in her ears. "We've been waiting for ever so long to meet you, haven't we, Saint Just? Do you mind? I have a question for you, not that I'm not completely grateful that you've allowed me to be a figment of your imagination and all of that. But, and here's my question, Miss Kelly — couldn't you have figmented me just a tad *thinner?*"

It was perfect. A perfect Sterling Balder question, right down to his self-conscious overuse of the phrase "and all of that." Maggie would have laughed, except that her gums were now going numb, along with her lips, her forehead, and three-quarters of her body.

"I — I created you," she said, her voice coming to her ears from far away as she stared at Saint Just once more. God, he was gorgeous! She really did do good work. "But you're in my *imagination,* not my living room. Who gave you permission to drop in for a visit? It sure wasn't me! But no. I take that back. You're not *really* here. You *can't really* be here."

Saint Just raised his quizzing glass to his eye, put one foot forward, one hand on his hip, and struck a pose. A perfect Saint Just pose based on a perfect Beau Brummell pose she'd seen reproduced in one of her research books. "Far be it from me to point out the error in that statement, Miss Kelly," he drawled in that wonderful young Sean Connery as James Bond voice, "but we most definitely are here. Now, if I may brook a suggestion, might I say that Sterling and I are most happy to excuse you while you . . . forgive me . . . *freshen* yourself?"

"Yes," Balder said, nodding. "Not to be insulting, but you do look a trifle hagged, and all of that. Probably do you good, a wash and a brush up."

Maggie looked down at her body, winced, pulled the edges of her robe

33

around herself. She did it without really thinking, but simply responding to Saint Just's arrogant remark on her appearance.

Arrogant. Yes, she'd made Saint Just arrogant. She'd had to, as no character is perfect, not even the perfect hero. In the end, she gave him a few other less than kind characteristics.

Arrogant, a bit sarcastic, perhaps a tad overbearing. More than slightly proud, a completely confident man who didn't suffer fools gladly. Those were the defects (could they be strengths?) she'd picked for the Viscount Saint Just. Not that it mattered. All she had to do was shut down her computer and he'd shut up, go away. At least that's the way it was *supposed* to happen.

And that was the way it *did* happen, damn it. Saint Just and Balder were not in her living room. They couldn't be. She was dreaming, that's what she was doing. She'd locked Kirk out, then lain down on the couch and fallen asleep and begun to dream.

"Ouch!" Okay. So pinching herself didn't wake her up, banish these imaginary intruders. Clearly she had to find another way to wake herself up, regain her sanity.

Maggie lifted her chin, just the way defiant heroines did, and commanded herself to walk forward . . . to put out one trembling hand . . . to poke a hole straight through the washboard-flat belly of this absurd, absurdly handsome figment of her imagination.

But before she could touch him, that figment of her imagination took hold of her hand, bowed over it, turned it at the last possible moment, and planted a kiss in her palm.

Maggie felt a rush of heat race up her arm and invade her cheeks. Her brain reeled as her senses danced, and her vision began to narrow, darken. The feeling was silly; she was silly. Because none of this was really happening.

CHAPTER 2

Maggie sighed, stretched, burrowed her face against the soft cushion beneath her head. How she loved napping on the couches, often curling up on her favorite after a long day of writing, happy to ignore the trip down the hallway to her usually unmade bed.

Eyes still closed, a smile playing around her mouth, she allowed herself to remember her dream. That silly, insane dream. Kirk was right. She obviously needed a vacation, and an island resort sounded just perfect — as long as it was six nights and seven days, Kirk Not Included.

But it had been fun "seeing" Saint Just and Balder, if only in her silly dream.

"Here it is, Sterling. Here's where she went wrong. But never fear, my dear friend, I can fix it."

Maggie's eyes popped open, then nearly popped out of her head. She struggled against the enveloping cushions, finally able to prop herself up on one elbow and peer over the facing couch, toward her desk in the corner.

And, sonofagun, there they were. Balder standing behind her desk chair, munching a KFC chicken leg, Saint Just seated, using the mouse to scroll through her manuscript as it appeared on the computer screen.

She got shakily to her feet, blinking furiously and rubbing her eyes. She pinched herself again. Nothing worked. She was still asleep, still couldn't wake up.

If she had really been asleep . . .

She looked down at her right palm, stroked the skin with the fingers of her left hand — and remembered the sensation. And the shakiness, the silliness. And the rapidly descending darkness.

"I fainted? Nah. I don't faint. I never faint."

"Um . . . Saint Just? It would appear Miss Kelly has risen from her swoon."

"Humm — what? Oh. Oh, yes. Well, that was only to be expected at some point, Sterling, now wasn't it?"

Maggie watched, knowing she looked like the proverbial deer caught in headlights, as Saint Just abandoned the desk chair and walked across the room. He stopped a polite three feet in front of her.

"Feeling more the thing now, Miss Kelly?" he asked, all concern, and yet unable to hide his amusement, the rat. "I must say, I haven't had the pleasure of catching up a swooning miss since *The Case of the Misplaced Earl*. Luckily for you, I was not too many years out of practice. My, you're still looking quite oppressed, aren't you? Would you care for a drink of water? Sterling — fetch Miss Kelly a drink of water, would you? There's a good fellow."

"Hold it, Sterling." Maggie poked out her arm and held it in front of her as she advanced on the pair of them. "Hold it right there for just one cotton-picking minute."

Sterling Balder was nothing if not an obedient sort, and he halted in his tracks.

This could work. If she was dreaming, then she could dream herself into being a fearless heroine. "And you," Maggie continued bravely, pointing her accusing finger at Saint Just. "Okay," she said, repeatedly nodding her head as she spoke, as she stepped forward, walking a complete circle around both men. Staring, nodding, jutting out her chin, she chanted inside her head: "Oh, yeah. We bad, we bad." She even rolled her shoulders a couple of times and ran one hand beneath her nose — doing her best to look intimidating. "You're groupies, aren't you? I knew I had fans, but not groupies. What's the matter, you figure the Trekkie conventions were too crowded? You didn't think you looked good in Mr. Spock ears?"

Sterling Balder nearly did an *Exorcist* imitation as his head all but rotated on his neck, watching Maggie's progress. "Saint Just — what is she talking about? And what is she *doing?* It looks painful."

"Stubble it, Sterling," Saint Just said, his smile maddening. "Although you might want to commit to memory just how one looks when one is making a total cake of one's self."

Maggie ignored the man's remark and just glared at him. "It was Socks, wasn't it? He let you in the service entrance in the kitchen. And to think I baked him homemade chocolate chip cookies for Christmas — plus the fifty bucks I stuck in the tin. Well," she ended as she planted herself in front of Saint Just once more, "that's gratitude for you, isn't it? And the rest is makeup, wigs, and costumes, right? I've seen *Cats*, you know. And *Phantom*. I know what you Broadway hopefuls can do with makeup. At least, if Socks knows you, I know you're not dangerous. Wacko, but not dangerous. Except that I'm dreaming, so none of this means anything, right?"

Saint Just reached beneath his coat and

extracted a slim cheroot, then stuck it between his straight white teeth, his lips caressing the thing. Just like Val Kilmer in *Tombstone*, damn him. She wouldn't have been the least surprised if he were to speak around the cheroot: "I'm your huckleberry." How would that sound with an English accent?

Instead, he inclined his head to her politely, then fished inside his jacket once more, coming out with her pink mini-lighter. "I'll assume you won't mind, seeing as we share our bad habits," he told her smoothly.

Maggie watched, fascinated, as Saint Just bent his head and lit the cheroot. "Ha!" she then said. "You've really blown it now, buster. And I don't mean the cigar. You've turned off my stereo. You've been fooling around with my computer — and if you've screwed up my book, no jury on earth would call it anything but justifiable homicide when I wring your neck. And now the lighter. Tell me, *my lord,* how did you know how to do all of that?"

He gave her a pitying look, which definitely made her want to strangle him. "I know this is probably difficult for you, Miss Kelly, but it is really quite easily explained. In fact, in time I think you'll come to realize how very flattering all of this is to you. After all, you've created characters so real, so well defined, that they have drawn breath, come to life. Perceive me, if you will, whilst I draw breath."

And then he did, drawing in on the cheroot, blowing out a thin blue stream of smoke. He continued: "A pity you didn't draw the character of Clarence quite as sharply, as I begin to realize that I will sorely miss the services of my loyal valet. The man's a wizard with boot blacking, you know. But we'll work on that, won't we? Among other slight problems in this latest effort which fail to show us in our best light."

"Shut up," Maggie said, pushing both hands through her hair, trying to keep her brain from exploding. "Just shut up, okay? Shut up, shut up, *shut up*."

"Well, now, strong hysterics won't benefit anything, Miss Kelly," Balder pointed out politely. "Not if you wish to understand. Please, if you were to only listen as Saint Just here explains everything to you? He's a right one at heart, and ever so good at explaining and all of that. Quite a treat to listen to, as a matter of fact. Splendid voice, with a rather delightful cadence."

"Thank you, my dear, good, and always

astute friend," Saint Just drawled, inclining his head in Balder's direction as Maggie shivered from head to foot, feeling as if she might soon crawl straight out of her skin. "Miss Kelly? That mulish expression really doesn't quite become you. However, it's early days yet, and we'll soon have this settled. If I might continue, that is, without further interruption."

"Oh, what the hell, go for it," Maggie muttered, retrieving a cigarette from the pack on the desk, then allowing Saint Just to light it for her. She sat down on the couch and waved for him to continue. Arrogant, condescending bastard. Then, belatedly, she glared at him. "What problems? What's wrong with my *latest effort?*"

"It's Quigley, of course," he told her, gracefully splitting his coattails and then seating himself on the facing couch, crossing one elegantly clad leg over the other, and not having the slightest difficulty with the soft cushions. "He's entirely too likable. None of your previous victims has been quite so affable. Readers can understand murder, even relish it in all its gory details, if the victim is a bit of a rotter. But not to concern yourself, as I've already discovered a flaw in dearest Quigley's character that will make his an unlamented demise."

Maggie tried to wet her lips, but there wasn't any spit in her mouth. Instead, she took a deep drag on her cigarette, then shakily blew out the smoke. "How — how do you know about Quigley? Nobody sees my work until I'm done with it. Nobody. Okay, nobody but Bernie, but I changed Quigley's name after I wrote the synopsis. So how — damn it, *how?*"

Balder leaned over the back of the couch, speaking beside Saint Just's ear. "I think she's listening now, don't you? And she doesn't look quite so fierce anymore. That has to be good, doesn't it?"

"Yes, thank you, Sterling," Saint Just said as he also accepted the ashtray his friend was holding out to him. "Now, Miss Kelly, to continue as, in Sterling's opinion, I have your attention. One, I am not an actor. And this is not a dream. I am a character. Your character, as is our dear Mr. Balder here. Everything we are, you have created. Every word that comes out of our mouths, you have put into them at one time or another — although I do hope to enlarge my vocabulary now that I'm here in earnest. Two, we have resided, as it were, inside your delightful head for the past five and more years — only while you're in this apartment and the computer is turned on, but we've learned quite a lot, as you rarely turn off your computer. Everything we are, you have made. Everything you are, we have learned, when we chose to listen, chose to observe."

Maggie didn't believe him. That didn't, however, keep her from pulling her bathrobe around her protectively and squeaking: "Everything? In this apartment? Everything that goes on? Here? *Everything?*"

"If that delightful blush concerns our knowledge of Mister Kirk Toland — the toad — then, yes, Miss Kelly. Everything. However, our memories are most adaptable when it comes to some of what has transpired over the years. We are gentlemen, Miss Kelly, and have been careful not ever to go along as you enter your boudoir or bath — or that one time, in the kitchen — so as not to invade your most intimate privacy." He pronounced the word as "*privv*-acy."

The kitchen? She'd never — wait. There was that one night, after the theater, when Kirk grabbed her in front of the sink. Oh, lordy, lordy. They knew about *that?*

Maggie swiveled her head toward Ster-

44

ling Balder as that man joined in the explanation. "Yes, the toad. Saint Just says you were right to send him to the rightabout, and none too soon, either. Man's a rotter. We both find it difficult to believe you would live like a nun for all these years, then let a scoundrel like that into your bed. Saint Just believes you may feel the years creeping up over you — a spinster, getting rather long in the tooth — and grabbed at the first male who paid you the least attention. But now you're alone again, and may be tumbling into a sad decline, which is yet another reason we're here, isn't it, Saint Just? We're worried about her, aren't we?"

"I am not going into a sad — I am *not* depressed!" Maggie protested. "And even if I were, it wouldn't be because of Kirk Toland. Like he was the first man to — well, yeah, right. In your dreams."

"Don't be critical, Sterling," Saint Just warned. "Miss Kelly's morals, or the lack of them, are really none of our concern."

"Oh, that's it. That is *it*. Playtime's over, boys." Maggie jumped to her feet, ran over to the door, and threw it open. "Out! The two of you! Out of my mind, out of my life, out of my fricking apartment. You've got five seconds before I call a cop. Before I call a whole damn precinct."

"You shouldn't have said that last bit, I don't think," Sterling scolded Saint Just, obviously seeing nothing to upset Maggie in his own comments. "After all, it was you who explained to me that her life is not our story."

"Of course, Sterling," Saint Just said, rising and depositing ashtray and cheroot on the coffee table. "I overreached, definitely, and stand corrected, thank you. But it's insulting, you know. These upstart Americans have put a man on the moon, Sterling. Certainly the woman should be able to understand *us*."

"One . . . two . . ." Maggie called out, still holding the door open to the hallway.

They continued to ignore her.

"Still, you're going to have to placate her somehow," Sterling said. "Much as I enjoy these clothes, we both know we can't be seen in them on the streets without raising untoward suspicion and all of that, eager as I am to experience the dissipations of town life. And money, Saint Just. We have no blunt, remember? I don't believe either of us would do well in the workhouse. A rare end, that, to all your grand ambition. Although there is always that YMCA place, I suppose."

"Three . . . four . . . YMCA?"

"YMCA place?" Saint Just frowned. "I'm sorry, Sterling, I don't recall —"

"You know. We've both certainly heard the song enough on that thing she calls a stereo. Something about every young man down on his luck being allowed to reside for a time at this estimable establishment? I've given it some thought and believe the letters stand for Young Man's Comfort Assembly."

"Oh, good grief . . ." Maggie gave the door a push, closing it with a bang. She then returned to the couch, sat down and glared up at Saint Just. "I'm nuts, aren't I?" she asked with a slightly sickly smile. "I've gone around the bend. My train's slipped its tracks. I'm two muffins short of a dozen. All of that. Because you're really here, aren't you? You're not actors. Not groupies. Socks didn't let you in. You just . . . just *poofed* yourself into my apartment, didn't you? Right out of my mind — and I'm damned well out of my mind."

She stood up and wrapped her robe around her. "Okay. I'll play the game. I'll pretend you're real, that you're really here. In fact, I'll go take a shower now, get myself some sleep. Is that all right with you guys? You just stay here, amuse yourselves, and I'll try to go find my mind. Help yourselves to anything you want, just as long as you're gone when I wake up. Is that a deal?"

"We are real, Miss Kelly, and it would be wise of you, and easier for you, if you were to fortify yourself to the likelihood that we will most definitely be here when you awake," Saint Just told her, his Sean Connery voice beginning to make her as mad as hell; it was just too, too perfect. Bernie would be drooling all over him by now. Except that Bernie wasn't here, and neither was Saint Just. "But I agree that you should get some rest. Sterling and I will amuse ourselves by correcting your errors on the manuscript."

Maggie shuffled past him, flapping her arms like a bird too tired to take flight, but still giving it the old college try. "Sure . . . sure . . . you just do that. Why not let my imagination finish the book? Other people have ghost writers, don't they? Hell, trust Maggie Kelly not to be *ordinary*. Oh, no. Wouldn't want that, would we? And hey, then, if you guys aren't gone by the time I wake up, at least I'll be well rested when I check myself into the local nuthouse. YMCA — *jeez!* See ya. Or not."

"That went tolerably well, don't you think?" Sterling asked as he sat back on one of the couches and began waging a losing battle with the Balder-devouring cushions.

"Not to belabor the point, Sterling," Saint Just drawled as he puffed on his cheroot, trying to nurse it back to life, "but that's rather like the man with his head in the noose saying the hanging went well because the rope didn't break."

Sterling looked up at his friend and frowned. "You know, I never did get the right of that one, I don't think. It's from *The Case of the Lingering Lightskirt*, ain't it? I wonder what our dear Miss Kelly meant by that."

Saint Just flicked at a bit of ash that had dared to settle on his waistcoat. "It doesn't matter, Sterling. As long as your dear Miss Kelly believes it to be amusing, and to sound even vaguely along the lines of Regency speech. Speaking of which, I've been longing to take a peek into some of her research books, haven't you? I'm particularly drawn to *The 1811 Dictionary of the Vulgar Tongue*."

He walked over to the piles of books on the floor, bent down, and selected one. "Ah, here it is. Buckish slang, university wit, and pickpocket eloquence. Sort of rolls off the tongue — buckish slang, university wit, pickpocket eloquence. It's a wonderment, as dear Clarence might say. Ah, well, we might as well dip the toes of our intellect into the gutter to pass the time until Miss Kelly comes back and has at us again."

Sterling dropped his chin (the second one) to his chest. "She doesn't believe us, does she?"

Saint Just began paging through the book, reading snatches of yellow-highlighted text. "Lord bless her, why should she?" he asked, then smiled. "Ah, here's one I haven't seen before now. Thingumbob. Or, Mr. Thingumbob, which, it says here, is a vulgar address or nomination to any person whose name is unknown, the same as Mr. What-d'ye-call-'em. A rather insulting term, I would imagine, if employed to greet a person whose name *is* known to one. Ah, and here's the plural, Sterling. Thingumbobs, meaning . . . testicles?"

He snapped the book shut. "Miss Kelly should not be reading this book. Psalms and sermons, that's what young ladies of good breeding read."

"Yes, but is she? Of good breeding, that is. We can't be sure. And she certainly isn't young. Why, she should have put on her caps years ago, resigned herself to being well and truly on the shelf."

"I wouldn't suggest you repeat that sentiment within the lady's hearing." Saint Just selected another book from the pile, this one a more scholarly tome, but at least it had pictures in it. Drawings, actually, of his supposed Regency contemporaries, their abodes and suchlike. "Sterling, do try to remember what we've learned from the television machine over there in the corner. Ladies today — women, that is — are liberated, equal, and fairly competent. Except, of course, for those who stick rings through their noses and eyebrows, have their bodies tattooed, and curse like Billingsgate fishwives as they physically attack low-born men who have had sexual consort with the female's sister and mother."

Sterling's chins went even lower on his chest. "I don't like those exhibitions. They're revolting," he said sadly. "It's the world, Saint Just, going head over ears into hell in a handbasket. All the violence, emanating from that large box. Imagine what awaits us *outside* this apartment. I may have to rethink any notion of gadding about, going out on the strut, and all of that. At least not until I acquire one of those oozing things."

"Oozing things?" Saint Just closed the book and looked at his friend. "Oh, of course. One of those *Uzi* things. A firearm. Personally, I find them ugly, totally lacking in panache. I much prefer my dueling pistols. Chased silver handles, built entirely to my specifications."

"You can shoot the pip out of a playing card at twenty paces," Sterling said, nodding. "Very admirable and all of that. But I don't think it matters here, Saint Just. Expertise isn't necessary with the weapons we've seen. There's no sport to it, no sport at all. Where's the pride? Oh," he moaned, then sighed deeply and laid his head back against the pillows. "Perhaps this was a mistake, Saint Just. We thought we'd make her happy, but we don't belong here, and Miss Kelly certainly wasn't even half pleased to see us."

"Miss Kelly will simply have to adjust her conceptions of what is and is not possible to include the very real fact that we *are* here, and we're staying here. She needs us in this pathetic bit of nothing she calls a life. We discussed all of this before we came. Besides, I'm out, Sterling, my own man now, and not just a reflection of Miss Kelly's imagination. I'm *not* going back."

"No, no, neither am I," Sterling said sincerely. "However, have we really worked this all out, Saint Just? As I said earlier, we have no clothes, we have no money. Even your dueling pistols have been left behind, and we're here with only the clothes we stand up in — or sit down in, as I'm sitting down. No matter, you know what I mean."

"Yes, and your point would be precisely what, Sterling?" Saint Just asked as he stubbed out his cheroot in one of the ashtrays, then shot his cuffs.

"My point," Sterling said, shifting uncomfortably in his seat, "is that we also have nowhere to live, Saint Just. Miss Kelly is an unattached female, living alone. We cannot stay here."

Saint Just's left eyebrow rose a fraction as he leveled his cool blue gaze at his friend. "Becoming dashed moral a little late in the day, aren't you, Sterling? Are you suggesting that either of us is about to ravish the woman? Trust me, old friend, I believe I can manage to tame my own animal instincts where Miss Kelly is concerned. One-and-thirty? Gods, it would be like bedding my own grandmother. So, unless long-in-the-tooth ladies of uncertain morals stir you to your marrow, Sterling, I do believe Miss Kelly to be safe on that head. She is our friend, nothing more."

"I suppose," Sterling said. "Not that I've ever been much in the petticoat line anyway. I don't know why, as Miss Kelly never said, but I'm not, you know. And pretty little heiresses have yet to try to run me into a corner and take advantage of me, more's the pity. But she thinks you're handsome, Saint Just. She *made* you handsome, and a great lover into the bargain. She may set her cap at *you*, or didn't you think of that one?"

Saint Just rolled his eyes, weary of the conversation, and not much liking where it was going. His true thoughts about Miss Maggie Kelly, romantic or not, would remain his own. He was, after all, a gentleman, a hero. The fact that he didn't feel quite as complete, emotionally, as he believed he should would not deter him from his main objective, that of being his own man. "Perhaps you, Sterling, should pen the next Saint Just mystery, as your imagination appears to know no bounds. Do you suppose Miss Kelly will rejoin us soon? I admit to feeling a mite peckish, and could enjoy a good kidney pie."

In one of his rare, but always wonderful bursts of brilliance, Sterling Balder threw back his head and laughed out loud. "God love you, Saint Just, do you really think

Miss Kelly is going to *cook* for you? She ain't tumbling over herself so far, to be nice to us. Perhaps you should go back to work on the book, and make Clarence more believable so that he can join us. Otherwise, my good friend, I do believe we're going to starve."

Saint Just stiffened slightly at this rebuke, most especially because he knew his friend to be correct. After all, they'd existed inside Maggie Kelly's fertile brain for over five long years, definitely enough time to learn that the woman was, in the main, incomprehensible.

She did domestic chores, but only sporadically. Mostly, she spent her time in these rooms at her computer, or lying, sloth-like, on one of the couches, watching the television machine — sometimes yelling at it, especially on Sunday mornings, when the talk became political. She read books, spoke on the telephone machine; she sometimes had friends come to call, and she confided in her cats, just like all the old maids.

In short, the woman was pretty much a dead bore except when she was writing. Still, she did seem to have a mind of her own, and that mind had apparently told her years ago that, if left to her own devices, she could do what she wanted, when she wanted, and the devil with the rest of the world.

Rather like himself, come to think of it.

Would he cook for this woman? Hardly. Would he play housemaid for her? Really, how could he even ask himself such a ridiculous question. So who was going to take care of him? Dear God, would he have to take care of himself? It was unthinkable!

And yet . . .

"We served on the Peninsula campaign, Sterling, remember?" Saint Just said at last. "Slogging through the mud, foraging food from the fields, standing up in the same clothes day after day, week after week. I shouldn't think we will fare all that badly here."

"Yes, but we only *talked* about how we served on the Peninsula, Saint Just. We never really *experienced* it. Miss Kelly never really *wrote* about it. We're babes in the woods, Saint Just. Why, you have never even shaved yourself."

"Nor have you," Saint Just said, lifting his chin slightly, stung to think that he might have some failings, or at least what would appear to be shortcomings now that he was forced to pit his imaginary skills against a very real, very different environment. But, then, the Viscount Saint Just loved a good challenge. "We will adjust, Sterling, we will adjust."

"We'll have to, or else we'll be cooped up in these rooms like moulting pigeons, not allowed outside. As you have said, we do know some things, and we will learn more. Otherwise, we'll be knocking about like the rawest of greenhorns, and I know you wouldn't like that."

"No, I most certainly — damn, that startled me," Saint Just said, wheeling on his heels and glaring at the telephone, which now rang a second time. He then turned to look at a second telephone on the table beside one of the couches. Which one to choose? "Sterling, do you suppose . . . ?"

"That you should pick it up? The way Miss Kelly does? Talk into it? Oh, no. Oh no, no, no. I don't think so."

Saint Just smiled. "On the contrary, my good man. We have to learn how to fend for ourselves. This is as good a time as any to begin." The small black box on the desk, the one with the long cord dangling from it, attached to a silly little hat-type thing Miss Kelly wore stuck over one ear as she talked into the other end of it did not appeal to his sense of fashion. He opted for the second phone, which (rather unfortunately, as it turned out) activated the moment it was lifted from its cradle.

Looking at Sterling, Saint Just lifted the machine to his ear and, relying on his memory of how Miss Kelly used the thing, said loudly and distinctly, "Joe's Bar and Grill." Then he grinned at Sterling and exclaimed, "Someone just said hello to me! Here, listen — maybe she'll do it again."

Sterling raised his hands and shook his head, as if warding off attack.

"Oh, very well, Sterling, if you're going to be missish," Saint Just said and put the phone to his ear once more. "Ah, yes," he said after a moment, "this is the residence of Miss Maggie Kelly, but she is not receiving today. May I possibly be of service to you, madam?"

The woman's voice shouted into his ear. "Not receiving? What do you mean, not receiving? She's *supposed* to be *writing,* damn it. Kirk, is that you? That can't be you. I was calling to warn Maggie that you were going to come bother her. Christ, Kirk, can't you keep it in your pants?"

"I beg your pardon," Saint Just said in what Maggie would have described as a "frosty tone."

"Oops," the female said, then giggled. "Not Kirk, huh? Sorry about that. Just

58

forget I said anything. So, who are you? You *sound* gorgeous."

And that was when Alexandre Blake, Viscount Saint Just, hero extraordinaire, realized that he might have been better served to think before he acted. Who was he? He was the Viscount Saint Just. Could he tell this woman that? To employ the vernacular learned from Miss Kelly — not in a million years.

He took refuge in his dignity. "Again, madam, I beg your pardon. I, most naturally, am the person who is speaking. And who would you be?"

"Me?" the voice said, sounding confused. "I'm Bernice. Bernice Toland-James, Maggie's editor. Is Maggie all right? Maybe I ought to run over there and —"

"Miss Kelly is working," Saint Just interrupted, "and does not wish to be disturbed. And, as you are her editor, I can only assume that you'll be considerate of her wishes."

"Well, yeah, sure, but — but who the hell are you?"

Saint Just cudgeled his brain for an answer. There had to be one. After all, he'd been listening to Miss Kelly talk, listening to the television machine talk, for five long years. "Pizza delivery," he mumbled, then quickly slammed the phone back into its cradle.

He looked at Sterling, who had a couch pillow stuffed against his face, although his ears were visible and quite red. "By my calculations, Sterling, we have approximately a half hour to rouse Miss Kelly, explain what just occurred, and then go hide ourselves under her bed. I'm prodigiously sorry for not listening to you. My apologies."

CHAPTER 3

Maggie lay about two inches above her mattress, every muscle taut, every nerve end jangling. She should be sleeping. She should be working. She should be standing in the shower, washing those two men right out of her hair — um, head. She should be on the phone to Doctor Bob, asking him to book her a rubber room at the nearest funny farm.

Because, the thing was, she was beginning to believe that Alexandre Blake and Sterling Balder *were* in her living room.

The fact that this was completely impossible was losing ground to the fact that she'd seen them, she'd talked with them, she'd touched them. Just how real could figments of the imagination get? In a sane person, that is.

Unless she was insane.

She wasn't insane. She didn't wear a tinfoil helmet to keep the FBI from listening in on her thoughts. She didn't hold heated conversations with space aliens as she walked the streets of Manhattan in her bathrobe, pushing a stolen grocery cart loaded down with all her worldly goods.

Of course, everyone knew that no insane

61

person thinks he or she is insane. They think they're just fine, just peachy keen dandy, and it's only the rest of the world that's walking around with all its screws loose. So, Maggie deduced, getting more nervous, maybe it wasn't such a hot idea to keep thinking of herself as sane. Maybe if she decided she might be a just a little bit nuts, that would mean she really was sane.

Was this making any sense? Any of it?

Nope.

Maybe she should get up, go back into the living room, see if Frick and Frack were still there. Except if she did that, and they *were* still there — then what would she do?

Screaming seemed like a workable option.

Maggie jumped as the phone rang on the nightstand next to her bed. The outside world, trying to contact her. Just what she didn't need right now.

The phone rang again, and Maggie glared at it. "Go away, nobody invited you," she grumbled. Obligingly, the phone stopped ringing. That was good.

No, it wasn't. The answering machine didn't pick up until after the fourth ring.

"Maybe it was a wrong number and whoever it was realized that," she told herself bracingly, then frowned. "And maybe not."

Gingerly, carefully, she reached out, snatched up the phone, and put it to her ear.

"Again, madam, I beg your pardon. I, most naturally, am the person who is speaking. And who would you be?"

Maggie slapped her hand over the mouthpiece, eyes wide as she listened to Bernie's reply. Bernie was speaking to Viscount Saint Just. She *heard* Viscount Saint Just.

How was that possible? Maggie had thought she was going crazy on her own. She certainly didn't think Bernie — or anyone else, for that matter — was coming along for the ride.

With her hand still over the mouthpiece, Maggie muttered incredulously, "Pizza delivery? *Pizza* delivery? Oh, God, we're dead meat."

She waited until she was certain Bernie had hung up on her end, then slammed down the phone and jackknifed off the bed. "Saint Just!" she bellowed — definitely a bellow — as she threw open the door to her room and stomped down the hallway, bathrobe flapping in the breeze she created. "Where are you, you stupid son of a —"

"Ah, Miss Kelly. How good of you to rejoin us," Saint Just said with what even her frazzled mind registered as marvelous sangfroid (that's what she would have called it in her dialogue tag, anyway). "You're looking . . . ah, well, I'd hoped you might have taken a small lie-down, but I see that wasn't the case. Pity."

Maggie wrapped her robe around her and glared at him. "The day I take a shower because a figment of my imagination *says* I should take a shower is — damn it, Saint Just, why did you pick up the phone?"

Saint Just struck a pose. Spine, ramrod straight. Chin lifted so that he looked at her down the length of his aristocratic nose. "Don't rattle me off in that high-nosed tone, madam," he said.

Maggie made a small, frustrated noise in the back of her throat as she jammed her fingers through her hair and spun in a tight circle. Then she pointed a finger at him, straight up at his face, and gritted out, "You know, I've listened to you, and listened to you, and had to come up with insipid comebacks like 'Oh, that's the outside of enough, Saint Just,' or even, 'I do not like that above half, my lord.' But now — *now* — I finally get to say what I've been longing to write for one of my heroines for five damn years, ten if you count all my historical romances. So stuff a sock in it, Saint Just!"

The silence in the room, as Maggie also had written time after time, was deafening.

Saint Just lifted one hand to his lapel and picked off an imaginary bit of lint. "If you're quite finished," he then drawled at his most maddening, "I do believe we needs must put our heads together to solve a small, almost infinitesimal problem that may have arisen."

"Oh, bite me." Maggie brushed past him, heading for the phone, and pushed the speed dial that would connect her with Bernie's office. "Come on, come on," she muttered as she paced the carpet, the phone stuck to her ear, only to hear Bernie's recorded phone message stating that she was either away from her desk or out of the office.

"Damn. Damn, damn, damn." Maggie punched the Off button and threw the phone in Saint Just's general direction. He neatly snagged it out of the air with one hand, while twirling his quizzing glass with the other. "Damn!"

"Shouldn't swear, you know," Sterling Balder piped up from his seat on the couch (or *in* the couch, as he seemed to have been half devoured by the loose cushions). "It really isn't ladylike, and all of that."

Maggie ignored him as she advanced on Saint Just once more. Looked at his clothing once more. Went so far as to stare at the front of his breeches, looking for a zipper, because zippers hadn't been invented until years after the Regency, but costume makers invariably used zippers anyway.

No zipper.

"One more time, guys, okay?" she asked hopefully. "You're not two of Socks's actor buddies, playing a trick on me? Are you *sure?*"

"Playing pranks?" Sterling said, obviously insulted. "We'd never do that, would we, Saint Just? Too shabby by half, pulling the wool over a lady's eyes and all of that. And terribly beneath us. Saint Just, can't you convince Miss Kelly that we are who we know we are?"

Saint Just lifted the quizzing glass to his eye and glared at Sterling. "You're wanting parlor tricks now, my good friend? Shall I quote chapter and verse of *The Case of the Disappearing Dandy*, which will be Miss Kelly's next effort? I don't think so, especially since the ideas floating around in her head are still a tad weak as to some of the major plot points — the method of murder, for one. You do call them plot points, am I right, Miss Kelly?"

"I . . . um . . . I . . ."

"Well said, Miss Kelly," Saint Just told her. "Such articulation, so impressive. Now, if you were to perhaps close your mouth before a fly finds its home in it? Just a suggestion, you understand, as I most certainly would never think to give you *orders*."

For the second time in as many hours, Maggie felt her limbs going numb, and her vision narrowed, darkened. She sat down quickly, right on the floor, and dropped her head between her knees until the dizziness passed.

When she dared to look up again, Sterling Balder was holding out a glass of water, and the Viscount Saint Just was sipping from a glass of his own.

"Dramatics completed, Miss Kelly?" Saint Just inquired, his polished voice dripping sarcasm. "Ah, splendid. Now, about this small problem we might have. Much as I long to make Miss Toland-James's acquaintance, I do believe neither Sterling nor myself is quite dressed for the occasion. Don't you agree?"

Maggie nodded, unable to find ¹ voice.

"Again, splendid. Therefore, I have decided that you will entertain Miss Toland-James on your own whilst my good friend and I stay most neatly out of the way. Agreed?"

Again, Maggie nodded. Then she frowned. Then she realized that she was being led around with a ring in her nose by a supercilious, posing, pontificating pain in her — "Whoa!" she said as she got back to her feet. "My house, Saint Just. I call the shots."

"Certainly, my dear woman. Call away. What would you have us do, as we are most definitely your obedient servants? I doubt Miss Toland-James would be at all confounded by our attire, now would she? And as to our names? Why, she'd probably not even blink as you introduced us as the Viscount Saint Just and his stalwart companion, Sterling Balder."

Maggie narrowed her eyes. "I could seriously hate you," she told him, then nearly jumped out of her skin as the buzzer beside the door announced that she had a visitor. "Stay there. Stay *right* there," she ordered, then went over to the intercom and pressed the button. "Yes, Socks, what is it?"

"Ms. Toland-James to see you, Miss

Kelly," the doorman told her. "Shall I send her up?"

Maggie looked at her "guests." Saint Just lifted his left eyebrow, the smile on his face infuriating her. Sterling was gnawing on his fingernails, looking nervous.

"Send her up, thank you, Socks. Oh, and Socks? Are you appearing in any plays this week? Off-off-off Broadway, that sort of thing? Maybe a historical play?"

"No, ma'am," the doorman told her. "Unfortunately, I'm appearing nightly at the McDonald's near the Village, working the fryers. And let me tell you, that's *no* way to meet men. Why? Have you heard of a historical play being cast? Where?"

"Never mind, Socks," Maggie said, and let go of the button. "You," she then said, pointing at Saint Just, "and you, Sterling. Into my bedroom, now. And *stay* there."

"Not the most gracious invitation into a lady's boudoir that I've ever received," Saint Just said, "but I do see the wisdom of it. Come along, Sterling. Much as it pains me to be written out of this scene, I suppose we'll have to allow Miss Kelly to untangle this particular coil without our assistance."

"But Saint Just," Sterling said in confusion as he followed his friend out of the

69

room, "isn't that just what you wanted? Miss Kelly to fix things for us? I mean, after your mistake in talking to that woman, your first thought was to appeal to Miss Kelly for —"

Saint Just stopped and turned on his heels to face his friend. "How you do run on, Sterling," he said, his smile intact even as his voice turned to cold steel. "I never said anything of the kind."

"But — but you looked positively *stunned* for a moment, and then you said we'd hide under Miss Kelly's bed, and —"

"Surely you misheard me, my good friend. Hide under a woman's bed? Do I look such a ninny?"

"Oh, would you just knock it off and get *out* of here!" Maggie exclaimed as the doorbell rang and she began undoing the locks. She didn't know whether she should scream or follow the two of them around with a notebook, taking down their every word. She waited until they had disappeared around a turn in the hallway, then slid off the chain and opened the door. "Bernie! What on earth are you doing here?" she asked as Bernice Toland-James burst past her, into the apartment.

"Where is he?" she asked, looking around the large room. "Where are you hiding him, Maggie? He sounded *gorgeous*."

It was so good to have someone normal in her apartment. Maggie watched her friend as Bernie went over to the Chinese lacquered liquor cabinet and poured herself a neat scotch. She looked at the clock on the mantel. Two in the afternoon. Normal?

Well, sort of normal, anyway. Marginally.

Bernie was Maggie's first and only editor, and a good friend. Bernie had nursed Maggie's career, given her advice to the lovelorn, and helped wallpaper her kitchen. In return, Maggie had worked her ass off for Bernie, listened to stories of her love life, and held the woman's head as she hugged the porcelain bowl — which she did a lot.

Bernie was fun, a lot of laughs, and only scary sometimes. Five feet, nine inches tall, and with great legs that went all the way to her neck, she had two eyes, brown, one surgically perfected nose, two collagen-injected pouty lips, a mane of carefully dyed, purposely frizzed-out red hair, and a constant weight problem.

Besides the nose job, she'd gone under the knife for one eyelid and brow lift, a mouthful of capped teeth, one face lift, two

71

liposuctions (the thunder-thighs, dear, the thunder-thighs), a tummy tuck, and a fanny booster. As Bernie said, if she got herself a new liver, Saint Peter wouldn't recognize her at all when she hit the Pearly Gates.

At forty-five, Bernie was still beautiful, although the battles to stay that way were getting harder, which was why the woman indulged in two other vices. One kept her Platinum MasterCard humming with bills from every health food store in the city, and the other could land her in jail.

Every morning, every evening, and once in the afternoon, Bernice Toland-James lined up her bottles of supplements and swallowed about two dozen different pills. Vitamins. Extracts. Beta-carotene whatevers. Saint John's Wort to fight depression. Garlic to keep her heart pumping. Ginko biloba to keep her mind sharp.

Bernie's body was her temple, and she worshiped at the shrine. But when those extra pounds piled on, Bernie went another route — only occasionally, but effectively.

She snorted coke.

Just once in a while, just to keep her appetite down, her energy up. Just a line here, a line there. Nothing horrible, according to Bernie.

Of course, when she combined the coke with the booze and the ginko biloba . . . ? Well, as a worried Maggie told her one day in disgust, at least there was the hope that Bernie would be able to remember where she was when she slipped into the coma.

"So? Well?" Bernie said now, spreading her arms. "Where is he?"

"Where's who, Bernie?" Maggie asked, avoiding her friend's eyes as she scrambled to figure out some sort of answer that wouldn't smell riper than five-day-old flounder. "I don't know what you're talking about."

"R-i-i-ight," Bernie said, winking one heavily mascared eye. "I get you. He's brand-spanking new, and you want to keep him under wraps. Okay, I can deal with that. Just as long as you give me something. Give me *some*thing, Maggie. A name?"

"A — a name? Oh, a name." Maggie crossed to her desk and grabbed her pack of cigarettes. Quit smoking? Sure. The minute she didn't consider the damn things the only real lifeline she had at her disposal. She took her time lighting the cigarette, partly to stall, partly because that damn Saint Just had her Mini-Bic and she had to find a pack of matches somewhere on her cluttered desk.

She put the match to the end of the cigarette, inhaled deeply, blew out the smoke, and watched it as if it were tea leaves, possibly containing an answer for Bernie. "A name. Sure, why not. It's . . . um . . . it's . . . Alex. Yes, that's it. Alex."

"Alex," Bernie repeated. "Alex what?"

"Is that a new blouse?" Maggie asked, quickly going over to Bernie and picking at the sleeve of the black silk creation she'd seen at least three times. "I really like this. It looks so good against your skin. Did you just have a facial?"

"Maggie," Bernie said warily. "What's up? Oh. Wait. He's still here, isn't he?" She lowered her voice to a whisper. "Where? In the bedroom? Oh, you sly dog, you. What is it? Is he married? You know I've warned you about that. Look what happened to me. Sylvia Leeds came after me with a butcher knife, for crying out loud. Pulled it right out of the butcher's hands when we met up at the meat market and chased me all the way down the street. Trust me, no man is worth being carved up like a rump roast."

"He's not married," Maggie said, using the ashtray. That was another great thing about smoking. It kept you busy, or at least looking busy. Lighting, inhaling, exhaling, flipping ashes . . .

"He's not? Okay, then what's wrong with him? There's got to be something wrong with him, if you're hiding him."

"Hello there," Sean Connery's voice said from behind Maggie, so that she stopped dead in the process of being very busy inhaling more nicotine, and began to choke on the smoke. "Maggie, my dear, how very remiss of you. You didn't tell me we had a guest."

"Well, hello there right back at you, Alex," Bernie said, bursting the just blown-up bubble of Maggie's hope that Saint Just was only visible to her. "Maggie? Aren't you going to introduce us?"

Maggie coughed a few more times, wiped at her stinging eyes, then turned to look at Saint Just. Yup. There he was. Dressed in a pair of Kirk's slacks, Kirk's tan sweater (and Kirk would have given his capped eyeteeth to look half so good in those clothes). Only his boots were his own, and the pant legs covered them to the ankle, so Bernie probably wouldn't notice. Especially since Bernie was too busy being taken in by the man's insufferable killer smile.

"Yes, Maggie, please. I should be very

honored to make this beautiful lady's acquaintance."

Muttering very unlovely things beneath her breath, Maggie stubbed her cigarette out in the ashtray on the coffee table before saying, "Bernice Toland-James, Alex. Alex, Bernice Toland-James. Now behave yourselves, both of you."

She watched as Saint Just approached Bernie, bowed over her hand, kissed it. Probably on the palm, too, the bastard. "It is my great pleasure, Miss Toland-James."

"Oh, please," Bernie gushed, blushing like a virginal schoolgirl, something Bernie hadn't been in a long, long time. "Call me Bernie. And I'll call you Alex. Alex — Alex what? I don't seem to get anywhere with that question, do I?"

"Ah, yes," Saint Just said, striking a pose. "A man of mystery. I do so enjoy a mystery. Don't I, Maggie?"

"I wonder how much you'll enjoy being tossed out of a ninth-story window," Maggie muttered as she walked by him, deliberately hitting his elbow so that he dropped his ridiculous, dandified pose. "Bernie, did I tell you that Kirk showed up here today?" she then asked, leading her friend toward the couches.

"Kirk? And did you throw him out the

window?" Bernie asked, still glancing back at Saint Just, exactly the way all the ladies in Maggie's books looked at him, because she had made him so magnificently handsome. Pulling Maggie down beside her on the soft cushions, she stage-whispered, "Don't be such a smart mouth, Mags. This one looks like a keeper."

"He *needs* a keeper, you mean," Maggie grumbled, then grabbed hold of herself and gave herself a mental shake. She had to keep her head, get through this, get Bernie the hell out of the apartment before Sterling Balder waltzed in and blew up what was left of her sanity.

"I had to invite Kirk to the party," Maggie pressed on, working over the pain in her head and the buzzing in her ears. "Do you mind?"

Bernie, obviously using tremendous self-discipline, pulled her gaze away from Saint Just, who was now pouring himself a glass of wine, his back turned to them both. "Do *I* mind? Honey, I'm not the one who was bumping bellies with the man, remember? Not for a lot of years. Therapy has pretty much erased that particular memory from my mind, thank you, Jesus. Besides, maybe it's a good idea. One look at Alex here, and Kirk will know he's been outclassed."

Maggie tilted her head to one side, considering Bernie's words. "Yeah. You're right. Kirk would really hate being cast in the shade by Alex, and he certainly would be, wouldn't he? Son of a gun."

"Well," Bernie said, slapping her palms against her thighs and then getting to her feet. "Now that I know you're all right — *boy*, are you all right — I'll just get out of your way and get back to work. I'm editing the new Felicity Boothe Simmons this week. The woman's endless supply of unnecessary adverbs is astounding. But, as long as she hits the *NYT* for six weeks with each book, who's complaining? Certainly not *moi*."

"Leaving so soon?" Saint Just said, taking Bernie's arm as the woman headed for the door. "And we were just getting acquainted."

Bernie, who would have had brass ones, if women had them at all, just about melted into the carpet. "Oh, I know, I know. It has been wonderful, hasn't it? But you'll be at Maggie's little party next Saturday night, won't you? That won't give me time for a chemical peel, but I could probably slip in another collagen injection in my lips. Oh, never mind me. I'm just thinking out loud. Toodles, Maggie. Finish that book!"

Bernie was halfway out the door before she leaned her head back in and mouthed the words "Call me!" to Maggie, who gave her a sickly grin, and a sickly wave to go with it.

Saint Just closed the door behind Bernie's departing back, then turned to smile at Maggie. "In the words of my esteemed friend and compatriot, Mr. Balder, that went tolerably well, don't you think?"

Something inside Maggie snapped with a loud, almost painful *twang*. "Are you out of your *mind?* What did you think you were doing? I should have tied you to the bed; that's what I should have done. You can't be seen, you idiot. Not until we get our stories straight. And give you and Sterling names, for crying out loud. I can't introduce you as Alexandre and Sterling. People *read* my books, you know. Or they will, until I kill you and Sterling off in the next one, if that's the only way to get the two of you out of my life."

She slapped her hands to her head. "What am I saying? This is not happening. I don't care if Bernie saw you; this is *not* happening."

"There she goes again, Saint Just, climbing for the treetops," Sterling said,

79

entering the living room. "Perhaps another parlor trick?"

"Absolutely not. Either she believes, or she doesn't. As long as *we* believe, that's enough to keep us here."

"Yes, but she's going to kill us off, Saint Just. She said so. Weren't you listening?"

"Not really, no. Histrionics are so fatiguing. Sterling? Perhaps you could show me the kitchens?"

Maggie watched them go, her characters, her creations, behaving just as she'd envisioned. One, she wanted to hug. The other, she'd always thought she'd want in her bed. Now all she wanted was to slap him until his ears rang.

Proud. Arrogant. Wittily sarcastic. They had all sounded so good at the time. A handsome, dreadfully handsome, marvelously talented, extremely intelligent man of the world. The perfect man of the Regency world, that is. Pull him out of the ballroom, or off the hunting field, and put him in a Manhattan apartment, and the man lost a whacking great lot of his appeal.

Maggie looked over at her computer, knowing that there was no way she'd work anymore today. Then she sighed, got to her feet, and headed for the kitchen, wondering how the Viscount Saint Just would

feel about peanut butter and jelly sand-
wiches. . . .

Just at midnight, a most civilized hour
for gentlemen of the *ton,* Alexandre Blake,
Viscount Saint Just, stepped onto the pavement outside Maggie's apartment. He was
still dressed in Kirk Toland's rather comfortable slacks and definitely comfortable
sweater. He wore his own boots, and had
tucked his ebony cane beneath one arm
before sauntering off in search of a bit of
fresh air and, just perhaps, adventure.

He'd left Sterling behind, happily snoring on one side of the bed in what Maggie
Kelly so quaintly termed her "guest"
room. Saint Just wasn't too put out by this,
as he and Sterling had been forced, on
more than one occasion, to share a bed-
chamber and a bed in some out-of-the-way
inn. He remembered the Boar's Head, in
Lincolnshire. He'd used his diamond
stickpin to carve his name into the win-
dowpane in his private dining chamber. A
lovely custom. Perhaps he'd do the same in
the "guest" room.

Stepping away from the doorway, and ignoring the liveried man who asked if he
could summon him a cab — as if the Viscount Saint Just would ever condescend to

81

a common public carrier — Saint Just stopped, looked left, then right, then set out down the street toward a blinking light in the distance.

The lights fascinated him. Red ones. Green ones. Dancing lights, blinking lights, nearly turning the night into day. Nothing like London after dark, where even strong, well-armed men took care to travel in groups. There could be no danger here, not with all this illumination.

First Saint Just followed the lights; then he followed his nose, advancing toward a delicious swirl of smells emanating from a huge metal cylinder stuck straight into the wall beside an establishment spelled out in brightest yellow lights: Styles Cafe.

The proprietor's name? A crafty statement? Did it matter? Food was food, as long as it wasn't haggis, and he was definitely hungry.

He slipped a hand into one of those most convenient pockets and withdrew a few coins, a few folded bills, both "borrowed" from Maggie's purse. He had felt bad about this, but not bad enough to risk venturing outside without at least a few pennies in his purse — or pocket, as was the case.

"Hey. You. Yeah — you. Got a buck for me?"

Saint Just looked up from his handful of money, straight into the eyes of a rather large, definitely unkempt young man who had stepped in front of his path. "A buck?" he said, not understanding the term.

"Yeah, a buck. Five bucks. For me, and for my friend here. Ain't that right, Snake? Money. *Dinero*. Bucks," the youth said, a toss of his head indicating the second youth, who somehow was now standing behind Saint Just.

"Yo. Right on, Killer, m'man, m'main man."

"Oh," Saint Just said, as the dawn broke over his confusion. "You want *money*. Excuse me, I didn't quite understand." He knew Homer had said that there is a strength in the union even of very sorry men, but the youth in front of him was sorrier than most, and his companion was probably just as pitiful. Amusement replaced any slight fear. His smile widened. "No. I don't think so. Now, if you'll just step aside?"

"You don't *think* so? Did you hear that, Snake? He don't *think* so. Now what are we gonna do?"

By way of answer, the young man named Snake clamped both hands down on Saint Just's shoulders, then rammed a knee into

83

the small of his back.

Perhaps Homer had been right. Saint Just went down on his knees, pain blasting through him. He was down, but he was by no means out. Not Alexandre Blake, Viscount Saint Just, hero extraordinaire.

The slim rapier so cleverly concealed within his cane came out with a *swish* and moved with a flourish as Saint Just pushed himself up and to his left, a whirling dervish of well-orchestrated movement, just as Maggie Kelly had described in Chapter Two, pages 26 to 30, of *The Case of the Pilfered Pearls.*

Snake howled — did snakes howl? — and grabbed at his bleeding cheek even as he ran back into the darkness. Then Saint Just turned the rapier in the first youth's direction, lightly pressing its tip against the boy's shirt, the one printed, quite apropos of the situation, with the words: Shit Happens.

"*En garde,* you blackguard!"

The youth backed up, one hand to the front of his jeans — a suspiciously dark stain forming at the crotch — the other raised beside his head. "Hey, hey, hey. Don't be goin' postal, man. It was just a question. I'm gone, I'm gone. See? I'm going. Going. *Gone.*"

Saint Just watched as the youth backed up, nearly tripping over his too-long jeans, then turned and ran off into the alleyway, following his cohort in attempted crime.

"Well," Saint Just said out loud as he sheathed the rapier, "that was exhilarating."

But then the two youths reappeared, and they seemed to have found reinforcements. Saint Just displayed the sword once more, which kept the group, now numbering four, at a distance as he walked — rapidly, but with dignity; certainly not at a dead run — back to his new residence.

He was a hero, after all. He wasn't brick stupid.

CHAPTER 4

"I refuse. I most completely and utterly refuse to do anything of the sort. I do hope that's sufficiently clear, Miss Kelly. If not, I am most certainly prepared to restate my objections."

Maggie glared at Saint Just across the breakfast table. Her hero. What a letdown. "You know, you'd look a lot more menacing without all that toilet paper stuck to your chin. You're just lucky I got to you in time to loan you my old electric razor, or you might have cut your throat with that disposable — which may not have been a bad idea, come to think of it. Oh, and would you give all this complaining a rest? It's only Kirk's underwear. And it's clean, damn it. It's not like I'm asking you to wear stuff I pulled out of the hamper."

"Hamper?" Sterling asked, his mouth full of Cocoa Puffs. "Keep food in a hamper, Miss Kelly, not smallclothes."

"Pic-nic-ing with unmentionables. How very original," Saint Just said, leaning back in his chair, holding a half-slice of buttered toast to his mouth. "Now, when do we visit the shops?"

Maggie sighed and put down her teacup. "Okay, okay, I get the point. You guys need clothing. Slacks, shoes, shirts."

Saint Just pulled the bits of dried toilet paper from his chin, wincing slightly as it stuck to his recent small wounds. "Fresh linen, my good woman. Most definitely fresh linen. We're not ragtag barbarians."

"Yeah, right. Except I didn't expect you to still be here this morning. So much for desperate prayers. But you can't go out to the stores. Especially you, Sterling, not dressed like that."

"I warned him that waistcoat was a poor choice. Canary yellow. Can you imagine anything more unsuitable?"

"One . . . two . . . seven — okay, lucky you, Alex — the urge to strangle you is passing," Maggie told him. "It was *my* decision that Sterling should be fond of yellow. Besides, you know that's not what I meant. There just is no way — no way — you two can go out in public until we get Sterling out of those clothes."

Sterling choked on his Cocoa Puffs. "Dashed mad you are, Miss Kelly, if you think I'm amenable to walking about stark, staring naked. Too chilly, for one thing. And I wouldn't want to upset the ladies."

"That's *not* what I meant, Sterling. I

meant — oh, hell," Maggie plopped her elbows on the table and dropped her head in her hands. Sterling and his literal way of thinking weren't half so amusing when she had to deal with him directly.

Not that it was any easier dealing with Saint Just. She could still shiver, remembering the cold look he'd given her earlier, when she'd asked him to carry the platter of scrambled eggs over to the table. Anyone would think she'd just asked him to stand on his head and sing three choruses of "God Save the King." Proud, arrogant, a totally early nineteenth-century gentleman.

And he'd obviously cast her in the role of his personal servant. A hero in a book was one thing. A hero in her apartment was definitely not nearly so romantic. Her readers wouldn't be so gaga over Saint Just if they knew he expected to be waited on hand and foot. She was going to have to evolve Saint Just a little in her next book. A little less Peter O'Toole, a little more Ben Affleck.

"Look," Maggie said, raising her head once more. "If you guys are going to be here — and I get the feeling that you are, at least until I'm committed — then we're going to have to come to a few agreements.

Starting with this one — *I'm* in charge. The boss. The head honcho. The one calling the shots and making the rules. You got that?"

"Saint Just?" Sterling asked, looking at his friend. "Saint Just, you've got that little *thing* working in your cheek again. See it, Miss Kelly? That can't be good. Last time I saw it, he was seconds from planting a facer on Lord Alton. Knocked two teeth from the man's mouth, as I recall. Perhaps you'd like to reconsider?"

"No, it's all right, Sterling," Saint Just said at last, putting down the piece of toast, then patting at his mouth with the paper napkin he'd called "an invention of a decidedly low-class devil" not five minutes earlier. "Miss Kelly is quite correct. We are far from babes in the woods, but we are in unfamiliar territory, possibly even dangerous territory for the unwary. Who knows what trouble we might stumble into out there, unawares. We probably should let Miss Kelly have her head for a while, until we're more knowledgeable. More knowledgeable, and in clean linen, if you don't mind."

"Really?" Maggie looked at him warily. "You mean it? You're actually going to shut up and let me get this show on the road?"

"A traveling show?" Sterling asked. "With wagons, and all of that? Why would we —"

"*Sterling,*" both Maggie and Saint Just said at once, and the confused gentleman prudently returned his attention to his Cocoa Puffs.

Maggie moved to stand up, and Saint Just immediately came around the small, glass-topped table and pulled back her chair, even as Sterling — mouth full of cereal — all but leapt to his feet.

Okay, so it wasn't *all* horrible. At least she'd invented polite characters. Her last blind date had walked through a doorway ahead of her, and let the door swing back, smacking her in the nose. His name was Robert Quigley, and she'd enjoyed killing him off in her current manuscript. Writing for a living had more perks than just being able to go to work in her bathrobe.

"Thank you, Alex," she said, heading into the living room with her teacup, Saint Just on her heels. "We could do this on-line, you know," she said, seating herself at the computer. "Ralph Lauren is on-line. Lots of designers are on-line."

"I'm confident you know precisely what you're saying, Miss Kelly, but I'm afraid I'm not comprehending a word of it."

She turned in her chair and smiled up at him. "No, you're not, are you? How much *do* you know about" — she spread her arms — "all of this? You know. This apartment, me, the world — *me?*"

"You're blushing, Miss Kelly," Saint Just pointed out, seating himself on the couch that faced the corner computer desk. "I imagine I should allay your fears. Sterling and I existed in your mind. We were born, grew, evolved, became real, in your mind. Slowly at first, then more rapidly, more fully, learning more, hearing more and, frankly, *wanting* more. And sometimes wanting a lot less. Such as your great deal of worrying about the size of your bosoms, which I, by the bye, believe totally unwarranted."

"Thank you, I — whoa! No, I don't thank you. But I'd thank you to get *out* of my mind from here on, okay?"

"That isn't a matter for thanks, as we're here now, most definitely *out* of your mind. Even more now than yesterday, as we're finding our feet here now, as it were. Shall I prove it yet again, Doubting Thomas?"

Maggie lit a cigarette with shaking hands. She was believing this guy, really believing him. Maybe because she wrote fiction and had an imaginative streak.

Maybe just because no other explanation fit — at least not one that didn't have her ending up in a padded cell. "Yeah. Prove it. I'd love for you to prove it."

"Certainly. Close your eyes, Miss Kelly, and tell me the setting you've chosen for *The Case of the Disappearing Dandy*. I'm willing to wager you can't."

"My next Saint Just Mystery? Of course I can do that." Maggie thought for a moment, then blinked. Stared at Saint Just. "I . . . I don't remember."

"Naturally, my dear lady. Sterling and I aren't in your mind anymore."

"But — but I remember that I'm the one who chose yellow as Sterling's favorite color. I remember *everything*."

"Everything that has happened, everything that you have written, definitely. But nothing that you *haven't* written. That spark of imagination as it concerns Sterling and myself, well, that now resides with us. You have talent and a store of information. We have the inspiration."

"You can't do that," Maggie said, her body cold with panic. "That's . . . that's *stealing*."

"Hardly." He lifted his right hand, cursorily inspecting his buffed fingernails. "You do remember giving me a brain, don't you?

I don't simply react, as does Sterling, the dear fellow. *I* act. Once I felt ready, *I* acted. For my own reasons, having much to do with self-preservation, I made sure that Sterling and I tidied up, as it were, before moving out of your mind and into this lovely establishment. You'll not see a single new idea for the Saint Just Myteries without us at your side, literally at your side. We are now, as you might say, *indispensable* to you, Miss Kelly. Collaborators. Cohorts in crime. Worthy associates." He looked at her and flashed his Val Kilmer smile. *"Partners."*

Maggie shot to her feet, began to pace even as Saint Just also got to his feet, the complete gentleman, damn him. *"Disappearing Dandy, Disappearing Dandy.* Just hold on a minute, I'll remember. You and Sterling were going to be invited to a house party — no! I'm going to set it in London. Aren't I? Oh, God, I can't remember!" She stomped across the room and glared at the infuriating figment of her imagination. "What did you do? What the *hell* did you do?"

"Do? Why, I did just what you created me to do, Miss Kelly. I took charge. Of myself, of Sterling, good but not too astute soul that he is, but always quite lovable,

don't you think? And so, although I understand, and even sympathize, with your desire to — what did you call it? — be the
head honcho? Yes, that's it. While I sympathize, I felt you should know that, if we
are nothing without you, you are nothing
without us."

Maggie pressed her hands to her
stomach. "My books . . . my career . . . my
God. This isn't happening. This *can't* be
happening to me."

"That's it, Miss Kelly, fight it. Pluck to
the backbone, you are, and so I've told
Sterling time and again. It's why I was so
sure you'd eventually come to grips with
our new . . . Shall we call it our new *reality?*
Yes, that sounds like something you'd understand, although why anyone would wish
to spend time and money to read about
someone else's idea of how to achieve internal peace, or outward success, remains a
total mystery to me, the Regency world's
greatest amateur sleuth. I especially disliked that book written by Doctor Bob
Chalfont, *Love Well, Live Free.*"

Maggie seemed to have lost verbal eloquence as well as her imagination, because
she only looked at Saint Just and said:
"Huh?"

"The book, Miss Kelly. *Love Well, Live*

Free. Poppycock. How could you read such nonsense? I'd nod off after half a chapter, just couldn't remain awake in the midst of all those ridiculous *tests* and *study exercises.* You did notice a lack of inspiration at those times, didn't you? You must have, as you never finished reading the book. Why would anyone take a *test* to see if they're happy? Just look in the mirror. If you're smiling, you're happy. That's all there is to it."

Saint Just's voice was like bees buzzing inside Maggie's head. They knew about Doctor Bob? Her therapist, Doctor Bob? The psychologist she'd introduced to Bernie, helped get a book contract? *That* Doctor Bob? Maggie pointed both index fingers at him, shook them once for emphasis. "Let me get this straight. When I read Doctor Bob's book . . . *you* read it with me?"

"Until I'd nod off, yes."

"Doctor Bob?" Sterling said, walking into the room, still munching on a piece of toast. "What a tiresome man. I much prefer Oprah, although Saint Just believes she's too puffed up with her own consequence. He's most partial to sporting events." He stabbed one arm into the air. "Let's go, Mets! Right, Saint Just?"

A whimper — not the first of the day — rose in Maggie's throat, and she raised both hands, signaling that she wanted silence. "All right," she said, taking a deep breath, releasing it slowly, "I think I'm getting this now. You two slowly came to life inside my head —"

"Becoming more real every day, until we felt secure enough to leave, yes," Saint Just cut in helpfully.

"Don't interrupt. You used to see the world through *my* eyes, but now you don't. I used to be sane, but now I'm not. How am I doing so far? Am I babbling yet, foaming at the mouth?"

"Sterling, if you'd give us a moment?" Saint Just asked, and Sterling, who was looking rather nervous anyway, gratefully retreated to the kitchen.

Maggie was in a flat-out panic. "Gone. It's gone. Every Saint Just idea I ever had. *Pffft!* And what did I get in trade? A handsome pain in my ass and his faithful companion. And I haven't seen Napper or Wellie since these two bozos got here. They've deserted me, and I don't blame them. Unless . . ." she said slowly, her cheeks going pale as she stared at Saint Just. "Oh God, you didn't. Please tell me you didn't *morph* into their little bodies or something like that." Maggie collapsed onto the couch, drew a pillow into her lap, and buried her face in it.

"Oh, yes, the cats," Saint Just said, lightly rubbing his hands together, his head down, so that Maggie didn't see his smile. "I had hoped to ease you into much of this, truly. But, about the felines, Miss Kelly . . ."

Maggie's head shot up. "What? I'm right? I can't be right. You *did* morph them, become them? Damn it, Saint Just, how could you do that to two defenseless animals?"

He looked at her thoughtfully, perhaps a little angrily. "Perhaps you might want a glass of wine?"

"Wine? Believe me, Saint Just, it's going to take a whole hell of a lot more than a glass of wine. I love those cats." She blinked back tears. "I really love those cats."

"To each his own, I suppose. But it was necessary, Miss Kelly. We had our minds, all the many gifts you gave us, but we needed that spark of life. Beating hearts, blood pulsing through the veins, that sort of thing. And yet, they're not really gone, not departed — not exactly. They're still here, but now we're here, too. Are you understanding any of this, Miss Kelly?"

Maggie felt her eyes growing wider, wide enough that she wouldn't have been surprised if her eyeballs popped straight out of her head. She hunted for words as she glared up at him, found none, and screamed. One great big, blood-curdling scream.

"Female hysterics aid nothing, Miss Kelly," Saint Just said with maddening calm. "It has nothing to do with anything not entirely sane and scientific. In a way. Now, if we might get back to important matters? Clothing, Miss Kelly."

But Maggie just sat there, trying to digest all that she'd heard, all that she'd learned. "Which one are you? Wellie or Napper? Do you *feel* like a cat?"

Saint Just rolled his eyes. "Most definitely not, because I am *not* a cat. This silliness has gone on long enough. I am your imagination, come to life, and I suggest you stop asking ridiculous questions and take a bow, Miss Kelly."

"Take a bow," she repeated dully. "Oh, sure. Right. I lose my mind, my career, and my cats — except the cats are still here, at least while you're here, right? In return, I get a guy who thinks he's God's gift, and his Cocoa Puffs-loving buddy. And my book isn't done. Believe it or not, through all of this, that's what really ticks me off. That book was supposed to be done."

"And it is," Saint Just told her. "We'd already agreed on how Shively should be punished after my so-brilliant unmasking of his dastardly deed — he was led off to face the hangman's justice. My good friend Sterling and myself accepted the congratulations of our peers, and we toddled off into the night to applause from the gentlemen and deep sighs from the ladies. Oh, and that correction concerning Quigley? I did that as well. I made him an insensitive boor, which you should have known to do, considering *his* inspiration was an insensitive boor."

"I hate you," Maggie said in all sincerity.

Saint Just shrugged his broad shoulders. "As Pilpay said, 'There are some who bear a grudge even to those that do them good.' Clearly, Pilpay knew whereof he spoke. So, now that you've run most entirely out of reasons to remain here, may I suggest we adjourn to the shops?"

Maggie's lip curled. "Why? To get you a new flea collar?"

"How very droll," Saint Just drawled, smoothing down Kirk's sweater, which still looked better on him than it ever had on

Kirk. "And how very unperceptive of you. Your felines, Miss Kelly, were last seen not an hour ago beneath my bed, snoring their heads off."

"You mean . . . ? Then they're not . . . ? You didn't . . . ? Oh! What a *bastard* you are, Saint Just."

"Yes, just as you made me. However, you must admit, you are a most wonderfully gullible audience. So gullible, it takes most of the sport out of it, actually. Now, if you can possibly wipe that nasty look from your face, shall we be off?"

Saint Just prided himself on all he had learned through Maggie Kelly as he prepared — studied actually — the reality he would soon be entering, the world in which he would live, hopefully thrive.

He'd picked and chosen information, some that suited him, some elemental, such as how to turn on a faucet, employ a light switch, use Maggie Kelly's computer, television machine, and even the telephone — although he doubted he'd try that one again anytime soon. He hadn't come off well there, and Saint Just did not like looking, or feeling, inadequate.

From the books that Maggie read, to the television programs that she watched, to

100

the discussions she and her friends had in the apartment, Saint Just had come to know the mores of the day, the freedoms women enjoyed (he couldn't agree with them, but he acknowledged them). He understood that man had evolved (or degenerated) into creatures who actually performed domestic chores. He knew that, for instance, if Miss Kelly lived a more bucolic life, rather than in this Manhattan apartment, *he* would be expected to dispose of the garbage, scythe the lawn, even shovel the flagways in winter.

Which was one of the many reasons he appreciated Miss Kelly's Manhattan address.

He may have been tied to this apartment, never out and about in the city until last night, but he felt sure he could manage, even excel, in his expanding environment. He was not a stupid man.

So he *knew*. He knew quite a number of things.

That didn't mean Maggie Kelly had to know he knew as much as he did, not when it was more convenient for him if she thought he was a babe in the woods, needing her protection.

Because he did. That small contretemps with Killer and Snake last evening had taught him that quite successfully. He was not ready to be on his own. He had no money, no place to lay his head. If he had skewered those two ruffians, he would be in jail, not a hero, as the laws of the modern world had also embraced this new "sensibility" he believed to be trying at times, laughable at others, and sometimes downright inconvenient. Still, last night's encounter proved once and for all that, if Maggie Kelly needed him, which he'd so wisely made sure she did, then he likewise relied on her.

So, for his creature comforts, he needed her. For his safety, he needed her. And she needed him, although he kept having to prove that to her. That business with the cats was mean, to a point, but once again she had proven to him that she needed a keeper. She trusted too much, believed too easily and, for all her mouthiness, her air of bravado, she became depressingly cowed whenever a stronger personality presented itself. For all her practiced courage, she was a babe in the woods, and the hero in him cried out that he must protect her.

So she needed him.

He needed her.

At the moment, he needed her to pay the bill for the separate, leaning towers of clothing (one for Saint Just, the other for Sterling) that threatened to slide off the counter and onto the floor of this place called Bloomingdale's.

"Are you sure this is enough?" Maggie said to him as Saint Just added yet another sports coat to his purchases. "I've got a ten thousand dollar limit on this credit card, and I think you're still about fifty bucks short of topping it out. Go on, get a couple more pairs of socks. Shoot the whole wad, why don't you?"

"There is nothing colder or less flattering to the giver than reluctant charity," Saint Just reminded her frostily, then wandered off to look at the socks. Comfortable-looking things, socks. Much more comfortable than his usual hose. He dropped a pair on the floor, then manfully suppressed a wince as he bent over to retrieve it; his lower back was giving him hell, thanks to Snake's none-too-gentle method of introduction.

What a lowering experience that had been. Chased back to his hole like a frightened hare, harried by ragtag scum of the earth. Hardly heroic. He had a score to settle with Mr. Snake and Mr. Killer.

"Alex? The clerk is ringing everything up now. Is there anything else you want?"

"Hmmm?" Saint Just murmured as he turned to see Miss Kelly standing beside him. "Forgive me, I was woolgathering. Do you recall, as I'm convinced you will, the time I was sauntering down Bond Street at some ungodly hour, and was accosted by ruffians hired to murder me?"

Maggie looked to her left, her right, and then whispered fiercely, "Would you shut up? Somebody might hear you."

"I believe I routed them quite nicely," he went on, ignoring her warning, "and there were five of them. Nasty brutes. But I sent them to the rightabout, and limping and whimpering as they went. Didn't I?"

"God, all you men are alike, real or imaginary. Always wanting a pat on the head. Stroke me, flatter me, tell me I'm wonderful, and I'll help you if you miss any of the smaller parts. Yes, Alex, you were magnificent. Banged two of their heads together, knocking them senseless, skewered one with your sword stick, brained another with the cane, and sent the fifth running away, hoping his nearly severed ear wouldn't fall off. I remember. It took me hours to orchestrate that scene. Hours."

"But *I* performed the deed, remember? I didn't run, didn't turn a hair. I simply dispatched the ruffians, adjusted my cravat, and continued on my way. Because *I*, Miss Kelly, am a hero."

"Yeah, yeah, yeah," Maggie agreed. "A hero. Shame they don't sell medals here, so I could pin one on your chest. Now, do you want to tell me what this is all about?"

Saint Just smiled, raised a hand to adjust the cravat that wasn't there. "Just a fond reminiscence, nothing more. Are we quite finished here?"

Maggie looked around as she ticked off items on one hand — then the other. "Slacks, shirts, socks, sweaters, pajamas, a suit for you — Sterling's will have to wait until he can come in and be fitted — shoes, ties, belts, handkerchiefs, underwear. Yes, I suppose that's it. We can take some of it with us and have the rest delivered. Besides, we still have to get you a razor, other toiletries. Comb, toothbrush, deoder— oh, shit."

Saint Just lifted one eyebrow. "I beg your pardon. There's no need to be vulgar."

Maggie grabbed him by the sleeve and pulled him behind a rack of sports coats. "It's Kirk. I don't want him to see me — you — both of us. Either of us. Oh, for crying out loud — where are you going?"

Where was he going? Most certainly not to hide somewhere else. Was the woman daft? He was the Viscount Saint Just. He did not hunker down behind haberdashery, hiding like nervously twitching vermin from the kitchen's best mouser. Besides, he'd been longing to meet Kirk Toland for some time. Toland was, when Saint Just was being honest with himself, one of the many reasons he had decided to find a way into Maggie Kelly's life. The man had hurt her, and Saint Just took that as a personal insult.

"Maggie?" he trilled rather loudly, deciding that the time had come for informality, now that Toland was within earshot. "You absolutely must see this tie," he said, grabbing one at random from a large display. "I believe it will be famous with my new ensemble."

Maggie's wince told him two things. One, she'd rather stay hunkered down in her hidey-hole and, two, he probably shouldn't have said *ensemble*. Ah, well, he was English. As he already knew, it often seemed as if the British and the Americans spoke entirely different languages.

"Maggie? Is that you? Good God, it is. I thought you were working on your book?" Kirk walked toward her, still holding a packaged dress shirt in each hand. "And who's this?" he asked, glaring at Saint Just.

"Who? Him? He's . . . I'm . . . we're —
hi, Kirk," Maggie ended brightly, also
glaring at Saint Just.

How he loved being the center of attention. And this time, he was prepared.

"Good afternoon," he said, extending
one hand, waiting until Toland shifted
both shirts to his left hand. "Alex Blakely,
late of London and currently Miss Kelly's
houseguest. M'cousin, you understand.
And you'd be — ?"

Toland allowed his hand to be shaken as
he looked Saint Just up and down.
"Toland," he said automatically, vaguely.
"Kirk Toland. Maggie? The man's wearing
my clothes. Why is he wearing my
clothes?"

"*Your* clothes? Oh, yes, yes," Maggie
sputtered, then laughed. "What a mixup.
My . . . my *cousin* only just arrived from
England last night. And . . . and they lost
his bags. The airline. Lost his bags. That's
. . . that's why we're here, getting Alex a
new wardrobe to hold him over. Weren't
we lucky that your clothes fit him?" She
took a deep breath, blew it out. "So, what
are you doing here, Kirk? Shopping?"

"What else would I be doing here?"
Toland responded, still looking at Saint
Just, who was silently applauding Maggie

Kelly's fertile imagination. The woman had a real flair for invention, bless her. But, then, he already knew that. He was here, wasn't he?

Maggie laughed nervously. "Shopping? Well, of course you are. You haven't forgotten the party next Saturday night?"

Toland ignored her. "You're English. Maggie's Irish. How did she end up with an English cousin?"

Maggie's grin threatened to split her face as she spoke through her clenched teeth. "Over to you, Alex," she said, waggling her eyebrows at him.

"Why, of course," Saint Just said, saluting her with a slight bow. "Although unwonted inquisitiveness from strangers is always so abrasive, isn't it? What was it Publicus Syrus said? Oh, yes. 'It is not every question that deserves an answer.' Good man, Syrus. But you Americans seem to thrive on gossip, as do we English, now that I think about the thing. Very well, Mr. . . . Thingumbob — sorry, I've quite forgotten your name — I'd be happy to satisfy your curiosity, although it's not a pretty story, or one of which either of us is very proud."

"Oh, go ahead," Maggie said, glaring at him again. "Tell Kirk the story. I love hearing that old story, really."

Impudent woman! He could very often admire her — what was the word? Oh, yes. Her *spunk*. "Very well. My English ancestors once held land in Ireland, land which conveniently came with Maggie's ancestral home already on it, as was so often the case in those days. My ancestors took the land, the house . . . the women, when they chose. My dearest cousin descends from that side of the family, don't you, Maggie? Conceived on entirely the wrong side of the blanket."

He vainly searched on his chest for his quizzing glass, his usual prop when about to make a damning statement. "Bastards, sir."

Her smile frozen in place, Maggie nodded. "There are some who would call the Blakely side of the family the real bastards," she purred, then grabbed Saint Just's elbow. "Come on, *cousin*, we have to get home."

Toland raised a finger as he said, "But — but you never said anything about this cousin before, Maggie."

"He's the black sheep," she gritted out as Saint Just spied a tie he really liked, and went over to look at it. "We never speak of him if we can help it."

Toland leaned closer to whisper in her ear. "Like Socks, isn't he? You know, light in the loafers? And there you were yesterday, acting so self-righteous. No wonder, with Blakely hiding in your closet."

From the counter a few feet away, Saint Just watched, unable to hear Toland, but convinced that the man had said something upsetting, because Maggie looked ready to spit, just as Wellington had done this morning when Sterling inadvertently stepped on the cat's tail.

"Miss Kelly?"

Everyone turned to see the clerk standing there with a thick stack of paper and a pen.

"I'll just need your signature right here, below the total, and then we're done."

"*Your* signature?" Toland asked, his eyes wide as Maggie signed the bill and accepted her charge card. "*You're* paying for this guy's clothes?"

"Excuse me, Mr. Thingum— whatever," Saint Just drawled, approaching yet again, "and remembering dear Syrus — if you could possibly tell me what concern it is of yours what my cousin does, and who she does it for, I would then probably give you an answer. Although I don't think you'd like it. Are we understanding each other?"

Toland took two steps in Saint Just's direction, lifting his chin, folding his hands into fists. "No, I don't think so. Why don't you give it to me in black and white?"

Saint Just puzzled on this for a moment, then shook his head. "Dear me, I was thinking more of black and *blue*. Or aren't we going to face off now, punch each other into jellies?"

"Punch?" Toland backed up a step, then two more. "We're in Bloomies, for crying out loud."

"Very well then, name your seconds, and a time and place. I'm amenable."

"Maggie?" Kirk pulled her to one side, away from Saint Just. "Is he for real?"

Maggie coughed, quickly recovered. "No, Kirk, I don't think he is. Be happy he didn't slap you silly and demand pistols at dawn. Or didn't I mention that the Blakely side of the family is sort of . . . How can I say this? Okay, I've got it. The Blakely side of the family is sort of *nuts*."

As Saint Just patiently waited, feeling much more the thing than he had since scurrying back to Maggie's apartment last evening, his tail at least figuratively between his legs, Kirk Toland worked at putting a smile on his face. Even summoned a laugh.

"Well, that was fun, wasn't it? Nothing like a little joke to get the blood flowing, eh, Blakely? Oh, wait. Alex Blakely? Maggie? Isn't your protagonist Alexandre Blake?"

Ah, time for *le coup de grâce*. Thank the good Lord his assessment of the man had been correct, for outwitting Toland clearly would take little effort. "Yes," Saint Just said quickly, "he is. And I cannot tell you how flattered I am that she chose my name — and rather outstanding physical attributes — to use as her English hero," Saint Just inserted smoothly, just as if he hadn't spent half the night cudgeling his brain for what he hoped would be a plausible explanation. How very good of Kirk Toland to show up and let him try out his lie for size. "And those of my good friend, as well, Sterling Balder, whom she met about six years ago, on our first trip here to the colonies. Although you lifted Sterling's name whole, didn't you, you sneaky little puss?" Saint Just ended, wagging a finger at Maggie.

"I . . . I didn't think he'd mind," Maggie said, shrugging, and actually getting some color back in her cheeks, as if she might

112

also be enjoying bamboozling Kirk Toland. "Such a great name, and Sterling is such a sweetheart. I used the names, the physical descriptions, everything. Besides, it was only on spec. I wasn't sure the series would sell, and by that time I'd got to thinking of my characters as Alexandre Blake, as Sterling Balder, and didn't have the heart to change them."

"You should have said something earlier, Maggie." Toland frowned. "Names *and* faces? You took both? Maybe I should run this past Legal," he said quietly, then smiled at Saint Just. "You're flattered, right? And your friend? He's flattered, too? No thought of taking us to court, or anything like that?"

"Not a single one, no," Saint Just assured him, then offered his hand once more, immensely grateful that the fellow was such a thorough nincompoop. "And now, if you'll excuse us? We left Sterling at home, at loose ends, and Lord only knows what mischief he'll get into during our absence."

"You're staying with Maggie?" Toland asked, his friendliness evaporating once more. "And you're cousins? What kind of cousins?"

"Oh, give it a rest, Kirk," Maggie told

him, having just accepted two large shopping bags from the clerk. "Come on, Alex, let's go home."

"I was brilliant, wasn't I?" Saint Just asked as he looked back over his shoulder, at a frowning Kirk Toland. "Kept him off his balance, in fear of his pretty face, and then I bamboozled him. Oh, I'm so good, Maggie. So very, very good."

"I wouldn't be patting myself on the back if I were you, sport."

Saint Just looked at her, disliking her tone of voice. "Is there a problem?"

"A problem?" Maggie asked, handing him one of the shopping bags. "You tell me. Kirk thinks you're gay."

Saint Just chewed on this a moment as they headed toward the street. "Well, I am by nature a happy man," he said at last.

Maggie stopped dead, threw back her head and laughed out loud. "Not happy, Alex — *gay*. You know," she said, holding out her arm, allowing her wrist to go limp. "*Gay*."

"I still don't compre— *what?*"

"It's the way you sort of *pose*, Alex. And the way you talk. It will look famous with my ensemble? Thingumbob? *Dear me?* Trust me, bucko, American men don't talk like that. Not that there's anything wrong with being gay, and I made you a very liberal, broadminded sort, and Sterling is sort of — not totally — maybe sort of asexual, when you get right down to it. But it's still kind of funny. A Regency hero, in his own time, is all man. But here in Manhattan? Oh, no, not hardly. Maybe you'd better get used to not having all the ladies fawning over you, Alex. Except for Bernie, of course. She'll just consider you a challenge." And then she laughed again.

Saint Just looked around, realizing that several passersby were eying him strangely. "That's not amusing," he said stiffly, and exited Bloomingdale's, definitely not a happy man.

CHAPTER 5

It was Monday morning, exactly one week (minus a couple of hours) since Maggie's home had fallen to the latest British invasion.

Saint Just and Sterling Balder were still in residence, very much in residence.

Sterling was a real cutie, trying to be helpful in the kitchen, making the bed every morning, and he had the most delightful giggle as he plunked himself down in front of the television in her bedroom, watching Nickelodeon for at least eight hours a day (*Gilligan's Island* had some special appeal for the man, probably because he highly identified with Gilligan).

Sterling was lovable, huggable, silly, and had only one bad habit — Saint Just. He damn near worshipped the man, which just went to prove that, although she thought she'd created two really neat characters, she had rather shortchanged Sterling in the common sense department.

Then there was Saint Just. Oh, God, was there ever. He didn't hang up his clothing — Sterling had taken over the role of valet. He saw no need to carry his dirty dishes to the sink. He pleaded innocence — haughtily — when she accused him of leaving the top off the toothpaste. He called out for pizza twice a day, and ate in front of the TV in the living room, having taken custody of the remote — just like any man.

In one week, he'd become a CNN junkie, when he wasn't watching the History Channel, the Discovery Channel, PBS, MSNBC, ESPN, A&E, and two home shopping networks. It had taken until last Saturday to realize that he'd lifted her MasterCard and run rampant through yet another credit limit, because Saturday was the day Socks had called her down to the lobby to pick up twelve — count 'em, twelve — packages.

She was now the proud owner of an electric shoe-polishing kit, a George Foreman grill with built–in bun warmer, a laptop computer, a gas motor-powered sidewalk scooter, a six-foot-tall "cat tower" for Wellington and Napoleon, an autographed jersey from Mets star catcher Mike Piazza (five hundred bucks!), and a rather stunning piece of Joan Rivers jewelry.

The scooter and shoe-polishing kit were for Sterling, the grill for Saint Just, because he was now convinced that, yes, men *can* cook, as long as it's meat and it's grilled, and the necklace was for Maggie — obviously a gift meant to keep her from killing the viscount, just on general principles.

The remaining five boxes contained videos of various programming on the History Channel and other channels. He'd gotten the full set of *Horatio Hornblower* from Arts and Entertainment, plus several editions of *Tales of the Gun*, as he admitted to being "fascinated with firearms." Now *there* was a thought to send her stumbling, screaming, into the night.

He'd shown absolutely zilch concern when Maggie grabbed the kitchen shears and cut the MasterCard in half in front of him, probably because he'd already memorized the number. But, then, as he'd told her (taken right from dialogue in *The Case of the Overdue Duke*, blast him), "A gentleman of means has a responsibility to support tradespeople with his custom."

Pointing out that he didn't have a damn cent of his own meant nothing to him. In his mind, he was rich, had always been rich, and spent accordingly.

Still, Wellie and Napper were happy in their new "tower," and Sterling was well on his way to mastering the scooter — although she'd have to have the nicks in all her doorways spackled and repainted. So how bad could it be?

Pretty bad. And all because of Saint Just.

Bernie had stopped by twice, on the flimsiest of excuses the first time, and saying only "you know damn well why, sugar," the second time. Saint Just kissed the woman's hand, poured her drinks for her, and complimented her hair, her skin, the way she held a cigarette, you name it. The next time Bernie showed up, Maggie half expected her to bring along one of those blow-up air mattresses, so she could give up any silly pretenses and plain move in. Saint Just could probably get her one for a good price on one of those home shopping networks.

But, over rough spots and even rougher spots, the week had passed. Saint Just and Sterling were still in residence and Maggie, although still harboring moments of doubt ("Am I nuts? Definitely nuts."), was actually beginning to get used to them. After all, she'd been living with both men for close to six years.

"Now, here's the drill, boys," she said as she addressed the two men that Monday morning at the breakfast table. "I'm going out, and you're not. Got that?"

Saint Just frowned at her and sat back,

brushing nonexistent toast crumbs from his Mike Piazza jersey (you had to see it to believe it, but the man actually looked *good*). "So sorry, Maggie, but I've already promised to take Sterling to the park, to practice on his scooter. You'd be devastated to have to postpone your outing, wouldn't you, Sterling?"

"Well, if Maggie says not to —" he began, then looked at Saint Just, who had quietly cleared his throat. "Brokenhearted, definitely. I'd really been looking forward to it, Maggie."

"No, no," Saint Just protested. "It's quite all right, Sterling. I had wanted to stop by the shops, select a few choice cuts of beef for dinner tonight, but it's of no matter. Up for another pizza, old boy?"

"Again?" Sterling said, sighing. "I'd really prefer the beef. Don't have a shirt left without tomato stains on it."

Maggie watched the two men as they went back and forth, Saint Just being so maddeningly accommodating, Sterling being Sterling.

"I'll pick up three steaks on the way home, and we'll *all* go to the park after lunch," she offered as Sterling began gathering the dirty dishes and carrying them into the kitchen. The man was fascinated by the dishwasher, still in disbelief that he could close the door on dirty dishes and open it an hour later to clean dishes. And the question of "does the light go out when you close the door" had been formed for Sterling Balder, as she'd caught him emptying the refrigerator so that he could climb inside, and check it out for himself.

"Would you? Oh, now you see, Saint Just? Maggie has it all settled, right and tight."

"Yes, she does, doesn't she," Saint Just said, neatly folding his cloth napkin (another shopping channel purchase) and leaving the kitchen, his spine ramrod stiff.

"Oh, that's not good," Sterling offered as he stood in the kitchen doorway, holding two dirty plates. "He doesn't take orders well. Bristles, and all of that."

"Let him bristle. He'll get used to it, Sterling," Maggie said, gathering knives and forks and carrying them to the kitchen. "Now, I promise not to be gone more than two hours, tops. Isn't there a *Brady Bunch* marathon on Nickelodeon today?"

Sterling visibly brightened. "Oh, yes. All day. I'm rather fond of Alice. Do you think I could write to her? I want to tell her that she's entirely too good and pure to be

121

chasing after that butcher fellow."

Maggie opened her mouth to explain, yet again, that Alice and the rest of the Bradys were, in their own way, as fictional as Sterling himself, and then just smiled and said, "Sure. Maybe this afternoon. Bye, Sterling." She leaned over and gave him a kiss. "Be good."

She went to her room, passed through to her private bathroom, pressed her palms on the sink, and looked at herself in the medicine-cabinet mirror. If she was smiling, that meant she was happy — wasn't that what Saint Just had said?

Okay, so she was frowning. Working on developing a permanent crease between her eyes from frowning. This meant she was not a happy woman.

Gee. Wonder why.

Maggie touched up her lipstick — she hated wearing makeup — ran a comb through her hair, and fixed the collar on her pink blouse.

It was time. Either now, or never.

She fished a small key from her pocket and unlocked the two-drawer cherry-wood personal file cabinet she used as a nightstand, removing her wallet, then locking the drawer once more on her car keys, a family-size bag of Good and Plenty, her private journal, and the box containing her diaphragm.

Shoving the wallet in her purse, and slinging the purse over her shoulder, she headed back down the hallway, past Saint Just, who was watching her old videotape of *Tombstone* for at least the fifth time.

He looked up at her and drawled, "I'm your huckleberry."

"Go to hell," she said, not breaking stride, and smart enough now to know that he *knew* where she'd gotten his lips, and why. "I'll be back before noon. Be sitting in that same spot, okay?"

He hit Pause on the VCR controller. "What are you going to tell him?"

Maggie hesitated, her hand on the doorknob. "Tell him? Tell who? Whom?"

"Why, Doctor Bob, of course. It *is* Monday. I know you canceled your appointment last week, as you were finishing our latest effort, but you see him every Monday at nine-thirty. I don't like the man, by the way, just in case you were thinking to ask. He makes you unhappy. So, what are you going to tell him?"

"Nothing," Maggie said after a moment. "I'm going to tell him absolutely nothing. And you don't like him? You've never met him."

"No, but I've watched you on your return from these Monday appointments. He sees your weaknesses, Maggie, and uses them to make sure you keep feeling that you need his counsel."

"That's ridiculous, Alex. Doctor Bob is a professional. He . . . he's helped me enormously."

"But you're not going to tell him anything about Sterling and me?"

"No way!"

"Ah, there's my huckleberry," Saint Just purred as Maggie yanked open the door and slammed it shut behind her.

"Oh, envy, envy! That is *so* frigid, man," Argyle Jackson said, coming to a halt in front of the building, putting down one foot to steady himself, then handing the scooter back to Sterling. "But you probably should get a horn. You know, so people know to get out of your way?"

"A horn?" Sterling repeated blankly. "But I'm not at all musical."

Saint Just stepped in front of his friend, and addressed the doorman. "A wonderful suggestion, Socks," he said, waving one hand behind his back, warning Sterling to silence. He slipped a hand into his slacks pocket and pulled out a small wad of

124

folded bills that had lately resided in Maggie's wallet. Not that he'd tell her that there were *two* keys to her little wooden cabinet, and he had one of them in his possession. "Here, please take what you'd need, and be so good as to purchase this . . . horn, you said?"

Socks took the money, counted it. "But . . . but you've got close to two hundred bucks here, man. A horn couldn't cost more than ten, fifteen tops. Here. I'll take a twenty, and bring you change."

"Not necessary, my good man. Just the horn will do, and you may keep the rest for your trouble. But I wonder. How will Sterling hold on to both the handles and the horn? I see a mishap in his future."

"No, no," Socks said, waving his hands. "The horn gets attached to the handlebars, see, and he only lets go for a moment, to squeeze it. You know — *ooo-ga, ooo-ga.*"

Saint Just smiled and nodded, hoping Socks didn't realize that he hadn't a clue as to what any of the man's last comments meant. "Ooo-ga, ooo-ga. Ah, yes. Rather more rude than a simple 'pardon me,' but I imagine that would be eminently successful in warning away pedestrians. Now, if you'd be so kind as to point out the direction of the nearest park?"

"Central Park? Sure, no problem. You're only two long blocks away once you're at the corner down there — you've gotta cross Broadway, too, in the middle of the first long block. Go straight down this street, then turn right when you see the park and go one short block. Tavern on the Green is right across the street, right at an entrance. That's a restaurant, Tavern on the Green. There's horse-and-carriage rides there, the whole nine yards. You can't miss it."

Sterling waved back at Socks as they walked along, not yet climbing onto the scooter. He looked left, right, and up. Definitely up. "Everything is so tall, Saint Just. I doubt Westminister is this tall."

"They're called skyscrapers, Sterling," Saint Just told him, bowing to an approaching woman, who quickly grabbed at her purse and kept moving.

"Skyscrapers? Is that because they —"

"No, Sterling, they do not. Why don't you get on your scooter now?"

"You don't want a carriage, Saint Just?" Sterling asked.

"What, on such a fine day? Besides, as Syrus said, 'An agreeable companion on a journey is as good as a carriage.' "

"She don't like that, you know."

"She? Maggie? She doesn't like what, Sterling?"

"She doesn't like that you keep using all those quotes she used to put in your mouth. Our contemporaries — that is to say, the gentlemen of Regency England — were always tossing off quotes, even spouting Latin, but nobody does that now. She says you come off sounding like a know-it-all. Yes, that's what she said, a know-it-all. She also said she's thinking of making some changes in us, for the next book. Are you worried about that?"

"Me? I never worry, Sterling," Saint Just said, squeezing the knob of his gold-topped cane. Squeezing it until his knuckles turned white.

Ten minutes, one small stumble with the scooter that put a tear in the knee of Sterling's new slacks, one irate Federal Express deliveryman, and one crate of oranges scattered on the sidewalk later, Saint Just and his friend entered the park.

"An oasis of calm in a mad, frantic world," Saint Just said, lazily swinging his cane as they strolled along, Sterling becoming more and more proficient on his scooter. "Why Miss Kelly would think we'd stumble into trouble while partaking of a leisurely stroll — well, the woman must learn to put more faith in us, Sterling, and that's the whole of it. We've made great strides in having her believe in us. Now we must convince her to accept us, trust us."

Sterling shot ahead slightly on his scooter, executed a neat turn, then wheeled back to Saint Just, making a full circle around his friend. "Look, Saint Just. There's a man selling ices over there. See him? I love ices. Would his be as fine as Gunther's, do you think?"

"Nothing surpasses a Gunther ice," Saint Just reminded him, but reached into his pocket anyway, this time removing only two five-dollar bills, which seemed sufficient, if Socks's assessment of the cost of minor goods could be used as a yardstick. "Come along, Sterling. We'll sample the man's wares."

Sterling chose the blue, which proved to be a good choice, gastronomically, but not ascetically, for within five minutes he had blue teeth, a blue tongue, blue lips, and yet another stained shirt. "I could eat these morning, noon, and all of that," he vowed, licking his blue fingers with his blue tongue once the ice was gone.

Saint Just handed him yet another napkin. "You look ridiculous," he said, un-

128

aware that his own tongue and lips had turned a bright cherry red. "And how will we explain your looks to Maggie, hmmm? Come along, Sterling, we'd better head back to the apartment."

Sterling, nothing if not an obedient sort, revved up his scooter, pushed off, and putt-putted ahead of Saint Just, rather proficiently weaving his way through the pedestrians and making the street a good one hundred yards ahead of the viscount — and just in time to startle a carriage horse making its way around the perimeter of the park.

It would have taken Maggie half an afternoon to set up, describe, and put the finishing touches on the scene that followed.

Saint Just, however, required only as much time as it took to break into a run on his long, strong legs, vault over a child's stroller, neatly skirt an elderly lady and her walker, and bound into the street, running straight at the head of the wild-eyed, plunging horse.

As Sterling bent and cringed, the hack driver yanked ineffectually on the reins, and the tourists in the open carriage screamed bloody murder, Saint Just grabbed at the horse's halter and began running alongside as the animal pounded off down the street, heading into the heavy vehicular traffic.

One hand on the bridle, the other fisted into the horse's mane, he took a deep breath, then hoisted himself up on the animal's back, landing safely just before the horse went up on its hind legs yet again, pawing the air.

"The brake!" he called out to the driver. "Put on the brake, you brainless twit. And stop sawing on the reins, I've got him."

And he did. "Get him," that is. As taxis honked and cars screeched to a halt, and a man talking on a cell phone, who'd stepped off the curb without looking, set the world's record for the backward long jump (if there were such a thing), Saint Just successfully fought to control the horse, bringing animal and carriage to a halt just before the intersection.

Nearly breathless, dragging the scooter and carrying Saint Just's cane, Sterling ran up to grab the horse's head as Saint Just dismounted. "First-rate, Saint Just!" he exclaimed as his friend walked back to check on the tourists — which was how he found out they were from Goddard, Kansas, that they had come to New York for a plumbers' convention, and if Saint Just ever

130

needed his drains snaked, all he had to do was call. Until Friday, when they'd go back to Goddard, taking with them several photographs of Saint Just and Sterling.

"Only one more, please," the tourist with the camera begged as Saint Just stood beside Sterling, the two of them flanked by the plumber's wife and daughter.

He shouldn't have tarried, should have just gone on his way, but the thrill of being feted as a hero — definitely his stock in trade — kept him on the scene as the plumber snapped pictures, as other tourists captured the remainder of the moment on videotape, and as the driver of the carriage threatened to "sue your scooter-riding ass into the next century. Where's a cop? I want a cop!"

As the sound of approaching sirens came to him, Saint Just politely disengaged himself from the Goddard daughter, a freckle-faced poppet who'd just given him a piece of her bubblegum. "Sterling, I do believe we should be on our way now, don't you?"

"My thoughts exactly, Saint Just," Sterling answered as the carriage driver pulled out a stub of pencil and a wrinkled piece of paper, demanding to know everybody's names and addresses, so he could "sue *all* your asses."

They walked briskly, not quite running, but definitely far from a leisurely stroll, until they'd gotten to the corner, at which time Saint Just told Sterling to get on his scooter and "proceed with prudent haste" back to Maggie's apartment. "Ooo-ga, ooo-ga, my friend."

"She'll never know, will she?" Sterling asked fifteen minutes later, as he scrubbed at his blue lips with a soapy washcloth.

"Not if you don't tell her, no," Saint Just said, peeking in the mirror to get a look at his tongue. "Too bad, really, as it was most exhilarating, wasn't it?"

"I suppose so," Sterling answered. "But if you don't mind, old friend, I don't think I want to be exhilarated like that again anytime soon."

"Come on, come on, come on," Maggie muttered under her breath as she checked her watch for the fifth time in as many minutes.

How could Doctor Bob do this to her? Okay, so she'd canceled last week only an hour before her session. Big deal. It wasn't as if he wasn't going to charge her for it. But to schedule someone else during *her* hour? That wasn't fair.

She checked the brown paper bag she'd

laid on the chair next to her, half hoping the juice from the three T-bone steaks had leaked through onto his white chenille cushions.

Was that passive-aggressive? Did she want to know?

No. She was still trying to figure out why she needed so much therapy, considering she'd never needed it when she couldn't pay for it. Being broke and unhappy made sense. Having money and not bouncing off walls in her glee wasn't quite right. Success certainly had its pitfalls.

She checked her watch again. "Come on, come on, come *on*."

At least she'd been able to run out and get the steaks, so that she'd be free to grab a cab straight back to the apartment after the session . . . which should have begun twenty minutes ago. He'd said an hour delay, that was all. Funny, she always thought a shrink's hour ran fifty minutes, not eighty.

At last the door opened and Doctor Bob smiled at her, waving her into his office. She didn't get to see his other patient, who presumably had left via the second door, because Doctor Bob didn't want his patients seeing each other. He said it was for personal privacy, but Maggie always wondered if he just didn't want his patients getting together, talking about his fees, which were only inches short of outrageous.

The smell of expensive perfume lingered in the room, which told her that Doctor Bob's previous appointment had been either a woman or one of his gender-dilemma patients. Gender-dilemma had been the title of Chapter Seven in *Love Well, Live Free*. Best damn chapter in the book.

"Hello, Margaret," Doctor Bob said, settling himself at his desk, which faced the wall. He motioned for her to sit down on one of the two chairs set at right angles to the desk, consulted an open manila folder on his desk, and then swiveled his chair to look at her.

She hated this part and never had gotten used to being only three feet from the guy in his tiny office. His claustrophobia patients really got a dose of tough love in this place.

"Hello, Doctor Bob," Maggie said back at him, forcing a smile on her face, and deliberately avoided looking either straight at him or at the handy box of tissues he kept on a small table between the patient chairs. She'd gone through her share of those over the past two years. "I'm sorry I had to cancel on such short notice last week. I'd been up all night, writing, and must have lost track of the time."

"And why do you think you did that, Margaret?" the psychologist asked, looking at her over the top of his gold-rimmed half-glasses. Shorter than average, rounder than many, Doctor Bob looked only marginally better now that he'd starting working out, but you had to give him credit. The man did try. He had to, for the book tour he'd gone on last fall, when *Love Well, Live Free* was on the bestseller charts.

You'd think he could afford a bigger office now, or more comfortable chairs. Or a better hair weave.

"I just said why I did that," Maggie answered, inwardly cursing because she'd allowed herself to be so immediately put on the defensive. "I was up all night, working."

"All night, Margaret? That's rather obsessive, isn't it? And I imagine you smoked while you were working?"

Maggie dipped her chin, tried not to feel like a ten-year-old called to the principal's office for putting chewing gum on the teacher's chair. "Yes, I was smoking."

"And are still smoking? I can smell it,

you understand. It's not very appealing, Margaret, which you already know. Isn't that why you want to give up the habit? Health should be your first consideration, but if it's the smell that worries you, then we work with that, that you find your habit socially repugnant."

Maggie's head shot up, as he'd hit one of her hot buttons. "Habit? Doctor Bob, we've been over this before. Chewing your fingernails is a *habit*. When you start digging through the waste can for a butt you can light, that's not a habit. When you stand outside in minus zero weather, in the middle of a snowstorm, to grab some nicotine after having dinner in a restaurant, that is not a habit. That's an *addiction*. Crackheads get more sympathy. There ought to be telethons for us," she ended, grumbling.

"Yes, yes, we certainly have been down that addiction road before, haven't we, Margaret? So much so that I won't bother discussing your need for oral gratification. Cigarettes, junk food. I blame it all on early weaning and an emotionally distant mother, as I've discussed with you."

"Oh, shove it," was what Maggie was going to say when she opened her mouth, but what came out was, "I know, Doctor

Bob. I'm trying to fight it. Really, I am."

What a wuss. She ought to be seeing a shrink because she was a wuss, and the hell with the cigarettes and all the rest of it.

"On a happier note, did I tell you that Bernice and I have come to terms on another book? And I have you to thank for it, Margaret."

Maggie grinned a little as she reached for a tissue. She didn't feel like crying, but she needed something to do with her hands. Why didn't Doctor Bob see that it was her hands that needed filling most of the time, not just her mouth? "Thanks, but I didn't do that much. I just introduced the two of you, that's all. And Tabby, my agent, of course."

"Yes, of course. I *did* write the book, didn't I? I didn't mean that, Margaret. We're going to contract for a smoking cessation and junk-food addiction treatise." He laughed shortly, ended it with a snort. "You'd better not prove me wrong and be able to quit your habit, Margaret, as you're going to be ninety percent of my composite Patient A, the one who swears she's trying and failing, but really isn't trying at all."

"Gee. Swell," Maggie said, twisting the tissue in her hands, wondering what

Doctor Bob would do if she rolled the tissue into a tube, then lit it. "Excuse me, but could we change the subject? I mean, we've been doing the smoking cessation now for over a year, and we're getting nowhere."

"Not smoking cessation, Margaret. That's only the buzz word. We're dealing with your deep-seated fear of rejection and your feelings of low self-worth. Creatively, your childhood is a gold mine for success, but emotionally every hole you dig is a dry well. Oh, wait. I mixed that metaphor, didn't I? Those were metaphors?"

"How should I know? That's why God created copy editors." Maggie leaned forward in her chair. "Look, Doctor Bob, I've got a problem. A *creative* problem, okay? It's a plot idea I want to run by you."

Doctor Bob sat up straighter and folded his hands in his lap, careful to let the diamond pinky ring show. "You're asking for my professional advice on a creative problem? How flattering, Margaret. Thank you."

"You're welcome." Maggie bit her bottom lip for a moment, then let him have it, knowing she'd never been worth spit at pitching an idea in person. Writers write; they don't talk. "All right, here it is. I've got this book idea, see? There's this writer."

"Ah. Like you and I?"

Maggie considered this, trying to put Doctor Bob in the same category as herself. "Okay," she said, nodding her head. "Like you and me. But the thing is, this writer, well, he has a problem."

"*He* has a problem, Margaret?"

"Yeah. He. I'm thinking about starting a new series, see, and my main character is going to be a writer. A mystery writer with, um, some personal problems."

"Write what you know," Doctor Bob said, sighing with satisfaction.

Maggie gritted her teeth and counted to five. "Absolutely, Doctor Bob. Here's the setup. I've got this mystery writer, okay? He's got a character in his book, the continuing character who solves the mysteries. You with me so far?"

Doctor Bob smiled benevolently. "I think I can follow this, yes."

"Good. So this guy — the writer in the book — turns around one day, after writing, oh, ten or so of these mysteries with this character and, bam, there's the character."

"Where's the character?"

The impulse to scream was back, and

139

Maggie had to bite her bottom lip to keep from letting one loose. "In his living room. The character. In the mystery writer's living room. This guy, this writer, he wrote such a strong, convincing character that the guy came to life. Poof! Right in his living room."

Doctor Bob smiled. "You *have* been putting in some long hours, haven't you, Margaret? Have you considered a vacation?"

Maggie squirmed in her chair. "No, no, we're not talking about *me*. We're talking about my book, my new series. Mystery writer and his imaginary character come to life. Would anybody believe it?"

"I can think of several of my patients who might believe it . . ." Doctor Bob said slowly, steepling his fingers on his ample belly. "Of course, a few of them are institutionalized and may not have access to fiction novels in their current condition."

"So it's not believable? Not plausible?"

"I'd stick with the Saint Just Mysteries, Margaret. Now there's a believable hero."

Maggie slumped in her chair. "Yeah. Tell me about it. . . ."

Hours later, snuggled against her pillows as Napoleon and Wellington lounged on

140

the bed with her, Maggie thought back over her day, and smiled.

Okay, so the Doctor Bob thing hadn't been grand, but at least he hadn't tried to have her committed.

She'd been able to take a nap in the afternoon because Saint Just and Sterling had decided to watch a movie on HBO rather than go out to the park, and dinner had been more than pleasant. She'd tossed a salad, serving that with baked potatoes, and Saint Just had actually not burnt the steaks in the George Foreman grill.

Leaving Saint Just in front of the laptop, surfing the net, and Sterling reading a Harry Potter book, Maggie had indulged in a bubble bath, painted her toenails bright pink, and crawled into bed to catch up on her own reading. Still, out of habit, she turned on the TV in time for the ten o'clock news.

The government was being sold to the highest bidder; nothing new there. Bus crash in Sri Lanka, soccer riots in wherever they were having soccer riots this week. Forecast for mild and sunny into the weekend, just as if these guys knew what would happen in the next ten minutes. The Mets playing a night game out on the coast.

Just the same old stuff. Hell, they could broadcast reruns of last week's news, and who'd know?

She picked up the channel changer, ready to turn off the TV, when the smiling anchor woman said, "And now, as promised, another look at our Central Park hero, as seen on the five o'clock edition of *Fox News*."

Maggie hesitated, her thumb on the Power button, and watched as a rather grainy, jumpy videotape played on the screen. A bolting carriage. A man leaping onto the back of a runaway horse. A Mike Piazza uniform shirt.

Her jaw dropped and she knelt on Napper's tail — the cat scratched her, but Maggie didn't notice — as she scrambled to the bottom of the bed.

"Out of nowhere," a red-faced man in a plaid shirt and bright blue *I Love New York* ball cap was saying now, nervously grinning into the camera. "A real hero, too, just like I told my Nancy. Wouldn't give his name, either, but just bowed — yeah, bowed, honest — and took off." He sighed, wiping a tear from his eye. "Saved our lives. Who says New York isn't a friendly city?"

"Friendly, indeed," the street reporter

said as she turned to face the camera. "We're going to run the tape provided by a tourist from Ohio one more time, in hopes that, if our hero won't come forward on his own, someone else might recognize him, as the mayor would like to thank him person-ally. Please, watch closely, and if you rec-ognize this man, call our station at . . ."

"Saint Just," Maggie whispered hoarsely, her throat tight as the grainy tape ran once more.

"Saint Just!" she called out, nearly falling off the bed, as she couldn't seem to drag her eyes from the screen.

"*Saint Just!* I'm going to *kill* you!" she bellowed, running down the hallway.

CHAPTER 6

"And one . . . and reach . . . and three . . . and feel the burn . . . and five . . . and —"

Saint Just pressed the Power button, turning the television screen dark just as Sterling reached for the sky one more time.

Arms still raised, jogging in place, and breathing heavily, Sterling swiveled toward Saint Just. "Now why would you go and do a thing like that? I was experiencing the burn. At least I think I was."

"Much as it pains me to admit this at times such as these," Saint Just responded, crossing one leg over the other as he sat on the couch, "I would sorely miss you, Sterling, if you were to pop an artery somewhere in your brain box and expire at my feet."

Sterling took three more huge, gulping breaths, then reached for the fluffy white towel hanging over the back of the facing couch. "Well, thank you, Saint Just. Again, at least I think so."

"You're welcome," Saint Just said, smiling. "Besides, our dearest creator — lower case, Sterling, as the woman is inspired but not godlike — decided that you were to be

144

. . . pleasantly plump. In order to rectify that, you'll have to convince her to *write* you smaller. We've only aged two years in the past five, because all our stories took place in that two-year time span. You do understand that, don't you?"

Patting at his sweat-shiny cheeks, Sterling walked around the couch and sat down all at once, allowing the cushions to envelop him. "About that, Saint Just. In case you've forgotten, Miss Kelly has been as mad as fire at us for the past few days, ever since that little incident in the park."

"I remember," Saint Just said, nodding his head. The woman had a considerable temper, when she put her mind to it. "What of it?"

"Well, there's a lot of it, actually. Think about what she threatened to do to us, Saint Just. And the thing is, she *could*. All she has to do is write it, and zap! We could be hunchbacked, shot in the bread box, hanged at Newgate."

Saint Just sighed and shook his head. "Sterling, Sterling, Sterling. She'd never do such a thing. Remember the story of the golden goose? We're her golden geese, Sterling. She can't kill us off, not if she wants to continue being a successful scribbler. And we both know how driven the woman is. That business with her longing for validation, and the rest of that drivel. We have Doctor Bob to thank for her believing that she needs success, although I still long to wring the man's neck for most of the nonsense he's been putting in Maggie's head."

Sterling wrinkled up his forehead, considered this for a few moments. "All right. Maybe she won't have us cock up our toes, be put to bed with a shovel, and all of that. But she could *hurt* us, Saint Just. Bend us, just a little."

Now it was Saint Just's time to consider, ponder. "Yes," he said slowly. "She probably could, couldn't she? But not without our consent, Sterling. Not now that we're here, carrying at least half the creativity needed for her to ever put pen to paper again as concerns the Saint Just Mysteries. Or so I've convinced her. And I have convinced her, Sterling. I'm a very convincing man, and our Miss Kelly can be lamentably gullible for such an intelligent female. She believes that she needs us in order to continue writing the Saint Just mysteries."

Sterling tried to get up, which only sank him further into the cushions. "And that's another thing. What if she decides never to write about us again, but just make up somebody else, write about somebody else? She's got talent, Saint Just. We've only got her."

Was there anything more distasteful than a man in short pants and a shirt that had "Brady Bunch Forever" stenciled on it telling him things he didn't want to hear? "All right, Sterling, you've made your point. Now, what do you propose we do?"

"Do? *Me?* I'm not the one with the brilliant brain, Saint Just. I thought you'd know. Don't you know? How depressing."

Saint Just got up and went over to the liquor cabinet, poured himself a glass of wine. He stared at the design on the lacquered cabinet for a few moments, then turned on his heels to look at Sterling. "Much as it pains me, Sterling, I imagine what we're going to have to do is to continue as we have for the past few days. In short, we're going to have to behave ourselves. At least until I can come up with a better plan."

Sterling nodded his head. "No more going out on our own. No more inviting Socks up here for a few hands of cards. She made you give the money back at any rate. And perhaps, and this is only a suggestion, Saint Just, but perhaps you might consider being more of a *help* around here."

"I beg your pardon." Where was his quizzing glass when he needed it? If he was struggling to hang on to his consequence, he could use at least one other prop than his wineglass. *"Me?"*

"Yes, Saint Just. You. Or haven't you noticed that Miss Kelly doesn't have upstairs maids, or kitchen maids, or even a tweeny to sweep the floors?"

"She's got you," Saint Just said with a small smile. "Or haven't I told you how endearingly domestic you have become? And all without Miss Kelly writing a single word placing you in the scullery. Watching this Alice person on the television has been a great benefit to you."

"I am learning a lot from Alice, yes. But being helpful just comes to me naturally, because I'm a gentle soul at the heart of it. And thoughtful." Sterling succeeded in fighting his way free of the cushions and stood up, pulling himself up to his tallest, his chins in the air. He looked most impressive, except for the dimples on his pudgy, dead-white knees. "You, my lord, are neither."

"Well, I'll be damned," Saint Just said quietly.

"Yes, Saint Just. Much as I hesitate to point it out, that's always a distinct possibility," Sterling said as he exited the living room, definitely in high dudgeon . . . leaving Saint Just with much to think about.

"Is there anything else I can do for you, Maggie?"

Maggie looked at Saint Just, still trying to figure him out after two full days of having the man be nice to her. Two full days of trying to figure out why she didn't like him so much when he was being nice to her. Saint Just was a hero. She'd made him a hero. And heroes didn't alphabetize a woman's spices, damn it.

Then she looked around the living room. Coasters on the tables. Bar set up on the fold-out leaves of the liquor cabinet. Crudites, potato chips, pretzels, dips on the coffee table.

"Yes, there is something," she told him. "Get Sterling's nose out of the onion dip, please."

"Hmmm?" Sterling said, dipping another potato chip. "M'nose? M'nose is nowhere near the — oh. Yes, of course, Miss Kelly. Leave some for the guests and all of that, right?"

"Yes, and all of that," Maggie said, her voice gentle as she spoke to Sterling, because it was impossible to be anything but gentle around the man. "And please, Sterling, and for the fiftieth time, my name is Maggie. I realize you don't believe in such informality, but no one will understand if you keep forgetting, calling me Miss Kelly. All right?"

His mouth full, Sterling nodded, even as he held up his index finger, silently asking her to wait until he swallowed. "There we go. Nectar of the gods, Miss — Maggie. But I do have a question. Must I say *Alex?* I — I don't think I can."

"I know, Sterling," Maggie said, slipping an arm around his shoulders. "I've been meaning to tell you that I've thought about that, your reluctance, and decided that you may continue to call him Saint Just. Just make sure everyone realizes that it's a private joke between the two of you, okay?"

"But then it wouldn't be private, if I told everybody."

"Here, let me try," Saint Just said, handing Sterling a napkin to wipe his greasy fingertips. "Sterling, listen carefully. Maggie used my name in her books. Used your name in those same books. You found that amusing and decided to call me Saint Just, exactly as the *character* Sterling Balder does in those books. It's a joke, between the two of us. A private joke, in some ways, but not a secret. One that can be shared. All clear now?"

Sterling began to breathe more rapidly. "Maybe . . . maybe I won't come to the party. I'm not especially good at parties, you know. Remembering names, talking about the weather and all of that."

Maggie took Sterling's hand and led him over to the couch, then thought better of it and pulled him along until she could pull out a chair at her game table. She motioned for him to sit down. "Don't worry about names, Sterling."

"Don't worry? But there's so many of them."

"Not that many. You know Socks, right? And Bernie's been here a few times, so you know her, too. Then there's Kirk, and you won't want to talk to him anyway. So there's only a few you haven't yet met. My agent, Tabby, and her husband, David, who's a Broadway producer. Say hello to Tabby, and she'll juggle the conversational ball for the next hour all by herself, trust me. All you have to do is smile, nod, and come out with the occasional, 'Is that right?' "

"Is that right?" Sterling asked, and Maggie reached over to give his hand a squeeze.

"Perfect. And don't forget The Trigger. Nelson Trigg talks to nobody he can't use in some way, so you're safe there. I only invited him because Bernie had this brainstorm last year about the Trigger handing over my completion check at these parties. You'll be amazed, Sterling, to see how fast Tabby grabs that thing from him. Never, never ever, get between Tabby and a check."

"Is that right?" Sterling said again, obviously believing that practice made perfect.

"Who else?" Maggie asked herself, tapping a finger against her chin. "There's one more, I know it. Oh — Clarice Simon, Trigg's personal assistant. She's nice. You'll like her, honest. Alex, tell him."

"You'll be fine, Sterling," Saint Just assured him, one eye on the television set, because the Mets were playing.

"Gee, that was encouraging," Maggie grumbled and went over to the set to turn it off. "You could be a little more help. Besides, I thought you were putting in a tape, recording the game?"

Maggie stood quite still as a distinct chill entered the room and her words seemed to hang there until frozen, then crack and fall to the floor. "What? You're mad about putting in a tape? What?" she asked, because Saint Just was looking at her in a way that defied descriptive words like *cold,* or *haughty,* or even *oppressive.* Oh, okay, *oppressive* sort of came close.

"I could be a *little more help?*" Saint Just said at last, each word dropping like ice cubes onto a stone floor, joining hers. "I beg your pardon. I've *not* been helpful? Madame, I have been a veritable *paragon.*"

Maggie laughed, stopping only millimeters from a snort. "Yeah. Right. You stayed out of trouble for a couple of days. Whoop-de-doo. Oh, and you vacuumed the apartment. I'll give you that one."

"I should hope so," Saint Just said, pulling at the cuffs of his sports coat.

"Except that you had way too much fun," Maggie added. "For a minute there, I thought you were going to dump ashtrays on the floor, just so you could pull out the vacuum again."

"I have an interest in machines, that's all. Now, if you'll excuse me, I believe I'll go begin to heat up my George Foreman grill."

Maggie watched as he left the room, moving with an almost leonine grace. God, the man was gorgeous. Who would have thought the creature she'd created to wear neckcloths and breeches could look so damn good in stone-washed jeans, a white dress shirt open at the collar, and a navy sports coat? Elegant, and sexy. Casual, yet sexy. In love with his George Foreman grill, but sexy.

"He is trying to be helpful, you know," Sterling told her after a moment. "So you won't kill us off in the next book."

Maggie, who had her back to Sterling, whirled around to look at him. "Kill you off? Why would I — oh, wait. He's *afraid* of me? But I thought I couldn't do anything without — oh. *Oh!* He was *lying* to me about that?"

"Not about your most recent idea. We did pack that up and take it with us," Sterling said, retrieving the bowl of chips and the onion dip. "He thought, if you couldn't remember the next idea, you'd believe you needed him — us — for any new idea."

"Oh, he did, did he? And I *fell* for it? Of course I fell for it. He was challenging my talent, and he knows how wishy-washy I am about that, how afraid I am that I'll wake up one morning and it all will be gone. How I *hate* that he lived inside my head. He knows way too much about me — the rat!"

Then a smile curled her lips, so that she was pretty sure that if she looked in a mirror she'd resemble the Cheshire Cat. Or Sylvester the Cat. One of the two. "So I am in control, right? That's the bottom line, I'm in control, and the big bad viscount can't do spit about it. Well, how about *that*."

"Oh, dear," Sterling breathed, reaching for another potato chip. "I suppose I shouldn't have said anything, should I? I'm sure I shouldn't have said anything. Not about shooting us, or hanging us, or just giving us the gout, if you're feeling particularly mean."

Maggie waggled her eyebrows — Saint Just wasn't the only one who could do that little trick. Ah, but could he wiggle his ears? Nope. She was one up on him in ear-wiggling. She was one up on him in a *lot* of things. "I could do that, too? Give him the gout? Saint Just made me think I couldn't do anything without him. I could really *do* that?"

"I don't really know, to tell you the truth. But what if you could? Saint Just seems to think you could, because he told me we had to behave ourselves for a while, especially after that little dustup in the park the other day."

Maggie rubbed her hands together. A weight had lifted from her shoulders, her

155

heart soared, and her mind flew free. She had her life back, her work back. She still had Saint Just in her apartment, but her life was again her own.

So what if he'd packed up her idea for her next book and taken it with him? That had only been one idea. She'd get another idea. She had a million ideas a week. For instance: She wondered if they had poison ivy in England; she'd have to look that up. How nice it would be to drop Saint Just off his horse and into a patch of the stuff. Except he was her hero. She wouldn't have her hero all itchy and pimply. But she *could*, and that was enough. She held the hammer!

"Oh, I like this," she said. "Sterling, between you and me — cross your heart and hope to die — I'd never do anything mean to either one of you. Honest. But that doesn't mean that Saint Just has to know that, right? I mean, I'm seeing taking out the garbage in Saint Just's future. Doing laundry. Scrubbing the kitchen floor on his hands and knees. Ah, Sterling, as you might say, the mind *boggles*."

"It must, Miss — Maggie, if you think you'll ever see Saint Just on his knees, with a rag in his hand. I do believe he'd rather die."

"Yeah, I suppose so. But a woman can dream, Sterling, a woman can dream. Oops, there's the buzzer. Looks like our guests are arriving. Chin up, Sterling, you'll be fine."

"Fine? Isn't that what Saint Just said in *The Case of the Pilfered Pearls*, just before ruffians grabbed me by the elbows and tossed me headfirst into the Thames?"

Maggie winced. "You're right. Scratch fine. You'll *survive*, Sterling. How's that?"

"I suppose it's enough. I should go fetch Saint Just, I suppose, except he'll probably wish to make an entrance only after all the guests are here."

"As long as he doesn't expect me to announce him," Maggie muttered, pressing the intercom button and telling the weekend relief doorman to send up her guests.

The "Yay! It's Done!" party was going along swimmingly, with the soundtrack from *Stand By Me* playing on the stereo on her desk shelf, the men gathered on one side of the room, the ladies on the other — and Clarice Simon kneeling down beside the cat tower, deep in a one-way conversation with Wellington and Napoleon while Socks looked at her as if she'd just lost a wheel off her cart. Well, no one had hit anyone else, or thrown up on her Persian rug, and Saint Just had so far very obligingly stayed in the kitchen, so Maggie figured she had a success on her hands.

Except now Bernie was looking a little intense. Taking a large sip of her wine, Maggie decided to listen in on the conversation between her editor and her agent, standing far enough back to avoid being drawn into an argument, close enough to prevent bloodshed.

There were never two more different people who had so very much in common, if that made any sense.

Bernie had married twice, divorced twice, then vowed that if she ever thought about getting married for a third time, she'd appreciate it greatly if Maggie would just shoot her. Tabby had dropped out of college to marry her childhood sweetheart, refused to see his faults, and had heard more lame "I didn't mean to cheat" stories than the IRS.

Bernie, if she'd ever been a mother, said she was pretty sure she would have eaten her young, the way guppies did. Tabby had twin sons and a wallet thick with photographs of them, of her husband, of their summer house on the island, of their collie, Boodles, etc., etc.

Bernie was tall, painted in brassy colors. A little too raw-boned to ever try to play at being frilly-feminine, she had a blunt, outspoken mouth and fought a constant battle of the bulge with diet, surgery, vitamin supplements, and the aforementioned occasional lines of coke. Tabby was a breathless blonde with great big green eyes and a five-foot, four-inch Venus de Milo body she dressed in flowing clothes, lots of similarly flowing scarves, and then drenched in scent. Maggie had decided that her agent must belong to the Overpowering Perfume of the Month Club.

Tabby hinted, occasionally sniped. Bernie laid it all on the line, in spades. Maggie smiled now as she remembered the day, years ago, right after her first historical romance had come out, when she'd asked Bernie how to answer when someone burst her balloon by saying (as someone had), "Romance? That bodice-ripper smut? When are you going to write a *real* book?"

Maggie, young and naive, had thought her editor would have some words of wisdom for her, something to do with how worthy romances were, their high market share, all that good stuff. Bernie's answer had been Maggie's real introduction to

New York: "What do you say? I've always found a simple Go Fuck Yourself to work."

Yes, Bernie steamrollered. Tabby cajoled. Bernie drank most of her meals. Tabby baked bread from scratch.

So dissimilar, and yet so alike in many ways, the main way being that they were both ambitious enough to crawl over the bodies of their newly sacrificed grandmothers to sign up a good writer.

Maggie leaned in a little closer, listening to Bernie.

"Granted, I sort of liked it. But then I realized, once I was finished, that I really didn't give a rat's ass if everyone lived happily ever after or fell off a cliff. Or am I wrong, and every shy, well-bred, Georgian-era Lady Whoever of twenty-seven climbs onto the hero's face and lets him have her for dessert? On page fucking *twelve*. Oh, yeah. Virgins always spread their legs and go for oral sex with a complete stranger first time out of the box. Sure they do."

Tabitha Leighton took another sip of wine, then said, "Bernie, her last book was *NYT* for six weeks in hardback, sixteen in paper. And you're complaining? A book doesn't have to have heart. Not if it has enough kinky sex."

"Heart? Who's talking about heart? All I want to know is, is it too much to ask for some historical *accuracy?* I'm an English History major, remember? If you want your heroine to act like a gutter wench, then make her a gutter wench, not a lady of quality who *acts* like a gutter wench. Not if she's your fucking heroine — and I use that term literally."

"Oh, Bernie," Tabby said, sighing. "Historical accuracy? Nobody worries about that anymore. And as long as the book carries us along, who cares about heart, character development? It's the same with graphic violence. We may never connect with the protagonist, but the tide of events, the blood and gore, carry us on, keep us turning the pages — and coming back for more. As a matter of fact, I heard the most interesting debate on just this subject three weeks ago, at the *We Are Romance* regional conference in Kentucky. Let's see, who was on the panel? Oh, yes, I remember now. There was — oh, hello, Maggie. Where have you been hiding? Bernie's already on her second scotch."

Bernie reached out and pulled Maggie to her. "Ah, thank God for you, Maggie. The only way I can keep editing Felicity Boothe Simmons is that I can always count on you to follow her up with another wonderful Saint Just mystery. Now, where did you hide your inspiration? I've been here for twenty minutes and, much as I'd enjoy another of Tabby's monologues, and hearing all about the latest WAR conference — yeah, right — I'm in the mood for red meat."

"Red meat?" Tabby asked, sounding confused, which was a good act if she could pull it off. "When did you start eating again, Bernie, red meat or anything else? The way I heard it, you gave that up in eighty-nine."

Maggie looked at her agent, who hadn't been nicknamed Tabby just because it was a natural diminutive of Tabitha. "Behave, Tabby, or we'll have you spayed."

She shrugged. "Works for me. Two children are more than enough. Robbie had his second speeding ticket up at Stanford last week, and Joey's on probation for having a girl in his dorm room. I remember when my biggest problem with them was when they began whidding in the sandbox. Besides, I'm much too young to have eighteen-year-old twins. It took me sixteen years to get my waistline back."

"Yeah, and that's just because I gave you the name of my plastic surgeon," Bernie said, patting her own flat stomach. "Saw him again recently, didn't you, Tabby? Or did David punch you one in the chops?"

Maggie frowned, looking at her agent. Damn. The woman's lips *were* fatter. Puffier. "Tabby?"

"What?" she answered, giving a toss of her blond hair. "Bernie's the only one who can have a little . . . enhancement? I'm forty, Maggie, and David is beginning to lift his head a little too much, sniff the air. I had to do something."

"Divorce is always an option, right after doing a Bobbit on him," Bernie said, and Maggie gave her a quick nudge with her elbow, because David Leighton's well-known straying was not a subject she wanted brought up at her party.

"Have you met my cousin Alex and his friend Sterling yet, Tabby?" Maggie said quickly. "Alex has been in the kitchen, fooling around with his George Foreman grill. Bernie, why don't you take Tabby into the kitchen and introduce her?" Maggie said, suddenly aware that Sterling was waving to her from the other side of the living room. "I think I have to rescue Sterling from The Trigger."

Poor Sterling. He looked so cute in his khaki Dockers and his plaid, short-sleeved shirt opened at the collar. Sort of like George Costanza in *Seinfeld*. Whoa! Why hadn't she realized that before now? He *was* George. Sort of George. A little bit George. A kinder, gentler, definitely more ethical George Costanza. Balding, pudgy, confused. And somehow content to remain in Jerry's — that is, Saint Just's — shadow.

Well, wasn't that great? She'd built the gorgeous hunk of this or any other century, and now she thought he was Jerry Seinfeld? What did that make her? Lady Elaine of the buck teeth and brown-and-white shoes?

"Not in this lifetime," Maggie muttered to herself as she approached Sterling and The Trigger. "I see you two are getting acquainted," she said, smiling at Nelson Trigg, which was an act of heroism akin to looking down the barrel of a .44 Magnum while armed only with a peashooter.

How she hated Nelson Trigg. The man had no soul, no passion. Build an author slowly, over time? Recognize talent and home-grow it? Not The Trigger.

Three books. That's what he gave anyone. Three books, and then either you're up or you're out. The guy thought he was selling soup. Chicken noodle's not cutting it anymore? Drop it, push tomato rice this week. Lately, at least for the last two years, he hadn't allowed Bernie to sign any new talent at all, and had her chasing name authors with a contract in her hand. Toland Books was rapidly getting a reputation for buying bestsellers, not building them.

What really got to Maggie was that, physically, The Trigger went so much against type. He should have been stoop-shouldered, rail-thin, with wire-rimmed glasses and a pasty complexion. A pocket protector, a pencil behind his ear, a calculator glued to his left hand. Or maybe short, his belt hidden beneath his paunch, his entire appearance sort of dirty, greasy.

Instead, The Trigger was actually handsome. Blond hair, fairly decent blue eyes — if a little too close-set to be hero eyes. He played tennis, had a treadmill and stair-stepper in his office, and walked around the offices while doing curls with ten-pound weights.

Clarice Simon adored her boss, which Maggie believed to be a bleeding pity. And embarrassing too, when she remembered Clarice's shocked expression when she'd asked if she wanted to ante up for the kitty being formed to hire a hit man and take The Trigger out.

"Miss — Maggie," Sterling said as Maggie, after a small detour to the liquor cabinet to grab a diet soda, joined him and The Trigger over near the desk. "So very glad you could join us. Mr. Trigg was just asking to see my identification."

"See your what?" Maggie asked, nearly dropping her soda can. "Nelson?"

"He says his name is Sterling Balder, Maggie," The Trigger informed her, somehow able to enunciate clearly with his nose forty feet in the air. "I asked him to prove it."

"And why should he have to prove it?" Maggie should have gone for the hit man. Definitely.

"Why? Maggie, the man says he's your *character*. I wasn't born yesterday, you know. Everyone else might believe this story I've just been told about your cousin and this fellow here, but not me. You're not going to find me calling him Sterling Balder all the night long, just so you can tell us you've hired actors to liven up the party — and make a jackass out of me."

"You need help?" Maggie said, suddenly wishing Saint Just were beside her, which just went to prove how desperate she was feeling at the moment. "I'm sorry, Nelson," she added quickly. "But asking for identification? What are you, the Manhattan branch of the Gestapo? His name is Sterling Balder. Honest to God, Nelson. It could have been George Costanza, which I only figured out tonight, but it's Sterling Balder. Scout's honor."

"Who's George Costanza?" The Trigger asked.

"My dry cleaner," Maggie said, rolling her eyes. "Come on, Nelson, I'll introduce you to Alex. My cousin, Alexander Blakely. Then maybe you'll believe it. I ripped off my cousin and his friend, turned them into my characters. I'm shameless, I admit it. But since they don't mind, I don't see why it should bother you."

"I don't know, Maggie. Maybe we should run this past Legal."

"Here we go again," Maggie grumbled, realizing that her career was skating on thin ice because the characters she made up in her head were now in her apartment, and it looked as though the characters in her books weren't hers at all. Or something like that. Whatever it was, she had Alexandre Blake, Viscount Saint Just, to blame for any trouble she was in now, damn him.

"Again, Maggie?" The Trigger repeated.

"Yeah. Kirk worried about it, too, but it's

all right. Promise. After all, it isn't like I lifted pages from someone else's book — and God knows that's been done, and rewarded, for crying out loud. These are *my* characters, Nelson. Alex and Sterling are real people; *my* Alexandre and Sterling are fictional. Totally. Same damp island, different centuries. Right?"

"You're asking my opinion?" Nelson shrugged his shoulders. "Never having found a need to read any of your books, I really wouldn't know, would I?"

"Just making me love you more and more every day, in every way, aren't you, Nelson?" Maggie said, her smile tight. "Now come on, it sounds like the party has moved to the kitchen."

CHAPTER 7

Saint Just exited the kitchen just as Maggie, Sterling, and a tall, blond man approached.

"Maggie, my dear girl," he said with a barely polite, definitely dismissive nod toward yet another stranger in his apartment. Although, knowing the guest list, he had a fairly definite idea whom he was ignoring, and a definite idea as to why. "I've just come to fetch you. It seems we have a bit of a development."

"Development? There's a problem? What did you do?"

He watched as she tensed, rather enjoying her reaction.

"Well, perhaps I overstate. Not precisely a problem. But it seems that Mrs. Leighton has decided that I, and I alone, can possibly make the final decision on the redecoration plans for her retreat in a place called Great Neck."

"You're kidding," Maggie said, pushing the blonde ahead of her, toward the kitchen. "Be right with you, Nelson."

"You could introduce me to your cousin, you know," The Trigger said, standing his ground.

169

"Ah, it speaks. Yes, my good man, she could," Saint Just said, unconsciously searching his chest for his quizzing glass. "But then, I would first have had to evince an interest in making your acquaintance. And I don't believe I did. So sorry."

Saint Just kept his expression blank as Maggie's foot came down on his instep. He couldn't understand why she was put out with him. After all, he was simply being Saint Just.

"Alex, cut it out," Maggie said, her laugh rather nervous. "I'm sorry, Nelson, but Alex is rather . . . um . . . formal? Alex, behave. Now, Alex Blakely, Nelson Trigg, Comptroller, or whatever, of Toland Books, the guy who handles the money, writes the checks. Nelson, my cousin Alex, who just moved here from England."

"Ah, that would make you The Trigger. You're the one who originally, and with malice aforethought, turned off my cousin from your publishing establishment, yes?" Alex said, refusing to offer his hand. "I don't think I like you."

"For God's sake, knock it off," Maggie whispered, then turned back to Nelson Trigg. "I'm sorry again, Nelson. I — well, I was pretty mad when you decided not to offer me a new contract, and I'm afraid I wrote to Alex about it. Except, when you get right down to it, you did me a favor. As a matter of fact, the Saint Just mysteries might never have happened, if you hadn't cut me loose."

She turned back to Saint Just and glared at him. "Or hadn't you thought of that one, cousin Alex?"

"That's my cousin Maggie," Alex said as Nelson Trigg's handsome face went beet red. "Such a forgiving sort. Very well. If she can excuse you, I suppose I'd be wrong to carry a grudge. Shall we cry friends, Mr. Trigg? You could help me with the hamburgers. We're having hamburgers, you know. Maggie wanted cold meats and cheese, but I convinced her otherwise. I may be wrong, but you have the look of a man who'd be a genius with ground meat."

"I don't cook," Nelson said, then turned on his heels and headed for the cat tower and the rather mousy-looking woman who was being entertained by Socks, who seemed to be reciting lines of Shakespeare to her. Badly. Two outsiders, definitely not feeling at home at this hodgepodge soiree, bound together by their mutual discomfort.

"Socks is being entertaining for the spinster," Saint Just said. "Perhaps, later, he'll sing for us? The young man has a tolerable voice, and to hear him tell it, you purposely invited him this evening so that he could impress Mr. Leighton. That may or may not have been kind of you, Maggie. Especially if he keeps hiding behind our little Miss Bashful."

"Would you forget about Socks? What the hell are you doing, being so rude like that?" Maggie asked when Trigg was out of earshot. "These are my friends."

"You number Mr. Trigg among your friends?" Saint Just gave it up, pulled his quizzing glass from his jacket pocket and lifted it over his head. "May I suggest that he'd be a poor choice to guard your back in any fight."

"Okay, okay, so he's my business acquaintance, and if I wanted to invite Clarice, which I did, I figured I'd have to invite him, too, or she wouldn't come, and if there was ever a woman who needed to get out more, it's Clarice. Besides, he brought the completion check, didn't he, so now I can pay all those bills you ran up on my charge cards. I may even allow you to charge again, in moderation. Is that better? So just leave The Trigger alone, all right? Now, what's this about Tabby and you and her house in Great Neck?"

Saint Just fingered the quizzing glass and sighed. "I haven't the foggiest idea. We were all talking, I was being my usual erudite, friendly, and witty self, when suddenly she grabbed at my sleeve and *demanded* that I give her my opinion on some draperies and other falderol."

"That's two," Maggie said, shaking her head. "Alex, Tabby thinks you're gay."

He whipped his head around in the direction of the kitchen, then glared at Maggie. "Don't be ridiculous. If we're going to be crude, Miss Toland-James has been trying to get her hand in my pocket for the past quarter hour, which is another reason I'm here with you and not minding my hamburgers. I had to put David Leighton in charge, and the moment he asked to wear your Kiss the Cook apron, I knew *that* had been a mistake. Now, tell me about this Great Neck place. Would I like it?"

"Probably. I don't know. Sure, why not? Hey, wait a minute! You're actually thinking about accepting Tabby's invitation? What are you, nuts? You're not ready for prime time."

"Perhaps. Perhaps not. But I am most definitely ready for a change of scene, and a flying visit to the country sounds like just the thing. Sterling and I would be out of your way, giving you some time to yourself, and we, in turn, will be able to enlarge our knowledge."

"And pick draperies," Maggie pointed out. "What do you know about picking draperies?"

"About as much as you know about a gentleman's need for independence," Saint Just retorted, feeling some righteous anger beginning to bubble beneath his carefully cool exterior. "Mrs. Leighton has offered to pay Sterling and me for our expertise."

"Shit." Maggie ran a hand through her hair and looked around the room, as if for outside help. "So there's no real reason to have this conversation, then, is there? You've already told Tabby yes, haven't you?"

"We leave Monday morning and return to the metropolis on Tuesday afternoon," Saint Just said, smiling. "Is Great Neck anywhere near the ocean? Sterling has put forth an interest in spitting into it, you understand. Maggie? Where are you going?"

"To get some aspirin," Maggie said, heading for the hallway to the bedrooms. "And maybe to kick something."

Saint Just watched her go, then shrugged his shoulders, not understanding the woman even a little bit, and headed back into the kitchen.

"Bravo! Bravo!" Saint Just called out as he clapped his hands and advanced toward Socks, who had just completed a medley of songs from something he'd called *West Side Story*. "Magnificent, my friend, simply magnificent." Then he turned to David Leighton, who was nursing his sixth vodka tonic. "Mr. Leighton? Wasn't he magnificent?"

"He wasn't bad," Leighton said. "And I still don't see why Tabby thinks you and your friend should be going out to Great Neck with her Monday morning."

Jackass. Saint Just patted Socks on the shoulder, then aimed him toward Clarice Simon, who had offered to push the correct buttons on Maggie's stereo so that Socks could sing along to the music tape he'd brought with him to the party.

"You'll not be joining us?" Saint Just asked Leighton, wondering how much longer the fellow would be able to speak without slurring his words. A dedicated drunk, that was David Leighton, a man used to giving the impression of holding his liquor, even while his liquor held him. "Now, that is a pity. I had hoped to discuss

Argyle's career with you, now that you've heard him perform."

"Huh?"

Oh, yes. Leighton's liquor was beginning to get the upper hand.

"I said, I am representing Argyle, looking out for his best interests, that sort of thing. I dabble a bit in the theater, among my other interests, you understand. We've been entertaining an offer from Lloyd Webber, but the man's a hit-and-miss talent at times, don't you think, for all his successes? Face it, I say. After *Phantom*, what has he done?"

"Andrew Lloyd Webber? *He's* interested in him?"

"Hmmm, yes. Andrew and I have worked together before, in London, naturally. Why, just last month, he and Cameron and I had lunch at this charming little place in New Bond Street, and —"

"Macintosh? Cameron Macintosh? You know Cameron *Macintosh?*"

"Ah, yes, you may stare. But times have changed, and it is now quite acceptable for those of the quality to rub shoulders with those in the theater. I, being a most ecumenical sort, number many theater folk amongst my acquaintance," Saint Just said, and he did, in a way, having crammed as much information about musical theater into his head as a mentally superior man could do in three days. *West Side Story* remained a mystery to him, but he was pretty well up to scratch on Lloyd Webber, Macintosh, and Wildhorn.

Leighton's eyes narrowed, attempting to focus. "And Lloyd Webber and Macintosh are interested in Maggie's *doorman?* I don't believe it."

"Well, goodness, old boy, no one asked you to, did they?" Saint Just responded smoothly. "May I freshen your drink?"

"No — wait. You're representing him, you say?"

"I may have said that. But please, good sir, don't pay me the least attention. It was nothing. Argyle's plate is rather full as it is. He's appearing nightly in a little something in the Village — cabaret, you understand — and with Lloyd Webber's latest to begin casting soon . . ."

"No. He's not casting soon. I would have heard."

Saint Just lifted his quizzing glass by its black riband and began lazily swinging it back and forth. *Gotcha,* as Maggie might say. "Really? You two speak? How strange that Sir Andrew never mentioned you. Of course, I'm not all that familiar with the smaller producers, especially on this side of the pond."

"Friday," Leighton said, rummaging in his pocket and pulling out a business card. "Have him at this address Friday, ten o'clock. There's this revival we're taking to workshop, and Argyle would be perfect for it, now that I think about it."

"Ah, but will it be perfect for him? But that's what life is all about, isn't it? Choices," Saint Just said, pocketing the card. "Now, let me freshen that drink."

All right, so the man could make a tolerable hamburger, even if George Foreman deserved at least half the credit. And her friends, definitely more used to deli meats and salads at her parties, seemed to have enjoyed the change.

But how did this all translate to Maggie, alone in her kitchen, doing all the cleanup while Socks serenaded her guests? Huh? How did that happen?

Maggie shook open another green garbage bag and headed into the dining alcove, ready to toss paper plates, plastic forks, and anything else that looked even marginally disposable. She didn't have to do this now, and Tabby would offer to help at some point — Tabby as the helpful sort;

Bernie wouldn't even realize that little cleanup fairies didn't do the work.

So maybe she just didn't want to be part of her own party? That's what Doctor Bob would say, and he'd be right, although not for the reasons he'd list. He'd say she was retreating into her shell, pretending to be busy so as to not have to interact with *real* people; that imaginary people, her characters, were more comfortable for her because she could control them. Make them talk when she wanted, say what she wanted, respond as she wanted, and leave her alone, not ask anything of her.

Fat lot Doctor Bob knew.

Yes, she was better on paper than she'd ever be in person. She'd rather write a complaint letter than make a phone call, say, "Hey, Bozo, you overcharged me for that last bottled water delivery." Because she hated confrontations, Doctor Bob said, while at the same time harboring an intense desire to have the world turn as she ordered. Hence the brilliant complaint letter, while she would rather pay three times the correct price than say a single word to a real live person.

And hence her career in fiction. Maggie's little make-believe world, where everyone said what she wanted them to say, did what she wanted them to do (and wanted to do herself, but didn't). Happy Endings by Maggie Kelly, that was what she did, what she dreamed, what she didn't live. Didn't have the courage to live, according to the hair weave, damn him.

It was that wuss factor again, rearing its ugly head. She was so far into wuss mode tonight that she was actually allowing Saint Just to step in for her, take on the role of host, while she auditioned for the role of Unnamed Cleaning Woman. That was so lame, and she hated herself. But she wasn't going back into that living room again until she had to, no matter how much she tried to tell herself that these end-of-the-book parties were "fun." Yeah, fun. Like having a root canal.

She liked people. Sort of. One at a time. But being responsible for everyone else's happiness? Nope. It just wasn't her thing, even though she'd been told she was a great hostess, and people like Tabby and Bernie thought she was funny, and bright, and good company.

If they only knew what it took to pull it all off, rather than just pull the covers over her head and hide.

These parties were part of her therapy, that's what they were. "Personal interaction," according to Doctor Bob, and necessary to her mental health. Was it any wonder she'd yet to send him an invitation to one of these therapeutic bashes?

Maggie angrily grabbed up paper napkins, wadding them together in one hand as she held the trash bag and leaned across the table.

"Surprise!"

Maggie sucked in her breath in shock; she would have jumped a good foot off the floor if Kirk's arms weren't wrapped so tightly around her waist. She closed her eyes, pressed her hands against the tabletop. "Let go, Kirk. Not funny."

The king of the brain dead, libido alive and kicking, leaned over her, nuzzling his lips against the side of her throat as he pressed his pelvis against her rear end. "Hmmm, you taste good. A little catsup, some mustard, and I'd have my own Maggie-burger."

Maggie didn't know how to pronounce it, but she knew how she wrote the word: *Blecch!* "Kirk, I said, knock it off. The table's cutting into my gut, for one thing, and you're turning my stomach, for another."

"You don't mean that, Maggie," Kirk said, but he did let her go, so that she could push herself upright again, turn and splay her fingers against his chest. "You're flushed," he said, making it sound like, "You're hot for me, babe."

"I'm cleaning up, Kirk. If you want to help, fine. Otherwise, please get out of my kitchen." *My apartment, my life, my solar system.*

Kirk Toland couldn't take a hint if it flew through his window wrapped around a rock and landed on his head. "Okay, I'll help," he said, taking the garbage bag from her. "Hey," he said, looking into the bag. "You've got forks in here. You're not saving the plastic utensils?"

Maggie lifted one hand to her face and pinched the bridge of her nose. "No-o-o. That's why they're called disposable utensils. So I can throw them away. If I wanted to wash a bunch of forks and knives, I'd have used the stuff in my drawers."

"All right, but you'll never get rich throwing things away," Kirk told her in a tone condescending enough to inspire a quick fantasy in which a Kirk Toland neatly skewered by at least two dozen yellow plastic forks played the lead role. "Do you know that when I was a kid we had a toaster at home that we had to unplug, then fish in it with a fork to get the toast out? Could we have replaced it? Certainly. But it still worked. Twenty years, Maggie. It's the Toland way, and the reason we have money."

"Gee. Wow. Too bad that story's too long to cross-stitch on a pillow," Maggie sniped, handing him a fistful of plastic forks. "But, wait. I'm a writer. Maybe we can do this. How about — 'If you aren't electrocuted first, you, too could be rich'? Yes? No? And then maybe you can explain the Toland yacht to me, and the Toland private jet, and the Toland house in the Hamptons, and the Toland limousine? You saved enough money not buying a new toaster for all of that?"

"Don't be facetious. The toaster is just one example. These forks would be another."

"And inheriting about fifty million bucks from your grandpa Toland figures in there somewhere, too, right?"

Kirk dropped the garbage bag onto a chair and stepped closer to her. "Why are we fighting, Maggie?"

"I haven't the faintest idea," she answered honestly. "I'm sorry, Kirk. I've had a rough couple of weeks, I guess."

He took another step and laid his hands on her shoulders. "I could help smooth you out, Maggie," he said, kneading her flesh with his long, semi-talented fingers. He tipped his head, aimed himself at her left earlobe, blew softly into her ear. "Come on, Maggie. You know we were good together. Don't say no."

Maggie closed her eyes, responding to the physical touch because she hadn't been touched in a while, because she was human, not a block of wood, and because she sure wished someone would hold her, love her.

But not Kirk.

"Stop," she said, pushing him away from her, then ducking down beneath his still stretched-out arms and scooting into the kitchen.

Kirk followed her, stopping in the doorway and propping one shoulder against the jamb. "I nearly had you, didn't I, Maggie?"

You had to give Kirk credit for knowing how to look good, because he sure looked good. Stuffed and mounted, he'd be spectacular. But she couldn't let him back in her life, because he did talk and move, and when he talked he said things that made her want to strangle him, and when he moved it was usually to cheat on her.

She ran the dishrag under the tap and

began wiping counters. "What's that old saying, Kirk? A miss is as good as a mile? You missed, Kirk. It doesn't matter by how much."

"Okay. Best two out of three?" he asked, pushing himself away from the doorjamb, heading for her once more.

"Kirk, no. Let's not." She dug down deep and came up with what she hoped was a gem: "Let's be content with our memories."

"Memories don't keep you warm at night, Maggie," Kirk said, somehow with his arms around her once more.

"It's April," she said against his chest. "We don't need heat."

He rubbed his chin on the top of her head. "Remember January, Maggie? My place? The hot tub on the roof terrace? Wine, soft music, the stars above us . . ."

Okay. So that wasn't a bad memory. Maggie relaxed slightly, still knowing she wasn't going to allow Kirk back in her life, but a little nostalgia never hurt anybody, right? Besides, she *had* been having a rough couple of weeks. Rougher than he'd ever know. Mind-boggling, even. Because it wasn't normal to wonder if one needed a condom if one had sex with a figment of one's imagination.

"Maggie?" Kirk asked when she said nothing, didn't move — toward him or away from him.

"I don't — *no*," she said, the small, still sane part of her knowing that she couldn't go to bed with Kirk and think about kissing Val Kilmer's lips . . . lips which also happened to belong to Saint Just.

Sean Connery's voice. Clint Eastwood's cheek slashes. Paul Newman's eyes. Val's lips. Kirk's hot tub. Saint Just and his quizzing glass.

It was beginning to feel as though she couldn't tell the players without a scorecard.

"Why not? Ah, Maggie, why not?"

"I . . . I'm thinking about becoming a nun," she said quickly, and just about jogged back into the dining alcove to pick up more dirty plates.

Kirk Toland might not be faithful, but he was sure as hell persistent. He followed her. "All right, Maggie, maybe I'm going too fast here. I know we had some problems —"

"We sure did. The lingerie model, the soap opera bimbo and, lest we forget — Miss February."

"But I'm sure we can work them out," Kirk went on, not missing a beat. "So let's start over. How about dinner, Maggie? To-morrow night, my place."

Maggie opened her mouth to say no. No way, no how. But suddenly Saint Just was in the room with them, Tabby draped on one arm, Bernie on the other.

"I'm here to deliver the scullery maids, my lady," Saint Just told her, looking at Kirk. "Happy volunteers, the both of them. Isn't that right, ladies?"

"Well, of course. I'll put these in the refrigerator before they go bad," Tabby said, disengaging herself from Saint Just, picking up small bowls of mayonnaise and pickle relish, and heading into the kitchen.

"Tickle her Martha Stewart button and she'll clean up anywhere. Me, I'm just along for the ride," Bernie said, leaning more heavily against Saint Just. She had his quizzing glass strung around her neck and raised it, stuck it to one eye, and trained it on her ex-husband. "What's the matter, Kirk? We interrupt something, I hope?"

"You look ridiculous. And you're drunk," Kirk said, his lip curling as Maggie wondered if her party was going to end with her doing a stint as referee.

"Drunk? Well, of course I am, darling," Bernie told him. "It's a party."

Saint Just retrieved his quizzing glass and turned Bernie by the shoulders. "Socks volunteered to call her a cab, as I believe he phrased it. If you'll excuse us?"

" 'Night, Maggie. Don't do anything I did," Bernie said as she was led away, so that Kirk and Maggie were alone once more, except for the sound of running water in the kitchen. Tabby obviously meant it when she said she'd help clean up, bless her.

"Maggie? Dinner?"

She rubbed at her forehead. "We probably do need to talk, get this settled once and for all," she said faintly, feeling her wuss factor kick in. "Okay, look. Not your place. Alex and Sterling are going to Tabby's on Monday, so we can have dinner here Monday night. You, me, and the clothes I'm going to pack up and you're going to take home with you."

"But, Maggie, I —"

"Take it or leave it, Kirk. And I wish you'd leave it."

"Found another volunteer," Saint Just said, once more entering the dining alcove so quietly that Maggie hadn't heard him coming. This time he had Clarice Simon on his arm, and the woman's cheeks were pink with embarrassment.

"I'm so sorry I didn't come to help sooner, Maggie, but Nelson spilled some wine on his jacket sleeve and I was in the bathroom, rubbing it with club soda."

Ignoring Saint Just and Clarice, Kirk bent down and kissed Maggie's cheek. "Monday night it is. Just you and me, right here, for dinner."

"Oh, how charming," Saint Just said, in a tone usually reserved for commenting on the nastiness one might step in after one of the Central Park carriages has driven by. "Come along, Miss Simon, and we'll see if we can assist Tabby in the kitchen, and leave these two cooing doves their privacy."

He still pronounced it as "*priv*-acy." And Maggie still wanted to choke him with the riband on his own damn quizzing glass.

Sterling lay on one of the couches, the bowl of potato chips and dip balanced on his belly.

Maggie sat at her computer, her horn-rimmed glasses balanced low on her nose, her back rudely turned to the room, playing game after game of Snood. Losing game after game of Snood, and giving some serious thought to going out first thing Monday morning and buying a new toaster, just because she didn't need a new toaster.

Saint Just hit the Stop button on the VCR after Mike Piazza struck out to end the ninth as the Mets suffered their second straight loss to the Philadelphia Phillies.

"Two o'clock," he said to no one in particular, consulting his pocket watch, then slipping it back into his sports coat pocket. "Many a London evening doesn't even begin until two o'clock. And here we are, the party over, the scraps and bits all tidied — save two bowls — and with enough melancholy hanging over the place to think we'd just hosted a Methodist wake."

"Your point?" Maggie asked from her corner, not turning around as she shot down a whole row of blue Snoods with a click of her trusty mouse. "I'm sure you have one. You always do. And it's usually self-serving." She missed her next shot and the screen filled with teeth-chattering skulls, signaling that she'd lost yet again. She swiveled her chair around to face him, giving up on her plan of never speaking to the man again. "God. I still can't believe it. You told David that you're representing Socks? How could you do something like that?"

"Told Mr. Trigg he's heavily invested in the Exchange," Sterling added, biting into yet another potato chip. "Told him to think water treatment plants, whatever they are. Man was taking notes, though."

Maggie slapped her hands on her knees, got to her feet. "Oh, God. He didn't. Please say he didn't."

"Ah, but he did," Saint Just told her, talking around the cheroot he'd just stuck between his molars. "A fool can see that this country, the entire world, is rapidly running out of clean water. I fully intend to double my own investment within six months."

"*Your* own investment?" Maggie crossed the room, stopped inches in front of him, and glared up into his face. "Explain. *Now.*"

"On-line investing, of course. But allow me to allay your qualms, as it appears you may have a few. That would be double my investment, taking into consideration repaying the monies you advanced to me."

"*I* advanced to you? And when did I do that?"

"When?" Saint Just frowned. "Let me see. Ah, yes. That would have been Thursday."

Maggie stepped back, waving away a stream of blue smoke from the cheroot. "You used my credit cards again, didn't you? You ripped me off — again."

"I transferred monies from your checking account, actually, but I prefer to see it as a loan," Saint Just told her. "I had to set up the account in your name, but I'm keeping detailed records of what will be my profit. Prodigiously unpleasant, punting on tick, but I'll soon have my own funds. Or did you think I'd be content to remain tied to your petticoat?"

"I'd like to see bits of you tied to every streetlight in a five-block radius," Maggie told him, and meant it.

"Please, Maggie, a little more elegance of mind, if you will," Saint Just said, walking over to the couch and selecting one potato chip from the dwindling pile in the bowl on Sterling's belly. "I make no doubt you're upset, but you'll see the wisdom in it all once I am independently wealthy and out on my own. If you're very good to me, I'll take Sterling along, unless you've gotten used to having him cleaning up after you all the time."

Maggie pressed both hands to her chest. "*Me?* Sterling cleans up after *me?* Oh, that's rich. What about *you?* You're so dedicatedly lazy, I'm surprised you don't have the man cut your meat for you. And *chew* it!"

"Oh! Famous!" Sterling cheered, sitting

up, levering his feet onto the floor. "And what's this about me choosing draperies, eh, Saint Just?" he asked, clearly emboldened by Maggie's words — or overdosed on onion dip and feeling braver than he otherwise might.

"You don't wish to accompany me on Monday, Sterling?" Saint Just asked, then shrugged. "Very well. Far be it from me to give you orders."

"No, I want to go," Sterling said, looking to Maggie as if for rescue. "Mrs. Leighton asked for me most expressly. Didn't she, Saint Just?"

The viscount looked toward the liquor cabinet, then the ceiling, then at the floor. "She did say that she thought my *significant other* might enjoy coming along," he said at last, and Maggie could swear the always so sophisticated, urbane Saint Just was turning a little red around the ears.

Maggie grinned. "Oh, there is a God, and She loves me," she said, dropping a kiss on Sterling's head and then patting Saint Just's cheek before she left the room.

CHAPTER 8

"My house," Maggie said as she turned the last dead bolt. She grabbed a cigarette from the pack on her desk, flicked her Bic, then did a quick hop-skip-and-jump onto her favorite of the two identical couches. Inhaled deeply, blew out a blast of smoke. "My house, my couch, my life," she singsonged, propping one arm behind her head and wiggling her bare toes. "Houses and couches and lives — oh, my. Hot damn!"

Sunday had been interminable — or, in her real world rather than in the formal Regency world — a real loser.

It had rained all day and she couldn't take Sterling to the park for another scooter ride, so the two of them spent most of the morning picking out the clothes he and Saint Just would wear on their overnight vacation. After much deliberation, Sterling chose khaki Dockers and cotton knit shirts for both men. Saint Just sauntered into the room just as Maggie was closing the suitcase and added two more pairs of socks, a striped tie and white dress shirt, two Hershey bars, and his snuff box.

In the afternoon, with the Mets game

postponed because of rain, Saint Just surfed the Net for decorating tips while Sterling took a nap and Maggie tried, without much luck, to work on a new Saint Just Mystery plot. She'd ask for his help, but first she'd have to find a sharp stick to poke out her own eye.

But now it was Monday morning, and Maggie was alone, blessedly, quietly alone.

She could take a nap.

She could strip naked, run through the apartment, screaming.

She could balance her checkbook and see if she still had at least ten bucks to her name.

She could move, leave no forwarding address, and Tabby could have her own live-in imaginary characters. No. Maybe not.

Besides, she had an appointment with Doctor Bob in forty minutes. Oh. Joy.

Sighing, knowing she'd cancel the appointment if she could get over her guilt at standing up Doctor Bob yet again — now there was a subject for the two of them to discuss one of these days — Maggie crawled out of the couch and headed for the shower.

Twenty minutes later she was heading for the door and hesitated when the phone rang, deciding if she should answer it or just let the machine pick up for her. Of course, if she did that, she'd only have to deal with whoever it was later, when she played back the message. It could be her bank, saying she was overdrawn. It could be a guy selling replacement windows. It could be her mother. Yesterday had been Sunday, and she always phoned her mother on Sunday. Except for yesterday. And maybe last Sunday, too.

"Oh, God." The only thing worse than a call from her mother was returning a call to her mother. Although, if she could spend the first ten minutes of the call apologizing for not being home to take her call, at least they'd have something to say to each other.

How pathetic. Having to script a phone call to her own mother.

Maggie grabbed the phone on the third ring. "Hello? What? I'm sorry, this must be a bad connection, I can hardly hear you. Oh, okay, that's a little better." Ridiculously relieved that it wasn't her mother or the bank — she was ambivalent on the replacement-window salesman — Maggie said, "Sure, no problem, although he should know already. Steaks smothered in Mr. Toland's favorite mushrooms and onions, baked potatoes, tossed salad with hemlock. No, no, I'm just kidding about that last part. So a red wine, I guess, right? Although I like that pink stuff better — white zinfandel? They call it white, but it's pink. He'll know. Uh-huh, sure, you're welcome. And you can tell your boss seven o'clock, all right? Thanks."

Maggie hung up the phone and headed for the door once more. Kirk was really going all out, having someone call just to doublecheck what she'd be serving, so that he'd bring the proper wine. There were times she could almost believe it would be all right to give the guy another chance. Luckily, the thought was always fleeting, and sanity returned with a reminder that the man had the faithfulness of Mickey Rooney when he'd vowed "this time it's forever" to each of his eight or nine brides.

Which is what she said to Doctor Bob when, ten minutes into their session, he asked her about her social life.

"And yet you're drawn to him?" Doctor Bob asked, taking notes. "Knowing it would end badly, you're drawn to him?"

"I'm not drawn to him," Maggie objected, doing her best to avoid reaching for the tissue box. "I was, but I'm not now. But I think I hurt him. If you'd asked me if Kirk could be hurt, I would have told you that's impossible. Yet I think he's really hurt. I . . . I don't like hurting people."

Doctor Bob sat back in his chair, steepling his fingers on his belly. "And, we're off," he said, smiling. "Little Maggie Kelly, making the world happier for everyone — except herself. Little Maggie Kelly, who identifies with rejection entirely too much. Little Maggie Kelly, who thinks she *should* be rejected, because nothing she's ever done has been good enough. Little Maggie Kelly, living through her stories, the perfect people of her imagination, making up happy endings for everyone — again, except herself."

"Oh, God," Maggie said on a sigh, reaching for the tissue box. "I hate this part." She pulled out tissues — one, two, three. "I mean, I really, really hate this part. . . ."

Maggie set up the dishes at the small game table in the corner of the living room, because the view from her living room windows was better than that from her dining alcove. In other words, the living room windows looked out over the street, and her dining alcove window faced a brick wall and somebody else's dining alcove. Next time she was in the market for

198

real estate, she'd open every closed drape before signing on the dotted line.

Thinking of drapes made her think of Saint Just and Sterling, and she wondered how they were doing at Tabby's house on the island. Had either of them tripped up, tried to explain themselves as imaginary characters come to life? No. Saint Just wouldn't be that stupid. Besides, no men in white coats had shown up on her doorstep to take Maggie away, so they still had to be safe.

Safe being a relative term. How safe could she be, with Saint Just playing hero in the park, running rampant through her assets, opening his big mouth in front of her friends as he passed himself off as an expert on everything from water rights to the perfect hamburger?

Still, much as she hated to say it, she missed the man. Missed both of them. She'd worked at her desk for three hours this afternoon, going through her stacks of notes — on paper napkins, Post-it notes, receipts — many of them just lines of dialogue, some of them headed by the handprinted words: SAVE — PLOT IDEA.

She had stacks and stacks of these notes, and with each one she read, more of her ideas came back to her. Saint Just had been pulling her leg with that business that she couldn't write, couldn't get an idea, without him. She'd bought what he was selling, and her imagination had frozen solid just as rapidly as her confidence in her own ability, never high, melted.

But he'd been right about Quigley, damn him. The additions he'd made had been in her style and his voice, and had worked beautifully. Bernie had accepted the manuscript as written, without a single "I love it, Maggie, it's brilliant . . . but." Bernie would have spotted the problem with Quigley if Saint Just hadn't fixed it. So she was grateful to him. Grateful to a figment of her imagination.

Couldn't she even give herself credit for imagining Saint Just in the first place, so that she could give herself credit for Saint Just's imagination because it had been her imagination all along?

Sure. Say that one fast five times, why not?

Man, the apartment was quiet. *Too quiet,* her writer's mind suggested.

Saint Just remained in his chair set in an oasis of mellow yellow light in his darkened study, pretending an interest in his newspaper while he waited for the killer to take the bait he'd dangled earlier that evening at Lord Alvanley's ball.

No, cut that into two sentences. Regency sentences were long, but Bernie only allowed her five really long sentences per book. She could easily make the break after *study*. Then it would be, *He pretended an interest in* — Maggie gave a small shiver of surprise as the intercom buzzed and she told Socks to send Mr. Toland up.

For reasons she didn't want to investigate, Maggie crossed to the mirror beside the door and checked her hair and makeup. Not too good, or he'd think she'd dressed just for him, yet not too sloppy because, after all, the man was bringing wine, for crying out loud.

His customary glass of wine at his elbow, Saint Just smiled slightly as he heard the scratching at his study door.

"Would you *stop!*" Maggie ordered her imagination, which clearly wasn't entirely in Great Neck selecting draperies. She'd only been away from her computer for about two weeks, yet she couldn't stop the voices, the lines of dialogue, the mental editing of bits and snatches that kept invading, bombarding, driving her back to work.

She could zone out anywhere, at any time, her little voices taking over, shutting out the world. She could walk straight past a familiar face, not seeing it, or catch a line of dialogue on a TV show and spend the next twenty minutes scribbling notes to herself about an idea that just wouldn't quit. Nobody understood that. Nobody except the few writer friends she'd met during the early years, when she'd attended the WAR conferences as a newbie.

To the rest of the world — like her mother, for instance — the constant noise in Maggie's head was dangerous nonsense. Fairy tales, escapes from reality, and not to be talked about in polite company. As her mother had said, countless times, it was all right to be a writer, but did her daughter also have to *act* like a writer?

Well, tough. This was her mind, and Maggie thought it was just fine, thank you. Of course she did. That's why she'd been visiting Doctor Bob every Monday for two damn years, just to end up with two parts of her imagination bunking in with her full-time. Better? Was she getting better, making any strides with Doctor Bob? She didn't think so.

Maggie grimaced, her eyes shut tight, and told her imagination and her inner voices to shut the hell up for a while, then opened the locks even before Kirk could knock on the door.

"Hi, Kirk," she said, quickly grabbing the brown paper bag he carried and heading toward the kitchen. "Oh, wine! Wasn't that thoughtful of you?" she said as he followed after her, still on the lookout for a welcoming kiss. "Red and zinfandel, just like always. And they're cold, too. All ready to pour."

When she turned to look at him, he took the opportunity to plant a wet one on her mouth. "That's chilled, Maggie. Beer is cold, soda is cold. Wine is chilled," he told her. "And the wine will need to breathe for about fifteen minutes before I serve it. It's my favorite, by the way, from a small vineyard in California."

Rhymes with Dick, rhymes with Dick. Maggie gritted her teeth and kept her smile. "And you've already had some before getting here, haven't you? I could taste it just then. Okay. Great. I'll put the steaks on now, and we'll be able to eat about the same time the wine is ready."

Such haste is unseemly, Miss Kelly. And that rhyming nonsense is excessively childish. The word, Miss Kelly, is prick. If you can think it, you can say it. And if you don't like the man, tell him, send him on his way. Or do you enjoy having him stick his tongue down your throat?

Maggie shook her head, shoving Saint Just back into her brain, or off the dock at Tabby's Great Neck house, whichever worked. "Here you go, Kirk," she said, handing him one of the bottles and a corkscrew she'd dug out of her junk drawer. "I've got two glasses *chilling* in the refrigerator. There. Did I use the right word this time? You do the honors when the moment is right, okay, while I finish with the salad."

Kirk took the bottle and corkscrew, but didn't move out of Maggie's way. "Let me guess. Steak again, right? With mushrooms and onions, baked potatoes, and salad. I really should have someone send over some of the cookbooks Toland Books publishes, just so you might try a little variety. Oh, and why the bum's rush, Maggie? Or do you expect me to drink, eat, and get out of here in the next twenty minutes?"

Maggie's shoulders slumped. "Oh, Kirk, I'm sorry. I don't know what's wrong with me, really I don't. But I've been on edge all day. Probably because I'm worried about Alex and Sterling. They went out to Tabby's Great Neck house, you know. It's the first time they've been on their own since . . . since coming to America."

"They're grown men, Maggie, and can take care of themselves," Kirk reminded her, still keeping her blocked between the counter and his body. "But, hey, if you have some crushing need to take care of someone, we could just forget about dinner and head for your bedroom."

"Kirk —"

"All right, all right, I'm sorry," he said as she pushed past him, headed for the refrigerator. "I promised to be good, and I'll be good. At least until after dinner."

And he was. Good, that is. Right up until the last bite of newly defrosted chocolate mousse pie.

Maggie was actually congratulating herself on a meal well cooked as she began to clear the table, a pleasant hour of back-and-forth banter, and the fact that even the center of the pie had defrosted in time, when Kirk went from pussycat to pouncing lion.

She had a stoneware dinner plate in each hand when he leapt on her, saying something about wanting a second dessert, and before she could think, she moved to slap his face. The edge of the dinner plate connected with his skull, and Kirk staggered back, tripped over Wellington, and hit the floor. Wellington gave him a swipe with his claws and ran out of the kitchen.

"Ohmigod, Kirk! Are you all right?" she asked, quickly shoving the plates onto the table and rushing to him, kneeling down beside him. "Here, take your hands away. Let me see."

"My eye! My eye!" Kirk kept repeating, holding both hands to the left side of his face. "Christ, Maggie, you could have blinded me!"

"Oh, I could not," she said, worried he might be right. "Come on, get up, and let me see the damage. Please?"

She helped him to his feet and pulled him toward the bright work light over the kitchen sink. "Here we go, Kirk," she said, speaking as if to a child. "One hand at a time . . . just let them down and let Maggie see. There. That's not so — oh, boy, I really got you, didn't I? So did Wellington."

His hands flew back up to his face. "Am I cut? Will I scar? Is there blood?"

"No, to all three. Except for those scratches, and they're not too bad," Maggie said, going over to the refrigerator to take out a bag of frozen corn. "But I think you're going to have a whopper of a shiner. It's already getting a little puffy and purple around your eye. Here, hold this to it," she said, leading him into the living room. "I'll get some antiseptic to clean up those scratches."

Kirk said a few nasty things about Wellington as Maggie dabbed antiseptic on his scratches, then grabbed the frozen corn and gingerly held it to his eye. "Just stay here on the couch, keep the ice on, and I'll clean up the kitchen, okay? Maybe it will be better by then."

"You owe me," Kirk called after her as she headed back into the kitchen, biting on her lips so she might make it to safety before bursting into giggles. Shiner? Oh, yeah, a real *big* one, too. Couldn't have happened to a nicer guy. And a bag of Niblets stuck to his face, as Saint Just would say, "lent nothing to his consequence."

"Wine!" Kirk called to her a few minutes later, as Maggie was scraping leftovers down the garbage disposal. "Maggie? This hurts like a bitch. How about some wine and some aspirin?"

"Your *whine* is my command, sir," Maggie grumbled, drying her hands on a dish towel, pouring the last of the red wine into Kirk's glass, and heading for her bedroom to get the painkillers.

"You really shouldn't have more wine, Kirk," she told him as he sat up on the couch and reached for the glass. "You killed off the whole bottle."

"You nearly killed *me* off," Kirk reminded her, downing two aspirin and the entire glass of wine. "Damn. Why did you do that, Maggie?"

She rolled her eyes. "You *grabbed* me, Kirk, when I wasn't expecting it. I'm Irish, remember. We have this way about us. Say or do something that shocks us, and we don't think, we react. I . . . reacted." *Knee-jerk reaction to the Kirk-jerk.*

"You know what?" he said, settling himself back against the pillows. "I give up. I don't care if Nelson says Tabby's making noises about shopping you around. I can't do this any more. I like you. You're okay in bed. But you're *weird,* Maggie."

Maggie sat down on the edge of the coffee table and blinked. Waited for Kirk's words to fully hit her brain, for her brain to process them. "Then . . . then you don't really want me back, Kirk? You're just romancing me because my contract is up and Tabby says she's shopping me?"

He lifted the ice bag a fraction to glare at her. "Right. Like you didn't know."

Maggie felt butterflies start exercising their wings in her stomach. Know? No, she hadn't known. Hadn't had a clue. She didn't even know Tabby was shopping her, and would bet she wasn't. At least not seriously. But Tabby could be a real barracuda when it came to negotiating. "And this was The Trigger's idea? You saying you wanted me back? This dinner tonight? All of it? He wants me that badly?"

Kirk lowered the ice bag once more and gave a small moan. "Nelson? He wishes you'd go away, never come back. Except he got rid of you once and ended up looking like a jerk. He doesn't want to look like a jerk twice. None of us do. Or do you really think he would have come to your party, if he hadn't had an ulterior motive? So a little romance, a little sack time, and once you'd signed on for another four books without gouging us too badly, I'd let you kick me out again. Simple. Damn, my head's spinning."

"Well, son of a gun." Maggie smiled. She actually smiled. "Maybe it's for all the wrong reasons, but you guys want me. I love it. Almost as much as I love the fact that you don't *want*-want me, Kirk, any more than I *want*-want you. In fact, now maybe we can even be friends. I've always been attracted to bastards."

He lifted the ice bag again and glared at her from between rapidly discoloring eyelids. "Yeah. Right. Friends. Can you shut up now? I want to try to take a little nap, if you promise not to beat me up again."

Maggie unfolded the afghan from the back of the couch, covered Kirk, and went back into the kitchen to finish cleaning up, humming all the way. Breaking into song, actually.

Once she'd turned out the kitchen light, she went back to the living room, checked on Kirk, who was snoring with his Harvard accent — honest — and then headed to bed. He had a headache, and in the morning he'd have a hangover, so she might as well let him sleep on her couch.

She'd sleep well tonight, too. Really well.

"Ooooh! Ooooohhhh! Oh, my God! *My stomach! My stomach!"*

Stumbling in the dark, Maggie bumped into the doorjamb as she banged out of her bedroom and raced down the hallway toward the living room.

"Kirk? Kirk! What's the matter?" she asked, flipping on a light to see Kirk doubled up on the couch, rocking from his side to his back. "Is it your head?"

"My *stomach!* Motherfuckingbastard-cocksucker —"

"Kirk! Control yourself, and answer me," Maggie ordered him, trying to sit down beside him. "It's your stomach? Are you sure?" It was a stupid question, but the guy had a black eye. What was this business about his stomach?

"My stomach, my stomach, my fucking stomach. Oh, God!"

"Appendicitis?" Maggie asked herself as she grabbed the cordless phone and pushed in 9-1-1.

The ambulance arrived fifteen minutes or seven hours later, depending on whether the question was asked of the ambulance driver or Maggie, and Kirk was strapped to a gurney and taken away.

Maggie bummed a ride up front with the ambulance driver, wishing she'd taken time to brush her teeth. Wasn't it always the little things — so much easier to concentrate on her four-in-the-morning breath than the idea that Kirk had just told the female paramedic trying to start an IV to suck his . . . yeah, well, nothing like a little appendicitis to strip the veneer off his Harvard accent.

211

Once at the hospital, Maggie told the emergency physician, a gum-chewing intern who looked to be all of twelve, "I think it's appendicitis. You should probably check his white blood count, stat."

The junior doctor blew a bubble, let it pop, tongued the gum back into his mouth. "Yippee, another expert. How lucky can I get? I blame those real-life trauma shows on the tube. Wait in chairs, lady, and we'll take a look at him." Then he followed Kirk's gurney into a curtained-off area of the large room.

"Smart-ass," Maggie grumbled under her breath, and found her way outside to indulge her nicotine addiction. She finally found the Designated Smoking Area, a partially glassed-in cubicle with a broken exhaust fan and all the charm of a six-by-twelve ashtray. She shared the cubicle with two teenagers who looked like they'd witnessed — or instigated — a drive-by shooting, two pretty ripe street people, a guy in scrubs who bummed a light from her, and a large sign that told her if she stopped smoking today her lungs would begin healing tomorrow.

"Right," she said, gesturing toward the sign. She was nervous, and she talked when she was nervous. Besides, signs like

212

this one always kick-started her temper. "That's such bull. I took my friend to the emergency room one time, and the doctor asked her if she smoked. Nope, she said. She quit twelve years ago, misses it every day, but never cheated. And you know what that doctor did? He made a face, shook his head, and said, 'Yeah, but you smoked. Too bad, the damage is already done.' Now what the hell is that supposed to mean? Quit and get better, quit and get lung cancer anyway? Why don't they make up their damn minds, get their stories straight, huh?"

"I have a better idea, lady. Why don't you shut the fuck up," the guy in scrubs suggested wearily. Maggie looked at his name tag. He was a doctor — chief of surgery, no less.

Maggie took one last drag, stepped on the butt, and headed back to "chairs." Smoking was such a glamorous addiction, and you met the nicest people.

"Miss Kelly?"

Maggie, who had been about to sit down in the only chair that wasn't directly beside someone with either ten earrings in each ear, tattoos on their neck, or who smelled of — God, she didn't want to know what they smelled of — happily trotted toward the junior doctor. "Yes? Was I right? Is it appendicitis? May I see him now?"

"Mr. Toland is being moved to Intensive Care, Miss Kelly. His condition is critical. I'd like to talk to you, if you don't mind?" Junior Doctor took her by the elbow and led her into a small room behind the nurse's station.

"Critical? Did you say critical? That's worse than Guarded or Serious, right? Less than Grave, but definitely not Good?" Maggie sat down in the hardback chair. "I don't understand."

"Neither do we, Miss Kelly, and that's a large part of the problem. It would seem that Mr. Toland ingested something that didn't agree with him — big time. And there's also the possibility of a closed-head injury. Do you know who hit him? He looks as if he's been in a fight. Those scratches? Are they your work?"

Maggie coughed, her mouth tightly closed as she made choking noises in her throat. "Hit . . . hit him? Um, yes, that would be me. But not the scratches. Those are from Wellington. Not the guy from Waterloo, my cat."

"Really?"

Could she go home, type it all up for him, bring it back later? No. She was going to have to wing it. "Um, yes, really. Kirk — Mr. Toland — is a friend, and we were having dinner in my apartment. And then he wanted to kiss me, and I was holding these really heavy dinner plates in each hand — my mother bought them for me for Christmas two years ago, and I hate them, and they're way too heavy for the dishwasher and I already broke two of those little wheels — you know those little wheels on the bottom of the bottom pullout shelf? But I have to use them because she gave them to me, which Doctor Bob says is yet another sign that I'm not ready to be my own person, no matter how well I come off looking like my own —" She sagged against the chair. "Yeah, me. I hit him. Maggie Kelly, in the kitchen, with the dinner plate. I'm *so* sorry."

"I see," Junior Doctor said, and Maggie had a funny feeling he did see. In fact, if he called for Security, she wouldn't blame him. "And you said you had dinner at your place? This was last night?"

"Well, yeah," Maggie said, confused for a second. And then she sat up again, like a hound going on point. "Oh, I get it. Concussion, reaction to concussion? I shouldn't have let him lie down, should I? Oh, this is all my fault!"

"Did he lose consciousness when you hit him? Complain of headache? Vomit?"

"Only the headache," Maggie told him. "That's good, isn't it?" she asked, hoping for a reprieve from her sudden, crushing guilt. "I gave him a bag of frozen corn and a couple of aspirins, put some antiseptic cream on the scratches. He took the aspirin with wine, and I'll bet he shouldn't have done that. But he was being such a *baby* about the whole thing."

Junior Doctor scribbled something on a chart, and Maggie tried to lean to her right to peek at whatever it was he'd written. He noticed and covered the chart with his folded hands. *Spoilsport.*

"I think Mr. Toland has a black eye and some superficial scratches, Miss Kelly, but that's all. From the neck up, that is. I'm much more interested in what else he did last night. What he had for dinner, because his stat blood tests are really screwy."

"Screwy? Is that the medical term?"

"Absolutely." He picked up his pen again and began to write once more. "You said he had wine?"

Maggie, aching to be helpful, nodded. "Wine, yes. Kirk brought the wine, and he had the red. I don't know the name; I don't pay attention to that stuff, I'm sorry.

And I made the dinner. Steak, baked potatoes, salad, chocolate mousse pie. But I'm
not sick, so it couldn't be food poisoning,
right?"

"I think you might want to stick to your
day job, Miss Kelly, and stop trying to
come up with a diagnosis of Mr. Toland's
illness, all right?"

"Good idea," she mumbled, wanting another cigarette so badly she could feel the
beginning of withdrawal pangs. "But did
you pump his stomach? He ate hours ago,
so I doubt that would help, right?"

"Miss Kelly?"

"Sorry. I — I'm a writer, you see, and
I've got all these bits and pieces of information, and a mind that keeps trying to
come up with scenarios. I'll stop, honest."

"I'd be grateful," Junior Doctor said, and
he didn't smile as he said it. "Now, let's go
over this one more time, all right? Steak,
you said. How was it prepared?"

Maggie mumbled, her chin on her chest.

"I'm sorry. I'm afraid I didn't hear that."

"I said, on a George Foreman grill. Me-
dium rare. It really works, you know."

"I know, I have one," Junior Doctor said,
and finally smiled. "Did you use marinade?
You can only use marinade once, you
know, can't save it, use it again after it has

been in contact with raw meat. I'm a doctor, you see, and I have all these bits and pieces of information, and a mind that keeps trying to come up with scenarios."

"Very funny." Then Maggie shook her head. "No. No marinade. They were New York strips, prime cuts. They didn't need marinade." Then she raised one hand and added, "But there were mushrooms and onions. Kirk loves mushrooms and onions, so I made a bunch for him. I don't eat those." She leaned forward, excited. "That's it, isn't it? That's the only thing that was different. Kirk ate the mushrooms and onions!"

Junior Doctor was scribbling again. "Mushrooms. Canned? Fresh?"

"Fresh. I got them down at the corner store. Mario's. I always buy my vegetables there. But surely —"

Junior Doctor stood up, holding the chart. "Thank you, Miss Kelly. I've got to go upstairs and give this information to the physician in charge."

"May I go with you?" Maggie asked, standing up herself.

He looked at her, then shook his head. "We'd rather you waited in —"

"Chairs, right. But first I think I'm going to go outside and have a cigarette. If you

218

need me, I'll either be in chairs, or in the smoking area, rubbing elbows with the elite."

"You know, Miss Kelly, if you quit today, your lungs would begin recovering tomorrow."

"Yeah," Maggie said, smiling weakly. "I think I read that somewhere."

Junior Doctor smiled at her again, then reached for his waistband, where his pager was vibrating. He looked down at the message just as the loudspeaker squawked and a woman's voice called out with absolutely no emotion, "Code Blue, Intensive Care, Three West. Code Blue, Intensive Care, Three West."

"Is it —" Maggie asked as Junior Doctor brushed past her, breaking into a run.

"Stay in chairs!" he called back at her as he ran down the hallway. "Hold that elevator!"

CHAPTER 9

Saint Just gave a final wave toward the Mercedes pulling away from the curb, then sighed, wondering if Tabitha Leighton had any idea how fortunate they all were that every other driver between here and Great Neck had managed to stay out of her way.

"Well, Sterling, that was an experience, wasn't it? I hesitate to call such a nice lady a cow-handed driver, but no more flattering term comes readily to mind," he said as they headed for the front doors of the brick building, only to have Socks push through one of them and walk toward them. "Socks. You're looking rather harassed on such a lovely day."

"Oh, she's not with you," Socks said, looking past Saint Just. "That sucks. I was hoping she would be."

"Well, that was cryptic, and probably in very poor taste. What are you talking about, Socks?"

"Maggie. Miss Kelly. She's not with you."

"And that was astute. You're a wizard of observation," Saint Just said, then frowned. "But I'm missing something here, aren't I?"

"Yeah. It's Maggie. When I came on this morning, the night guy told me she'd gone away in an ambulance, around four. Her and a guy. But the idiot couldn't remember if it was Maggie on the litter, or the guy. Probably because he was smoking a reefer, like usual. Can't get good help anymore, Mr. Blakely. You just can't."

"I see," Saint Just said quietly, his mind whirling. Ambulance. He knew that word. A cart used to transport the sick to hospitals. "Did the man say where the ambulance driver was taking Miss Kelly?"

Socks shook his head. "I'm figuring Lenox Hill, but I called there a while ago and there's no Maggie Kelly listed as a patient. I was hoping you knew something."

Saint Just felt his blood stir. A mystery. He could solve a mystery. It was what he did, not choose draperies. "And I do," he replied, pushing through the doorway and heading for the elevator, Sterling a few steps behind him, as he'd taken time to buy a pretzel from a street vendor with the pin money Saint Just had given him to keep in his purse.

"What are you going to do, Saint Just?" Sterling asked as he and Socks rode up to the ninth floor with him.

"We are going to enter the apartment.

Sterling, you are going to prepare tea to soothe your jangled nerves. You, Socks, are going to employ the telephone over there to make contact with this hospital again, and inquire if a Kirk Toland is a patient there. And I, of course, am going to think," Saint Just said, extracting the key Maggie had given him from his pocket and inserting it in the first lock.

"Don't bother. Door's open," Socks said, leaning around him to turn the knob. "I checked earlier, but without a key, I couldn't lock it up."

"Maggie must have gone off in quite a hurry," Sterling offered, dropping the suitcase just inside the door. "Look at this mess, Saint Just. Table turned on its side, everything spilled onto the floor. This doesn't look good, does it?"

Saint Just stood and observed the scene, his every sense alert. "Perhaps there was an altercation?" he suggested, and Socks opened his eyes wide.

"You mean, like a fight?"

"I mean nothing, Socks. It's early days yet. Any conclusions would definitely be premature. Ah, a clue," Saint Just said, poking at a white plastic bag lying on the carpet. "Corn?" he said, picking up the bag and examining it. "And warm. As it is now closing on toward noon, and the warning on the package reminds us that it is to be kept in a frozen state, I would say that this corn was removed from the kitchen at least twelve hours ago. Do you concur, Sterling?"

"Huh?" Sterling asked, righting the coffee table and picking up white paper packets that appeared to have been ripped open. Saint Just could read the words "sterile gauze" on one of them. "Oh. Oh, yes. We did that little experiment, didn't we? Measuring how long it would take for an icicle from the roof to melt, so that we knew how long ago the man stabbed by one had died. Brilliant work, Saint Just."

Socks, holding the phone book, stopped paging through it and looked at Saint Just. "What did he just say? You're a detective? I thought you were an agent."

"I dabble in many areas," Saint Just said, sparing a moment to glare at Sterling.

"I . . . I'll just go check on the kitchen, Saint Just," Sterling volunteered. "Start the tea, clean up, that sort of thing."

"Yes, do that," Saint Just agreed, wishing the man out of the room. "Now, Socks, I do believe you were about to make that telephone call?"

"Oh, yeah. I've got the number right

here. This time I think I'm going to pretend I'm a doctor. That should work."

"Excellent. Be imperious. I've always found physicians to be imperious, even though most of them know next to nothing," Saint Just said, doing his best not to pace. Not to panic. Had something happened to Maggie? And, selfish bastard that he was, what would happen to him and Sterling, if something had happened to Maggie?

Fiends take the woman — how could she be so inconsiderate?

"Then he's all right? I mean, I can still hear the machines beeping. That's a good sign?"

Junior Doctor — except now they were being more informal, and she'd begun calling him Dr. Thompson — took Maggie by the elbow and led her away from the glass cubicle and the sight of Kirk Toland lying on a narrow bed behind that glass, hooked up to about a dozen different tubes and monitors.

"He's still unconscious, I'm afraid. And I'd ask how you got in here, except then I'd know the answer, wouldn't I? And I might not like it."

"I told the nurse I'm Kirk's sister,"

Maggie admitted, still looking back over her shoulder as a technician left the cubicle carrying several vials of blood. "And a nurse. An intensive care nurse, who wouldn't scream or faint or throw up or something."

"In other words, you lied. I told you, Miss Kelly, I didn't want to hear that."

"But he's all right. No more of that code-blue stuff?"

"We got him back, yes, but since we don't know why he had the arrest . . . well, let's just say we're not happy. He's in a coma, his renal output is just about zilch — another complex technical medical term — and it looks like his systems are starting to shut down, one by one. As fast as we try to put out one fire, another one starts somewhere else."

Maggie blinked back tears. "That's not good."

"That's exceptionally bad, Miss Kelly. We've drawn blood cultures, but the funny thing about those is that, by the time the cultures grow and tell us what we're dealing with, the patient is usually either recovered or dead. Now, how about you go on home, and we'll call you if there are any changes. I hesitate to say this but, in my medical opinion, you look like hell."

"I feel like hell," Maggie said as they pushed through the doors and left the ICU. "If Kirk dies because I cooked him dinner . . ."

"We don't know that, Miss Kelly," Dr. Thompson assured her. "Still, if you could bring us some of those mushrooms?"

Maggie brightened, having been given a job. "I could do that. I'll go right now, to Mario's, and get you some."

Dr. Thompson shook his head. "No, I didn't mean for you to go shopping, Miss Kelly. I mean, can you bring us some of the mushrooms you served to Mr. Toland last night? Mushrooms not used and still in your refrigerator? A bit of leftovers?"

Instantly deflated, Maggie shook her head. "They're gone. Kirk ate most of them, and I put the rest down the garbage disposal. I could have put them in the refrigerator, waited until they got moldy, and then thrown them out, but I gave up on that plan the last time I had to toss half a grapefruit that was growing penicillin all over it. Still, I should have saved them, because maybe Alex or Sterling would eat them. Wish I'd thought of that before I tossed them."

"Alex and Sterling? They live with you? Cats? Dogs? People?"

"Um-hmm," Maggie said absently. "But they weren't home last night. They were out in Great Neck, with my friend, picking draperies."

"Which pretty much eliminates cats and dogs," Dr. Thompson said, and Maggie looked up at him quickly. He said, "You have two male roommates?"

"What?"

"Nothing, Miss Kelly. I'm just trying to go over the events of last evening. So you have two roommates, male, and they were out of town, at which time Mr. Toland, male, came to have dinner. And you prepared the mushrooms and onions? Not either of your roommates? Did they have access to the mushrooms and onions?"

"Don't give up your day job, Dr. Thompson," Maggie said in disgust. "Like you said, they have my number at the nurses' station. I've already called his ex-wife, and she said she'd send flowers but a visit is out of the question, and there really is nobody else, so I guess I'm the one you guys have to call. I'll be back around six. See ya."

She stomped off, indignant that Dr. Thompson would even *hint* that Saint Just or Sterling had done something to the mushrooms and onions because they were jealous of Kirk, or something like that.

It wasn't until she was riding down in the elevator that it hit Maggie. If Dr. Thompson (Junior Doctor turned Junior Detective) was thinking somebody put something in Kirk's mushrooms and onions — and it wasn't either Sterling or Saint Just — who did that leave?

"This is *not* turning into a good day to give up smoking," Maggie said, already reaching into her purse for her cigarettes as she crossed the lobby and headed for the nearest taxi stand.

Two o'clock. Saint Just longed to throw something at the clock sitting on the mantel above the fireplace, but that would have been entirely out of character for him, so he didn't. Instead, he glared at Sterling as that man walked by, carrying a white plastic garbage bag and wearing Maggie's Kiss the Cook apron.

"*Now* what are you cleaning?" he asked. "And far be it from me to complain, but you look ridiculous."

"At least I'm being useful," Sterling retorted, showing a lot more spunk than usual, as if the man had gained new courage by the simple act of having somehow picked a drapery fabric Tabitha

228

Leighton said had been precisely her own choice.

"I don't *do* menial tasks, Sterling. Gentlemen never do menial tasks."

"And that's another thing. You really are high in the instep, Saint Just. Or have you forgotten? We aren't in Regency England anymore. We're in Manhattan, the Big Apple, and we have to sing for our supper around here or land in the street."

"She'd never do that," Saint Just said. "I've convinced her that she needs us."

"Really. And she's convinced herself that she does *not* need us."

Saint Just eyed his friend, watching a hot flush stain Sterling's cheeks. "What did you do, Sterling?" he asked, outwardly calm.

"Do? Me? Um, nothing. Nothing." He put down the garbage bag and sighed. "Well, I might have done, said, something. Possibly. Maybe."

"I see," Saint Just said. "So, if I am deducing correctly, you *may* have, might *possibly* have knocked the pins straight out from under us. You may have, might have, just possibly could have told Maggie that, although we took her most recent idea with us when we departed her mind, her imagination is still her own? Would that, could that possibly be what happened, Sterling?"

"She . . . forced it out of me?" Sterling supplied hopefully.

"Of course she did, Sterling. What was it? The rack? Thumbscrews? Oh, the audacity of the woman." Saint Just gave a wave of his hand. "I believe you were on the way to dispose of something?"

"Saint Just," Sterling said, wringing his hands. "I'm sorry. Really."

Saint Just sighed, then nodded. "No matter, Sterling. I'm relieved, actually. Keeping up that particular ruse was becoming fatiguing, at best. And we have much more important matters to deal with now."

"Mr. Toland. Socks told me his condition is as well as can be expected. That doesn't sound good, does it?"

"If he dies, Sterling, Maggie will be devastated. We know her, know her tender heart. The fact that she doesn't really like the man much will make it even worse. Guilt, Sterling. The woman is riddled with it."

Sterling picked up the bag of garbage and tossed it over his shoulder like Father Christmas preparing to make his rounds. "Guilt? Why?"

"Simple, Sterling. Maggie has wished the man gone from her life, numerous times. If he goes — expires — she will feel she wished it on him. Females. They think that way."

"Oh. I hadn't thought of that. You're so smart, Saint Just. Well, I guess I'll go dispose of this bag down the chute and then unpack our clothing. I'm much too nervous to simply sit, as you are doing, and I can't think of anything else to do."

"Yes, you do that," Saint Just said with a small smile. "Oh, but Sterling? If you could wait a moment? Do you by chance have any of your pin money left?"

"I do. But I don't need it to push this bag down the chute."

"No, of course not. But if you were to also step down the street to Mario's, the way Maggie showed you? Then perhaps you could purchase some sort of cake — something — to serve with the tea, should Maggie return soon."

Sterling brightened. "Those small ones, covered in chocolate? With the white squiggles on top?"

"Yes, those sound perfect," Saint Just said, happy to see his friend smiling once more. "And don't worry, Sterling. We're here. We won't let anything untoward happen to Maggie. Not while we still draw breath."

Seemingly satisfied to leave all his worries behind with Saint Just, and probably eager for the small chocolate-covered cakes, Sterling was out the door and gone within seconds, leaving his friend to sit, and to think.

Saint Just was ashamed of himself. Nearly his first thought upon hearing that Maggie might have been taken to the nearest hospital had been for himself. His survival, his and Sterling's.

He should be horsewhipped.

Still, it was a logical leap for his very logical mind to take, because the only reason he existed at all was because he had existed in Maggie's mind. Had that changed the moment he and Sterling had made the greatest leap, from mind to reality? He didn't know, and he'd have to ponder it at some point, but not until he knew more about what had happened in this apartment.

Which he wouldn't learn until Maggie returned to this apartment. Blast the woman. Where was she?

Saint Just gave in to his urge to pace and began walking off the steps that took him from one end of the Persian carpet to the other, then back again. In his mind's eye he could still see the overturned table, the debris left, as Socks had informed him, from the people who had ministered to Kirk Toland before carting him off to the hospital.

Socks had also informed him that bags of frozen vegetables were often employed to soothe bruises, knocks on the head, that sort of thing.

Who had been knocked on the head? Maggie? Had Toland accosted her? Had she retaliated? Had she dealt him a mortal blow?

He hated making assumptions, but there was so little fact, and so much to assume.

There were no stains on the carpet. No bloody clothes had littered the floor. His only clues remained the bag of Niblets, the tube of antiseptic he'd found on the kitchen counter, and the bits and pieces Socks had provided him after contacting someone at Lenox Hill Hospital. Maggie was not a patient; Toland was.

He had just decided to go downstairs, grab Socks, and have him take him to this Lenox Hill Hospital when the door opened and Maggie walked — nearly staggered — into the apartment.

"Oh," she said, looking at him with eyes

that didn't really see him. "You're back."

"As are you," Saint Just said, watching as she dropped onto one of the couches and began rummaging in her purse for her cigarettes and lighter.

"Allow me," he said, withdrawing his own lighter, a black one he'd purchased at Mario's, as he could not bring himself to keep appropriating Maggie's pink one for himself. A gentleman must maintain standards.

She leaned her head forward slightly, allowed him to light her cigarette, then drew in deep and blew out a stream of smoke as she collapsed her head onto the back of the couch. "When did you get back?"

"Two lifetimes ago, at the least," Saint Just said, pouring them both full glasses of wine. Never the most fashionable dresser, unlike her editor and agent, Maggie had outdone herself this time, wearing the dark blue T-shirt she slept in over a pair of wrinkled, not quite clean jean pants. The left shoelace of her sneakers was in a hopeless knot, she had not bothered with hose or socks, and it appeared as if she had combed her hair with a rake. "Here, take this, and drink it straight down."

She looked up at him and took the glass. "You know?"

"I know many things," Saint Just said, not willing to beg, to plead with her to tell him what had happened . . . and manfully controlling a most worrying impulse to gather the sad-looking, rumpled Maggie in his arms, comfort her, kiss her, hold her tight. "Why don't you tell me what you know, and we'll compare our information?"

"Okay." She looked around the room. "Where's Sterling?"

"I sent him on an errand. He'll be back soon. Now, you were saying?"

"Did you two pick draperies for Tabby?"

Saint Just drew in air through his nose and let it out slowly, tamping down his anxiety, his temper. "Sterling chose them, as a matter of fact."

"Yellow?"

"Yes," Saint Just said, at last finding some small reason to smile. "Yellow. Mrs. Leighton is delighted. Now, about Toland?"

Maggie sat forward, placing her empty glass on the coffee table. "It's awful, Alex. Awful. His heart stopped. They got him back, but his *heart* stopped. He's so sick."

Saint Just felt himself marginally relax. "Then he's ill? Not injured?"

Maggie stubbed out her cigarette. "Oh,

well that, too, but it's only a black eye and some scratches. Serious enough, if it weren't for everything else."

"Yes, everything else," Saint Just said, not knowing what in the devil he was saying. "Just how bad is everything else?"

"Pretty bad. He's really, really sick," Maggie told him, reaching for another cigarette and unearthing her pink lighter from the depths of her purse. "I think they think it was the mushrooms I cooked him for dinner last night. Nobody said so, but I think that's what they're thinking, because he ate them and got sick, and I didn't eat them, and didn't. I don't like mushrooms."

She looked at the lighter, the cigarette, and tossed both on the tabletop. "He could die, Alex. And it would all be my fault."

There were times when Saint Just was not pleased when he was right. This was one of them, as he watched Maggie shrink into a tight little ball of guilt. "Don't be ridiculous, Maggie. It wasn't as if you went to the park and *picked* toadstools. I was with you Sunday afternoon, remember, when you shopped at Mario's? If anyone killed him, the mushrooms did, not you."

Maggie looked at him and gave him a wry smile. "Haven't you heard, Alex?

Mushrooms don't kill people. People kill people."

He watched as she stood up, went over to her desk, and picked up the headphone to her telephone as she sat down. "I've got to call Bernie," she said as she punched in numbers. "She said she wouldn't visit him, but I think she has to go with me when I go back to the hospital tonight. I mean, he was — is — her ex-husband."

Saint Just watched as Maggie swiveled back and forth in her desk chair, waiting for Bernie to answer on her end of the line. At least, if she spoke to Bernie, he'd get to hear as well, and maybe he'd learn something else, something important.

"Damn," Maggie said, pulling off the headset and tossing it back on the desktop. "She's not at the office. I know she said she was going to some big lunch meeting with Sales, but I didn't think she'd actually do it. Not with Kirk so sick."

"Obviously, she doesn't like him enough to be concerned."

"Like him? She hates him. He broke her heart, not that she'd ever admit it."

Saint Just filed that information away, trying to balance it with the growing certainty that, if Toland ingested poisonous toadstools in place of innocent mushrooms, *somebody* had to have served them to him or found a way to place them in Maggie's refrigerator so that she would serve them to him. Ms. Toland-James had a key to the apartment, he remembered. Had Maggie gone out at all Monday, leaving the apartment unoccupied? Yes, she had. Her weekly appointment with Doctor Bob.

"Don't concern yourself with Ms. Toland-James," he told her, taking her hand and guiding her toward the hallway leading to the bedrooms. "I shall be accompanying you on any further trips to visit Toland."

"Oh, yeah, right," Maggie said, looking up at him. "Just what I need. You asking questions, deducing, lining up possible suspects. This is just an adventure for you, isn't it? I don't think so, Alex. This isn't one of my plots. I don't already have all the answers."

"True. I doubt we even have all the questions," Saint Just said, ignoring her sarcasm. "Now go. Nap, freshen yourself, and we'll be off. Right after you have some tea and cakes, because Sterling has convinced himself that you need both. Had you realized you'd given the man motherly instincts?"

Maggie smiled. "Tea and cakes. That's nice. Sterling's such a sweetheart."

"Ah, there it is, that most winning smile. Good. And yes, Sterling is a marvelously considerate soul, isn't he?" Saint Just said, giving her a small push in the direction of her bedroom. "I, on the other hand, am the heartless brute who cares only for himself."

"I didn't mean that, Alex," Maggie said, her steps dragging as she headed off down the hallway. "You can't help what you are. I made you; it's my fault."

He was running hot and cold, and he knew it, knew himself to be caught between wanting to hug Maggie and to shake her. "Sterling stubbed his toe on a rock yesterday afternoon while exploring the beach," he called after her. "Am I to assume that was also your fault?"

Maggie stopped, her back to him, and lifted her shoulders, then dropped them again. "Probably. Oh, God, I'm exhausted. I think I'll take a nap. Don't forget to wake me around five, okay? I want to be back at the hospital by six."

Now he'd been put in the role of servant, ordered to wake his mistress at five? How dare she!

"Of course. It would be my pleasure,"

Saint Just said, swallowing his pride, which left a bitter taste in his mouth — and an unfamiliar warmth around his heart.

Maggie showered, brushed her teeth, and fell into bed after dragging on clean underwear and an old T-shirt, only to wake abruptly at the sound of voices in her living room.

Raised voices.

Angry voices.

She stumbled from her bed, pushed both hands through her hair, and climbed into a clean pair of slacks before heading down the hallway.

"And I, *Left*-tenant Wendell, have told *you* that Miss Kelly is resting and may not be disturbed."

"Alex?" Maggie said, walking into the living room and grabbing onto the back of one of the couches when she saw Saint Just standing nose-to-nose with what could only be one of New York's finest. Unless that black wallet flipped open to show a gold shield meant that their visitor was here to show off his brand new Chicken Inspector badge. "Alex?" she repeated, as both men turned toward her.

"Ms. Kelly? Ms. Margaret Kelly?"

"Ohmigod," Maggie breathed, making

her way around the couch, still holding onto it, then falling into the cushions. "He's dead? Kirk's dead?"

"Leaping to conclusions is my cousin's favorite pastime, *Left*-tenant," Saint Just said, stepping back as the police officer brushed past him.

"No, ma'am, Mr. Toland is not dead," he told her, and Maggie looked up through her tears and into the greenest eyes she'd ever seen. "Please, allow me to introduce myself. I'm Lieutenant Steve Wendell, and I've caught — that is, I've been assigned the job of collecting your garbage."

"What . . . what department are you from?" Maggie asked, her ears buzzing. "Is there a police department of garbage collecting?"

"Homicide, ma'am," Lieutenant Wendell told her as he flipped his wallet shut and shoved it in the front pocket of his badly creased khakis.

"Homi— *homicide?* But you said Kirk wasn't dead."

"Yes, ma'am, but I was available, so here I am. Lenox Hill notified my captain, asking for assistance, and I was up next."

Maggie wanted to keep him talking. That way, she wouldn't have to hear what he had to say. "I see. No, I don't see. Ho-

241

micide? You guys don't get the scut jobs."

Lieutenant Wendell's smile lit his emerald eyes. "They do, ma'am, if they're on desk duty because they might have punched a fibbie in the chops because the idiot screwed up a case they'd been working on for six months."

"You decked an FBI agent?" Maggie asked, actually diverted for the moment. She looked at the lieutenant again, took in his lanky height, his light brown hair that hung below the collar of his blue-and-white striped dress shirt (sleeves rolled up, collar open, no tie). Definitely over thirty, under forty, he looked about as professional, and as dangerous, as Socks . . . and the complete opposite of the always well put-together Saint Just of the ramrod-straight posture and impeccable wardrobe.

"I'm not proud of it, ma'am," the lieutenant said.

"Yes, you are," Maggie said, reaching for her pack of cigarettes and lighter still residing on the coffee table. "So, okay, Dirty Harry, sit down, tell me what's going on. And Alex? Stop *hovering* and glaring and get out of here."

"You're going to allow this . . . this Bow Street Runner in your apartment?" Alex shrugged. "Very well. But I will chaperone you," he said, sitting down next to her. "*Left*-tenant? As I recall it, you have told us that Mr. Toland is very ill, which we already know, and that you've been commissioned to come here, gather up garbage, and transport it to the doctors in charge of Mr. Toland, which is, I'm sure, a reflection of your level of competence. Am I correct so far?"

Steve Wendell looked at Maggie as he jerked his head toward Saint Just. "Got a hell of a poker up his ass, doesn't he?"

"He's English," Maggie answered, figuring that was probably as good an answer as any other. "My cousin, actually. He and his friend, Sterling Balder, are staying here with me."

Wendell shifted his weight and reached into his back pocket, coming out with a bent-up notebook and a stub of pencil. "Uh-huh. Alexander Blakely and Sterling Balder. I got that much from the doorman. That and the news that if I think Maggie Kelly did anything bad to anyone, ever, I was out of my gourd, and it's no wonder this whole city is going to hell."

"Socks," Maggie said, smiling weakly. "Sorry about that."

"And I'm sorry to hear that your

cousin's friend already destroyed any evidence."

Maggie drew in her breath sharply, as Saint Just laid a hand on her arm and squeezed it. "Mr. Balder, *Left*-tenant, disposed of the garbage. However, since I'm convinced that you're a perfect bulldog of an investigator, may I suggest that you toddle off to the cellars and indulge your forte, digging through offal?"

Wendell used the blunt end of the pencil to scratch at the side of his head. "Yeah, I figure that's next." He got to his feet and looked down at Maggie. "You aren't going to confess to poisoning the guy and save me from this, are you? No, didn't think so. They never do."

"I didn't —"

"Let me show you to the door, *Left*-tenant," Saint Just said before Maggie even knew what might come out of her mouth next, then stood up, motioning for Wendell to precede him to the door.

But then Wendell stopped and looked at Saint Just once more. "Not that any of this is probably going to go anywhere, you understand. The guy got some bad mushrooms or something, that's all it's going to turn out to be. Still, and knowing my captain, I guess I should at least pretend I'm making an investigation. So, got any ID on you, Blakely?"

"ID?" Saint Just stiffened. "I beg your pardon?"

"Okay, okay, never mind. I'm not going to push. Next thing you know, you'll be lawyering-up. People from addresses like this one know all about lawyering-up. Then your lawyer calls the mayor, and he calls the chief, and he calls my captain, and I'm back on the shit list. Can't win, you know? I'm just glad this assignment got me out from behind that desk. But I am going to have to check you out, just so it looks like I'm doing something. You, your friend, Miss Kelly. Especially if the guy croaks." He leaned around Saint Just and waved his notebook at Maggie. "Nice meeting you, Miss Kelly."

Maggie waved weakly and waited until the door had closed behind the lieutenant before she leapt to her feet, looking about her wildly, as if for somewhere she could hide. "Who *is* that guy? Man, has he ever seen too many *Columbo* episodes. Hi," she said, singsonging, as she began pacing, unable to stand still. "I'm just this dumb, rumpled, good-looking nobody know-nothing from Homicide, so don't you go worrying yourself about me, because you're so smart and I'm such a blockhead, I wouldn't know if you were the murderer if I caught you with the bloody knife in your hand. Yeah, sure, right. Like wrinkled clothes, too-long hair, and that *duh* act would have gotten him into Homicide? My God, my God, he asked you for *ID.*"

Saint Just handed her a glass of wine, which seemed to be his answer to any sort of problem. A part of Maggie's mind — the writer part — took a note to switch Saint Just to lemonade before she became an alkie.

"Yes, that did take me aback for a moment. But then I recalled what it means. Identification, correct? The *left*-tenant wishes to see our papers."

"Stop saying *left*-tenant," Maggie all but shouted at him. "It's *lieu*-tenant, *lieu*-tenant. Got it? You sound like such an ass sometimes, Alex. And where's Sterling?"

"Sterling is having a small lie-down, at my suggestion," Saint Just informed her, his tone dripping icicles. "Now, if you'll explain to me just what these identification papers are all about, perhaps we can put our heads together and find a way to produce some for Sterling and myself? Or would you rather just stand there, being vulgar and unlady-like as you insult me for being who I am."

"Oh, God," Maggie said, stabbing her fingers through her hair as she collapsed onto the couch once more. "I'm sorry, Alex. It's just . . . it's just . . ."

"Toland is ill, perhaps mortally ill, and the police are at your door, asking questions about mushrooms, questions about us, about Sterling and me. I understand. It is a bit of a muddle. However, allowing ourselves to panic will aid nothing. Now, first things first, since it has only just now gone four, and we're not scheduled to be at Lenox Hill until six — tell me about this ID business."

Maggie lifted her hands, then let them drop into her lap. "ID. It's ID. Identification. You know, driver's license, birth certificate, voter registration card, Social Security number. ID. Oh, wait a minute. You're not American. You're English. You wouldn't have any of that stuff."

"Really? Then why did the *left* — the *lieu*tenant, ask for them?"

Maggie's mind was skipping over itself as she tried to figure out just *where* on the internet she could find a forger. "Hmmm? Oh. No, you'd still have papers. A visa, a green card — something. Plus all your English citizenship papers, your passport that you needed to get here, that kind of stuff." She dropped her head against the back of the couch. "That's it, Alex. We're dead. We're dead meat. I don't have the faintest idea how to get ahold of stuff like that. I mean, we'd need a criminal, a forger, somebody with connections."

Saint Just sipped from his wineglass. "Socks?" he suggested.

"Socks?" Maggie laughed sourly. "Socks can't even get me theater tickets, for crying out loud. No, Alex, we'd need a crook, a bad guy. Someone who, for a price, can put us in touch with someone else who knows how to make up fake IDs."

"I see," Saint Just said, looking thoughtful. In her books, whenever he looked thoughtful, he was about to do something outrageous.

"Alex? What are you thinking?" she asked, just as the telephone rang. "Damn, I have to get that. Hold that thought, okay?"

But when she picked up the telephone, only to hear Nelson Trigg on the other end, she forgot that Saint Just had been giving her "that" look.

"Nelson? How did you — yes, it's true, he's in the hospital. But how did you — oh, Bernie. Okay. Lenox Hill. I'm going back over at six." She made a face, but did the right thing, asking, "Do you want to come along?"

Trigg's next words staggered her: "That's impossible," he said. "I have to stay here, take charge."

"Why?" Maggie shook her head. "Who the hell are you, Alexander Haig? What do you mean, *take charge?*"

"Maggie," Trigg said, his condescending tone making her teeth hurt, "Toland Books is a one-man operation. No board, no officers, just Kirk Toland. Someone has to take over, step up, calm fears."

"Whose fears?" Maggie asked. "No board, no officers — no stockholders. It's not like the CEO of Microsoft just went down."

"Employees, Maggie. Of course, you wouldn't consider them, would you? They need a feeling of stability. Until the heirs, whoever they might be, step in and assign someone permanently to run Toland Books. Until then, Maggie, I'm in charge. Do you understand now?"

"More than you think, Nelson. But just a small suggestion here — you might want to wait until the body's cold, or else Kirk could come back, hear what you've done, and fire your pompous ass," Maggie gritted out, then slammed down the phone.

She whirled around to face Saint Just, who was just then putting down the portable phone. "You heard?"

"Every word. The man could barely keep the glee from his voice. And, as you said, the body is not yet cold. Very interesting."

"Ghoulish is more like it. Look, I'm going to change my clothes and head back to the hospital. Call out for pizza for Sterling and come with me. I know you said you would, but I need to ask anyway. I really do want company."

Saint Just bowed from the waist. "It would be my most distinct pleasure, Miss Kelly. As always, the Viscount Saint Just is on the case."

"Oh, God," Maggie breathed, and closed her eyes.

CHAPTER 10

"You couldn't lose the cane? Leave it at the apartment?"

"My cane? Don't be ridiculous. This cane was given to me by my Great-uncle Sylvester on the occasion of my twenty-first birthday."

Maggie pressed her hands to her temples, where her headache throbbed. "Oh, it was not. I gave it to you as a prop, an affectation, and a weapon. And it looks stupid with khakis and a golf shirt. I mean, it looks really *bad*."

Saint Just looked at her as they walked toward the entrance to the hospital. "And now I believe I must protest. Have I said anything in the least derogatory about that *feedbag* you carry slung over your shoulder? I think not."

Maggie stopped on the pavement, blinking back tears. "I'm sorry, Alex. I'm just . . . I'm just . . ."

"Fretting about Toland, I know. And you're right to worry. If he expires, I would imagine that Lieutenant Wendell will feel the need to run tame in our living room, which is an exceedingly depressing thought.

But it's not to concern you, Maggie. I'm here now and will protect you. Isn't that wonderful? How clever of me to show up just as you need me. My timing remains, as always, impeccable."

"I could shoot a few holes in that assumption, if I had an hour, but I don't," Maggie muttered, once more heading for the double doors that led into the main lobby of the hospital. "I only hope someone lets me go upstairs to see Kirk."

"There could be a problem?"

Maggie rolled her eyes. She didn't have time to lead Alex by the hand and run him through hospital protocol. "Yeah, there could be a problem. Kirk's in Intensive Care, for one, and they usually only let family members in there. Two, I'm a suspect, remember? There's probably a sign taped outside his cubicle — No Attempted Murderers Allowed."

"I see," Saint Just answered, then brightened as, through the crush of people clogging the foyer, he spied the Information desk. "Remain here, if you please. I'll handle this."

"Stay — what? Are you out of your — Alex, come back here. I — ah, hell," she said, as he'd already "toddled off," swinging that damn cane, and all she could do was follow after him, like some dumb puppy.

She got to the desk just as Alex was introducing himself to a blue-haired woman with the chin of a Marine drill sergeant. ". . . so you *will* assist us, won't you, dear lady? We only received word of this distressing development two hours ago, at which time we raced here pell-mell from Great Neck. Our poor brother. The doctors . . . the doctors say his situation is quite grave and advised us to hurry. Please, can you help us? Direct us?"

The little blue-haired lady, who should have been oozing compassion at this point, merely blinked and said, "Name of the patient?"

"Oh, of course, of course. Toland," Saint Just supplied, watching as the woman paged through a thick computer printout. "Kirk Toland. We used to call him Kirk the Jerk, isn't that terrible? Ah, the callousness of youth. And now he's so ill. Our oldest brother, our rock, our foundation. We must speak with the doctors at once."

"Uh-huh," the woman said, running her finger down one green-and-white-striped page. "Here he is, Toland, Kirk. Intensive Care, Three West. You can't see him now."

Saint Just took one step back. "I am not

allowed to see my own brother?" he pronounced loudly. "Madam, that cannot be correct."

"Oh, you can go up there, call in from the Waiting Room, but I don't think they'll let you in, at least not until the top of the hour, and then only for ten minutes. But a nurse could probably page one of the doctors for you." She shifted to one side, looking past Saint Just. "Next?"

"Now see here, my good woman —"

Maggie grabbed his elbow and pulled him away. "Who said charm will get you anywhere?" she asked, leading him toward the elevators.

"Charm got me Toland's location," Saint Just pointed out, looking around at the crush of people. "Why are half of these people dressed in pajamas?"

"They're doctors and nurses, and those aren't pajamas. They're scrubs." At Saint Just's blank look, she said, "Uniforms. They're uniforms."

"They're green, and they're wrinkled. A person should have some pride. However, that said, the mission has not been a complete failure. We now know Toland's location. All in all, I think I did very well."

"Not really. I already know where Kirk is, smartass. And they already know that

I'm his sister, because I used that lie earlier to get up to see him."

Saint Just smiled his Val Kilmer smile as he drawled in his Sean Connery voice: "How droll. Your imagination is my imagination." The elevator doors opened and there was the usual free-for-all of people trying to get in the elevator before the people already inside could get out. Saint Just stood back politely as a woman pushing a baby stroller barreled through, using the stroller as a weapon, then bowed three more women into the elevator as the doors slid shut.

Maggie's headache continued to pound in her temples. "Excuse me for saying this, Alex, but you might have already noticed that we're not in the elevator?"

"Ladies first, Maggie. I am nothing if I am not polite. We'll take the next one to arrive."

Maggie turned to look at the crowd behind her, all of them ready to trample their young in order to get on the next elevator. "We'll take the stairs," she told him, already walking toward the Exit sign, so that he had no choice but to follow.

As they climbed the three flights, Maggie issued warnings to Saint Just. "I talk, you stand there and look handsome and appealing. We're Kirk's brother and sister from Great Neck, just like you said, and we want to see him. We want to know his condition. We want to talk to a doctor. We do *not* want to charm everybody because people in places like this do not charm. Polite gets you nowhere. So just shut up, and watch and learn."

They stepped out of the stairwell and found their way to the Intensive Care Unit and the waiting room that held the phone Maggie had used earlier. Gathering all her courage, as she hated talking to middle management — they were always so damn *sure* of themselves — she picked up the phone, impatiently waited for someone to come on the line, then barked out, "Maggie Kelly and brother, to see Kirk Toland. Dr. Thompson said I could see him at six."

She cupped a hand over the phone and turned to smile at Saint Just. "She said just a minute. Did you hear that tone I used? Charming doesn't cut it. Authoritative, that's the way you have to go. I just acted like I *know* I'm going to be let in to see him. Confidence, that's what you need when dealing with these guys. They take orders, they're used to taking orders, so if you just act like you're — *what?*"

She took her hand off the phone and turned her back to Saint Just. "What do you mean, I can't come in there?" she whispered fiercely. "Please let me in there. I was told I could see him at six, and — oh. Oh, okay."

"Is there a problem, General? Are the troops in revolt?" Saint Just asked as Maggie hung up the phone, keeping her back to him.

She turned slowly and glared at him. He had no idea how she had forced herself to be firm, show some guts, take on one of the nameless horde of gatekeepers. Then again, maybe he did, considering he'd lived inside her head all these years. And that made it worse! "Shut up. Just shut up, okay? Kirk's not there. They took him somewhere for another test. Nuclear Medicine, I think she said. But Dr. Thompson left a message that they're to have him paged when I show up. They're getting him now."

"Ah, mission half accomplished. How I thrill to figuratively sit at your feet and watch, learn."

"You're getting on my nerves, Alex," Maggie said, grabbing a six-month-old copy of *People* and collapsing into a hard chair. "Sit down. We'll probably have to wait a while."

"Actually, I believe I'd like to stroll around a little, gain familiarity with the territory and all of that."

Maggie shot to her feet again. "No way, Jose. You're not going anywhere by yourself. I've got enough problems as it is. Bernie won't come to the hospital, *you* will . . ."

Saint Just shrugged. "Very well, Maggie. As my attempt at polite vagueness has failed, perhaps you can assist me in my search for the nearest water closet."

"You . . . you have to go to the bathroom? Why didn't you just say that? Oh, never mind. Go ahead, go to the bathroom. But it won't say Water Closet on it." She led him out into the hallway, looking around for a Rest Room sign. "There'll just be a sign saying Men, or maybe a stick figure that looks sort of like a man. Wait, I'd better come with you."

"If you are insinuating that I cannot navigate a few simple corridors on my own, madam, might I remind you that I am a grown man who has competently traversed every thoroughfare and alleyway in London? I am not without my talents. Although, if you wish me to leave a trail of bread crumbs, I suppose I could manage that. If you'll supply the bread crumbs.

Why not look in your feedbag? It is possible, you know. Everything else is in there."

"Except my money, because you have all of that, don't you? Oh, okay, okay, and I'm sorry I insulted you. Go, go. I don't want you here when Junior Doctor shows up anyway. I can't even begin to think about all the stupid questions you might ask him."

"Your lack of confidence in me is rather condemning of you, considering that you created me. Ah, someone approaches, perhaps Dr. Thompson? What's that he has emerging from his mouth? It looks like a pink bladder."

"Bubblegum," Maggie said on a sigh as she watched the doctor approach. "I'm dealing with a doctor who blows bubbles. Poor Kirk."

"Ah, yes, bubblegum. I believe I do remember seeing that somewhere. Not that you want to be reminded at the moment, I'm sure."

A nurse in green scrubs, a stethoscope hung around her neck, pushed through the doors from the Intensive Care Unit and headed for the elevator.

"Ah, and here comes someone else. And in pajamas, too. How nice," Saint Just said. "Well, I'll be off."

Instead of heading down the hallway, Saint Just approached the elevator and stood beside the nurse. He bowed, introduced himself, and Maggie got a sudden stomach-flipping feeling. She took a step toward the elevator before Dr. Thompson blocked her view, stepping in front of her. "Ms. Kelly?"

"Huh?" Maggie said, watching as the elevator doors opened and Saint Just ushered the nurse — the giggling nurse — into it. He waved to her, a sort of salute he made with his cane, as the doors closed. "Oh, boy," Maggie said, closing her eyes. "I knew I should have tied him to the bed frame."

"Yeah? You into that? There must be a lot of it going around. S&M, kinky toys, nooses, small fuzzy animals in places you wouldn't believe," Dr. Thompson said, apparently a man who didn't ruffle easily. "You wouldn't believe the stuff we see downstairs. I could tell you stories —"

"I didn't mean it that way," Maggie said quickly, then looked into the crowded waiting room. "Do we have to talk in there?"

"Actually, we have to talk out here. Patient confidentially only goes so far in a place as overcrowded as this. Besides, I really don't have much else to tell you. Mr. Toland is still failing fast, and we can't stop it. We have him down in Nuclear Medicine right now, doing a kidney scan, which is where I was when I got the page. Doesn't look good. Nothing looks good. And the cop came up empty."

"The — oh, Lieutenant Wendell. He came to pick up my garbage."

"So did the City of New York, unfortunately," Dr. Thompson said, shaking his head. "Where's a good garbage strike when you need one?"

Maggie didn't know whether this was good news or bad news. "Then they can't tell if I gave him bad mushrooms?"

"Seems that way. But that's what happened, at least according to our resident guru. Mr. Toland's showing all the signs of mushroom poisoning. We've even got it narrowed down to two of them that grow locally. I didn't know there were such deadly things around here, did you? Muggers in the parks, that's a given, but poison mushrooms? Blows your mind, doesn't it?"

"Fascinating," Maggie agreed, gnawing on the inside of her bottom lip. "How does your resident guru know this?"

"Like I said, the symptoms. That, and

knowing you fed the guy mushrooms. That was a pretty big clue. We have to be up on this stuff because of the magic mushrooms, you know. Hallucinogenic. People will try anything for a high these days. But the guru doesn't think it's magic mushrooms, because Mr. Toland didn't go ape before he slipped into the coma. He didn't go ape, did he?"

"Hallucinate, you mean?" Maggie shook her head. "No. He cursed a lot."

"You would too, if you had a gut full of poison mushrooms. Okay, that narrows it down to one."

"And that's good, right? If you know which one it was, then you have an antidote or something?"

Dr. Thompson tongued his wad of bubblegum into his left cheek as he tipped his head and looked at her. "Are you sure Mr. Toland has no family?"

Maggie felt her body begin to tingle, and not pleasantly. "No, no family. Except his two ex-wives, and one of them is married to a count or something now, and living overseas. Why?"

The doctor took a deep breath, then let it out slowly. "I hate this part. Look, Miss Kelly, I know you're not family, but you did bring him in here, so I guess you're the one I tell. There is no antidote. Mr. Toland is dying, and there's not one goddamn thing we can do about it."

"Oh, God." Maggie staggered where she stood, reached out, and grabbed some wall. "No, that's not possible."

"Hey," the doctor said, taking hold of her elbow and leading her into the waiting room to sit down. "I'm sorry. He's going fast, probably because he ingested such a large amount of the poison, and he's already in a coma. Believe it or not, that's a bonus, because it can be a very painful death. But his organs are failing, one by one — liver, kidneys, circulatory system. We don't expect him to make the night. Damn near textbook mushroom poisoning."

"Oh, poor Kirk," Maggie said, blinking back tears. "I killed him."

"Damn, and me without my tape recorder. Isn't that always my luck."

Maggie looked up through her tears to see the sloppily handsome Lieutenant Wendell standing behind the doctor. He'd be reasonably adorable, if he didn't carry a badge. "No, I didn't *kill* him. I mean, I didn't *mean* to kill him." She hopped up from her chair. "Where's a phone? I can't use my cell phone — it says so on signs all over this place. I have to call Bernie."

"Your lawyer, Ms. Kelly?" the lieutenant asked, helpfully pointing to a small beige phone hanging on the wall. "No rush, I'm not here to arrest you. But I would like you to come downtown with me, on your own, for a few questions. I mean, it's either you or more desk duty, and I've already got enough paper cuts to put me in one of the beds here."

Maggie picked up the phone and realized she couldn't remember Bernie's number. She could barely remember her own name. "You're taking me in for questioning? For murdering Kirk?"

Wendell nodded. "Sounds like a plan."

Dr. Thompson clapped his hands together a single time. "Well, I'm outta here. Good luck, Ms. Kelly. Oh, and a word of advice. Don't say anything."

Maggie nodded, pressing her hands to her cheeks, wishing there weren't at least a dozen pairs of inquisitive eyes concentrated on her. Hey, at least she'd taken their minds off their troubles. After all, it wasn't every day you got to see someone hauled off to the slammer. "I'll need to . . . to find my friend who came here with me."

"Damn, I hope it isn't that Saint Just guy," Wendell said as he handed Maggie her purse. "I have a feeling he could be a real pain in my ass."

"Finally, the guy's good for something," Maggie muttered as she headed toward the elevators.

Saint Just sat in the cafeteria, watching Mindy O'Donnell devour French fries smothered in sticky yellow cheese. She picked them up one at a time, licked the cheese off the potato, then slowly sucked the crispy stick into her mouth.

He believed he just might be being seduced.

"So you're from England, huh? I've never been. My sister and I went to Italy once, but it rained all the time, and there were all these old buildings everyone else was going nuts over. Me, I didn't get it. But I got some great leather in Florence, so it wasn't all bad." She licked another French fry, sucked it into her mouth. "You been?"

"I beg your pardon?" Saint Just said, as he'd been rather fascinated, wondering what would happen if she sucked too hard, and the potato lodged in her throat. "Oh, Italy," he added, smiling. "Yes, I've *been*. Fascinating country. You were saying that you've got a very interesting patient in your . . . unit, was it?"

Mindy nodded. "Oh, yeah. We're already getting calls from the press, if you can believe that. I don't know how they got our unit number, but they always find a way. Big muckety-muck in publishing or something. And handsome, too, or at least he would be, if he didn't have nine million tubes sticking in him and his eyes rolled back in his head. Handsome or not, they all look like hell in a hospital bed. Dying, too. It's a shame."

"Dying," Saint Just repeated, reaching for his missing quizzing glass. "Is that right? Accident?"

"Mummumph-mummph," Mindy mumbled, holding up one finger and pointing at her mouth as she chewed, then swallowed. "They don't think so. They think his girlfriend poisoned him, and there's no antidote. He must have pissed her off royal, you know? Man, what a way to go."

Saint Just picked up a paper napkin and dabbed at some cheese that had stuck to Mindy's lip, leaning forward intimately as he did so, smiling his best smile. "Arsenic, Mindy?" he asked, and the word sort of slid off his tongue, as if he were really saying, "My place or yours?"

"Oh, no, no," she said, blushing to the

roots of her blond hair. "I saw it on the chart," she said, leaning forward herself, whispering. "It's not final, and won't be until the autopsy and pathology, and all of that, but the head honcho thinks it's — well, I don't remember the Latin, but Sylvia, the unit clerk, told me it translates to Destroying Angel mushrooms. Man, the tabloids are gonna pick up on that and run banners, betcha. Destroying Angel Killer. Isn't that bizarre? Um, you sure you're not married?"

"Positive," Saint Just said, watching as Mindy looked beyond him, at something or someone who made her frown.

"Hello, Maggie," Saint Just said without turning around. "I see you've found me."

"Let's go, Alex," she said, poking him in the back with his own cane, which she'd grabbed from its place, propped against the table. "Lieutenant Wendell wants to take me to the police station and question me."

Saint Just blinked, just once, his only reaction to this news. "Mindy," he then said, smiling. "It has been a distinct pleasure."

"You'll call me soon?" she asked, looking up at him as he stood and turned to glare at Lieutenant Wendell, his attention now entirely on that man.

"I'll call you anything you like, my dear," Saint Just said with a wink to Wendell, then took Maggie's arm — she shook off his hand — and headed out of the cafeteria. As they walked along, he leaned down, whispering, "You are not to say a word to the lieutenant, Maggie. He thinks you poisoned Toland with a deadly mushroom."

"I know," Maggie whispered back at him, turning her head to look at Wendell. "Kirk's dying; they can't save him. I don't . . . I don't know what I'm feeling, what I should do. . . ."

"Must you go with him?"

Maggie stopped just outside the cafeteria and blinked up at Saint Just. "I don't know. He hasn't read me my rights, arrested me." She waited for Wendell to catch up with them — he'd stopped to buy a doughnut — and asked, "Do I have to go with you?"

Wendell took a bite of doughnut, leaving a ring of white powdered sugar around his mouth. "No, ma'am, you don't. But it would look better if you did. Cooperate, and all of that."

"But you cannot force her to accompany you, isn't that right, *Left*-tenant? If Miss Kelly does not wish to go to this police station with you, she is not obliged to go?" Saint Just pressed, hiding a smile as Wendell muttered something under his breath. Saint Just believed it was something like, "Damned Englishman."

"She wouldn't be helping her case by refusing," Wendell said, looking at Maggie.

"No," Saint Just corrected smoothly, "she wouldn't be helping *your* case by refusing, *Left*-tenant Wendell. Maggie, let's go home."

"I don't know," Maggie said, looking toward Wendell, back at Saint Just. "I have nothing to hide."

Wendell stuck the last of his doughnut in his mouth and spread his hands, talking around his mouthful: "Then let's go, get it over with. Just make a statement, that's all, Miss Kelly. You'd be back home in a couple of hours."

"Maggie, as your attorney, I refuse to allow you to accompany the lieutenant," Saint Just said firmly.

"You're her lawyer?" Wendell asked. "You never said you were her lawyer. Damn, an English barrister. I didn't know that about you."

"You would be shocked and amazed at the many things you do not know about me, *Left*-tenant," Saint Just said, pushing the button for the elevator. "And now, as Miss Kelly values my professional opinion, good evening to you."

"Miss Kelly?"

"Um . . . good evening, Lieutenant," Maggie said as the elevator doors opened and Saint Just all but knocked down an old man with a walker, pulling her into it before the doors closed, with Wendell still standing in the hallway.

They stood with their backs to the wall until the elevator opened on the ground floor, then walked rapidly out onto the sidewalk before Maggie said, "My attorney? Where did you get that from?"

"Television, of course. Sterling asked me to watch something called *Miami Vice* with him the other day, so I know that you are allowed to have an attorney present during questioning. I also know that once the coppers have got you, they rarely let you go. You could learn a lot watching television, Maggie. And Wendell could too, perhaps pick up a few pointers on his wardrobe from Mr. Sonny Crockett."

"The coppers," Maggie repeated. "You sure are broadening your vocabulary, Alex."

"Police, coppers, pigs. There's nothing new in that, surely."

"I never used *pig,* even though it was around in the Regency. It sounds too modern. Nobody would believe me," Maggie said, watching as Alex put one foot in the street, gave the slightest crook of his right arm, and had a taxi screeching to a stop in front of him. "How do you do that?"

"Expect service, Maggie, and you get it. I could barely stand to watch you hopping up and down, whistling, yelling, as you attempted to get us transportation here to the hospital. Not ladylike at all."

"Well, pardon me," Maggie said as she climbed into the backseat of the cab and gave the driver her address. Then she leaned against the shabby leather seat and closed her eyes. "Kirk could be dead by morning, and I could be arrested by tomorrow afternoon, for his murder. It's a nightmare, Alex."

"I'm here, Maggie," Saint Just told her. "Nothing untoward will happen now that I'm here, I promise. How do I know this, you might ask? The answer is obvious. I simply won't allow it."

Maggie's laugh was hollow. "You said that to Lady Sylvia in *The Case of the Overdue Duke.*"

"And did I save Lady Sylvia, solve the

murder, and bring the killer to justice, all while romancing Lady Sylvia and maintaining my usual sangfroid?"

"Yes, you did." She squeezed her eyes shut against the tears stinging her eyes and allowed him to pull her against his shoulder, hold her, stroke her arm, all the way back to the apartment.

It was good to be a hero.

Socks ran out to the cab as it drew to a stop two car lengths from the apartment door, and motioned for Saint Just to roll down the window. "Tell the guy to go around back, Maggie," he said, leaning his head into the taxi. "We've got reporters in the lobby."

"Already?" Maggie reached for Saint Just's hand. "What do they want?"

Socks rolled his eyes. "Pictures of you holding a bloody knife would be my guess. Alex, get her out of here. I snuck Ms. Toland-James up a while ago, in the freight elevator, then left it unlocked for you guys."

"Thank you, Socks," Maggie said, hitching herself forward on the seat to direct the driver around to the rear of the building.

"Yes, thank you, Socks. Now, if you will be so kind as to stand back, we'd like to exit this hack."

"Alex?" Maggie glared at him. "Didn't you hear Socks? There's a bunch of reporters in the lobby. Cameras, lights, *questions*. I can't face them."

"Yes, my dear, you can. You can hold your head high, keep your step steady, and allow me to speak for you. This is, after all, the twenty-first century. We are civilized creatures, and I'm sure reason will triumph, if we simply cooperate. I'll speak to them, and then they will go away."

"Oh, yeah, right. That'll work," Maggie fairly spat. "Are you *nuts?*"

"Uh-oh, too late, they spotted us," Socks said as a half-dozen reporters burst through the door, like hunting dogs who had picked up the scent of the fox. And everybody knows what happens to the fox when the dogs get to it.

"Ms. Kelly! Over here, Ms. Kelly! Is it true? Did you poison him?"

"He dropped you, right? A woman scorned? How'd you do it?"

"Holly Spivak, *Fox News.* Just look into this camera over here, Ms. Kelly."

"Police sources said you'll be arrested as soon as Toland croaks. Who's this? Your new lover? Does he let you cook for him, huh?"

Maggie bowed her head, hoping to be

able to push through the small mob with the usual "No comment," knowing she'd look like a first-class felon on the ten o'clock news, but Saint Just seemed to have other plans.

He stopped on the pavement, held up his hands for quiet, and damn if he didn't get it. Maybe it was the cane. Reporters aren't much for being threatened with bodily harm, and Saint Just certainly did look dangerous.

"Ladies, gentlemen," he called out, only lowering his arms when they stopped asking questions. "Ms. Kelly is devastated by Mr. Kirk Toland's sudden illness. She has just returned from hospital, and now has the unhappy duty of giving the most grave news to Mr. Toland's former wife. Ms. Kelly is cooperating with the local constabulary and has not yet even been questioned by them, let alone arrested. Mr. Toland's illness is an accident, an unfortunate accident. Now may I suggest that you all disperse, return to your — well, wherever you wish to go."

"Who the hell are you?" one of the reporters yelled, still scribbling in his small notebook. "You her lawyer?"

"Hey!" It was Holly Spivak, *Fox News.* "I know who that is. God, I must have watched that stupid tape a million times. It's the mystery guy from the park. Remember? The guy who jumped on the runaway carriage? Spike — get him on tape, now!"

"This may have been a mistake," Saint Just said out of the corner of his mouth as the reporters started yelling again and pressing closer, closer.

"Gee, what was your first clue, Sherlock?" Maggie said as Socks grabbed her, pulled her into the lobby, and locked the doors, leaving Saint Just on the sidewalk.

"Wait! Socks, he's still out there. We can't leave him out there. They'll eat him alive."

"All right," Socks told her, "but first I get you on the elevator, okay? Then I'll let him in. And maybe I'll sing something from *Gypsy*. I mean, all those microphones and cameras? Who could resist?"

Maggie shook her head, watching as Saint Just edged toward the locked doors. "In Regency times, this was called a farce," she said, apropos of nothing. "Just get him in here, okay?"

The elevator door was sliding closed as Socks opened the door and Maggie heard the first strains of "Everything's Coming Up Roses."

CHAPTER 11

It had just gone midnight. Bernice Toland-James was softly snoring on one of the living room couches, and Maggie had finally given in to her headache and gone off to bed after what had been a very forgettable evening.

The ten o'clock news had been the worst, as Holly Spivak had spent what Maggie had said was an enormous amount of time giving out non-news on Kirk Toland's situation, considering there was no official word from the police or the hospital to back up anything she said.

Still, a picture was worth a thousand words, and the tape of Maggie, head down, racing toward the doors of her apartment building was, to be polite, not very flattering.

Ms. Spivak still had no name to put to the split-screen video of Saint Just outside the apartment building and Saint Just's feat of derring-do at the park, but that didn't keep her from celebrating her coup on air.

And then there was Felicity Boothe Simmons (wasn't there always). Somehow — probably because she phoned the television station and volunteered — the woman had gotten herself on camera as a colleague of Maggie's, also published by Toland Books. After pretty much disassociating herself from Maggie professionally, the woman had added, as if forced to speak, that it had been said — not by her, of course — that Maggie Kelly had slept her way to the top at Toland Books, as everyone knew she was boinking (yes, the woman said *boinking,* on air) "poor Kirk." Until he'd broken it off, of course.

"*He* broke it off? He did not. I did, damn it! Try doing your research, Felicity — there's a first time for everything! Look at her, with her name plastered across the bottom of the screen. Felicity Boobs Simmons, *New York Times* Bestselling Author. She's got the three names, the Os, the implants. God, I hate her."

Maggie had then hit the Off button on the remote and thrown the thing at the television set, at which point Saint Just had remarked that the treachery of one's friends is always a shock.

"Yeah. Fuck her," Bernice had said, lifting her head from one of the couch cushions, but that was all she said, as she was already nursing her fifth double scotch.

"Friend? She's not my *friend*, Alex, damn it," Maggie had protested hotly. "And she can't write her way out of a paper bag, either. She just got lucky with one idea. Hell, she's been writing that same one idea for the last ten years."

"I'll second that motion," Bernie said, saluting with her glass before taking another deep drink.

"Now, Maggie," Saint Just had said soothingly. "You may be a little overvolatile right now. . . ."

"Overvolatile? Hell, I'm *pissed!* Wait, I'll prove it to you. Over there." She pointed rather wildly. "On my bookcase. I get them straight from Toland Books, not that I've read any in the past five years. Get me one of her books, Alex, any one of them. I bet you I can tell you the whole plot if you read me the first line. You want to know why? Because it's always the same plot, that's why! God! How I detest that woman. Boinking? *Boinking?* I need chocolate."

"Food. Yes, an excellent idea," Saint Just had soothed as he and Sterling followed Maggie into the kitchen, where she pulled a carton of chocolate ice cream from the freezer and a box of short waffle cones from the pantry cabinet.

Maggie deposited a scoop of ice cream

in two separate cones, then stuck one on top of the other, ice cream sticking to ice cream, and mashed it all down, while Sterling followed after her, putting the carton away, rinsing the scoop under the faucet.

Holding the stuck-together ice cream cones in each hand, Maggie stomped back into the living room, licking at the ice cream in between.

"Now I'm going to get fat," Maggie groused. "And it's all Felicity's fault."

"Not a pleasant-looking person, Miss Simmons. You cast her quite in the shade, Maggie, you know," Sterling said nervously as he took up residence on the facing couch, watching Maggie eat her rather odd snack.

"Thank you, Sterling," Maggie had told him, then burst into tears.

Ah, yes. A very forgettable evening. But now it was time for action, time for the men to be out and about, taking charge as was their right, their duty.

Saint Just stopped on the pavement, turning to look at his friend. "Sterling, you're dawdling. Don't dawdle."

Sterling hurried to keep up, still peering into every darkened doorway. "Saint Just, I think this may be a mistake. Maggie wouldn't like it, not by half."

"Maggie has other things to occupy her mind," Saint Just answered, peering into an alleyway as they stepped from one slab of pavement to the next. "Bernice Toland-James, for one. If she can keep that heartless woman from throwing a party the moment Toland turns up his toes, we'll all be grateful. Beware the woman scorned, Sterling."

"So you think she did it? You think she poisoned Toland?"

"I think there is an excess of likely suspects, Sterling," Saint Just said as they approached the Styles Cafe neon sign he had not quite reached the last time he'd dared the Manhattan streets after midnight. "Nelson Trigg, for one. He's ambitious. Cassius, you'll remember, was *ambitious*. As Will Shakespeare described Cassius, so is Nelson Trigg. 'Yond Cassius has a lean and hungry look. He thinks too much: such men are dangerous.' Ah, yes, Sterling, I will have to explore just how Toland's death will affect our dear, ambitious Mr. Trigg. From what I overheard on the telephone, I believe he expects Toland's heirs to put him in charge of the publishing concern. And as history tells us, Sterling, heirs apparent often murder their way to the top."

"So that's one. Who else?" Sterling asked, his mood improving as he caught the heady scent of greasy French fries.

"That's two, Sterling. You're forgetting Bernice. She's entirely too delighted at the moment."

"Oh, I don't think so, do you? She seems too happy in her own skin, not at all jealous of our Maggie when she was . . . consorting with the man. She didn't like Mr. Toland, but I don't think she hated him."

"True, but I believe I'll reserve judgment. I just know that Maggie did not poison Toland. She doesn't have murder in her soul."

Sterling nodded, then stepped back a pace as two figures separated themselves from the shadows. "Saint Just? We have company."

"Ah, wonderful! I thought this was their usual stomping grounds, thieves being more or less creatures of habit, but I didn't think we'd get so lucky so soon." With his cane held very obviously in both hands, ready to unsheathe the sword hidden within, Saint Just squinted at the two figures. "Mr. Snake? Mr. Killer? How lovely to see you both again. I daresay it's been an age."

Snake — the one with the row of surgical stitches in his cheek — growled low in his throat and took one step forward; something shiny appeared in his hand as Saint Just heard a faint click. "Been waiting for you. I'm gonna cut you, man. I'm gonna cut you *bad*."

From his new position behind Saint Just, Sterling made a small sound that sounded a lot like *"Urp."*

"Good heavens. Being rather dramatic, aren't you?" Saint Just inquired, his hand tightening on his cane. "Your abused sensibilities to one side, Mr. Snake, if you recall, as I most certainly do, you accosted me. I merely retaliated. Mr. Killer? Isn't that correct?"

"He's got you there, Snake. You hit him first."

"And from behind," Saint Just added. "Not very sporting, Snake, now was it? But I forgive you. As a matter of fact, I especially sought you out this evening, with the possibility that I may . . . um . . . throw a small task your way? I believe that's the term. You'd be generously recompensed."

Snake looked at his friend. "Whad'd he say?"

"Dear, dear, dim-witted Snake. Obviously the despair of his afflicted parents, don't you think, Sterling?" Saint Just said quietly out of the corner of his mouth. He was enjoying himself most thoroughly.

Killer, obviously the brains of the two — although cursed with a weak bladder — scrubbed a finger beneath his nose and stared at Saint Just. "A job. He wants us to do a job for him."

Snake fairly danced in place. "A job? No way, man. I ain't fuckin' workin' for *nobody*. No time, no how. *Ever*."

"Yes," Saint Just drawled. "I had rather sensed that about you. A gentleman of independent means. I applaud you. But this is quite an easy task, I assure you."

Sterling stepped out from behind Saint Just. "It's true, gentlemen. Saint Just here is a capital fellow and wouldn't tell you anything that wasn't the purest truth, and all of that." Snake took a step forward, growled low in his throat as he flashed his knife, and Sterling receded once more behind Saint Just . . . who somehow had the tip of his own blade now neatly tucked beneath Snake's weak chin.

"Thank you, Sterling," Saint Just purred. "As always, my staunchest supporter. How good of you to guard my back while trouble stands in front of me. But I believe I can take it from here. Snake, my good man? I think it only fair to inform you that I am excessively fond of my friend here. Do not even think to hurt him, for my revenge might very well terrify you."

And then the blade was gone, hidden inside the cane once more, and Snake was standing very still, trying to look like a choir boy.

"Thank you, my prudent friend. Now, back to business. It would seem my dear friend and I are in need of something, and it is my greatest hope that you can assist us in procuring it. We are, you see, in need of a criminal, as it happens, and I immediately had the happy notion that I might apply to you for assistance."

"Shit, man, talk American!" an obviously frustrated Snake exploded (so fatiguing, being a choir boy), and Saint Just felt Sterling's hand grabbing at the back of his waistband.

"Yes, Saint Just," Sterling agreed. "No need to set the fellow's back up."

"Yes, very well. Gentlemen, I am of course trusting you to keep this confidential?"

"We ain't tellin' nobody we saw you and that damn stick of yours," Snake said. "Next they'll think we saw the fuckin' Easter Bunny."

"Ah, a joke? How wonderful, we progress. I doubt we'll cry friends, share a meal, crack a bottle together, but then, one can't have everything in this life, can one? Killer? I was told that if I wished to procure certain identification papers — passports and the like — I would be advised to seek assistance via the criminal community."

"Hey! I got that one," Snake said, his hands balling into fists. "He just called us criminals."

"Yeah?" Killer said, giving his friend a shove on the shoulder. "And what would *you* call us, Snake? One of those suits down on Wall Street?" He looked at Saint Just. "You want paper? That'll cost you."

"I imagine it will. Do you know how to get us this . . . paper?"

Killer took Snake by the arm and the two turned their backs and conferred with each other. There was a lot of head shaking, some arm waving, and more than a few whispers, before they turned around again and Killer said, "Sure. We knows somebody."

"Splendid. Take us to him, please."

"Yeah, right. No way, man. You go through us, ain't that right, Snake? Give us the money, and we'll get you the paper."

Saint Just looked at Sterling. "Sterling, my dear friend," he drawled amicably. "Do I look as if my wits have suddenly gone a-begging?"

"No, Saint Just," Sterling answered. "But that thing is jumping in your cheek again. That's not good." He looked at Killer. "That's really not good."

Once more the two youths conferred, this time the conversation ending with a slap to the back of Snake's head.

Killer hitched up his sagging jeans and said, "Okay, here's the deal. We knows this . . . person. But we have ta call her . . . um, this person, see if this person wants ta see youse. You could be cops, you know."

Saint Just raised himself stiffly to his full height. "It wanted only that. Now you insult me? A Tatony Street pig? I should say not. I am merely a man in search of identification. However, I begin to believe you cannot help us. I should have realized that you are only petty criminals. Why not run off now, rip the purse from some unsuspecting octogenarian, and consider yourself successful. Come, Sterling, we're going back to the apartment."

"I should just about say so," Sterling said, giving one last look at Snake and Killer.

"Hey!" Killer called after them. "*Hey!* Come back here tomorrow night, same time, and we'll have the guy here. But we want some bucks up front. Fifty bucks. Each!"

"And how would I know that you won't just take the money and never return here? Tell you what, gentlemen. Snake, I'll have that knife."

"No way," Snake said, shuffling where he stood. "My mom gave this to me."

"Ah, how wonderful. Some mothers knit scarves." Saint Just stood his ground. "The knife, Snake. Now. You'll get it back tomorrow night."

"Hand over the fuckin' knife," Killer said, giving Snake a hard shove.

"Yeah? Well then, you give him your fuckin' watch. The one you took from that guy last week. I'm not the only one who's giving up stuff."

Killer look at Saint Just, who merely held out his hand, the one with the crisp one hundred dollar bill in it.

"Oh, shit — here. But you'd better be back here tomorrow night, 'cause this person is gonna be real pissed if she comes here and you don't show."

Maggie had been awake since five, sitting curled up on one of the couches, both cats tucked in close to her, a cup of tea in her hands, her eyes on the door.

At eight, the buzzer rang and she stiffly uncurled herself and pressed the button that connected her with Socks. "Yes, Socks?"

"It's the cop with the great buns, Maggie. I have to let him up, okay?"

Maggie nodded, then realized Socks couldn't see her. Good enough. She didn't have to rubber-stamp Steve Wendell's "permission." He probably had a search warrant with him anyway.

She shot a glance toward the hallway leading to the bedrooms, for once thankful that Saint Just felt it his obligation to his class, or whatever, to be a late riser.

Opening the door before Wendell could knock, Maggie stepped back, waved him in, then returned to the couch. Wellie and Napper had already fled, probably because of some sixth sense cats had about trouble heading their way.

Once again the lieutenant looked like the kind of man Maggie would take special notice of in a social situation, the kind of guy she'd like to date. Tall, lean, not overly impressed with himself. Those great buns Socks had noticed. She liked his slightly shaggy, too-long brown hair, even the morning beard that set off his slightly squared jaw. And he had the greatest green eyes. Too bad they were looking everywhere but at her. And how sick was she, checking him out as if he could be a possible dinner date?

"It's over?" she asked as he walked around the room, stopping at her computer.

"Around four this morning, yeah," he answered, hitting the Return key on her computer, waking it from sleep mode. "Never regained consciousness, never said anything. I know, because I was there."

"I thought I recognized those clothes. You've been up all night?"

He activated her America Online and clicked on her address book, scanning it as it popped down. "Autopsy's scheduled for ten, and I have to be there, too. This is just my lucky day."

"It hasn't been great for Kirk, either," Maggie said into her teacup. She wasn't crying. Maybe she'd cried herself out last night. "Then what? Are you going to arrest me?"

"Nope. We don't have any evidence, we don't have much of a probable cause, and only an idiot would admit to giving the guy poison mushrooms."

Maggie felt all of her air shoot out of her in a rush of relief.

"Still, my boss says you're the only suspect we've got, and I tend to agree with him." He pulled a Hershey bar from his pocket, unwrapped it, and bit off nearly half. A fellow chocoholic; they had so much in common — unfortunately most of it was Kirk. His mouth full, he asked, "Mind if I take a look around?"

"You already are. Besides, I thought you had a search warrant."

"Yeah, I don't know where the doorman got that idea. Do you want me to go get one? I probably could, since the guy damn near died right here. And, word of advice off the record, you really have to stop saying you killed the guy. Anyway, then we'd have about a half a dozen cops pawing through your stuff, carting most of it off, not to mention a bunch of techs dusting everything. We're not a neat bunch. So, who do you think killed him?"

"You watched *Columbo* a lot, didn't you?" Maggie asked, reaching for her cigarettes and lighter. "The rumpled clothes, the Gee-I'm-only-a-dumb-flatfoot routine. Right down to sucking in the suspect, making him — her — think she's being a big help to the clueless cop. Right up until the moment you slap the cuffs on her. Sorry, I won't play. I don't have the faintest idea who could have killed Kirk, because I don't think anybody did kill him. I think he got bad mushrooms from Mario's. Have you checked on that? Is anyone else in New York dying of mushroom poisoning?"

She craned her neck as she watched him place the cursor over her Favorite Places and pull down that menu.

"Nope. Toland's the only one. Oh, and we did pick up all the mushrooms at Mario's to have them tested. He's in the clear. Man, you've got more favorite places than the *I Love New York* guide. And nice and neat, too, all in nicely labeled folders."

"I do a lot of research on the net," Maggie told him, not really paying attention. "Did Bernie call and say she'd claim the body? She said she would." *Right before she passed out,* she remembered. But when Maggie had awakened this morning, Bernie was gone, probably heading back to her own apartment to shower and change and medicate herself for her hangover.

"I wouldn't know about that. Sure do have a lot of websites marked," Wendell said, scrolling down the menu. "Clothing, furniture, transportation, maps. Here's a good one — Shakespearean curses."

Maggie inhaled on her cigarette and blew out a stream of smoke, still trying to calm her nerves. She just couldn't seem to get her mind around the fact that Kirk was dead. "Thou dissembling, tickle-brained coxcomb."

"Huh? What?"

Maggie stubbed out her cigarette. "Nothing. Just a sample of a Shakespearean curse. I mix and match them all the time. What are you looking for?"

He turned to her with his boyish smile. "Ever hear the expression, I'll know what I'm looking for when I find it?"

Maggie lit another cigarette, even though her chest hurt and the damn thing tasted really bad. That was one way to quit smoking: smoke until you couldn't stand smoking anymore.

"And, as they said in the gold regions, hardly Shakespearean — eureka! I've found it. Everything should be this easy."

Hopping from the couch, Maggie crossed to the desk, peering past Wendell's shoulder. "Found it? Found what?"

And then she saw it. He had another folder open, the one she had labeled Weapons. Running down from the opened folder were other folders that included hotlinks all over the Internet, to sites about firearms, sites about axes and instruments of torture, sites about knives, about famous murder cases . . . about poisons.

"Research," she said, feeling nervous, wondering if she sounded nervous. "That stuff's only for research."

"Really? Then how about we research?" Wendell said, and opened the folder titled Poisons. "Arsenic, belladonna, yadda-yadda, yadda-yadda, and bingo! Poisonous fungi." He turned, grinned at her over his shoulder. "That would be mushrooms. Fungi, mushrooms. I know this, because that's what the doctor called them."

"Bully for you." Maggie stared at the screen as he clicked on Poisonous Fungi, and America Online neatly signed on and took them to the site. "I don't even remember saving this," she said, shaking her head. "I'm not saying I didn't, because it's there. I'm always researching murder methods. I write murder mysteries, for crying out loud."

A full-color, and fairly ugly, photograph popped onto the screen. Beside it, the headline read: Destroying Angel (*Amanita verna*) and Death Cap (*Amanita virosa*). There were probably other mushrooms mentioned, but these two had gotten the headline.

"Mind if I sit down? I can't read the smaller print," Wendell said, already pulling out her chair.

"Is that it? Is that the mushroom that killed Kirk? Destroying Angel?"

"We won't know for sure for a while, but the doc's money is on Destroying Angel, right."

"It looks like any other mushroom, doesn't it?" Maggie grabbed her glasses and leaned over the lieutenant's shoulder, reading along with him. The physical description of the mushroom came first, although she couldn't figure out what the gills were, or the spores, or the volva, which sounded faintly indecent.

Next came the location where Destroying Angel mushrooms were found. It was pretty broad: throughout North America. That had to include Manhattan.

Maggie kept reading, and suddenly she smiled. She smiled, and then she gave Wendell a pretty good smack on the back. "I didn't do it! See it? See it right there? I didn't do it." She pressed a finger on the screen, tapped it on the screen. "See? It says, right here, that the whole damn mushroom is poisonous. 'Amanitas must be handled with gloves.' I didn't do that. I just made a face and chopped them up. And I'm not dead, am I?"

Wendell turned slowly in the chair. "You have a witness that can testify that you weren't wearing gloves when you chopped up the mushrooms?"

"Shit." Maggie pushed her hands through her hair. "I hadn't thought of that. I mean, I know I didn't wear gloves, but nobody else knows that I didn't wear gloves. I'm still the main suspect."

"But not the only one," Saint Just said from about two feet behind her, jolting Maggie half out of her skin. "Good morning, *Left*-tenant. I thought I heard your not-so-dulcet tones, so I stumbled out of bed — and here you are, just like the proverbial bad penny. Penny? Is that why they call you *coppers?*"

"Alex, you have to stop creeping up on people," Maggie said, heading for the couches once more. "I could have a heart attack, and then the State of New York would be cheated out of a death penalty case."

Saint Just, dressed in navy slacks and his Mike Piazza shirt, his hair still damp from his shower, sat down on the facing couch. "I would imagine there's no more tea in there?" he asked, pointing to the thermal carafe.

Maggie just shrugged, not having or even caring about the answer. "What did you mean, I'm not the only suspect?"

"Simple enough," Alex said. "I did a little snooping about late last night. You do remember that I did some investigating of my own at the hospital yesterday?"

"The blond nurse?" Maggie asked, then shook her head. "Of course. That just goes to show how distracted I've been. She wasn't at all your type. I should have known you weren't just hitting on her."

"Yes, you most certainly should have. I imagine orangutans have better table manners. But now let us concentrate on the Destroying Angel mushroom or, to be more precise, the *Amanita verna,* a most deadly form of fungi. I once courted an Amanita, didn't I? No, that was Araminta, although, as I recall, she was rather deadly herself — in that case, a deadly bore."

"Alex, would you cut it out," Maggie warned, rolling her eyes toward Wendell.

"Sorry, I fear I digress. How very bad of me. *Left*-tenant? Continue reading, if you please. I have no idea if you're on the same site I visited on my laptop last night, but facts are facts. Please. And aloud, if you don't mind? I'm convinced that, if you were to concentrate on your enunciation, you'd have a lovely speaking voice. There you go now. Try not to trample on your vowels."

Wendell looked at Maggie more as an ally than as a suspect. "I told you. *Big* pain in my ass." Then he turned back to the computer screen and scrolled down the page. "Okay, here goes. Pay attention, class. 'Poisoning usually happens when inexperienced harvesters gather them accidentally . . . a distinctly unpleasant experience . . . severe abdominal upset . . . liver, kidney and circulatory system failure . . . usually fatal . . . no known antidote . . . symptoms onset within ten hours, but sometimes as long as ten days . . .'" He stopped reading and sat back in the chair. "Ten hours? Ten *days?*"

"Exactly," Saint Just said, preening a bit, Maggie thought, but since she was considering flinging herself across the coffee table and giving him a huge hug and kiss, he was probably justified in his reaction. "Ten hours, which is about as long as it took if Maggie had fed Toland the mushrooms, but also anywhere up to ten *days,* in which case most anyone could have fed him the mushrooms. I assume you'll be leaving now, *Left*-tenant? Right after you apologize to Miss Kelly?"

Wendell was shaking his head. "Nobody told me any of this," he said, almost to himself.

"A prudent man does his own investigating," Saint Just said as Maggie frantically waved him to silence.

"Lieutenant? Are you saying that I could have fed Kirk the mushrooms, but so could anyone, at any time, for the past ten days? That the whole thing could be a coincidence?"

Wendell pressed his fingers against the bridge of his nose. "I don't believe in coincidence. Especially in this case. It's too neat. You feed him mushrooms, and ten or so hours later, he's sick as a dog. When did you eat? Six? Seven?"

"Around then, yes. And he woke me up at four. That's around ten hours."

"If I might interrupt?" Saint Just got to his feet and stood with his hands linked behind his back. "It occurs to me that Maggie was — pardon me, my dear — the dupe. Someone decided to kill Toland and used Maggie as his or her dupe. Such an unflattering word, but I fear I can't summon a synonym. But I believe my meaning is clear."

"Go on," Wendell said, and Maggie could see that, although he didn't want to, he was paying close attention to Saint Just . . . who was obviously on a roll, bless his imaginary little heart.

"Yes, thank you, I had already planned to, as a matter of fact. You'll recall that simply handling the mushrooms is often fatal. Not to put too fine a point on it, if Maggie had prepared or injested the mushrooms, she, too, would be dead, which eliminates any notion that someone tippy-toed in here sometime Monday while Maggie was out, and exchanged Mario's mushrooms for Destroying Angels. No, somebody fed Toland the fatal mushrooms, then sent him off here to become ill. *Left*-tenant, I believe even you can understand that Maggie here is no more a suspect now than anyone else in this lovely city, or the state, or perhaps all of the colonies put together. She is, instead — if you still believe that the mushrooms she served were poisonous — another potential victim. Of course, you'd have to be a total ass to believe that, as Maggie is still here, isn't she? Which leaves us to deduce that Toland ingested the poison elsewhere, then arrived here, to sicken and die."

Maggie held up both hands, mutely

asking for silence. Something was going on in her head, something knocking on the door of her brain. Something important. Something vital. Something —

"I've got it!" she exclaimed hopping off the couch and grabbing Saint Just in a bear hug. "Oh, Alex, you're a genius!"

"Perhaps not a genius," Saint Just said, patting her back gingerly, then pushing her away from him. "But, please, don't let me stop you. What is it you've just realized?"

She fairly danced across the carpet, stopping in front of Wendell. "I got a phone call, okay? The morning before Kirk came to dinner — same day, that morning. Monday morning." Maggie took a deep breath, trying to calm herself. "It was somebody, a woman, asking what I was serving for dinner, because Kirk wanted to bring wine. And I *told* her. I told her about the mushrooms! I'm sure I did."

"A woman," Wendell said, pulling out his notebook. "Did she say she was calling from Toland Books? Did you recognize the voice?"

Maggie shook her head. "No. It was a really bad connection. And I was in a hurry, going out, and honestly didn't pay much attention. I almost didn't answer the phone, but it could have been my mother, so I did." She looked at Wendell, stricken. "My God. If I hadn't answered that phone, Kirk might not be dead. Doctor Bob is right. If you look hard enough, you can always trace all of your problems to your mother."

CHAPTER 12

Maggie sat nursing a Caffeine Free Diet Pepsi (no ice, no fruit), lost in her small corner of the large room tucked inside the Waldorf Astoria.

It was Thursday afternoon, just past four, and Kirk Toland sat center stage in the room in his fairly flashy, trashy gold urn. After being sliced and diced by the medical examiner Wednesday morning, bits and pieces of him preserved for posterity, he'd been carted away and cremated.

Ashes to ashes, dust to dust, publishing magnate to tacky centerpiece. What had Napoleon said on his way home from Russia? Something about how moving from the sublime to the ridiculous is just a step? Or a couple of mushrooms . . .

"I should have had them put something alcoholic in this," she said aloud to herself, looking into her glass.

"Are you all right, Maggie?"

She looked up, smiled at Sterling. He looked so cute in his brand new navy blue suit. "I'm fine, Sterling, thank you. How are you?"

"Rather amazed, bewildered, and all of that," he said, motioning to her for permission to sit down at the small table. "The man only cocked up his toes yesterday morning. This haste to have the ceremonies completed? Well, it's unseemly, don't you think? Even in my time, we knew to pack bodies in the ice house and have time to gather the relatives."

"Jewish people do it all the time."

"Oh, he was Jewish?"

Maggie shook her head. "No, he wasn't. He was a devout atheist, or at least that's what Bernie told me. His lawyer contacted Bernie late yesterday, told her that a letter he had in his possession from Kirk stated that there were to be no services, and his ashes should be scattered at his tennis club before the annual end-of-the-season tournament, right on the court, just like his father and mother before him."

"For people to tramp on, you mean?"

She tried to be nice. "Kirk loved to play tennis. I think he saw himself as always being part of the club, something like that."

"Oh, then that's all right. Actually, it's rather touching, don't you think?"

So much for being nice. "No, I think it was pretty cheap. You don't know how badly I wanted to send a bouquet of plastic forks."

"I beg your pardon?"

"Oh, I'm sorry, Sterling. I know I'm being snarky. And I'm really glad Bernie had this all done so fast. There was barely any press, and she decided that inviting no one from the Social Register was the only way not to invite all of Manhattan. So far, it seems to have worked. There couldn't be more than what — seventy-five, eighty people here? And no Playmates of the Month. God does grant small favors." She sat up slightly, for she'd been slouching in her seat. "Where's Alex?"

"Saint Just?" Sterling stood, looked out over the black-clad crowd, all of them circling the buffet table like carrion crows. Soon the only things left would be some cheese and the lettuce garnishes. "I'm not sure. Last time I spied him, he was introducing himself to everyone. I believe he is — what was it they said on *Miami Vice*? Oh, yes, rounding up suspects. That's what he's doing. Rounding up suspects."

Maggie sighed and got to her feet. "I should have guessed that, shouldn't I? Okay, I'm off to find him. You stay here, okay?"

"Gladly. Although I do believe I'd like

another of those shrimp-on-a-stick things. I never realized how many different foods could be impaled on a stick. Or asked why anyone would want to do that."

"Go for it," Maggie told him, grabbing her purse and heading into the crowd, most of whom she recognized, for they were the employees of Toland Books, a smattering of literary agents (Tabby had offered some excuse not to come; she hated funerals), and about another half-dozen authors who lived within cab, car, or train distance of the city. Felicity Boothe Simmons hadn't received a telephone invitation, thanks to Bernice.

If Bernie had held off, gone the two-day viewing route, the big church service route, there could have been thousands there, most of them people who knew Kirk Toland socially, those who barely knew him but who would come because of their curiosity, and those who had downright disliked him.

This way, the only people here were those who had disliked him.

"Liquor," Maggie told herself at that thought. "You really do need liquor. The man's dead, for crying out loud, and you boinked him, to quote the unquotable Ms. Felicity Boobs Simmons. Stop being so mad at him because he put you at the top of Wendell's Perps to Arrest Today list."

Maggie smiled to sales reps, copy editors, assistant-assistant vice presidents (there were about five of them now, all eyeing each other like mortal enemies). She kept her eyes peeled for Saint Just, finally spotting him talking to Nelson Trigg and Clarice Simon.

Nelson was wearing a blacker-than-black suit, nattily cut, and a rep tie. He held a sweating glass wrapped in a paper napkin in his hand and stood very straight, as if expecting his picture to be taken at any moment.

Saint Just, as the saying went, "cast the man terribly in the shade," with his own ensemble — not because his suit was superior, but because of the ease with which he stood up in it. And the black armband he'd fashioned was, as he'd told her earlier, an inspired touch.

Clarice, poor kid, looked as out of place here as she would in a strip club, and just as uncomfortable, her black pantsuit and white blouse making her look like a faintly agitated penguin as she nervously shifted her unfortunately deep-set hazel eyes between the Trigger and Alex.

No wonder. Maggie could feel the electricity from where she stood, ten feet away. Sliding her purse strap onto her shoulder, she headed in, ready to bust up a fight if it came to that.

"I see no reason for you to fly up into the boughs, my good man," Saint Just was saying as Maggie approached. "I merely asked you if you had any suspicions as to who might have poisoned the late lamented guest of honor. It was a simple enough inquiry, given our location and our reason for being gathered here. I didn't think it would be half as appropriate to, for instance, inquire as to how you think the Mets are doing this season."

"I don't watch baseball, and I still resent your question," Nelson Trigg said hotly. "I don't even remember who you are."

"Oh, dear. Haven't been paying attention, have you?" Saint Just drawled, and Maggie quickly stepped in front of him to say hello to Trigg . . . only to be attacked by the agitated penguin.

"You! How could you even show your face here?"

"Clarice?" Maggie asked, a part of her trying to identify this suddenly wild-eyed young woman. "I didn't kill Kirk. Honestly."

"Yes-you-did!" she fairly shrieked,

307

pointing a finger at Maggie, her raised voice causing more than a few heads to turn (Maggie caught a quick glimpse of Felicity Boothe Simmons, grinning like the anorexic, painted, top-heavy skeleton she was). *Gate-crasher,* she thought for a half-second, but then Clarice was at it again, her voice rising even more.

"You even *said* so! I called you that morning, and you said you were making Mr. Toland a salad of *hemlock.* You did, you *did!* And that's just what I told the police, too."

"That was *you?* I didn't recognize your voice."

"Mr. Toland asked me to. The very last words he ever said to me," Clarice whimpered. She reached into her pocket, pulled out a sad-looking wad of tissues, and blew her nose. "He was so happy, going to dinner with you. He wanted everything to be just perfect, he said so. And now he's *dead.*"

"Clarice —"

"Allow me, please," Saint Just said, tugging on Maggie's elbow, pulling her half behind him. "Ms. Simon," he said, offering her his own pristine white linen square, then manfully limited his involuntary flinch as she blew her nose in that, too.

"What, exactly, if you please, did you tell the police?"

Clarice sniffled, looked around, saw that she had an audience. "I . . . I probably shouldn't say."

"Oh, don't be silly. You've already made a general announcement, my dear. No reason to stop now."

"I . . . I suppose so," Clarice said, turning her too-deeply-set eyes on Maggie. "I told them I called Maggie and that Maggie told me she was cooking steak with mushrooms and onions, baked potatoes, and a hemlock salad." Those hazel eyes narrowed. It was like being stared down by a particularly ferocious guppy. "And then she laughed. How could you have laughed like that?"

"Mind if I take notes?" Felicity Boothe Simmons said from just behind Maggie's left shoulder. "I could probably use this in one of my books."

Maggie turned on her and growled low in her throat. "Don't be ridiculous, Felicity. That head of yours couldn't possibly hold more than one idea, the same one you've been milking for the past ten years."

"Why, you —"

"Now, now, ladies, please," Saint Just interrupted just as Maggie wondered if Felicity was wearing a wig, and what would happen if she gave it a pull, just to find out.

"She started it," Maggie said, then winced. Man, dialogue like this could get her the head writer's job on a soap opera. But she couldn't help herself. "Well, she did."

"Perhaps, but I believe you're both finished now," Saint Just said, staring hard into Felicity's eyes. Unbelievably, the woman blinked. Maggie hadn't known sharks ever blinked, even had eyelids.

"Oh, all right," Felicity said, sighing. "Besides, we must hear more about this hemlock salad. I read this morning that it was mushrooms."

"It said that in the newspapers?" Maggie asked Saint Just. "You said Sterling threw ours out by mistake, before I could read it, and I let you think I believed that because I wasn't up to reading the papers anyway. But I also thought you'd convinced Wendell that I'm not a suspect. What else did the article say?"

"You're not to trouble yourself with the scribblings of the gossip-mongers, my dear," Saint Just said quietly. "Although I would, if I were you, phone my mother later."

Maggie's head was buzzing. "Why? Am I getting married?" She held up her hands. "Scratch that. I make jokes when I'm scared out of my mind."

"Yes, I know. Rather bad jokes," Saint Just purred, giving her elbow a reassuring squeeze. "But now, because our audience is waiting to be titillated, and because I must admit some small curiosity myself, I believe I'd like to hear a little more from Ms. Simon." He turned to Clarice, who was now sheltering rather comfortably under the protective arm of Nelson Trigg.

"What?" she asked, looking frightened. "I told the police everything."

"I'm assured you did, Ms. Simon, but as I've already said, now that you've told us some of it, I believe we should be likewise gifted with the rest. You phoned Miss Kelly, she told you the menu, and you told Mr. Toland. In person?"

Clarice pushed herself slightly away from Trigg as she frowned at Saint Just. "No-o-o," she said slowly, as if reliving the event. "His secretary, Betty, is out on vacation, but I didn't mind helping him. I didn't see him again. I . . . I just wrote the menu in a note, and put it on his desk."

"I see," Saint Just said, smiling at the gathered guests. "And what time would that have been, Ms. Simon?"

"Time? I don't know. Around eight-thirty, quarter of nine. Early."

"How interesting. And you obtained entrance to Mr. Toland's office with a key? Or is the door left open, with anyone able to walk in and out willy-nilly, read items left on his desk? All, of course, without the, I'm convinced, very efficient Betty there to guard his privacy?"

There was the beginning of a low rumbling of voices around Maggie, and she began to relax, even enjoy watching her creation do his magic in the flesh. She was even beginning to get a kick out of the way he said "*priv*-acy."

"Well, I suppose so. We're pretty informal in the offices . . ." Clarice said, looking at Maggie rather apologetically.

"Just as anyone could have overheard Mr. Toland beg the favor of calling Miss Kelly from you in the first place? Where were you when he approached you?"

"In the coffee room. There were about six or eight of us in there, I guess. He asked me to find out the menu, then leave a note on his desk. And then I mentioned something at lunch, to some of the other secretaries. I thought it was sort of funny, that hemlock thing. I guess lots of people knew about it, and they could have told people about it . . ." Clarice's little face crumpled, and she reached out to Maggie, flinging her arms around her. "Oh, I'm so sorry, Maggie. Maybe you didn't do it."

"Well, that's over. How boring, almost as boring as your books, Maggie," Felicity said, turning on her three-inch heels and pushing her way through the already dispersing crowd.

Maggie couldn't even care that Felicity had insulted her, again. She was fully occupied with the now weeping Clarice. "Hey, it's okay, Clarice. I would have thought the same thing, really." *Not in a million years, you trouble-making little twit!* "Nelson, could you help me out here?"

"Come, Clarice," Trigg said, peeling his assistant off Maggie, so that she turned and latched her whimpering self onto him. "Now the entire staff is under suspicion, Maggie, thanks to you. There will be no work accomplished for weeks. No matter what, I think you and your friend here should leave. You're upsetting the legitimate mourners."

"Would that include you, Mr. Trigg? Are you in mourning?" Saint Just asked, striking a pose. "Now how could I have missed that? I'm usually such an observant fellow.

Perhaps I was led astray by the fact that you climbed into Toland's chair — used a ladder, did you? — even before the man breathed his last? A wont of respect, I should say, or a surfeit of . . . ambition?"

"I could sue you for that," Trigg said, his face suddenly beet-red as he held onto Clarice, either to comfort her or to hide behind her.

"Sue me? Wouldn't you rather punch me? How terribly civilized you must think you are. Yet murder, I have found, is rarely civilized."

Okay, so now Clarice was left to stand or fall on her own, because Trigg pushed her away and stepped toward Saint Just. "Are you accusing *me?*"

"You won't benefit by Toland's death? Or, to allow me to rephrase that, you don't *hope* to benefit from Toland's death?"

"Yo, Felicity!" Maggie called out, feeling pretty good all of a sudden. "Over here. You're missing this."

"I most certainly do *not,*" Trigg declared, his nostrils sort of flaring, or jiggling, or something — whatever it was, it made him look fairly horse-like. "It is up to Kirk's heirs to choose someone to lead Toland Books. Any fool would know that."

"Yes, of course. His heirs. Forgive me.

And who, do you think, might they be?"

"That's none of my business, and most definitely none of yours," Trigg said, then turned on his heels and pushed his way through the crowd, Clarice following close behind him.

"I do believe I've finally succeeded in insulting the man, after several tries, I must admit," Saint Just said as he steered Maggie back through the crowd, which parted as they approached. "I also believe, sadly, that we have now been witness to the wimp factor, if I have the term correctly. Sue me? No, Nelson Trigg couldn't kill anyone. He hasn't the bottom for it."

"Great," Maggie pointed out sourly. "But we need more suspects, Alex, not fewer of them. Unless you want to blame Clarice?"

"That watering pot? Oh, I don't think so. Although I do believe I'll have to speak with her again. Before you arrived on the scene she was being quite flattering about your books, and about me. She's delighted that I look so much like the *real* Saint Just. A more immodest man would say she's even attracted to me. I'll be able to use that."

"God," Maggie said, collapsing into her chair once more. "Roll up your pant legs,

Sterling, it's too late too save the shoes."

"I beg your pardon?" Sterling asked, distracted from his current project, which seemed to be constructing a small tower from his shrimp sticks. "Is there something on the floor?"

"Yeah. Alex's immense ego. We're ankle-deep in it. Oh, here comes Bernie."

Saint Just turned around. "Listing slightly to port, isn't she?"

Maggie watched her friend approach. She looked fabulous, her halo of bright red hair like a flame above her black, raw-silk designer suit. Only her face was pale, unnaturally pale, and her gait definitely was unsteady. That was unusual, because Bernie could hold her drink better than most sailors on their first shore leave in six months.

"Bernie? Is something wrong?" she asked as the editor collapsed into the chair Saint Just held out for her.

"Wrong?" Bernie repeated. "I don't think you'd call it wrong. I just talked to Kirk's lawyer, over next to the clam dip. Jesus, they're going through that like Grant through Richmond. Anyway, you know, the guy who told us how Kirk wanted to be incinerated and sprinkled? He says Kirk never changed his will after we divorced, even after he married the bimbo. He wants me to come back with him to his office, to read the will. But that's only a formality, because I get everything."

She sat looking at Maggie, but obviously not seeing her. She blinked twice, then sighed. "Everything. His condo on Park Avenue, all the houses. The limo, the jet, the yacht. The *business*. My God," she said, slumping in her seat. "I should have sprung for a classier urn."

CHAPTER 13

Maggie dragged through the door to her apartment, her entire mind concentrated on a hot shower and a bed. She'd no idea memorial services could be so exhausting.

Saint Just, on the other hand, was still looking as fresh as a daisy — scratch that analogy; it was too effeminate. She was having enough problems with the modern world's perception of Regency manners and speech. Especially after Socks had drawn her to one side as she entered the building, asking if she thought Sterling would have any objections if he "pursued Alex. He is *so* hot."

Wellie and Napper threaded through Sterling's legs, welcoming home the good and caring man who fed them and groomed them, as Maggie aimed herself at the hallway leading to her bedroom. She dropped her purse on one of the couches. She toed off her shoes as she slogged along, gamely struggling until her last breath to reach her goal.

Her body ached, her temples throbbed, and her toes had gone numb inside the uncomfortable heels.

"Maggie? The light on the machine is blinking," Saint Just said, his words robbing the last of her strength. "Maggie? You are going to contact your parents, aren't you?"

"No. No, no, no," Maggie moaned, slowly turning around, shoulders slumped, looking at the answering machine. "God, look at the way that thing's flashing. I can almost hear her from here. Pull the plug, okay?"

"Bad news doesn't improve with keeping," Saint Just suggested, and then pushed the proper button.

"You have three messages," the disembodied voice announced, then beeped cheerfully and rattled them off:

"Maggie? Maggie, are you there? Dad and I just read the paper when we came back from a late breakfast on the boardwalk, and we're so sorry to see that Kirk is dead. I had so hoped — well, never mind, but you'll remember that I've always told you it's as easy to love a rich man as a poor one. Maggie? You know how I hate talking to a machine. But what is this ridiculousness about *you?* Maggie? Evan, she's not answering. Well, how should I know where she is? She's your daughter, too, you know. Think, Evan, before you speak. Maggie, pick up. Maggie? Maggie? Oh, all right. I'll call again later."

Click.

Second message.

"Maggie? Maggie, your father and I are very worried. You were on the noon news. You need a haircut, by the way, and those streaks make you look cheap. I know the services for Kirk are today, and I imagine that's where you are. That is where you are, isn't it? Call me."

Click.

Third message.

"Margaret, it's four o'clock. They could have buried fifty people by now. If I don't receive a phone call from you by six, your father and I are driving up there. You know how your father hates driving after dark, so have some consideration and call me."

Maggie, suddenly very much awake and alert, shot a quick look at the mantel clock. "What time is it? What time is it? Shit! Six-ten." She leapt the couch in the proverbial single bound, grabbed at the portable phone, hit Number One on the speed dial. "Come on, come on, come on, *answer*, damn it!"

"Hello?"

"Daddy," Maggie said, collapsing onto the couch, then talking as fast as her mouth could move. "Thank God I caught you. Don't come up here, please. I'm fine. Honestly. I don't know what was on the news or in the papers, but it was all a mistake. Kirk accidently ate some poison mushrooms, that's all. I mean, that's enough, because he's dead and everything, but it has nothing to do with me. I'm fine. So don't come here, okay?"

There was a slight pause, and then Evan Kelly said what Evan Kelly always said: "I'll get your mother."

"No — Daddy —" Maggie said, leaning forward, as if ready to reach out, catch him, keep him from passing the phone to Alicia Kelly.

"Margaret? Well, it's about time. Another moment, and we'd have been out the door. As it was, we were in the car a moment ago, but your father remembered that he had forgotten his denture cleanser."

"Gee, I really needed to know that," Maggie muttered under her breath. More loudly she said, "Daddy wears dentures?"

"Only a partial," Alicia said. "Not that it's a secret. And, speaking of secrets, how long did you think you could keep this one from us? Kirk Toland dies in your apartment? You're a *suspect* in his murder?"

"No, Mom, I'm not, I'm not. Really. I mean, I *was,* but I'm not now." She looked at Saint Just, who was shaking his head in a rather pitying manner. "I . . . I was just a dupe."

"Margaret, have some self-respect," her mother commanded across the miles. "You're not stupid. You're my daughter, and you're innocent, although I will agree that your brother, Tate, got most of the brains, leaving you girls a little short."

Maggie rolled her eyes. If the woman would just break down and get herself a damn hearing aid. And she could have lived forever without having her mother praise Tate one more time at her expense.

"Not a dope, Mom, a *dupe.* Somebody used me, set me up, made everyone believe I poisoned Kirk. But that's all over now, okay? The police have agreed that I'm not a suspect anymore, and they still can't be sure it wasn't an accident, so there's no reason for you and Dad to come up here when I know you're so busy down there with your pinochle group and everything. Really, there's not," she ended, wincing as she heard her tone edge toward a whine.

"You're quite sure?" her mother asked, sounding disappointed. "A girl needs her mother when she's . . . when she's . . ."

"Being indicted for murder?" Maggie said helpfully. "I know, Mom. But since I'm not, you don't have to come. Besides, it will be dark soon, and it takes well over two hours to get here from Ocean City."

"True, true," Alicia Kelly said, and Maggie relaxed, just a hair. "But we are all packed and everything. Hold on, Maggie. Evan? Do we have any comp nights at Harrah's? So go *look*, why don't you, instead of just sitting there saying you don't know. Wouldn't that be logical?"

Two minutes later, after wishing her parents luck at the casino, agreeing to have her hair cut, and promising to call if there was any more news, Maggie pushed the Off button and looked at Saint Just. "Ever wonder why my brother and sisters all live more than five hours from New Jersey? I don't. I just wonder why I'm not living in Seattle. Lots of writers live in Seattle, probably because their parents live in New Jersey."

She frowned, exhausted once again. "But it rains all the time in Seattle, and I'm not that crazy for fancy coffee."

"You did convince her not to come to Manhattan," Saint Just said, handing her the glass of wine he'd poured for her. "A small accomplishment, but an accomplishment all the same. Tell me, Maggie, why are you afraid of her?"

Maggie took the glass and automatically drank from it. "Afraid of her? I'm not afraid of her. She's my mother, for crying out loud."

"She's a bully who rides roughshod over anyone she considers weaker than herself," Saint Just said, seating himself on the facing couch, sipping brandy from a snifter Maggie hadn't known she owned. She probably hadn't, two weeks ago. "Do you know that you spent the last several minutes of that distressing phone call saying yes, yes, yes?"

"Yes?" Maggie winced. "I mean, don't be ridiculous. I couldn't have done that. And my mother is not a bully."

"Really? I beg to differ. You had moments of spark, early on, but you degenerated into yes-yes-yes, as you always do. I was in your head, remember, for a very long time. I've heard those phone calls. The woman is a harridan."

"She is *not!*" Maggie said, pushing herself up from the couch, then falling back into the cushions once more. "Okay, so she's got a strong personality."

"And your father has none," Saint Just supplied, sipping from his snifter. "Your mother has been allowed to browbeat him for decades, and the rest of you either run away and hide, bow down to her, or try to act as peacemaker. You, in fact, have even taken it a step further. You bow down to anyone who speaks in pronouncements."

Maggie narrowed her eyes at him. "Pronouncements? What the hell is that supposed to mean?"

Saint Just stood and began to pace. "Allow me to rephrase that. You have a tendency to defer to anyone who seems more sure of himself, or herself, than you do about *your*self."

Maggie downed the last of her wine. "Oh, that. That's only because I'm a Well-Maybe."

"I beg your pardon?"

She gave a dismissive wave of her hand. "I mean it. I've figured it out. I've figured out that there are only two types of people in this world, and they're either Yes-Definitelies or Well-Maybes. There could be Almost-Alwayses and Hell-No-Nevers — sort of hybrids — but for the most part, there's just Yes-Definitely and Well-Maybe. You with me so far?"

"Not at all. Go on."

Maggie was warming to her subject, because she'd given it a lot of thought, especially when writing up character descriptions for her books. "Okay. Yes-Definitelies — they're sure of themselves. Completely and absolutely sure of themselves, their convictions, the *rightness* of their positions, twenty-four-seven, without fail. Like they got it all on tablets on some mountaintop. Like, well, okay, like Republicans. Are you paying attention?"

"I'm, *like*, riveted, my dear. Continue."

"Ha-ha, very funny. All right, so we have the Yes-Definitelies. It's true because I said it's true, period. And now we have the Well-Maybes. They're not so sure."

"They're not? Why?"

Maggie smiled, happy to share. "Because they see all sides of an argument. They think they're right, but they're willing to listen to argument, even congratulate the Yes-Definitelies if they make a point. They're tolerant."

"They sound weak to me," Saint Just said, taking up his seat once more.

"No, they're not. But they just can't say *stuff it* to people who — what did you call it? Oh, yeah — *pronounce*. They can *think* it, they can *write* it — like I do; they can discuss, rationally. But they can't declare unequivocally, because they don't see anything as unequivocal. Nothing is black and white, everything is gray. Everyone has a point. Or something like that. It's a personality thing. Then there's the whole physically intimidating thing. Yes-Definitelies are mostly big. Well, not actually big, but they *act* big. Fill the room, swagger. Well-Maybes get nervous around them."

"That was a very long, convoluted way of agreeing with me, Maggie. You're afraid of bullies," Saint Just said, tying all her meanderings up into one condemning package. "Your mother, a bully, trained you to be afraid of bullies. It's why you can talk to some people and be terrified of others. It simply amazes me how you can be so talented, so beautiful, and yet so unsure of yourself when confronted with a bully. Although I am pleased that you haven't been cowed by the *left*-tenant."

Maggie had caught one word, and she hung onto it. "Beautiful? Did you say beautiful?"

Saint Just put down his snifter and stood up once more. "That's neither here nor there, Maggie. Now, informative as this conversation has been, I suggest you take yourself off now, have an early night of it. Your mother still may very well travel here on her broom tomorrow, and you'll need your rest."

Maggie followed him down the hall. "Do you really think she'll show up?"

He smiled down at her. One excruciatingly handsome hero on a stick. Much more appealing than shrimp on a stick. "No, I do not. But Bernice will, at three o'clock. I would have asked her to arrive earlier, but there is the matter of Socks's audition, you understand. I imagine she'll be only the first of many visitors."

"I'm lost. Why's Bernie coming here?"

"My dear girl, I thought you wrote murder mysteries. Put on your Well-Maybe hat and consider all the possibilities, look at the crime from every angle, from Bernice's angle."

Maggie shook her head, trying to clear it of lingering memories of her mother. "Oh!" she said, her eyes growing wide. "Bernie has a motive, doesn't she? Ohmigod, I hadn't thought of that. Bernie has a motive."

"A whacking great motive. Approximately fifty million dollars of motive, according to Bernice, and that's figuring conservatively. I believe the *left*-tenant also may see it that way, and I pointed out as much to Bernice, who is naturally not a happy woman at the moment. We've therefore decided to put our heads together, as

328

it were, to draw up a list of others who might benefit by Toland's demise. I would appreciate your assistance."

Maggie nodded. "Sure, sure. Oh, poor Bernie. I know just how she feels. Wendell will be all over her once he finds out about the will. And she's innocent, of course. We have to help her."

"And so we shall, my dear," Saint Just said, damn near *pronounced,* except that, although he had some of the rather annoying attributes of a Yes-Definitely, he also had enough of Maggie in him to be at least a little bit flexible. "And so we shall. Trust me, I have everything very much in hand."

Imagine for a moment that Maggie Kelly, writer, has decided to branch out into time travel (a sub-genre, with a small but steady following, and one not without appeal and the occasional bestseller). Further imagine that she has decided that her two most successful creations, Alexandre Blake, Viscount Saint Just, and his faithful companion, Sterling Balder, should become her time travelers in a lighthearted farce.

Imagine Maggie using all of her experiences of the past weeks to goose her imagination, create characters and scenarios (that would be her companions in the smoking kiosk, in "chairs." Well, you'll see. Everything is fodder).

Now imagine this brave, at times fool-hardy Regency duo transported to mod-ern-day Manhattan. Imagine them out and about, doing their possible to obtain pa-pers (forgeries, that is) establishing their identity.

Oh, go ahead. Imagine . . .

The April evening was passably pleasant, if one was accustomed to the fog and mist of London, and Saint Just felt al-most comfortable as he strolled the dark, wet pavement, assuring Sterling yet again that the goblins most probably would not "get them and boil them for dinner." As he had explained numerous times, "The ex-pression is Gotham, Sterling, not Goblin, and it's only a word."

"You say the that calmly enough, Saint Just, but I notice that you keep your sword cane at the ready." Sterling cast his nervous gaze from side to side, walking with a rather hesitant step, as if he wasn't sure if his feet should be propelling him forward or backward. "And this Snake person. I didn't like the way he looked at me last night."

"I imagine you didn't, Sterling," Saint Just said soothingly. "However, as we are not in pursuit of a lifelong friendship with the man or his cohort, I should disregard it. Ah, I believe our friends are here."

"Friends? I thought you said they weren't our friends."

"Sterling," Saint Just said evenly, "attempt to get a grip, please." Then he took three more steps forward and bowed to Snake and Killer as Sterling pretended an interest in the heel of one of his new high-top sneakers with the reflectors on the back. "Gentlemen. How good of you to be so prompt. But I don't believe I see anyone else with you. Has there been a problem?"

"Yo, m'man," Snake said, holding out his hand. "Got my knife?"

"Yes, I do," Saint Just said, looking at Killer, whose eyes kept shifting to his left, as if in silent signal. Bless the boy; Saint Just had hopes he might end up stumbling one day onto the straight and narrow. "Your knife, and my new watch, will make tolerable additions to my rather meager store of belongings. But we'll be off now. Good evening, gentlemen."

"Hey! No, man, don't you be goin' anywhere," Snake objected, reaching out a

331

hand to Saint Just.

The viscount took the hand, along with most of the arm, pulling the youth toward him, twisting Snake's arm behind his back, and then tickling his nearly hairless chin with the tip of the switchblade with "To Vernon wit luv Mom" scratched on the hilt (obviously, the engraver had charged by the letter . . . or perhaps spelling and punctuation hadn't been his fortes).

"If you were to please advise the person lurking in the shadows that Snake would appreciate his presence, rather soon, I imagine, I should be most obliged," Saint Just said to Killer, who was once more showing a distressing tendency to grasp his private parts whenever startled.

"Do it, do it, do it," Snake begged.

"Sterling? Retrieve my cane, if you please," Saint Just said as he backed up a few steps, dragging the trembling Snake with him, until the viscount's back was securely against the plate glass window of a used-book shop. "Yes, thank you, Sterling. Perhaps you might wish to unsheathe it as well, brandish the thing about a bit in a threatening manner?"

"Me?" Sterling sighed the sigh of the horribly oppressed. "Oh, very well. But

I'll probably kill somebody."

"Yes, that would be one thing to do," Saint Just agreed, smiling. "As long as it's neither of us, feel free to attack anyone you wish. Killer? Vernon here is getting deuced heavy to hang on to. I fear the knife might slip, do him some irreparable harm."

"Jesus, Georgie, get her out here!" Snake shouted. "These guys are nuts."

Killer, alias Georgie, danced into the alley, his eyes trained on Snake, christened Vernon by his loving mother, and appeared a few moments later, dragging a young woman who had diligently worked and worked until she'd cornered the market on earrings.

In the yellowy light of the lamppost a half block away, Saint Just estimated that the young lady had punctured her ears at least a dozen times each, then dealt with her excess inventory by piercing both eyebrows, one nostril, her chin and . . . yes, unbelievably, her navel. One more bit of glitter revealed the pointed blade in her left hand. She hefted it as if she knew how to use it.

Very disconcerting, Saint Just decided, to a man used to women who held fans and simpered.

She stood not quite five feet tall and weighed no more than a feather, her arms and legs delicate twigs, her bared midriff pinched almost hollow. The triangular scrap of cloth that hid her nonexistent bosom was bright yellow; the slacks precariously clinging to her narrow hips dragged a good three inches on the ground as she shuffled into view.

Saint Just was nonplussed, perhaps for the first time in his memory. His agitation came at the realization that, outrageous as the young woman was, she was also one of the most beautiful creatures he'd ever seen. A wood sprite. A pocket Venus. Well, if he squinted, pretended not to see the piercings, the ridiculous costume, the almost malnourished body . . .

"So? What you lookin' at, old man?" she said by way of greeting.

"Pardon me, madam," Saint Just said, releasing his grip on Vernon, who stumbled forward a few feet, then stood close beside Georgie as he rubbed at his tender throat. "It is just that rarely have I seen such lovely eyes, such a smooth cheek, so *unusual* a hair style. Would that color be called pink?"

"What's it to you?" she said, closing the knife and slipping it into a pocket, then shoving her hands onto her hips.

"An impertinent question, my dear lady. I most sincerely apologize. Allow me, please, to introduce myself. I am the Viscount Saint Just. Beside me, just now with his mouth at half cock, is my boon companion, Mr. Sterling Balder. Sterling, close your mouth, please." He then made a most elegant leg, his bow so graceful, women had been known to swoon when gifted with the honor.

"Hey, I don't care what names you want, Vic. Just show me the green, okay?"

"Saint Just? Is she real? And wouldn't that *hurt?*"

"Quietly, Sterling," Saint Just warned. "We are in Rome, now, and we must do as the Romans do."

Saint Just retrieved his cane from Sterling and was about to reach into his pocket for the list he'd written of everything he required when Sterling tugged on the sleeve of his black sweater. "What is it, Sterling?"

"Manhattan. I thought you said we were in Manhattan. In New York, in the United States, and all of that. Everyone here speaks English, I think. I vow, Saint Just, I don't know if I'm on my head or my heels. It's all just too confusing."

"And entirely my fault," Saint Just apologized. "We are in the city of New York, Sterling. I was merely —"

"Hey! You! You with the mouth — we gonna do this or not? I ain't got all night."

Saint Just bowed once more, only a slight inclination of his head. "Forgive me, madam, I —"

"And don't call me madam, neither," the girl cut in, cupping her hands around a lighter as she lit a cigarette, one eye still on Saint Just. "Name's Mare."

"Mare? Oh, I think not. A mare, my dear young lady, is a female horse."

"Told ya, Mary Louise," Georgie said, giving the girl a push on the shoulder. "Told you it was a stupid nickname."

"Yeah, *Killer*," Mary Louise shot back, giving Georgie a push on the shoulder, one that sent him reeling toward the curb. "Come on. Either somebody buys me a burger and fries in the next two minutes, or I'm outta here."

Saint Just felt control of the situation dissolving at his feet. He didn't like the feeling. "I should be honored to purchase a meal for you, Miss Mary Louise."

Mary Louise tossed her cigarette toward the street. "Yeah? And I'd be *honored* to bust you one in the chops if you call me that again. Kapish?"

"Well, maybe they don't all speak English," Sterling said bemusedly as they followed Mare and her friends Vernon and Georgie down the street toward the Styles Cafe.

Saint Just avoided the problems he'd encountered the first time he'd visited this particular establishment the previous day — he'd cooled his heels for a good twenty minutes before realizing that no one was going to serve him — by handing Georgie a twenty-dollar bill and asking him to place their order at the counter.

Vernon went off to help carry the trays and load his pockets with complimentary packets of mustard and ketchup, leaving Saint Just, Sterling, and Mare sitting in a booth near the back of the restaurant.

"So," Saint Just said, ignoring the beautiful blue eyes, the cupid's-bow mouth, the creamy, silken skin. Strangely, the pink hair was rather exciting. "You're a forger?"

"Jesus H. Christ," Mare hissed, crossing her arms on the tabletop and lowering her head as she looked out into the restaurant. "Say it a little louder, why don't you?"

Beside him, Sterling covered a giggle with a cough.

"I'm so sorry," Saint Just said, realizing that he somehow had turned into a man who apologized for every other word out of his mouth. He had to take control. "You have credentials, of course?"

"Sure. You want proof I'm who I say I am? Whaddya want? I can make anything you want . . . jerk."

Now Sterling picked up a napkin from the pile that had been left on the table and shoved one into his mouth to stifle his laughter. Saint Just pretended not to notice, as it seemed to be the first spot of fun the man had had since they'd left Piccadilly.

"I mean it, Vic. What do you want? You're English, right? You want dual citizenship, because I can do that, but it costs extra. Passport? Green card? Student visa? Nah, not a student visa. You're too old for that. Five hundred bucks for each of you, for the works. Double that for dual citizenship and driver's licenses, voter registration cards, Social Security cards, stuff like that. But no Visa or MasterCard, get it? I don't go that route. You gotta be wacko to do that stuff."

Saint Just hesitated, then thought: What was the point? He could go back and forth all the night long, trying to convince himself that Mare and her cohorts were honest — or as honest as thieves and forgers could be — or he could take a leap of faith, pretending it had nothing to do with a pair of blue eyes filled with such a mixture of bravado and innocence that his heart ached to look at them. It could be a trial at times, being a romantic.

"Look," Mare said, obviously getting impatient as Saint Just remained silent. "Wrap your mind around this, Vic, okay? Georgie's my cousin, and a real loser right now. He came to me because he said he needed help and he thinks I'm the brains of the family. He's right, I am. I'm a grad student at NYU. Honest. Computers, graphic arts, you name it. I can do this. I can get you any identification you want. Piece of cake."

Sterling leaned forward. "Cake? Where?"

"Be quiet, Sterling," Saint Just warned absently.

"He's sorta cute," Mary Louise said, jerking a thumb at Sterling. "Anyways, I can do this. Hell, the real stuff will look fake next to what I can make for you. I mean, I am *good*. I do this for Irish kids down in the Village all the time, when they don't want to go back when their visas are up. No sweat. Okay?"

Saint Just heard everything, understood part of it, and believed Mare's blue eyes. He didn't really have any other choice. He reached into his pocket and withdrew three gold coins out of the several dozen still his possession. "These will be yours when we have what we need. I've already sold two of them, and, I assure you, the proceeds from the sale of these will more than cover your fees."

Mare took one of the coins, turned it over in her fingers. "Looks real enough," she said, slipping the coin into a small pocket just beneath the waistband of her jeans. "I'll check it out with my brother the banker. He knows all about that stuff. Me, I know paper. Now, either give me the information or not. I don't care."

Saint Just unfolded the paper containing his notes and handed it to her.

"Good, good, but I need DOBs."

"I beg your pardon?"

"DOBs — date of birth."

"Oh, well, that's easy enough, isn't it Saint Just?" Sterling leaned his elbows on the table and said, "I was born in the year of our Lord, Seventeen hun— ouch! Saint Just, you kicked me."

"Don't be ridiculous, Sterling. Why

would I do something like that?" Saint Just smiled at Mare. "We're of an age, Sterling and I, both five-and-thirty. But feel free to pick any date you like. Is there anything else you might need?"

"Yeah," Mare said, pulling a pen from her pocket. "Eye and hair color, height, weight." She looked at Sterling and began taking notes.

By the time Georgie and Vernon came back with the food, the deal had been struck. Mare had Saint Just's list, which included both their names and their address at the YMCA, along with her own scribbled notes. She'd snapped photographs of them both with a small disposable camera, telling them she could scan and upload the pictures, cut out the background, then superimpose their photographs on a plain background that looked more official. Another "piece of cake."

And then they were done. They were to meet in three days' time for Mare to turn over the papers and the coin, for Saint Just to give her two thousand dollars, "in regular money."

Everything had gone very well, in fact. Right up until the moment Saint Just asked for one more service to be provided by any of the trio or their assorted felon-relatives.

"Oh, yes, by the bye," Saint Just said as Sterling apologized for the rude noises he made as he slurped the last of his strawberry milkshake through a straw, "if it wouldn't be too much trouble, I'd also like a gun."

"A gun?" Georgie said even as he smacked Vernon on the back, for the young hoodlum was choking on a bite of his hamburger.

"Yes, a gun. A pistol. Why? There must be someone in your so estimable family who deals in firearms, correct?" He looked from Mare to Georgie and smiled. "Is there a problem?"

Well, that's the way Maggie might have written it.

In truth, except for the time travel and the gold coins, it went down pretty much that way. . . .

CHAPTER 14

There were days, and then there were *days*.

This was turning out to be one of "those" days. Everyone knows "those" days. Maggie knew them well. She sometimes had whole weeks of "those" days. In fact, she was going for a new personal record, a whole month of "those" days.

She barreled down the pavement at nine o'clock Friday morning, head down, pushing through the early morning rain, muttering to herself. Big deal; everybody in New York muttered to themselves.

"Oh, yeah? Oh, yeah? Well, you and whose army, huh, huh? Could have said that. It's pretty weak, but I could have. Or a simple fuck-you. Neat, succinct, to the point. That's what Bernie would say. Could have done that, too. But, no-o-o. I go, bam, straight to Wimp City. I just say *okay, sorry,* and walk out. *Okay?* Okay, hell! What I should have — *oof!*"

"Whoa, slow down, Ms. Kelly," Lieutenant Steve Wendell said, holding on to her shoulders, steadying her. "What's your hurry? I don't think your imaginary friend can keep up with you and he might miss what you're saying."

She looked up at him, blinked at the rain that splashed into her eyes, and saw Mr. Laid Back and Gorgeous grinning down at her, his hair wet and plastered against his head, his eyelashes dark, curly spikes. His teeth whiter than white. So adorable. She could strangle him.

"Don't be cute," Maggie warned, pushing his hands away and continuing her head-down walk, with Wendell right beside her. "I'm mad, I need a target, and you don't want to be it. Trust me in this. I don't blow all that often, but when I do, it can get messy."

Wendell took hold of her elbow, steered her into a reluctant U-turn, and headed her back down the sidewalk, toward the coffee shop.

"I said, *no.*"

"Yeah, I know. You also have the right to remain silent," Wendell said, still pulling her along.

Maggie dug in her heels, as well as anyone can dig sneakers into cement. Why wasn't she cowed by this guy? He carried a badge, for crying out loud. Yet, him she could insult. But Mario? Him she ran from. There just wasn't any justice in this world, at least in Maggie's world. "You're reading me my rights? I'm under arrest?"

He grinned. "Nope. I just thought you might want to stay silent, at least until I can put a hot cup of coffee in front of you. You don't look so good."

Maggie shrugged her shoulders, let her breath out in a rush, and then gave in. "Okay. But you're buying. And then you can tell me what you're doing here."

"Sure," he said, holding open the door for her, and she gratefully got herself out of the rain. "Right after you tell me why you're so piss— er, upset."

Wendell held up two fingers to the waitress as he slid into the booth, facing Maggie. "Want a doughnut, too? I want a doughnut."

"No, I don't want a — oh, all right," she said, pushing her fingers through her wet hair. She probably looked like hell. No, she definitely looked like hell. Hadn't he already said so? "Glazed. With sprinkles."

"That'll be two glazed, with sprinkles," Wendell told the waitress, who was unhappily plunking two mugs down on the tabletop. "And smile. You look so pretty when you smile."

Maggie closed her eyes, reran his last words inside her head, then looked at the waitress, who was walking back to the counter, her hips waggling, her head turned back so that she could smile at Steve Wendell. "God, that's so lame," she said in disgust, committing the line to memory, to use it for Saint Just's dialogue in her next book. "I don't know which is worse, that crap you fed her or the way she lapped it up."

"Hey, don't complain. I'll bet we get the biggest doughnuts. I'm a doughnut gourmet, you know. It's a cop thing."

"Cut it out. Nobody likes a stereotype." Maggie dug into her pocket and came out with her cigarettes and lighter.

"You can't do that in here," Wendell reminded her. "We're a non-smoking restaurant town, remember?"

"Sid seceded from the union," Maggie said, lighting up. "He says he makes his own laws now. One of them is the right to smoke. I like Sid," she said, blowing out a stream of smoke. "So does the cop on the beat, who comes in here for cigarette and coffee breaks."

Wendell scratched at his left ear. "I really wish you wouldn't tell me stuff like that. I'm an officer of the law, remember?"

"You're homicide," Maggie reminded him.

He shrugged. "So? Cigarettes are killers, right?"

"Oh, please, not you, too. I'm going to quit, I really am. Not because I want to, but just to shut everyone the hell up about my damaged lungs, their damned allergies, and because I can't find a place to smoke anymore. Besides, cigarettes will soon cost more than cocaine, if they don't already. So, hey, stick around, because when I do quit, I probably will be pretty damn dangerous. Homicidal."

"Speaking of which . . ." Wendell said, leaning back against the booth. "You were pretty hot when you nearly mowed me down out there. What set you off?"

Maggie looked at the tip of her cigarette, then stubbed it out in the ashtray. She had to give up her crutches — cigarettes, junk food, talking to herself. As it was, she'd be awake at two a.m., going over all the brilliant comebacks she could have made to Mario, and didn't. That was what she liked best about writing. Not only could she feed straight lines to her characters, she had all the time in the world to make up snappy comebacks. In real life, it didn't work that way. Real life sometimes sucked.

"I went to Mario's to get some cigarettes," she told him. "I'm almost out. Except he *threw* me out." She looked across the table. "Mario. He threw me out. I've been shopping in his place ever since I moved in here, paying his ridiculous prices. I give his wife autographed copies of my books. I always give a penny and never take a penny. Okay, so hardly ever. I let his damn dog sniff me — well, I don't really let her. Sheba's a Great Dane."

She waved her hands, nearly knocking over her mug. "But that's not the point. I'm a customer. A *good* customer. And he threw me out. It was so embarrassing. He says I'm bad for business. Can you believe that?"

"Hoo-boy, that's tough. It's the mushrooms, right?" Wendell said, taking a large bite of doughnut. "I guess having two squad cars pull up, confiscate all his mushrooms and other vegetables and salads sort of upset him. Probably bad for business."

"They took *all* his vegetables? And his salads? I didn't know that. Why'd they do that? But still, it wasn't *my* fault," Maggie said, blinking back tears. "And it was the *way* he did it. Yelling at me, with the place stiff with other customers. Calling me a troublemaker, saying I'm taking the bread out of his kids' mouths because of the bad publicity. And me? I didn't say a word. Not a damn word! I just stood there, looking stupid, feeling stupid, and then I sort of mumbled something, then sort of *slunk* away, like a dog with his tail between his — *two* squad cars? My God. Mario must have been having fits."

"What can I say? We're the NYPD, and we love our sirens and lights. We probably watch too many cop shows on TV. So," he said, leaning his elbows on the tabletop, "feeling better now?"

Maggie rolled her eyes. "Are you *nuts? No-o-o,* I'm not feeling better now. I just got kicked out of my corner grocery store. It's humiliating. It's also two long blocks to the next corner grocery store, it's raining, and I still need cigarettes."

"Two blocks, huh? Man, and with your smoker's lungs, that's probably too far to walk, right? So maybe it's a good time to quit?" Wendell suggested, then ducked when Maggie hefted the rest of her doughnut, ready to sail it at his head. "Okay, okay. Maybe today isn't a good day to quit. You seem to be pretty stressed today. Maybe tomorrow?"

"You're going to have the case solved by tomorrow?"

"I said we watch a lot of cop shows, Ms. Kelly. I didn't say we can produce miracles before the last commercial and still have time left over for the obligatory nude scene."

Too bad, and him with those great buns.
"So that's a no, right? Have you actually ruled Kirk's death a homicide now? I mean, it's definitely not an accidental death?"

"Do you think it was an accidental death?"

"Oh, no. My shrink answers questions with questions. I don't play that game."

Wendell drank the rest of his coffee, threw a bunch of ones on the table, and slid out of the booth, Maggie following him after quickly downing the last of her coffee. "You go to a shrink?" he said. "Why?"

"That's personal," Maggie told him as he held the door open for her. "And, unless I'm still a suspect, private. Even more so if I am. Privileged conversations, right? Isn't that what they're called?"

"Sorry, I was just curious. We have these periodic meetings with the department shrink, especially if we end up on a shoot. I hate talking to those guys. I can't imagine why anyone would actually pay down cash money to go to one on their own."

"Yeah, well I only go to stop smoking," Maggie told him as she held out her hand, palm up, happy to see that the rain had slowed to a damp mizzle.

"Really. How long you been going?"

"Two years," Maggie answered, then winced, realizing she was automatically reaching into her pocket for her crumpled pack and her lighter. "But we're making . . . we're making progress."

"I sensed that," Wendell said as they approached the door to her apartment building. "Well, here we are, and I haven't told you anything."

Maggie stopped outside the doors and turned to look at him. "You came here to *tell* me something? *Confer* with me on Kirk's case?"

Wendell grinned, showing those damn white teeth again. "Hell, no," he said. "I came here to tell you that I can't find spit about Blakely or Balder. Nothing. Zilch, zip, nada."

"Oh," Maggie said, then sucked on her cigarette. She could make a break for it, she supposed, race upstairs to warn Alex and Sterling. But what good would that do? Not much, unfortunately. She had the feeling Steve Wendell was a bit of a bulldog, and would follow right after them, hunt them all down. Like *The Fugitive*, except that she couldn't picture Wendell in the role of Lieutenant Gerard, saying, "I don't care," when she proclaimed her innocence.

"But you know what, Ms. Kelly? I don't care."

Maggie's head jerked up. "Huh?"

"I said, I don't care. Your cousin is a hero. That runaway carriage thing, remember? The mayor already said so, for the media. If I yank him in because he's here illegally? Well, then the tabloids pick it up, get front-page photos of our latest hero being led off in chains by the INS. The mayor looks bad. He looks bad, and I look worse. Nope. I'm on the Toland case, and that makes me happy. Anything that gets me off desk duty makes me happy. Besides, they'll be going back to England soon, right?"

Oh, if he only knew . . .

"Well . . . I . . . um . . . why not?" Maggie said, then grinned and shrugged her shoulders. "They're only here on a visit, after all. If they were going to stay, I'm sure they'd have the right . . . um . . . the right papers. And they do. They do have the right papers. I'm sure there's just been some — oh. Hi, Alex. Sterling." *Go away, Alex and Sterling. Run away, run away, the coppers are after you.*

Oblivious to her mental message, Saint Just opened a large black umbrella and held it over Sterling and himself. They were both dressed in the suits they'd worn to Kirk's memorial service the day before, minus the black armbands, Alex sporting the diamond stickpin in his tie.

"Maggie," Alex said, with a small, formal inclination of his head. "*Left*-tenant."

"Blakely. Balder," Wendell said, grinning as he imitated Saint Just's bow.

Maggie wasn't so upset or so far inside her own head that she didn't notice the friction — Alex would have said "a marked friction" — between the two men. What was their problem? Could it be her? Could she have something to do with it? Two very different, yet both drop-dead gorgeous guys, squaring off, sparing, over little Maggie Kelly? Could that really happen? *Nah . . .*

"Did anyone tell you guys that you don't exist?" Wendell asked, his tone pleasant, his blue eyes steely and rather cold.

Saint Just stepped back a pace and struck a pose, his expression one of amused dismay. "Ah, dagger glances, and so early in the morning, too. Perhaps your spleen is off, *Left*-tenant? You might want to consider seeing someone about that."

"Excuse him, Lieutenant. As Saint Just always says, he's not at his best before noon, so this is simply a little early

353

morning crustiness. Very natural," Sterling said placatingly, then turned to his friend. "No need to insult the man. Right, Saint Just?"

"Yeah," Maggie said, glaring at Saint Just. "No need at all. Don't you two have somewhere to go?"

"Not until Argyle presents himself, no," Saint Just said, pulling out his pocket watch, consulting it, and pointedly ignoring their pleas for him to restrain himself. "In the meantime, perhaps the *left*-tenant would wish to elaborate on his earlier statement? I confess to being quite interested in anything he has to say. Confounded, amazed, even vaguely embarrassed to think I could care, but there it is. Please, *Left*-tenant. Expound."

"Sure. I said, you don't exist. Your names aren't in any system anywhere. No ID, no papers."

"Nonsense. We don't exist? Sterling, did you hear that? We don't exist. You're not really standing here; I'm not really speaking to you, or listening to such drivel. In fact, the good *left*-tenant must be talking to himself, because we aren't here." Saint Just smiled at Wendell. "I wonder, *Left*-tenant, if you plan to arrest us? Haul us away in chains, or whatever? Because of this, you say, lack of papers?"

"I should. But not in chains. A gag. That's what I'd really like to use."

"How droll. Maggie, the man is attempting to set himself up as a wit. Failing badly, but bravely making the attempt. I suppose we must commend him, for all his misconceptions about Sterling and me."

"So you're saying you're *not* here illegally?" Wendell asked.

"Illegally? My goodness, *Left*-tenant, you do imagine the oddest things. I am pressed for time at the moment, and will be for the next few days, but if you wish, I would be — Sterling and I both would be — more than happy to present ourselves at your constabulatory on Monday — say two o'clock? — to present you with enough paper to, um, paper something."

"Alex," Maggie gritted out.

"Two o'clock?" Wendell grinned. "You've got it."

"Oh, splendid. And might I possibly bring Miss Holly Spivak along with us? Lovely woman, if a tad pushy. She has been ringing me up almost constantly, pleading for an interview. This might be just the sort of thing that would interest her, yes? She said she wanted us to meet somewhere that there were good visuals, as

I believe she termed it. Yes, I think your place of employment would do splendidly, don't you?"

"God, Blakely, you're a pain," Wendell said with some feeling.

"No, sir, I am insulted, a reaction you do not yet appear to have grasped. And you, my dear man, are very lucky that I have lately taken a vow against all violence, although some might consider Miss Spivak a weapon of sorts."

"Okay, okay, I quit. No more questions about your ID," Wendell said, just as Maggie thought she might never breathe again. Saint Just had *offered* to show Wendell ID? Was it a bluff? Or had the man *done* something? She decided on the latter — the man had *done* something. She also decided she didn't want to know what that something was. Ever.

"Just one more thing, okay?" Wendell then asked, just as Maggie began to relax. "Just tell me what it is you two do. Sterling here has said some things that don't make sense. So humor me, okay? When you're doing what you do — what do you do?"

Maggie shifted her gaze between Wendell and Saint Just, also waiting for his answer.

"Your boorish inquisitiveness knows no

bounds, does it, *Left*-tenant? Very well, if you must know, Sterling and I are inspectors of public buildings."

Maggie snorted, then tried to turn her snort into a cough. Inspectors of public buildings? She knew what that meant. It was an old joke the Irish used to confound the English: unemployed persons, with no roof over their heads, walked the streets all day, became "inspectors of public buildings." She had to hand it to Saint Just — he could deliver a punchline with the best of them.

"Oh," Wendell said, nodding. "So you work for the city, right? London?"

"You said one more question, *Left*-tenant. Your investigative skills lack a certain delicacy, I must tell you. Too cow-handed and obvious by half. I find I cannot trust you to push on, alone, in this investigation of Mr. Toland's murder. Oh, yes, indeed, sir, you may stare, but I've decided to solve the crime leading to Toland's untimely demise, ferret out the perpetrator and bring him to justice, etcetera, etcetera. What ho, Maggie? Have I said something to upset you? I must say, that mulish expression doesn't become you. But it's of no matter. I've decided to solve the case, and so I shall."

"*You're* going to solve the case?"

"I have just recently dedicated myself to that end, *Left*-tenant, yes," Saint Just said, flicking a nonexistent bit of lint from his jacket sleeve. "In point of fact, I have already begun. I have engineered a small gathering of some of those persons associated with the late Mr. Toland, at which time we will discuss motive, opportunity, method . . . I say, perhaps you'd wish to join us? We'll be convening at three today, in Miss Kelly's apartment. You could attend, possibly learn something? Bring your little notebook?"

Maggie looked around, but saw no convenient hole in which to hide herself. "Alex," she said, her lips tight, "knock it off, okay?"

"No, no," Wendell said. "I'd like that. Really. I mean, how often do I get to watch a great mind at work. You do have a great mind, right, Blakely?"

"I should just about think so. He's as sharp as needles," Sterling said staunchly. "Why, he's solved half a dozen —"

"Sterling," Maggie interrupted, thrusting a ten-dollar bill into his hand. "Be a dear and go down to Mario's, buy me some cigarettes. Two packs. And get yourself a candy bar."

Sterling accepted the money, frowning. "But I thought you said that's where you were heading when you left the apartment. To Mario's, for cigarettes."

Now would be a good time for Maggie to keep her mouth shut, and she knew it. It would be an even better time to lie, say she'd met up with Wendell, never made it to Mario's.

But she was still so *mad.* Mad enough to tell the truth.

"I did go, but Mario kicked me out. He says I'm bad for business, and I'm never to come back in his store. I've been *banned* from Mario's." She looked at Saint Just. "Can you believe that?"

"You were asked to vacate his establishment? Because his name was reported in the newspapers and on television, I would suppose, in reference to the mushrooms? Is that it, Maggie? You may as well tell us the whole of it."

"Not me," Maggie said, knowing she was figuratively closing the barn door way after the horse had already bolted. "I'm not saying another word. So forget it, Alex. Just forget it."

"Saint Just?" Sterling said quietly. "You've got that thing going in your cheek again. Are you all right?"

Saint Just motioned for Sterling to step back under the canopy leading from the apartment building to the street, then held the umbrella high as he tucked his cane beneath his arm. "If you'll all excuse me? I do believe Mario and I needs must have a small conversation."

"Alex, no!" Maggie called after him as he walked down the sidewalk, his back ramrod straight, his intention clear. "I don't care. Really, Alex. I don't — oh, hell. Me and my big mouth. Great. Here we go, pistols at dawn."

"Pistols?" Wendell took a step in Alex's direction, then turned back to Maggie. "You didn't really mean that, did you?"

"Mean? Me? No, of course not," Maggie said quickly, dragging her gaze away from Alex. "Sterling?"

"On my way, my dear," he said, quickly jogging after Saint Just. "After all, he might forget my candy bar, and all of that."

Which left Maggie standing with Wendell, and nothing left to do but smile at him and shrug her shoulders. "He's very protective. Alex is. Protective. I shouldn't have said anything."

Wendell scratched at the side of his head. "I don't know. I think you should have said something. You did, to me. And I should have done something about it. Paid Mario a visit, explained things. Your cousin isn't a violent man, is he? I mean, I sort of get the idea he's a little . . . but then I don't think so. I guess it's because he's English?"

Maggie coughed into her hand. "Yup, that's it. He's English. Very civilized. Not gay at all."

"Gay? I didn't say gay, did I?" Wendell said, then frowned as he looked down the street. "He's not? Too bad."

Maggie decided to ignore Wendell's last statement, although that, too, was packed away in her brain, to think about later. After shifting foot-to-foot for about a minute — or an hour — she spoke again just to break the tense silence, trying to explain herself a little while she was at it. "Alex won't hurt Mario. *I* would have hurt Mario, I think. Except I didn't. That's probably a good thing. Doctor Bob says I have a lot of suppressed violence in me, which is nonsense. I'm a total wimp. Oh, here they come already. And Sterling's carrying a bag. Wow, that didn't take long."

Maggie waited impatiently as Saint Just and Sterling leisurely made their way back up the street, then pounced when they got into earshot. "What happened? What did you say? Did you say anything? He's got to know you're with me, because we've been in there together, right? Did he try to throw you out?"

Saint Just, his cane still tucked under his arm, occupied himself in closing his umbrella, then handing it to Sterling. "So many questions, Maggie. You'll worry yourself halfway to Bedlam one of these days. And there's really nothing to report. Just two gentlemen coming to an agreement, nothing more."

"Mario? I didn't see Mario. Must have missed that when I was picking out my candy bar," Sterling said, carefully peeling the wrapper from his Milky Way. "Just Mrs. Mario." He shook his head. "Ah, you should have seen it, Maggie. Saint Just had her near to swooning."

"He *yelled* at her?"

"No, Maggie. Saint Just never yells. Goodness no. He just talked to her, bowed over her hand. That sort of thing. She gave us your cigarettes for free. Two packs. Here they are," Sterling ended, handing over the small bag.

"You were charming?" she asked Saint Just.

"Am I not always charming? And you, my dear, are once again one of Mario's most cherished customers, which includes this afternoon's gathering, for which Mrs. Mario will be preparing trays of food at no small cost," he answered, shooting his cuffs, and Maggie gave it up. What worked, worked. Saint Just as charming, worked. Ordering trays of food hadn't hurt, either.

Besides, she had already been distracted. "Oh, wow, here comes Socks. Would you look at him!"

Maggie's doorman was heading toward them at a near run, dodging the raindrops that had begun falling once more, covering his head with a section of the *Daily News*. His hair curved against his head in precise cornrows. His white shirt with full sleeves was open nearly to his waist, showing a rather impressive chest Maggie hadn't known he had. His slacks were black latex — nearly as thin as a leotard — molded tightly to every curve of his six-foot, three-inch dancer's body. He wore black high-top sneakers, and there was a red sash around his waist. He looked . . . he looked . . . He didn't look like a doorman.

Socks stopped about three feet away, spread his arms, and did a neat pirouette. "So? How do I look? I heard on the street that it's going to be a Caribbean musical. Do I look Caribbean? I got hit on three times in the subway, so I guess I look pretty good, huh? Man, I'm nervous."

"And tardy," Saint Just said, motioning for the acting doorman to hail a cab for them. "Shall we be off? Sterling? Are you coming?"

Sterling just stood there, his teeth sunk into his Milky Way, and stared at Socks. At the sound of his name, he lowered the candy bar and blinked. "Exquisite, Socks," he said in some awe. "Truly exquisite."

"Sterling!"

"Coming, Saint Just," Sterling said, his eyes still stuck on Socks — and not on his socks. "Oh, and I say, is that lip rouge? Are you wearing lip rouge?"

"Stage makeup, Mr. Balder," Socks said, motioning for Sterling to precede him to the curb. "All actors wear it."

"Oh, of course. I knew that. Just never thought I'd see a man painted up like a tart, that's all. It's very . . . becoming, Socks, really," Sterling said, and allowed himself to be helped into the backseat of the cab.

If Saint Just had been hoping for Manhattan's version of Covent Garden in its heyday, he was sadly disappointed, for the small theater — using that term loosely — was next door to being condemned, and rightly so.

The stage was no more than a raised platform. The seats were wooden folding chairs past their prime. Bare bulbs hung suspended from the ceiling. And the entire building smelled like boiled cabbage.

"Ramshackle past reclaim," Saint Just said, prodding one of the folding chairs with the tip of his cane. "Come, Argyle. We're leaving."

"What?" Socks danced in place. "Leaving? You're kidding, right? I mean, this is it. *It*. A real rehearsal hall." He clasped his hands to his bared chest. "Just think about the feet that have trod these boards. The voices that have lifted to these rafters. The *talent* that has been discovered here, born here, taken its first steps to Broadway here. Leave?" He rounded on Saint Just. "Oh, no, Mr. Blakely. I'm here to worship at the shrine."

"Quite the flair for the dramatic, eh, Saint Just?" Sterling whispered, then flinched, shocked to learn that, although not aesthetically pleasing, the building didn't lack for fine acoustics, as his voice seemed to come back to him from every corner. "Oh, my. I thought it was only Socks, emoting. I think we'd better cover our mouths, step outside, and all of that, if we feel the need to be private."

Saint Just motioned with his hand, effectively shushing Sterling. "Argyle? Impressed as I am by these rather uncalled-for and yet curiously delightful raptures of yours, are you actually saying that this is a *good* place?"

Socks's head bobbed enthusiastically. "Are you kidding? I'd give my best tap shoes and half my Judy Garland collection just to stand on that stage."

"The mind boggles," Saint Just said, extracting his quizzing glass from his pocket and sticking it to his eye as he walked further into the nearly bare room to pass his gaze over the knot of people standing to the rear of the small stage. He needed to get his bearings, compose himself, be prepared to take charge, because that was what he did. "And who might those people be, Argyle?"

"The enemy, I suppose," Socks said, nervously smoothing his shirt. "I mean, the other actors here to audition. I guess I should go join them, huh?"

"Absolutely not. You are a rare talent, Argyle, not one of the hoi polloi," Saint Just said, holding out his cane to block Socks's advance. "We will wait upon Mr. Leighton. However, you might wish to fortify yourself to the likelihood that I will not allow you to perform in such sad surroundings. Kean would not have done so. Siddons would not have done so."

"Who?" Socks asked, frowning. "Oh, hey, it's cool. Here comes Mr. Leighton now, and he's got some other guys with him. Wait — yes! Ohmigod, I'm going to faint. That's him. That's the director, Frank Fortune! Oh, man, this is going to be big. I mean *big*. This one could go to Broadway."

"Yes, yes, restrain yourself, Argyle. We don't need Mr. Fortune. Mr. Fortune needs us. Remember that, please. Now, if you'll excuse me, I do believe I'll go speak with Mr. Leighton. Argyle, perhaps you could join the others on the stage now, just to be polite."

"Gotcha," Socks said, and trotted down the aisle, his rather impressive hindquarters making a statement of their own encased in the tight spandex, and bounded onto the stage.

"Like an overgrown puppy, entirely too eager to please," Saint Just said to Sterling, sighing. "Yes, well, I suppose it is time to drop a few hints in Leighton's ear about Sir Andrew and whomever else I can remember. Oh, yes. Wildhorn. I should probably let that name casually dribble off my tongue as well. So fatiguing, this subterfuge, but necessary."

"I'll wait here, if you don't mind. I tend to color up when you start spouting shocking rappers, and I wouldn't want to give the game away," Sterling said. Saint Just nodded and went off to beard Leighton in his own den, as it were.

"Ah, Leighton," he said insinuating himself into the group of four that was standing in the only other aisle in the jungle of folding chairs. "Are you prepared to be dazzled? We have another appointment in an hour, you understand. Wildhorn. Couldn't put him off. Rather pushy of the man, don't you think? But Argyle seems impressed. Good morning, gentlemen," he added quickly, bowing to them. "Introductions, Leighton, if you please."

David Leighton curled his upper lip and jerked a thumb at Saint Just. "This is the guy I was telling you about. Blakely, I think. He's repping the big black kid."

"I beg your pardon," Saint Just said, stiffening. "I represent Argyle Jackson. Dancer. Singer. Actor. That's sufficient definition, don't you believe?"

"Yeah, whatever," Leighton said, and Saint Just detected the odor of liquor on the man's breath. Did the man gargle with the stuff, that he used it so early in the morning? Pitiful. Shively drank, as he recalled, and that was what had led him to murder Quigley. Never turn your back to a man who drinks strong spirits before noon. "Alex Blakely — Josh Norton and Rick Raines, my partners for *Hot Night in the Tropics*. And Frank Fortune. I don't have to tell you who he is, right?"

"Indeed, no. Your fame precedes you, Mr. Fortune. Good morning, gentlemen," Saint Just repeated, bowing again. "A delight, I'm sure. Now, shall we be on with it? What is it you propose for my door— er, client? We will only consider a substantial role in any production, of course."

"It's an ensemble cast," Frank Fortune told him. "No names, no stars. If you don't like it, leave it."

"All right," Saint Just said smoothly, looking deep into Frank Fortune's eyes. "We'll be leaving it. Good day, gentlemen."

He'd barely gotten his cane tucked under his arm when Leighton put a hand on his arm. "Ah, come on, Blakely. Cut the crap. We know what you're doing. Trying to up the ante." Still holding onto Saint Just's arm, he looked at the stage, where Socks was standing center stage, his hands on his hips, looking around the theater. "God, if I'm right . . . Okay, here it is. First we see what he's got, and then we talk. That's the best I can do. Frank? You okay with that?"

"I'm okay with anything that gets me out of here by noon," the director said, pulling one of the folding chairs into the aisle and sitting down, facing the stage. "Just get this thing moving."

"Okay?" Leighton asked Saint Just, who was looking down at his sleeve, at the producer's hand on his sleeve. "Oh. Sorry," Leighton said, letting go. "Man, you're weird, you know. Were you really going to walk?"

"Saunter," Saint Just corrected. "I much prefer to saunter. Now, if you'll excuse me, I believe I'd also much rather sit with my good friend, Mr. Balder. A man eats, drinks, and goes to the theater with friends."

"How did it go?" Sterling asked a few moments later, as Saint Just took up his seat in one of the folding chairs. "Have they hired Socks?"

"Not yet, but they will," Saint Just said, unbuttoning his suit jacket and easing himself against the back of the chair. "His color seems to interest them. I'm not sure if I like that, but I understand it. The Caribbean, and all of that, I suppose. Ah, here we go."

Leighton took charge of the audition, walking to the front of the theater and inclining his head to the young woman standing next to a large black box.

"You, the black kid. Yeah, you. Did you bring your own music?"

Socks shot a worried look toward Saint Just. "Um . . . no, sir. Nobody told me . . ."

"Okay, okay. Mimi, whaddya got? Got any *West Side Story*? Right. Crank it up. Go ahead, kid."

The woman called Mimi hunted through a small suitcase filled with tapes, located what she wanted, and inserted it in the black box.

"Oh, a stereo, like Maggie's," Saint Just said to himself. "All right. This makes sense. I had wondered where Leighton hid the orchestra."

"Shhh!" Sterling warned. "Socks is going to sing."

"My apologies, Sterling," Saint Just said, stifling a smile as he folded his hands across his chest, prepared to enjoy himself. He was already enjoying himself. There was nothing quite so exhilarating as watching a man like Leighton grovel. With any luck, he'd see it again, shortly.

Socks sang for about a minute, no more, before Leighton drew a finger across his neck, signaling Mimi to cut the music. "Okay, that's good. And you dance?"

"Yes, sir," Socks said eagerly. "Tap, some ballet. Modern, jazz. I did a little Fosse, um, in community college."

"Good," Leighton said, turning away from the stage, and Saint Just came to attention. That was it? That was all?

"Oh, yeah, one more thing, Jackson," Leighton said, looking straight at Saint Just. Smiling at Saint Just. "Strip off for us. Down to the skin."

Sterling grabbed Saint Just's arm. "What did he say? Saint Just? Did he say — oh, my Lord, would you look! No, don't look. Stop him, Saint Just. Please say he's never going to — good Lord. The boy's taking off his clothes."

Saint Just kept his attention on Leighton, who was making his way toward him, a rather nasty grin on his face. "Leighton," he said as the man sat down beside him. "You're about to explain something to me?"

"What? You never heard of *Oh! Calcutta!* on your side of the *pond? The Fully Monty?* And don't forget Nicole Kidman, right?

Nudity sells. After all, we're doing a *hot* night in the tropics, remember? Your boy's big, so I'm hoping . . . ah, well, shit. Maybe we do have a star here."

" 'Pon my word," Sterling breathed in awe, sitting forward and staring at the stage, his eyes wide, as if he needed to stretch his eyelids in order to see all that appeared before him. "I don't believe I've ever seen anything quite like that . . ."

Saint Just slanted his gaze at the stage, to where Socks was standing, as naked as he came into the world, and blessed with the most enormous piece of equipment. Truly remarkable. Outstanding. Literally.

Then he turned to Leighton, amazing himself with his own sangfroid in the face of such an enormous . . . surprise. "Whatever you'd planned to pay Argyle, Leighton, I believe the ante, as you termed it, just went up."

CHAPTER 15

What to do, what to do. She could write. Right. With her imagination on Stun? She didn't think so.

She could clean up the place, wash out the refrigerator, straighten the linen closet, put away the rest of her winter clothes. Yeah, sure.

Go shopping. Take a bubble bath.

Organize her file cabinet, coordinate her research, index her file cards. Now there was a joke.

So. What to do, what to do.

She could eat everything in the kitchen, then call out for pizza.

She had to do something, or else she'd do that other thing, and she wasn't going to do that other thing, not ever again.

She was strong. She was woman. Watch her evade.

Maggie walked to the stereo, turned it on, stepped back and began banging her head to the beat as Garth Brooks's voice blared into the room. She danced to the center of the carpet, wailed along with him.

Okay. This was something. She was doing something.

Snapping her fingers, shaking her head, two-stepping with her invisible partner. Losing herself in the music, the beat, the fun of the song. Slowing down as the music slowed . . . moving her hips suggestively . . . waiting for the windup, grinning at the guitar riff, doing a little Twist, a little Swim, a little Mashed Potatoes.

"Ba-da, ba-da, ba-da." She danced back over to the stereo, hit the button, started the song again, danced back to the center of the room, getting breathless as she sang, danced, made faces that looked almost painful. Eyes closed, she raised her arms high above her head; her hands drawn up into fists hammered at the air as she swiveled her hips. "Ain't going down 'til the sun comes — *hey!* What happened?"

She looked over toward the desk, to see Saint Just standing there, smiling at her almost indulgently, his finger still on the Power button. She stood there for a few seconds, blinking at him, then realized her arms were still up in the air and quickly brought them down, tugged on the hem of her T-shirt.

Busted. Busted, and embarrassed. Mortified.

"When did you get back?" she asked, her heart still pounding, her breathing slightly labored. She collapsed onto the couch, wishing she lived alone, on a mountaintop. In Tibet.

"Just now," Saint Just said, and Sterling gave her a small wave as he headed for the kitchen. "Exercising?"

Maggie bent her head and scratched at the back of her neck. "Yeah. Exercising, exorcising. Pick your description."

"You do it very well," Saint Just said, pouring her a glass of lemonade, as she'd begun keeping cans of the stuff in the liquor cabinet, so she wouldn't become an alcoholic, with Saint Just offering her wine every five damn minutes. "You always have."

"You've seen me do this before? Oh, shit, of course you have." She slapped her hands against her knees and stood up. "Well, if you'll excuse me now, I have to go kill myself."

"Don't you want to know how Argyle's audition turned out?"

She sat back down, looked at him. He was preening. Nothing obvious — he wasn't waving a sign saying, "I'm the greatest!" or anything like that. But he was pleased. He had this certain smile when he was pleased. A special twinkle in those killer blue eyes. She should know, she'd spent enough years describing both. "He got the part? Really? What is it, exactly?"

Some of the gleam went out of Saint Just's eyes. "I'm not familiar with all the particulars, and the production isn't, as Leighton termed it, a sure thing. This is only a workshop, where they will try out different scenarios, scenes, whatever. It's early days yet, with a lot still to be determined."

"Uh-huh," Maggie said, waving a hand at him, signaling that she wanted to hear more. She also wanted to see more of that strange flush that had invaded Saint Just's cheeks. She'd never written him a tendency to blush. "And what's Argyle's role? So far, that is?"

Saint Just busied himself pouring a glass of wine. "He's . . . he's to be the Lord of the Tropics, I believe," he said, then lowered his voice, so that Maggie had to lean toward him to hear him. "The Love Lord of the Tropics."

"The — the *Love Lord?*" Maggie grinned. "Oh, I gotta hear this. What does the Love Lord do?"

Saint Just took a sip of wine and placed the glass on Maggie's desk. "The usual, I suppose. He sings, he dances. He dances quite a lot, actually." He averted his head.

"Lots of jumping, leaping . . . that sort of thing."

"Uh-huh," Maggie said, still waving a hand at him, trying to draw out the rest of it. "Jumping, leaping. That's good, right?"

"Argyle seems to think so, yes," Saint Just said, then began fiddling with the stereo. "Is this the recording that includes the song 'Friends in Low Places'? I rather enjoy that one. It has a certain . . . panache."

"Alex? There's something you aren't telling me, isn't there? I mean, you should be doing some jumping and leaping of your own, getting Socks this chance. Really, I never thought you'd pull it off. David Leighton can be such a prick sometimes."

Saint Just, who had been taking another sip of wine, coughed and choked for a moment, then said, "Much as I am the first to encourage you to speak your mind freely, I do believe I would appreciate it greatly if you could restrain yourself from using that particular word."

"Alex? What's going on? Something's going on, isn't it?"

"Nonsense. Argyle auditioned for a role. He was taken on by Leighton and this other man, Frank Fortune. Silly name.

There's really nothing else to —"

"Hello, Maggie," Sterling interrupted. "Sorry I didn't do the pretty earlier, but I was in a rush to get myself a glass of water. Thirsty work, sitting around that barn of a place for hours. Did Saint Just tell you about Argyle?"

"I told her, yes," Saint Just cut in swiftly.

"Isn't that just the outside of enough? Parading around a stage, for all the world and his uncle, stark, staring naked."

Maggie sat back in the corner of the couch, propped her elbow on the arm of it, and dropped her chin onto her hand as she looked at Saint Just. She waggled her eyebrows a time or two. A slow smile curved her mouth. An evil smile.

"Argyle's going to perform naked? Gee, you didn't mention that, Alex. Funny how it slipped your mind."

The smile spread. "Jumping . . . leaping. How did he look? I'm trying to visualize this, you understand, strictly from an intellectual viewpoint. Naked. Jumping. Not to mention leaping. Can't forget the leaping."

"Stubble it, Maggie," Saint Just said imperiously, then ruined it all by nervously running a finger under his shirt collar. "It would seem that the only reason Leighton agreed to the audition was because Argyle is a black man, and he'd hoped that he would be . . . that he would be . . ."

"Hung. Big feet, big —" Maggie said, then bit her bottom lip. "Sorry. It's just that I know how David Leighton thinks. What does Socks have to say about that?"

"He's pleased," Saint Just said, getting himself back under control once more. "He's not unaware of Leighton's base reasons for taking him on, but he says that any way in the door is better than standing outside it, looking in. Argyle is a pragmatist, I believe. And he is confident that his talent — his singing, his dancing — will be noticed and praised."

"Oh, yeah," Maggie said, trying not to giggle. "They'll notice his singing and dancing. But I'm betting they'll really notice the leaping." And then she threw back her head and roared, watching as Saint Just's lips drew into a tight line. "Oh, lighten up, Alex. This is New York."

"Sodom and Gomorrah, more like," Sterling muttered, shaking his head. "Embarrassing, that's what it was. I didn't know where to look."

"Ah, poor Sterling," Maggie said, sobering. "I imagine it was a bit of a shock to your sensibilities, wasn't it?"

"Enough to send a fellow to the dogs directly," Sterling agreed, just as the buzzer sounded. "I'll get that, Maggie."

Saint Just pulled his watch from his pocket and consulted it. "Only two-thirty. Perhaps it's the food trays?"

"Nope. They're already in the fridge. Tuna salad, potato salad, some shrimp salad. And one other thing. Alex? Did you forget to mention something about your conversation with Mario's wife?"

"Possibly," he said, draining his glass of wine. "We were rather rushed, what with the audition and all of that. Why?"

"Why? Oh, I don't know, Alex. I know it was just a little thing. Barely worth mentioning. Just one small speech to Mario's wife's women's group. Some free, autographed books. I can see how it slipped your mind."

"Yes, of course," Saint Just said, waving away her words. "I do seem to recall something like that. Sterling? If you'd get the door? Someone of our summoned group appears overanxious to appear, plead his or her ignorance and innocence."

Maggie got up from the couch and walked over to give Saint Just's shoulder a small push. "The Rainy Day Readers and Salsa Dancers. That's the name of the group. And if *they* perform naked, I'm going to have to hurt you, Alex, I really am."

"The depths of your gratitude underwhelm me, Maggie," Saint Just said, just as Sterling opened the door and Bernice Toland-James breezed into the room.

"Darlings, how do I look?" Bernie said, turning in a slow, full circle, her arms outstretched.

"Black-and-white stripes, Bernie?" Maggie said, shaking her head as she took in her friend's broadly striped pants and matching thigh-length top, her mass of frizzed red hair. "You look like Donna Karan's version of a convict."

"Perfect! Just the look I was after," Bernie said with a toss of her frizzed red hair, collapsing into one of the couches. "Sterling, be a dear, and pour me something alcoholic. At least three fingers of it. I want to be well and truly blitzed before they haul me away to the slammer."

"A little dramatic, aren't you?" Maggie said, picking up her glass of lemonade as she sat down beside the editor. "Besides," she said, squinting, "I think you're making me dizzy."

"Dramatic, Maggie. Oh, I don't think so. My attorney called me an hour ago to tell me the police were there this morning, checking up on the will. I have m-o-t-i-v-e, with a capital M. My attorney stalled, demanded a search warrant or writ or some other legal mumbo-jumbo, but I have to appear on Monday, to make a statement or something. I mean, I don't *have* to, but we all know how bad it looks if I don't cooperate. Can we all say Patsy Ramsey? Leave it to Kirk to screw me from the grave."

"Imagine Kirk leaving you the Toland fortune, not to mention Toland Books," Maggie said. "I would have thought you'd be grateful."

"Oh, and I am, I am," Bernie replied, taking a glass half full with brown liquid and ice from Sterling. "Thank you, you sweetheart. Will you visit me on Sundays? Bring me chocolate torte with a file in it?" She took a large sip of scotch. "God. I can't believe this is happening. But, hey, at least I'll be able to pay for a top defense lawyer, right? And pay myself a seven-figure advance to write the story of my trial — if I'm acquitted, that is. Can't profit from a crime, and all of that." She lifted the glass again, her trembling hand betraying her show of bravado. "Cheers."

Maggie looked at Saint Just, who was standing behind the other couch, watching

Bernie. "Alex? Do you really think Bernie's in trouble?"

He tapped a finger against one lean cheek, then said, "Possibly. As Cicero said so well, 'Who stood to gain?' "

"And I'll drink to that, too," Bernie said, tipping her glass slightly toward Saint Just, then looking at Maggie. "Follow the money, right, Alex? And the money leads straight to *moi*."

"You most probably are the odds-on favorite among the bettors at the moment, yes," Saint Just said with maddening calm.

Maggie concentrated, picking up the thread of Saint Just's comment. "And everybody knows you didn't like him, that he ran around on you the whole fifteen years you two were married, then left you for that bimbo."

"That's it, Maggie, keep piling it on. Next someone will say they saw me pinching off Kirk's air hose while he was in the hospital."

"I'm sorry, Bernie, but I'm beginning to see your point. And John did disappear mysteriously five years ago. Have they asked about that?"

"Oh? More? Maggie, you ought to call the District Attorney's office, tell them everything you know. I'll bet they'd love to hear from you. John? Jesus."

"Ladies, please, if you would cease and desist?" Saint Just interrupted. "Now, I have summoned everyone here today to discuss just what we are discussing now, but I'd rather we wait until everyone is — John? Who, may I ask, is John?"

"Whom, I think, but don't quote me. And it's John Livingstone James," Bernie said, holding up her glass for a refill. "Husband number *dos,* if we're counting. He went sailing one day, and didn't come back. Two more years, and he's officially dead and I officially inherit the two pennies he had to rub together when he disappeared. His debts, I got right away. Two dead husbands. Jesus, I should own stock in widows' weeds, shouldn't I?"

Maggie blew out a breath. "Bernie, nobody thinks you killed John. He went out in bad weather, that's all. I doubt Lieutenant Wendell will even mention it. John's disappearance has nothing to do with Kirk's murder."

Bernie grinned up at Saint Just. "Isn't she cute? Writes murder mysteries, you know. A steel-trap mind. And all the naiveté of a two-year-old. You can bring a gal to the Big Apple, but you can't get the New Jersey out of her soul."

"New Jersey isn't the back of beyond, you know," Maggie said, offended. "We're sophisticated."

"Uh-huh. Nickel slots and *The Sopranos.* I'm all impressed." Bernie picked up the pack of cigarettes from the coffee table and held them out to Maggie. "Mind if I borrow one?"

"Go ahead," Maggie told her. "I slapped on another patch about an hour ago. I quit." She glanced up at Saint Just. "I've even started exercising."

"Hah!" Bernie flicked the lighter, drew in a lungful of smoke, blew it out. "Hide the knives, boys. Maggie's quitting again. Alex, who else is coming to this little soiree? I got The Trigger to agree, right after pointing out that refusal wasn't an option. God, I love being boss. Probate may still be a long way off, but Nelson got the point, believe me. It's be nice to Bernie or hit the bricks."

"Splendid," Saint Just said. "Miss Clarice Simon will also be here, along with Mrs. Leighton, and *Left*-tenant Wendell. I'm convinced there are others who should be here, but as I know none of them, this is at least a start."

Sterling's deep sigh had everyone looking at him as he sat enveloped in sofa cushions on the facing couch. "It's so sad," he said on yet another sigh. "The man is barely dead, and yet here we are, moving on with our lives. One minute laughing, talking, and the next . . . snuffed like a candle. It makes a person think, wonder. Was he happy? Had he accomplished all that he wished to accomplish? Did he have any regrets?"

Maggie blinked back sudden tears. "You're right, Sterling. We've gotten so caught up in solving his murder, that we've pretty much forgotten about poor Kirk."

"What?" Bernie said, looking at Maggie, Sterling, and Saint Just, who were all looking at her, waiting for her reaction. "Now you want me to be a hypocrite, sit here bawling my eyes out? I'm not glad he's dead. I was married to him, re-member? But I also hated his cheating guts. He died, folks, but that doesn't auto-matically qualify him for sainthood. Maggie? He cheated on you, too, right? Are you telling me you're in *mourning* for the guy?"

"No, not exactly," Maggie admitted, eying the pack of cigarettes, trying her best to surreptitiously inhale some secondhand smoke. It smelled like ambrosia. "Kirk wasn't the nicest guy. Still, he was cut down right in the prime of his life. It's sad."

Sterling nodded and said, "It's a worriment, isn't it? Thinking you'll live forever, or at least for a good long time, and then, suddenly, you could be gone. Back to where you came from. And without doing so many things you wanted to do. I mean, what's the sense of prudence and abstinence, if you could be gone — poof! — in a heartbeat?" He worked his way out of the cushions and stood up. "Excuse me, if you please, ladies. There's a piece of cake left in the kitchen. I wasn't going to indulge, but that would be a regret, wouldn't it?"

Maggie watched him go, biting her bottom lip. She hadn't realized it until now, but Sterling had to be concerned that he might not be here permanently, that something could happen, some glitch in whatever cosmic blip had allowed his and Saint Just's appearance, and the two of them could zap right back into her books, her mind — and out of her apartment. Poor guy. "I think perhaps I should go talk to him?" she said to Saint Just.

"Sterling seeks his own comfort — in this case, a three-layer banana cake from Mario's," Saint Just said just as the buzzer went yet again. "Ah, more suspects —

guests, that is. Good. I'm eager to begin."

Maggie rolled her eyes. "Try to contain yourself, okay, Alex? This isn't a parlor game."

He gifted her with a small bow. "I shall be a pattern card of discreet sensibility, my dear lady," he said as he pushed the button on the plate at the door, giving his permission to have their guests sent up in the elevator. "If you ladies will do your part, which is to sit quietly and observe, I would be most appreciative."

Maggie curled her lip at him, automatically reaching for her pack of cigarettes before remembering that she'd just quit smoking. "Oh, screw it," she said, ripping off the patch she'd only been wearing for about an hour. "Who am I kidding? I can't quit now. Not with Sherlock fricking Holmes in my living room."

Half an hour later, Bernice was doing her best to become the life and soul of the party — drinking her late lunch, smoking Maggie's cigarettes, and hanging on Saint Just's arm as if she couldn't remain upright without his support.

Saint Just allowed it, because strong spirits often make for loose lips, and if Bernice had anything interesting to say, he wanted to be close enough to hear it. Because he needed clues, any clues at all, and Bernice had been married to the victim, had inherited a considerable fortune from the victim.

Still, he was hard pressed to believe the woman guilty of anything other than an appalling lack of concern for her own self-preservation. She'd already toasted Kirk's memory three times, none of those toasts particularly prudent, especially: "Here's to funky fungi. Drink up, everybody!"

Now, as the rest of their small company was finishing up their meal of cold salads and seeded rolls, Bernice reached into Saint Just's pocket and pulled out his quizzing glass, draping it over her head.

"Here, now, Bernice," he scolded, "I'd rather you didn't do that. I feel positively naked without my glass."

Bernice gave him a sloppy smile. "Not yet, gorgeous. Here," she said, reaching for his shirt, "Let me help."

"Okay, playtime's over," Maggie said, peeling Bernice off Saint Just and leading her toward the hallway. "Time for a little nap, sweetheart." She looked back over her shoulder. "I hope you're happy, Alex. Look what you've made her do."

"Me?" Saint Just said, pressing both

hands to his chest. "The woman is a dedicated drinker, without my help. What did I do to — wait. She's got my glass. I need my glass."

"Yeah, yeah, you need your props," Maggie said as Bernie burst into song. "Get started without it, why don't you? Wing it. I'll be back as soon as I can."

Saint Just fiddled with a button on his shirt as he turned to look at the other occupants of the room. Except for the *left*-tenant, everyone was here. The moment he had been waiting for had nearly arrived, and he, the greatest sleuth Regency England had ever known, was about to take center stage.

He felt as naked as Argyle had been a scant two hours ago.

He had no lines. He hadn't a clue. There was no outline, no synopsis. There was no Maggie. None of her ideas. How did he begin? Whom did he speak to first? Could he do this?

Of course he could do this. Was there ever any question? He was the Viscount Saint Just, hero extraordinaire. He could do anything.

He could, for one, head for the liquor cabinet, aware that he could not overindulge like Bernice Toland-James, that becoming pot-valiant would aid nothing. Still, as Samuel Johnson had said, "Claret is the liquor for boys, port for men; but he who aspires to be a hero must drink brandy."

"Sterling? A brandy, if you please," he said as his friend was pouring himself a glass of lemonade. "And then we shall begin, as I do not wish to wait on the *left*-tenant any longer. Ah, yes, thank you, my good friend. And here comes Maggie with my quizzing glass. Splendid."

"Saint Just?"

"Hmmm?" Saint Just said, sipping from the snifter.

"You seem . . . I don't know. A trifle flustered?"

"Nonsense, Sterling," Saint Just said, lifting his chin. "I confess to be slightly disappointed that Bernice is no longer one of our party, but I will simply have to push on, won't I?"

"God's teeth, I think I've got it! You don't know what to say, do you?" Sterling asked quietly. "You don't have the faintest idea. You called for this gathering because that's what you always do, but now you have nothing to say. How embarrassing. Perhaps if we were to appeal to Maggie for her assistance? She is the one with the imagination, and all of that?"

"Appeal to Maggie? I should say not," Saint Just scoffed, neatly catching the quizzing glass she tossed in his direction before she did a sharp U-turn toward the game table and the trays of food loaded on it. He watched as she grabbed a roll, slammed a large scoop of tuna salad on it, *smushed* the closed bun unmercifully with the heel of her hand, then bit down on the abused creation as she glared at him. "This may not be a good time to appeal to her for anything."

Passing his gaze around the room, he paused at Tabitha Leighton, smiling slightly as he watched Maggie's agent trying to avoid Wellington, who seemed to wish to be attached to her hip. Maggie had explained that Mrs. Leighton was allergic to cats, a circumstance both Wellie and Napper seemed to sense with some glee as they alternately jumped on her lap, walked the length of the back of the couch behind her, and rubbed against her legs. At the moment, Mrs. Leighton was shooing Wellington with one hand while opening a packet of pills with the other.

Saint Just liked Tabitha Leighton, although he'd yet to take her up on her invitation to address her as Tabby. Why a woman would encourage such a silly appellation he would never know, but then, why a woman with any sense at all would remain bracketed to a supercilious twit like David Leighton was also beyond him. There just was no accounting for the vagaries of women when their hearts were involved.

That thought took him, quite logically, in his opinion, back to Bernice Toland-James. Now there was a woman who did not allow her heart to be touched. Not anymore. Kirk Toland had run roughshod over her heart ten years ago, and her second marriage hadn't sounded any happier. Although Maggie had vowed that her friend didn't usually drink quite so much as she had these past days, Saint Just couldn't help but wonder if she drank to cover her still easily injured heart, or to hide from her crime. *Crimes,* he corrected, remembering the disappearing John Livingstone James.

Except that Bernice was Maggie's closest friend. He wasn't quite sure why, but to Saint Just, that took Bernice out of the running as a suspect.

Odd. He had thought he was one of Maggie's Yes-Definitelies, fashioned from the hopeful part of her that was sure, confident. Now he realized he must be one of those hybrid sorts she'd skimmed over so casually. Damn inconvenient time for the Well-Maybe part of him to show up, to confuse him with sentiment.

He took another sip of brandy. That settled it; Bernice Toland-James was back in the running.

Now. Who else? And why was he hiding his deductive mind under a bushel, as it were? The Viscount Saint Just did not sit and stew, worry and wonder. He *acted*. He strode to the center of the room, commanded everyone's attention — not even needing words to do so, just his presence was enough — and set about voicing theories, watching, waiting, for reactions from his audience of suspects.

Yes, that was how it was done, how Maggie — he — had always done it. That was how he would do it now.

Putting down his snifter, Saint Just moved to stand in the centermost part of the room, which happened to be between the two couches, just to one end of the coffee table. He struck a pose, waited, watching as Nelson Trigg frowned, consulted the gold watch on his wrist; as mousey Clarice Simon stood in front of the bookshelf, reading the titles of Maggie's research books; as Tabitha Leighton sneezed and blew her nose; as Sterling made himself yet another shrimp salad sandwich; as Maggie curled up in one corner of her favorite couch, wearing a pained expression that did not bode well for her cooperation in his investigation.

None of them, not even Sterling, paid him a whit of attention. Lords and ladies were easier, definitely.

There was nothing else for it; he'd have to speak first, draw them all in with his brilliance, his suppositions, his deductions.

And wasn't it a bleeding pity that he had so few of them.

"If you'll please direct your attention to —"

The buzzer sounded and Sterling, who was standing closest to the door, told Argyle to send up their last visitor, the *left*-tenant.

That had been a mistake, inviting the man, all but daring him to appear. Saint Just wished to be taken seriously, and the lieutenant seemed to view him as a joke, the sort of comic relief that was supposed to be the role assigned to Sterling.

"You were saying, Alex?" Maggie prodded, licking her fingers as she finished her sandwich.

"We'll await the *left*-tenant's pleasure," Alex told her with a small, formal inclination of his head that, he was sure, she could interpret as the reprimand he meant it to be. Surely the woman didn't want her own creation to fall flat on his face?

"Yes, let's wait for the lieutenant," Maggie said, grinning. "So he can pull out his *little notebook* and write down all your brilliance. Isn't that right, Alex?"

All right, so she did want him to fall flat on his face. That was gratitude for you. "Sterling? The door?"

A moment later, Lieutenant Steve Wendell walked into the room, looking pleased with himself . . . and dressed for an afternoon on a couch somewhere, swilling beer and watching the baseball game. Rumpled khaki slacks, a navy T-shirt with the words *Cops Do It Better In Blue* emblazoned on the front, and his usual unkempt hair and boyish smile. He made Alex's teeth ache, especially when he directed that boyish smile straight at Maggie.

Wendell then looked around the room, his gaze finally landing on Saint Just. "Damn. Looks like the show's already started. Did I miss much?"

"*Left*-tenant," Alex said shortly. "So very glad that you're eager to listen and learn, as quite obviously you didn't come here to be amusing."

"No," Wendell said, his smile growing slowly, moving all the way up to his eyes. "I came here to be amused. So far, so good."

"Okay, even I'm going to drink to that one," Maggie said, abandoning her lemonade for a trip to the liquor cabinet and a glass of wine.

"What am I missing here?" Nelson Trigg asked, his brow furrowed, his gaze searching the room. "I thought we came here to talk about Kirk. And where's Bernie? This was her damn dumb-ass idea, wasn't it?"

Saint Just shook his head and sighed. "In the words of Publicus Syrus, Trigg, 'Let a fool hold his tongue and he will pass for a sage.' I suggest you consider that option."

Trigg put down his wineglass with some force, nearly snapping the stem. "You know, Saint Just, I've had just about enough of you. I'm leaving. I didn't want to be here in the first place. Clarice, are you coming?"

Sterling, obviously knowing his lines, and his reason for existence as it had been for the past five books, stepped in front of the door, effectively blocking Trigg's exit. "Please reconsider, Mr. Trigg. Saint Just has promised to be brilliant. You wouldn't want to miss it, now would you?"

"What is this?" Trigg asked, glaring at Maggie. "Is this one of your stupid writer tricks? Gather the suspects, point an accusing finger? And *I'm* a suspect? The hell I am!"

"Well, why not you, Nelson?" Bernice said as she leaned a shoulder against the wall at the entrance to the living room, her makeup rather smeared, her eyes a little bleary, but her mind probably clearer than anyone save Saint Just would believe. "Or aren't the rumors true?"

"Rumors? What the fuck are you talking about?"

"Oh, I don't know," Bernice said, brushing against Saint Just's shoulder as she slowly made her way to the couch and sat down beside Maggie. "Something about lots of trips to Atlantic City? A few bad runs at the craps table? Probably nothing to it, right?"

"I gamble. So what? And what would that have to do with Kirk's murder?"

Bernice shrugged her elegant shoulders. "I was married to the man for fifteen years, Nelson, which includes the year when his father died and Toland Books collected on the five million dollar insurance policy that had been taken out on the old man. Now, the way I see it, there's bound to be the same sort of insurance policy on Kirk, payable to the company on his death. If I was short on money, and needed to take a little from the company to cover my debts, a really great way to balance the books again would be with a lump-sum payment handed right to me, the business manager, to divvy up as I thought best. Am I making any sense here? I have a bitch of a headache."

Trigg stood up very straight and pushed out his chest. "I invite anyone to look at the books, and I defy anyone to find anything wrong with them. And I highly resent being insulted in this way. Embezzler? Murderer? Kirk Toland was my friend. It seems everyone has forgotten that. I'm as anxious to find his murderer as anyone else." He turned to Wendell. "Lieutenant? May I go now?"

"What, leaving so soon?" Saint Just drawled, eying Trigg through his quizzing glass. "I am, of course, devastated, although I do believe I shall be able to refrain from having to lay myself down on my bed, prostrate with sorrow at your defection."

"Fuck you, Saint Just. Lieutenant?"

Wendell, his back turned as he stood at the table, gave a lazy wave of his hand as he finished making a sandwich. "Hey, it's not my inquisition. If Saint Just says you can go, who am I to stop you? I'm just here for the tuna salad." Then he turned, smiling. "So we can look at the books, Ms. Toland-James?"

"Bernie, don't answer that," Trigg said hastily, and Saint Just watched a dark flush run up the back of the man's neck. "The last thing we need is for the police to be poking about in a family business."

"The man does have a point," Saint Just said consideringly. "However, and what is a great deal more to the point, as it is not *his* family's business, I would think that the new proprietor — that would be you, Bernice — has the right to make such decisions."

"I'll resign first," Nelson declared as he stared at Bernie.

"Oh, shut up," Bernice said, pressing both hands against her temples. "Nelson, you're a shit, but you've always been a competent shit, according to Kirk. I'm not going to invite the police into our books. Besides, the auditors will be there in about two weeks. At least that's what the lawyer told me. It's customary, or something like that, to run an audit at times like these. Surely, Nelson, you aren't going to object to that?"

Saint Just counted silently, *one . . . two . . . three,* before Trigg said, "Of course not, Bernie. I'll begin getting everything ready. And now, if you don't mind, I really do want to get back to work. Not everyone leaves the office at noon on Fridays, you know. As it is, I'll be working the weekend as well. Clarice?"

Clarice, who had been doing her best to be invisible, lowered her head and began walking toward the door.

"Oh, give her the rest of the day off, for crying out loud," Bernice said, sinking back against the couch cushions. "Clarice, please stay. Besides, I want to hear what Alex here has to say about everything, everyone. It's just like one of Maggie's books, and could be fun. You like murder mysteries, Clarice, right? So stay. But you're excused, Nelson. Go away. Please."

Sterling bowed the man out the door, then returned to his plate of food. "Never before met a man who gave me such a bellyache," he said, shaking his head. "I say, Saint Just, do you think he doth protest too much, and all of that? You know, like Shively?"

"Possibly, Sterling," Saint Just said, lazily swinging his quizzing glass as confidence flowed through him. He could do this. He was *born* to do this. He *would* do this: be a hero, save the day. "I do believe I may decide to pay a call on our friend Trigg tomorrow, beard him in his den, as it were, since he said he'd be at the offices. The man bears watching."

"I believe that might be my job," Wendell pointed out neutrally.

"Ah, yes, the so estimable *left*-tenant," Saint Just said, turning his glass on the man. "Then you consider Mr. Trigg a suspect?"

"Nope, but it's still my job to follow up leads, not yours. Right now, my money's on the lady with the money," Wendell said, jerking a thumb toward Bernice, who slid low on the couch, moaning.

"I see," Saint Just responded, motioning for Maggie to remain silent, as the dear girl looked ready to pounce. Still, how nice that she might be taking the *left*-tenant in a bad odor. "What an astonishingly nonsensical conclusion. And you're sticking to that conclusion buckle and thong, I suppose?"

"For now, yes, but I am here, Blakely. If you want to convince me I'm wrong, I'm all ears."

Saint Just stopped just short of preening. "Yes, you most certainly are, but one should not feel compelled to apologize for their physical failings."

CHAPTER 16

Maggie didn't let go of Saint Just's elbow until she had dragged him all the way into the kitchen, at which time she turned, glared at him, and demanded he explain himself.

"I don't understand, Maggie," he said in that maddeningly calm way of his. "I'm being who I am. Nothing more."

"You're being a jerk," Maggie shot back at him, giving him a none too gentle shove in the chest. "That's a cop out there, Alex. A *cop*. You have to stop baiting him, trotting out every insult I ever put in your mouth. Or do you really think you're helping Bernie? Investigating Kirk's murder is *his* job."

"Yes, and if I believed for even one moment that he could do it, I would be a happy man."

"Hey," Maggie said, pacing the tile floor, "think anything you want to think. Just stop *saying* it, okay? The lieutenant is being nicer than he has to be. I mean it, Alex. I think it might even be a crime to impede a police investigation, which is probably what you're doing — if he wants to stretch things a bit. So back off. Just back off."

She watched as Saint Just's jaw set, as the small tic began working in his cheek. "Alex? Don't be insulted, please. I know you mean well."

"It's what I do, Maggie. It's who I am."

Maggie rubbed at her forehead and sighed. "I know, Alex. But do you have to be such a wise-ass about it? What's wrong with you? You and the lieutenant are like cats in a sack."

"He annoys me," Saint Just said, pushing at the salt and pepper shakers so that they were aligned more neatly on the tabletop.

"He doesn't take you seriously," Maggie countered, pretty sure she was correct. "And you probably don't like the way he dresses, right? Or the way he talks?"

"Or the way he looks at you," Saint Just said quietly, then seemed to snap to attention. "Yes, Sterling?"

"Maggie. Saint Just. So sorry to interrupt, and all of that, but it's Bernice. She's a trifle up in the world —"

"Drunk," Saint Just agreed, nodding. "Go on."

"Well, yes, drunk. Although maybe not as deep in her cups as she would have everyone suppose, I think, because I caught her outpouring the last one in your ficus plant, Maggie. In any case, she is presently disporting herself in a way that . . ." He hesitated, sighing. "I suppose you'll have to see for yourself."

"Of course. Oh, and my congratulations, Sterling. I thought I'd been the only one to take note of Bernice's pitiful attempt at subterfuge. Maggie, are you coming?"

Maggie waved him on his way, not really hearing anything either he or Sterling had said. How could she, when all she could do was listen as her brain replayed Saint Just's shocking comment: "Or the way he looks at you"?

Was that what was going on between Alex and Steve — Lieutenant Wendell, that is? How difficult to believe that these two men could be like cocks scratching in the barnyard, ready to fight over her. Her. Damn.

And what was she going to do about it? How did she feel, about Alex, about Lieutenant Wen— oh, hell, about *Steve?*

She didn't have the faintest idea, Maggie realized after a full minute of intense concentration. Not the smallest idea. She only knew one thing: It was a real kick!

Shaking herself back to the moment, which effectively wiped the inane grin from her face, Maggie went back into the living room, just in time to see Saint Just helping Bernie back onto the couch, coaxing her into lying down on it.

"What happened?"

Wendell grinned. "Do you know your old movies, Miss Kelly? Mrs. Toland-James was doing a little Cagney for us. 'Top of the world, Ma, top of the world!' She was pretty good, too."

"Maggie," Bernie called out weakly, lifting an arm so that Maggie could take hold of her hand. "I'm a goner, Maggie. My life of crime has come to its ignoble end. Nothing left for me but the chair or a bullet." She lifted her head from the pillows. "Hey, copper, got a gun I can eat?"

"Shut up, Bernie, and stop pretending you're smashed, because I know you're not," Maggie pleaded, looking at Saint Just. "But she is getting hysterical. Are we done now? Can everyone please just leave, so I can take care of her?"

"No, no," Bernie protested, elbowing herself into a semi-sitting position. "Let's get it all out. All the reasons the lieutenant thinks I'm the one who killed Kirk. I want to hear them."

"Are you sure?"

"Maggie," Bernie said, levering her feet

onto the floor and pushing her frizzed mane of red hair back from her face, "I'm most definitely sure." Then she grabbed Maggie in a bear hug and whispered, "The best defense is a good offense, darling. First I learn what they have against me, and then my lawyer and I can counter it. Understand?"

Nope, the woman definitely wasn't drunk, Maggie decided as Bernie gave her a last squeeze, then let her go, already calling to Sterling to bring her another drink. "All right," Maggie said, getting to her feet. "Alex? This is what you wanted. Let's do it."

"Certainly," Saint Just said with a small inclination of his head, once more stepping to the center of the room, one hand on the small golden hilt of his quizzing glass. "*Left*-tenant? This might be the time for your notebook?"

"Sure," Wendell agreed, pulling a small, battered spiral pad from his back pocket. "Wouldn't want to miss a word."

Again, Saint Just bowed, just the faintest inclination of his handsome head. "Very well. Let us begin. Mrs. Leighton? Clarice? If you'd please take seats on this couch?"

Tabitha Leighton, stifling a yawn, sat down at once, but Clarice first had to replace a book she'd been reading before coming around the couch to sit down beside the agent.

"Perfect. I wish to preface everything by admitting that I have asked you ladies — and the now absent Mr. Trigg — here today simply because I know of no one else to invite. For all we know, the ground could be thick with suspects, those who may have wished Mr. Toland underground.

"However, all of you attended Maggie's little party, and, therefore, all of you knew that Maggie and Toland were to have dinner here that fateful night, so you all have some faint suspicion hanging over you. Suspicions we will hope to dismiss before this small gathering is dispersed."

Tabitha Leighton raised her hand. "Will it take long?" she asked, then had to cover another yawn. "These damn antihistamines put me to sleep."

Saint Just smiled, and Maggie looked at him curiously. Tabby? He considered Tabby a suspect? Why? She'd thought he'd invited Tabby and Clarice just so Trigg and Bernie wouldn't be the only ones. After all, the man did enjoy having an audience.

"In that case, shall we push on?" Saint

Just nodded to Sterling, who produced a glass of wine and offered it to him. "Thank you, my friend. Detecting is such thirsty work. All right, here we go. And, because of her deep concerns, we will begin with Bernice."

"Lucky me," Bernie said, her smile rather sickly. "Go ahead, Alex. Sock it to me."

Saint Just began to pace, keeping his gaze on Bernie's face as he uttered a single word. "Jealousy."

"Huh?" Bernie asked, shaking her head. "Me? Jealous? Jealous of what? I thought my motive was money."

"And it would have been, as the so-worthy *left*-tenant erroneously concluded," Saint Just explained, "except that, unless you're much more devious than I believe, and I am considerably less perceptive than I flatter myself to be, you had no idea until the other day at the memorial luncheon that you would inherit Toland's money, Toland's business — none of it. Did you?"

"Not a clue," Bernie said, and Maggie saw the ghost of a smile on her friend's face.

"Which leaves jealousy," Saint Just continued, and Bernie's smile evaporated. "You were married to Toland, correct?"

"So what? Everybody knows that. I dropped out of college to marry the bastard. Gave him the best fifteen years of my life, and then he dumped me. If I were going to kill him, I would have killed him then. I sure thought about it."

"You were crushed," Saint Just said, then paused to take a sip of wine. "You were a part of Toland Books, didn't want to leave. But where did that *leave* you? I would say it left you to watch as Toland married his second wife, as Toland dangled all the young women he romanced beneath your nose. That would be depressing and infuriating enough for any woman, but for a woman so concerned with her own fading youth —"

"Hey!" Bernie cut in. "Interrogate me, okay, but don't insult me."

Maggie sat silently, watching as Saint Just moved on, obviously on a roll.

"And then, just to put the capper on your humiliation, cursed man, he turned his sights on Maggie, your best friend. Quite a wedge that must have driven between you, the former wife and the beautiful, young, successful writer."

"Maggie's my friend," Bernie said, reaching out to take Maggie's hand in hers. "Kirk couldn't possibly come between us."

"You were happy for them?"

"Hell, no," Bernie said, liquor or her own nature compelling the truth when a lie would have been so much better. "Kirk was a slug. I knew he'd hurt her. But Maggie broke it off months ago."

"Which pleased you."

"I did a jig in Neiman Marcus," Bernie said, sipping her drink. "Hell, yes, it *pleased* me. Hey!" she called out, swiveling on the couch to look at Wendell. "You're scribbling in that notebook. Cut that out! Don't scribble in your notebook." She downed the remainder of her drink and stuck out her glass. "Sterling? Hit me."

Maggie pinched her lips together, tried not to laugh, and waited. Sterling didn't disappoint.

"Oh, I say, Bernice, I don't do that. I don't mean to be disobliging, always try to do my possible to be amenable, and all of that, but I really can't . . ."

"A drink, Sterling," Maggie told him, her eyes watering. "She wants you to get her another drink."

Sterling looked at Maggie, then to Bernie, then to Saint Just. "I don't have to strike her?"

"Of course not," Saint Just said soothingly. "But I would suggest a cup of your excellent coffee, Sterling. I believe Bernice would agree. Wouldn't you, Bernice?"

"Oh, all right. But one more crack about my fading youth, and I'm going to have Sterling hit *you*." She pushed herself to her feet. "Now, if you're done tearing me apart, I think I'll go lie down again. Maggie, please ask Sterling to bring the coffee to me."

"I'll help her settle in," Tabitha Leighton said, still wiping at her dripping nose as she also stood up and followed Bernice. "Put a throw over her, sit with her for a few minutes."

"Losing your audience," Wendell commented, walking around the couch to sit down beside Maggie. "Too bad Trigg isn't still here. I'd like to hear more about this gambling problem."

And that's when another precinct was heard from, as Clarice hopped to her feet, her cheeks mottled pink and white, to declare feelingly, "I think you're all horrid! Nelson Trigg is the most honest, ethical, wonderful man I know. Just because he won't . . . *shower* money on authors or agree to a new office building, or computerize the royalty department, does *not* mean that he is irresponsible, that he'd ever even *think* to steal from the company.

He *loves* Toland Books."

"And has a great ally in you, Clarice," Saint Just said, motioning for her to seat herself again. "I commend your loyalty, and applaud it. But Maggie has told me something that you may not know. It would seem that not only did Mr. Trigg know that Toland would be here for dinner last Monday, but he also had *ordered* him to instigate those dinner plans."

Clarice looked to her right and left, then at Saint Just. "He did? I don't believe it. Why?" she asked in her usual subdued tone.

Maggie sat forward on the cushions. "It's true, Clarice. Nelson heard that Tabby might be shopping me, and he didn't want me to leave Toland Books."

"Well, that's silly. He doesn't even like you."

Maggie smiled. "Gee, doesn't that make me feel all warm and cozy. And, yes, Clarice, I know I'm not Nelson's favorite author. But he'd looked bad when he cut me off years ago, and he didn't want to listen to the gossip that would follow if he lost me again now that I'm *NYT.* You know this business, Clarice. It's almost incestuous. Nelson told Kirk to romance me, get me back into bed, actually, so I'd stay at Toland Books. Kirk told me so, that night." She looked down at her hands. "Right after I decked him with the dinner plate."

"I still wonder about that," Saint Just said, taking up his pacing once more. "Why would Toland be subservient to Trigg? Why would he take orders from him?"

"Oh, that one's easy," Tabitha Leighton said as she reentered the room, rubbing her red eyes. "Nelson knew that Kirk had raided the Toland Books accounts to invest in some theater project last year. Such a sad experience, too. David told me all about it. The investors lost every penny."

She looked at Maggie. "You know the Blue Men? Those guys with the blue faces, who play with paint? This project was going to be the Pink Ladies, or something like that. A real bomb, never got anywhere near Broadway. Anyway, Kirk had Nelson write it all off as a business expense, so Toland Books lost money, but Kirk never did." She sat down and pulled out another tissue. "Kirk told David all about it, one day at the tennis club, in confidence, of course. I doubt he'd want the whole world, and the IRS, to know. Leona Helmsley, remember? That has to be it, doesn't it?"

Maggie looked at Tabby in awe. "I live in Manhattan, I think I'm pretty smart, or at least not stupid, but there's a whole world out there I know nothing about, isn't there?" she said quietly. "So Kirk was dancing to The Trigger's tune?" She directed her attention to Saint Just. "Then why isn't Nelson dead, and Kirk still alive and kicking? It doesn't make any sense."

"We keep eliminating Trigg as a suspect," Saint Just said, pulling out a chair from the game table and sitting down. "Still, I do believe a visit to the man is in order."

"Why?"

"Because, Maggie, I don't like him, just on general principles. Sorry, Clarice."

Clarice nodded. "That's all right, Mr. Blakely. A lot of people don't like him. But that's because they don't know him the way I do."

Tabitha Leighton squeezed Clarice's hands, which were primly folded in her lap, then said kindly, but with that show of claws Maggie had come to treasure, "What an absolutely sweet and loyal thing to say. You've really got to get a life, Clarice."

Maggie coughed into her hand, then looked at Saint Just. "Is that it? Are we done now?"

"Not entirely, no," he answered. "Mrs. Leighton? Tabitha? We have yet to discuss your motives for murdering Toland."

"My — *my* motive? I don't have a motive for killing Kirk. Why would I have a motive?"

"I have no idea," Saint Just answered, and Maggie immediately knew what he was doing. He was throwing out hopeful lines, hoping someone — in this case, Tabby — would take the bait.

It wouldn't work. That kind of thing only worked in books, where you could feed lines to a character, make them do what you wanted them to do.

"Well, I don't," Tabitha said, squirming slightly in her seat. "Not that he wasn't a bastard. He . . . he had this way of leading people on, making them think . . ."

"Tabby?" Maggie asked as her agent's voice trailed off and her throat flushed an unbecoming red. "Don't tell me *you* —"

"Oh, all right, all right," Tabitha said, as if Saint Just and Maggie had just brought out the thumbscrews, "as long as we're being honest here, though why we are still doesn't make any sense, I had an affair with Kirk, two years ago. A very small one. I caught David cheating and stupidly cried on Kirk's shoulder one day, and he said the best revenge would be to have an affair of my own, and the next thing I knew — well, he dumped me a month later. There. Happy now?"

"You slept with Kirk?" Maggie closed her eyes, didn't like the images her imagination immediately conjured up, and opened them again. "Does David know?"

Tabitha resorted to her wadded-up tissues once more, even as she glared down at Wellington, who seemed to have designs on her lap again. "He didn't. But then Doctor Bob said I'd probably never sleep nights again unless I got it off my chest, and —"

"Whoa!" Maggie interrupted. "Doctor Bob? You're seeing Doctor Bob?" The memory of heavy perfume, lingering in the psychologist's office, made her feel slightly sick to her stomach.

"I am his agent, Maggie, remember? You should. You sicced him on me. He said I seemed sad, and offered me some counseling, gratis, after I got him this new contract."

"Gratis? He does counseling gratis? Man, that's even a bigger shock than hearing you were sleeping with Kirk. You didn't happen to pick up a last-minute appointment a couple of Mondays ago, did you?"

"Maggie, you're digressing," Saint Just told her, and she looked up to see that he was standing once more, swinging that damn quizzing glass. "I do believe the more important questions would be when Tabitha confessed her indiscretion to Mr. Leighton, and how he may have reacted to that confession. *Left*-tenant? Do you agree?"

"Yeah," Wendell said, scratching at his left ear. "Actually, I do. Good work, Saint Just. I have to admit, this is getting interesting."

"What?" Tabitha looked from face to face, then suddenly gasped. "No! You can't think that David killed him."

"When did you tell him about Kirk, Tabby?" Maggie asked, still remembering the smell of perfume in Doctor Bob's office. When had she smelled that? Not the day of the dinner. Had to have been the week before, right? If she was right, and Tabby went home and did the bare-her-breast bit to David — did that leave time for David to come up with the mushroom scenario? Probably.

"When?" Tabitha shrugged. "I don't know. A couple of weeks ago. And David couldn't have cared less, if you must know. I suffered for nearly two years, and he couldn't have cared less."

Wendell turned over a page in his note-book. "Where were you, Mrs. Leighton, the night Kirk Toland was poisoned?"

Tabitha quickly pointed at Saint Just. "I was with him, in Great Neck. I was, wasn't I?"

The lieutenant scribbled on the clean page. "Uh-huh, we can check that out. And your husband? Was he in Great Neck with you?"

"David?" Tabitha's cheeks went pale. "No. No, he wasn't. He was here, in Manhattan." Then she sat forward on the couch. "But he wouldn't. I mean, he didn't even *care*. Oh, this is ridiculous," she said, jumping up from the couch as Napper rubbed against her legs. "The cats, this silliness. Maggie, I don't like this party. I don't like it at all, and I'm leaving. I'm sorry I can't stay to help you clean up, so please put the salads away before they go bad. Lord knows you wouldn't want to *poison* anyone." She grabbed her purse and was gone, leaving only her perfume behind her.

"I'll never understand how she can be allergic to cats and not have her nose go ballistic over all that perfume," Maggie said, gingerly picking up a wad of used tissues and depositing them in the trash basket under her desk. "Tabby and Kirk. Wait till Bernie hears this one."

There was silence, a rather uncomfortable one, in the room for a few moments, before Clarice stood up and smoothed down her below-the-knee skirt. "I really should be going," she said, looking at Maggie rather desperately. "I really shouldn't have been here, heard any of this."

Maggie gave her a quick hug. "I'm sorry, Clarice. It hasn't exactly been a great time, has it?"

"No, and all I did was phone you to ask about the menu. That's all I did. I — I have to get back to the office now."

"Poor thing," Sterling said, shaking his head after Clarice left. "A pigeon amongst the hawks."

"And then there were three," Wendell said, smiling at Maggie. "I'm not counting Mrs. Toland-James, because I think she's pretty well out of it for the next couple of hours. I mean, even if she only drank half the drinks she pretended to drink, she still downed enough to knock her out for a while. Miss Kelly, you might want to flush out that plant over there, before it starts smelling like scotch."

"You saw that as well?" Sterling asked. "I thought Saint Just and I were the only ones. Very good, *Left*-tenant."

"I have my moments. Miss Kelly? Maggie? If I could see you in the hallway for a moment?"

Maggie looked at Saint Just, then mentally kicked herself for looking to him for what — approval? Consent? Like hell! "Sure, let's go. Oh, wait. It's nearly five. Alex, would you do me a favor and call Doctor Bob's office, cancel my appointment for Monday? I don't think I want to see him right now, and he charges if I don't give twenty-four-hour notice."

"Oh, yes, your reluctance to speak to his rather ill-humored secretary. I remember. Certainly, Maggie. One must earn one's keep, mustn't one? *Left*-tenant, it has been a pleasure. And, hopefully, you now have more than one possible perpetrator to take your interest?"

"If by that you mean, am I going to be working the weekend, you're right. You know, if we don't solve most homicides in the first forty-eight to seventy-two hours, we don't solve them at all. But this one's different. Not a crime of passion, not with the mushrooms. Poison is a more deliberate crime. We're going to solve this one.

We've got time, and boy, do we have suspects. For now, though, I have to tell you, I'm stumped."

"Yes, you are, and it is a frequent occurrence with you, I imagine." Saint Just bowed. "Happy to have been of service, *Left*-tenant."

"Come on," Maggie said, glaring at Saint Just as she all but pulled Wendell to the door, then slammed it behind her, turned, and smiled at him. "You wanted to talk to me?"

He bent his head slightly and scratched at that spot behind his left ear. He looked so cute when he did that. Sort of shy, and boyish, and, well, darn cute. "I was wondering, Miss — Maggie, if you'd like to go to dinner with me tomorrow night?"

"Dinner?" Maggie blinked. "You and me, tomorrow night? Well, sure, sure. That . . . that would be very nice, thank you."

He visibly relaxed. "Great. I didn't know if you and Blakely, well, you know."

"No! I mean, no, of course you might think that, but — no. He's my cousin, remember?"

"I do," he said, and Maggie looked at him curiously. "Hey, I'm a cop. I notice things. I notice, for instance, how he looks at you."

"Oh, that," Maggie said dismissively. "He's just overprotective, that's all. Really." *Really?*

"Yeah, well, he's also not the idiot I thought he was," Wendell told her. "You know, we've been over Toland's office, his Park Avenue condo, his place in the Hamptons, and we came up with nothing. We don't have a clue as to who wanted him dead. Or at least we didn't, except for your friend, Mrs. Toland-James, and your cousin pretty much blew that one out of the water for me today. Not that she's off the hook, because fifty million dollars is a hell of a motive, but now I've got suspects all over the place."

"Except for me, right? This is a dinner, not another chance to question me when Alex isn't around?"

His smile flashed, and Maggie's knees went a little weak. "Oh, this is a date, Maggie. Trust me on that one. I'll pick you up around six, okay? I know it's early, but I've still got to work on the Toland case, and I've got to be at the office again on Sunday."

"Okay," Maggie said, then watched as he walked over to the elevator and pushed the button. Knowing it could take long minutes for the elevator to show up, and knowing all she could do would be to stand there grinning like a loon until it did, she opened the door to the apartment and stepped inside, her smile pretty sloppy.

"He's gone then," Saint Just said as he sat at the coffee table, leaning over his ever-present laptop. "Good. The man operates under considerable handicaps you know, Maggie. For one, he can't find his brains with a lantern."

"Um-hmm, that's nice," she answered vaguely as she passed by the couch and headed, still smiling, for the kitchen. It was only after she'd begun cleaning up, and Saint Just's words echoed in her head, that she grinned, saying out loud, "God, I am *so* shallow, to love this."

"Interesting," Saint Just said as he paged through a book after dinner, while Maggie worked at her desk — played Snood at her desk. But that was work, she had assured both Saint Just and Sterling. She did some of her best thinking while shooting down Snoods.

"Hmmm?" Maggie asked, not turning her head. "What's interesting?"

"This book," he said, walking over to her and putting the book down in front of her.

Maggie picked it up, read the spine. "So?

It's one of my research books. What of it?"

"Clarice was reading snatches of it this afternoon. This one, and a few others, I believe. There were several of them out of place. I know, because I organized those shelves just last week, in a thankfully passing fit of domesticity, remember?"

"Along with my spices, yeah," Maggie said, frowning at the title of the book: *Motive, Method, Opportunity.* "Clarice likes murder mysteries. She's crazy about the Saint Just Mysteries, and I always make sure to get her a copy in galley stages. She once found a technical error for me, as a matter of fact, before it could get into print. I called something a mace, and it was something else. She knows a lot about weapons."

"And you don't find that curious? That a little mouse like Clarice Simon is fascinated by weaponry?"

Maggie shrugged. "She's single, alone a lot. A hobby is a hobby. There are people who'd find it curious that I talk back to the television."

"Yes, that's true enough," Saint Just said with a small smile. "What is that saying? If you talk to God, that's praying. If you think God talks to you — immediately take yourself off to a doctor to have your brains examined. I imagine it's much the same for television. But you don't think the television is really talking to you, do you, Maggie?"

"Nope," she said, glaring at him. "I only think two of my fictional characters have come to life and are living with me, asking stupid questions. I'm sane as all hell, right?"

"Don't be peevish, my dear; it isn't becoming. But now, to get back to Clarice and her interest in your research books. Do you think she's fairly well acquainted with other weapons? Firearms? Poisons?"

"Clarice?" Maggie handed him the book. "Now you're stretching. Clarice wouldn't say boo to a goose. Her only failing is that she's so bonkers over The Trigger."

"Loves him, does she? Worships him from afar?"

"She'd kill for him," Maggie said, shooting down a whole block of red Snoods with one well-placed shot, then sighing in satisfaction.

"Indeed," Saint Just said, looking at Sterling. "Your opinion, if you please?"

Sterling furrowed his brow for a moment, then shook his head. "I don't see it, Saint Just. According to Mrs. Leighton, Mr. Trigg held something over Mr. Toland's head —

that business about pink females, remember? How would it then advance Mr. Trigg to have Mr. Toland out of the picture? No. I don't see it."

"Thank you, Sterling," Saint Just said, carefully replacing the book on the shelf. "My conclusion exactly. Unless, of course, Mr. Trigg's venture into the world of gambling is more extensive than we know, and Mr. Toland was about to expose him for embezzlement? Then I could see why Mr. Toland's removal from this mortal coil might be an advantageous exit for Mr. Trigg. Which, happily for me, brings the motive straight back to dear Mr. Trigg."

"Not Clarice?" Maggie put her computer to sleep and headed for the couch, to plop down into the comfortable cushions. "Good. For a minute there, Alex, I thought maybe you'd lost a screw or two. But I can buy The Trigger as the murderer. Definitely. I'm going with you tomorrow, right? When you talk to Trigg?"

"Oh, I think not, my dear. This will be a conversation between gentlemen — allow me to correct that. One gentleman, one cur. To be blunt, you'd be terribly in the way."

"I love you, too," Maggie grumbled, pushing herself up to her feet. "I'm willing to bet The Trigger won't talk to you anyway, so how much harm could you do? And the other reason I'm not fighting you on this, Alex, is because I'll be spending most of tomorrow getting ready for my date with Steve Wendell. Oh, and I'm going to be staying with Bernie Sunday night, before her interview with the police on Monday. Moral support, and all of that, as Sterling would say. She said I didn't have to, but I volunteered."

Saint Just nodded his approval. "As Theophrastus, I believe, said, 'True friends visit us in prosperity only when invited, but in adversity they come without invitation.' I approve. Indeed, I find myself to be inordinately proud of you, Maggie. You are a true friend."

Maggie's cheeks flamed. "Why . . . thank you, Alex. That was . . . that was very nice of you. So you don't mind being on your own Sunday night, you and Sterling?"

"I'm sure we'll be able to find something to amuse ourselves. Don't worry about us for a moment."

Take Thursday night, add three days, and come up with *Sunday*. Sunday night at the Styles Cafe with Mare.

No. Saint Just didn't mind. He didn't mind at all. . . .

CHAPTER 17

Whistling bits of "Merry Month of Maying," the Viscount Saint Just exited Maggie's apartment building and stepped into the sunny Saturday afternoon, lightly swinging his cane, bowing and tipping his Mets cap to the ladies. He regretted that Sterling hadn't deigned to join him, but understood the man's reluctance to leave the apartment, considering that Sterling was edging into hour five of a twelve-hour Bewitched marathon. A man did have to have his priorities.

Armed with his pocket map of Manhattan, he walked over to Central Park, as he had done on his first excursion in the city, and turned to his right on Central Park West. At the first corner, across from the entrance to the Park and Tavern on the Green, Saint Just paused to listen to a rather wild-eyed man standing on an overturned box. The man was yelling through a bullhorn that Armageddon would destroy the planet on May thirteenth.

A few passersby lingered for a moment or two, many of them throwing bills or loose change in the wicker basket sitting on the sidewalk.

"Excuse me, my good sir," Saint Just said as the man stopped for lack of breath. "May thirteenth? Would that be tomorrow?"

The man yelled through the bullhorn. "Tomorrow! Yes! Tomorrow! The Four Horsemen will ride out — Death, Famine, War . . . um, all of them!"

"Pestilence," Saint Just supplied helpfully. "You probably wanted to say Pestilence. And all in one day. My goodness me, won't they be busy little bees. But, not to beg the question, sir, if the world is going to end tomorrow, why are you collecting money today? There doesn't seem to be much point to it, does there?"

The man shut off the bullhorn and leaned down from his box to whisper in Saint Just's ear. "Bug off, buster. This here's my corner."

"Really." Saint Just's face lit in just a ghost of a smile. "Your corner. And you are allowed to set yourself up here, bellow your opinions to the populace, collect money for your trouble?"

"Yeah. Now scram. You're hurtin' business."

"Of course." Saint Just took out a ten-dollar bill and held it in front of him, just out of the man's reach. "One moment more of your time, if you please. How much money do you collect, standing on this corner, pontificating?"

The man reached for the ten, but Saint Just quickly moved his hand behind his back. "Ah-ah-ah. Don't be greedy. An answer first, if you please."

"And then the sawbuck, right? Okay. How much do I pull in? More than I did hawkin' T-shirts and watches. No overhead, nothin'. And a better neighborhood, too. Nobody tryin' to mug me if I get out of here before dark. The hicks think I'm bonkers, and toss in the coins, even take pictures sometimes. I'm probably in photo albums all over the Midwest."

He waggled his fingers as he shook his head, then raised his voice an octave or two. "And here's George, standing with that man from the corner who said the world was going to end soon. We gave him a dollar, poor sick man. I tell you, Mabel, New Yorkers are just *insane*." Then he narrowed his eyelids and glared down at Saint Just. "Why do you want to know?"

"Oh, nothing. I was merely curious," Saint Just said, handing over the bill. "I'm always interested in ventures that produce a profit for very little expenditure. And then there is the added fillip of knowing that the people who would give this money are addlepated idiots who don't deserve to have two pennies in their pockets. Well, let us just say that such amusement adds to the enjoyment of the farce."

The man looked at him. "Huh?"

"I imagine standing on a box, reciting some Shakespeare, for instance, might bring a similar monetary reward?"

The man rolled his eyes, as if trying to look inside his own mind where, hopefully, an interpreter was waiting to help him. "Oh," he said after a moment. "They do that up across from the museum these days. Museum of Natural History. Juggle, play the sax, do some actin' and singin'. And those damn white-faced guys who are always tryin' to get out of an invisible box. Give me the creeps."

Saint Just chewed on the man's last statement for a moment, then smiled. "Oh. Mimes. Irritating, aren't they? But to get back to the point here, if we might? A man of enterprise, such as yourself, if supplied with a stirring speech, has the possibility of earning money, just for giving that speech? And, for the sake of argument, a dozen, two dozen of your fellows, each giving the same stirring speech on those dozens of street corners, could also earn this money?

With a small commission paid to the author of this stirring speech, naturally. The author, a gentleman, who would not wish to soil his own hands with anything smelling the least like the shop. But this, this would be a form of theater, correct? Totally acceptable. A gentleman, you understand, must be true to his station in life."

"I didn't get that last bit, sorry." The man took another look around for his internal interpreter. "But as for that other stuff? You mean, like, make a whole business out of it? Franchises, like? Like McDonald's or something? Yeah. Okay. You can make money that way. You can make money any way at all in New York. Not much, but it beats nothin', you know?"

"Yes, I've always rather thought that something defeats nothing. But not very much, you say? I definitely need more than not very much. Still, it was a thought, one I may investigate further, for there are quite a lot of street corners in Manhattan, aren't there? Thank you, good sir. I won't keep you. Oh, but if I might brook a suggestion? At no charge, of course."

The man spread his hands and shrugged. "You'd shut up if I said no?"

Saint Just smiled. "My suggestion is that

you change the date for Armageddon. Make it, oh, perhaps *next* May thirteenth? Imminent death doesn't call for throwing money at the doomsayer, while the hope of salvation through gifts of money has always held a great appeal. Ask any of the clergy."

Now the man's eyes all but crossed, but he got some of it, at least enough of it to finally smile and say, "Yeah. Yeah, you're right. Thanks."

"My pleasure. A fine day should contain good deeds," Saint Just said, twirling his cane as he set off once more, walking the short blocks, watching the street signs. Soon he was turning into one of the buildings along Central Park West between Sixty-second and Sixty-first, the one marked with a few brass plaques, including one reading: Toland Books, Established 1924.

Saint Just was stopped, never stymied, by the uniformed guard on duty at the pair of elevators, but the simple application of a twenty-dollar bill to the man's outstretched palm had him on his way again, riding up the elevator to the fourth floor.

Money, Saint Just had decided, was the grease that kept the metropolis moving along. Money, he had also concluded, finding a way to have it come tumbling into his hands, was his most pressing concern after settling this Toland mess, which had certainly put a crimp in his plans to enjoy his new, expanded life.

He stepped from the elevator, into an area decorated by someone with a marked lack of imagination, as it contained nothing more than a desk, a few display cases holding copies of books published by Toland Books, and a few sad-looking blue leather couches.

Saint Just smiled as he saw the Saint Just Mysteries displayed prominently. When no one came to greet him, he decided that he would simply have to hunt Nelson Trigg down by himself, and took the corridor to his left, which looked promising.

Following the smell of coffee, he passed several uninhabited, doorless offices that looked as if New York had solved its waste problem by sending all its paper to Toland Books. In each small office, the desks were piled high with paper; the floors were stacked with it. A computer sat on each desk, and there were a few personal items, photographs and ivy pots in with the clutter, but nothing could override the feelings of claustrophobia the weekday occupants must surely experience every day.

Then the offices became larger, even came with doors. He saw Bernice's name on one of them, then a few others, and then a heavy oak door that stood ajar, open just enough to alert Saint Just that someone was inside, for he could hear the whir of a motor. He looked at the brass plate on the door and saw Nelson Trigg's name.

So far so good. The man had been true to his word, and was doubtless inside, working his manicured fingers to the bone, diligently slaving over financial statements or some such thing. Possibly *arranging* the accounts more to his liking, more to the auditor's liking?

He pushed open the door with the tip of his cane, to see Nelson Trigg dressed in a grey T-shirt and navy shorts, running in place on what Saint Just (thanks to Sterling's affection for early-morning television) knew to be a treadmill.

Trigg's face was red, with white spots high on both cheeks. His blond hair stuck damply to his head, and he never lost a step as he picked up a squeeze bottle of water and sprayed some into his open mouth. The whirr of the treadmill motor, the pounding of Trigg's sneakered feet, the rapid breathing that told Saint Just the man was either woefully out of shape or deep into his exercise program, were the only sounds in the room. The only smells were of freshly brewed coffee and, unfortunately, perspiration.

Saint Just stood quietly, watching Trigg for some moments, then cast his gaze around the large corner office. Trigg had two desks, big ones, each with a computer sitting on top. He had two couches, several tables, three file cabinets, and some paintings made up of splotches of color, which he must have purchased to go with the rather uninspired color scheme of burgundy and blue.

Besides the treadmill, Saint Just saw two other exercise machines he didn't recognize, as well as a wrought-iron stand holding several hand weights, also recognized from early-morning television.

Such an obsession with fitness confused Alex, who maintained his own impressive physique through horseback riding, boxing at Gentleman Jackson's saloon and, mostly, thanks to the fact that Maggie had described him as a Corinthian, a man of sleek, not bulging muscles, a man with a body men envied and women adored. And, as long as Maggie kept writing him that way, that would be how he would stay, just as poor Sterling would remain his sweet, plump self.

Which was a good thing, because Saint Just knew he would rather stand on a street corner, mouthing "To be, or not to be," in order to put food in his belly than ever look as asinine as Nelson Trigg did at this moment.

At last, Trigg noticed him. Frowning, he hit a button on the treadmill that slowed it, so that he was now jogging along like a child rolling a hoop, rather than running as if the hounds of hell were after him, and gaining quickly.

"Good afternoon, Mr. Trigg. How are you?"

"What the hell are you doing here?" Nelson asked, pressing the fingers of his right hand on his left wrist, obviously taking his own pulse.

"Why, yes, I do enjoy my customary good health, thank you so much for asking," Saint Just said as Trigg hit another button and the treadmill slowed even more. Rather, Saint Just thought, like walking a horse before leading it back to the stables. "I did, however, spend a decidedly unquiet night, worrying about Toland's murder, and wondering if the culprit will ever be exposed for the bounder he is. I'm convinced you did the same?"

"Hardly." Trigg put his feet on the bars on either side of the treadmill, then shut it off. He reached for a snowy white towel, wiped his face with it, and rubbed at his hair. Now he smelled like a hamper and looked like a porcupine. "That meeting of yours yesterday? Ridiculous. I'm leaving the investigation to the police, Blakely. I suggest you do the same."

"True, true," Saint Just said, walking over to one of the machines. "What is this one?"

Trigg came over, flung the towel over the handlebars of the exercise machine, and climbed aboard. "It's a stepper, of course," he said, adjusting the tension, then starting his exercise.

Saint Just watched, fascinated. "What does it do?"

"It . . ." Trigg took a few quick breaths, ". . . it simulates stepping. Stairs. Great for the legs."

"Yes, I would imagine so. But aren't there stairs in this building?"

"This is more precise. I can measure how many calories I've burned, how many fat calories. Monitor my heart rate and — why the hell are you here?"

"I can't imagine that myself," Saint Just

said, walking over to the table to pour himself a cup of coffee. "It would appear I'm about as popular as smallpox with you, Trigg. I may go into a sad decline. No sugar?"

"There's raw honey in that cabinet under the coffeemaker," Trigg said, once more doing the take-his-pulse routine before picking up two small black dumbbells and commencing to do curls, first his left arm, then his right. "White sugar will kill you."

"Oh, I imagine you're doing a pretty good job of killing yourself, without the sugar. You look quite wretched, you know. Is all this perspiration really worth it?"

Trigg bent his left elbow and watched his own bicep bulge. "You tell me."

Saint Just cocked one eyebrow as he looked at the man. Hairy, bulging legs. A reasonable chest, tolerable arms. The charm and charisma of a doorstop. "Perceive me as overwhelmed, incapable of coherent speech. Now, if you have a moment between tortures? I'd like to discuss Kirk Toland's murder."

"You don't get it, do you?" Trigg asked, putting down the weights and picking up the towel once more. "I don't want to talk to you. Even better, I don't have to talk to you."

"Not even about your small problem with the dice? So many of my contemporaries had to flee to the continent, to escape their own debts. Gambling. It's a curse. Or am I misinformed?"

Trigg threw down his towel and headed for the nearest desk. "I'm calling Security. I don't know who let you up here, but I know who's going to toss you out on your ear."

He nearly had his hand on the phone when Saint Just brought his cane down on it, holding it in place. "I'd as lief you didn't do that, Trigg, old man. Oh, dear, now a frown. You don't like me, do you? I can't think why, as I'm a wonderful fellow. But I do ask the most embarrassing questions, don't I? There, I just did it again. Shame, shame on me."

"What the hell do you want from me?"

Saint Just removed the cane, tucking it beneath his arm once more. "And here I thought I was being so clear, so concise. I want, dear man, for you to tell me that you had no reason to murder Kirk Toland."

Trigg's hands closed into fists. "I don't need Security. I can break you in half with my own two hands."

"People imagine the silliest things," Saint Just drawled, drawing the sword from his cane and smiling as Trigg looked at the blade with eyes gone wide. "Not that I am adverse to breaking several of your bones, Trigg, but this," he said, indicating the blade, "makes it all so much easier and civilized, don't you think? Much too fine a day for dramatic confrontations."

"I didn't kill him," Trigg said, his gaze still on the thin sword, his tone definitely more amenable. Objects with sharp points, aimed toward one's belly, Saint Just thought, seemed to have that affect. "I gamble, okay? Bernie already told everybody that one. And maybe I fudged the books a little once in a while, took a small advance for myself a time or two, but I always put it all back. No big deal."

"Only once in a while?" Saint Just asked, flicking at some of the papers on Trigg's desk with the tip of the sword, enjoying himself probably more than he ought to. "And now? You say you've put it all back? Are you saying that the books, as I believe you called the accounts, will now stand up to any scrutiny?"

"I didn't say that, no. There . . . there could still be a few problems; nothing that can't be corrected," Trigg continued, edging around the desk in the direction of his inventory of hand weights.

"Ah-ah-ah," Saint Just warned, employing the sword stick to wave him back behind the desk. "Having the upper hand, as it were, I have decided to keep it. Selfish of me, but there it is. So? How large is this current problem?"

Trigg mumbled something Saint Just couldn't quite hear, and didn't need to hear. The fact was that the man had embezzled funds from his employer, and now his employer was dead. How convenient. "But like I said. Nothing that can't be fixed, probably just errors. I'm going over the books myself, have been for a couple of weeks. Nothing . . . nothing major. I know my job."

"How commendable, I'm sure. But the original — what did you call them? Oh, yes, *advances*. The ones that numbered more than a few dollars, the ones you paid back penny for penny? Did he know? Toland. Did he know?"

Trigg shrugged, his eyes still on the blade. "I don't think so. And even if he did, I wouldn't kill him. And he wouldn't want to let it get out that he'd been ripped off. Kirk was an ass, more worried about his reputation than anything else. I'd agree to resign, take a golden parachute, promise to go to some clinic for my gambling addiction, get another job with Kirk's recommendation. Nobody does time for white-collar crime, especially since I paid it all back. They sure as hell don't kill for it."

Now Saint Just was confused. He didn't quite understand everything that Trigg had said to him, some of the nuances, but he did understand the tone. Trigg was telling him the truth. He didn't know if Toland had ferreted out his dishonesty, but if Toland had, Trigg wouldn't be all that upset.

It might even be a relief to him to have it all out on the table, so to speak. The fellow did seem to confess with very little encouragement. But what were these "problems" he had alluded to, these "problems" he'd been looking into personally for the past few weeks?

Saint Just put away his blade. "I must tell you, my good man, that I am mightily disappointed in you. How nice and neat it would have been. You send Toland to Maggie's for dinner — and I already know you did, and why you did, so we won't waste time haggling over that, all right? Your assistant phones Maggie for the menu. You somehow slip the dreaded mushrooms into the wine sometime during

446

the day, he becomes ill at Maggie's, and suspicion falls everywhere but on you. Are you sure you don't want to confess? Everyone would believe you, if you did. I could even have talked the *left*-tenant around to it, I'm sure. He's so thick-headedly concentrated on poor Bernice. And now, with you out of the running, I suppose she's the only suspect we have left. How depressing."

"Yeah, well how about you get the hell out of my office?" Trigg said, pointing toward the door. "Oh, and if you try to tell anyone I said I ever fooled around with the books, I'll deny it. I'm respected in this business, Blakely, and you're nobody. Hell, I'd even take you to court, sue you for slander, libel. Your cousin can afford the freight."

Saint Just struck a pose, smiling. "What an enigma you are, my friend. First you want to sue me, then you refuse to fight me, then you threaten me with bodily harm, and now you're back to wishing to take me before your courts. I wonder. Were you bluffing a few minutes ago? If I were to strip off," he said, putting down his cane and beginning to unbutton his shirt, "would you stand and fight, or run like the toothless barking dog I believe you to be? Tell me, which way would you really go, if itch came to scratch?"

Trigg looked, for a moment, as if he might be about to cry. Then he pointed one shaking arm toward the door. "Just get out. Get out! You get out of here right now or I'll call the cops, tell them about that stick of yours."

"Most happily," Saint Just said, picking up his cane. He got as far as the door, then turned around, looked at Trigg, and dredged up one of the smashing put-downs Maggie had fed into him over the years. "Oh, and before I go, I recall that you condemned Toland as an ass. Has anyone ever told you that you also are an ass? If not, please allow me to be the first. Good day to you."

He rode down the elevator with a small smile on his face, feeling quite invigorated, although he would so much more have appreciated Trigg if he'd dared to raise a hand to him. But, then, one couldn't have everything.

He stepped out into the bright sunlight and turned to his left, happy to be walking back to Maggie's apartment on this lovely day. Paying scant attention to anything more than cursorily scouting out possible corners for soapboxes — the idea still held some appeal — he stopped at a busy corner about two blocks from the Toland Books offices, waiting with a crush of pedestrians for the light to turn so that he could proceed.

A bus came down the street, heading for the stop at the corner. The pedestrians stepped back as the bus pulled against the curb.

And Saint Just felt two hands sharply collide with his back, pitching him forward, directly into the path of the bus.

Maggie left Sterling behind to pay the cab driver, barreled through the doors of the emergency department of Lenox Hill Hospital, and slammed herself against the reception desk. "Blakely, Alexander Blakely. Hit by a bus."

"I'm sorry, miss, but you'll have to wait in —"

"Dr. Thompson! Yo! Dr. Thompson!" Maggie saw the resident as he walked through the automatic doors, a bright blue stethoscope with a small stuffed animal tied to it draped around his neck, his hands shoved deep into the pockets of his white coat.

"Oh, shit," the good doctor said when he saw her, and turned tail, running back inside the emergency room.

Maggie ran straight for him, catching up to him before the doors could close behind him.

"Hey, you're not allowed back here," he told her. "But since you're here, please tell me you need a boil lanced or something like that. I don't like that minor stuff, but in your case, I could make an exception."

"Not me, my cousin. Blakely. Alexander Blakely. He was hit by a bus."

"Were you driving it?" Dr. Thompson asked, blowing a bubble. "I'd give odds you were driving it. I've been on duty the last couple of days, so I haven't had a chance to read the papers. Are you out on bail?"

"I'm not a suspect, damn it." Maggie was caught between wanting to strangle the young doctor and her need for information on Saint Just. "Alexander Blakely. Do you know who I'm talking about? Are you treating him? May I see him?"

"Yes, yes, no. Clear enough?"

"But I'm . . . I'm his cousin."

"And you were Kirk Toland's sister. I remember. Look, I've got a good chance of getting this one out of here alive. I don't need you around to screw up my success rate anymore, okay? A guy could get a complex."

"Then he's all right? How badly hurt is

he? For God's sake, give me something. Look," she said, lifting her sleeve to show the nicotine patch on her upper arm. "I'm a woman on the edge here."

"Oh, all right. Never let it be said I pushed a woman back into a habit that's sure to kill her. Come on, he's back here. And, hey, if you promise to take him out of here in the next, say, twenty minutes, I'd probably even be grateful."

"He's giving you trouble?"

"He keeps calling me a leech. I'm not a vain man, but, yeah, he's starting to get on my nerves. That, and the quoting."

"Quoting? Oh, wait, let me guess. Was it 'Cured yesterday of my disease, I died last night of my physician'? That's Matthew Prior, from *The Remedy Worse Than the Disease*."

"Nope, not that one. Probably only because he didn't think of it. I think we started with 'physician, heal thyself,' and went on from there. The worst one went something like, 'I often say a great doctor kills more people than a great general.' Something like that."

"Just like that," Maggie said, grinning. "That's Baron Gottfried Wilhem von Something-or-other. Alex is obviously alert, talking?"

"Insulting, complaining, telling me what to do. Now that I think about it, he probably is your cousin." He stopped in front of a privacy curtain and yanked it back. "There he is. Now let me go sign him out before I change my mind and send for a psych consult."

"Alex!" Maggie exclaimed, seeing him lying on one of those ridiculously narrow litters, a white blanket draped over most of his long body. One small part of her mind registered the scar on his left shoulder, left by a bullet she'd had shot at him in the second Saint Just mystery. "Oh, my God, are you all right?"

"That, my dear, would depend on how injurious one considers having one's clothes removed without permission, only to have oneself stuffed inside a *gown*. Between the King's English and your American, the word gown, I believe, suffered somewhat in the translation. You, leech," he called after Dr. Thompson, who was once more beating a hasty retreat. "Wouldn't you be pleased to do something useful? My clothing, good man. Now, if you please."

Maggie walked to the head of the litter, biting her bottom lip, knowing she should shut up Saint Just, but also delighted that he was healthy enough to so obviously give Dr. Thompson fits. "You're supposed to be deferential to doctors, Alex. Not order them around like servants."

He cocked one eyebrow at her. "Leeches, my dear, are for the most part inferior drunks with superior attitudes, and they kill far more than they cure. As it is, I doubt I'll be back to my normal robust health for weeks, considering all the blood this particular leech removed from my body in a vain attempt to ascertain what his eyes could have told a village idiot — that I am perfectly fine. Ah, my clothes. Splendid."

"Yeah, my pleasure," Dr. Thompson said, tossing the plastic bag containing Saint Just's clothing onto the bottom of the litter, following it up with the cane. "Someone has to watch him for twenty-four hours. We can't rule out concussion, not that he let us run any tests."

"No tests?" Maggie looked at the doctor. "No CT? No EEG? No MRI?"

"Sorry, Dr. Kelly," he said with a grin that had Maggie ready to choke him. "He refused to let us touch him after the blood test. Except for the ABC."

"What's that?"

Dr. Thompson grinned. "Oh, goodie, I

453

stumped the writer. It's simple. I say A-B-C, and if he answers D-E-F-G, he gets to go home. Here," he said, pushing a clipboard at Saint Just. "Sign this. It says you're leaving here against my better judgment. And bon voyage, I won't miss you."

"Impertinent twit," Saint Just said after Dr. Thompson had handed Maggie a list of instructions, then walked away with the clipboard, sliding the curtain shut as he went. "I told everyone I wasn't injured, but they dragged me here anyway. I'm perfectly fine. Just a small headache, and some soreness."

"Soreness? Where?"

"On his backside," Dr. Thompson sang out, obviously not beating that hasty a retreat. "Right smack on his ass."

"Your backside?" Maggie asked as Saint Just pulled his wrinkled clothing from the bag, muttering about the sad condition of his slacks. "You ended up on your backside?"

He looked up at her, shaking his head. "*The Case of the Pilfered Pearls.* Remember? Henderson came up behind me, pushed me into the street just as a coach was coming by? You had me fling out my arms, hit the coach flat-handed, and spring backward, rather than fall to the street and be run over like a dog. My reaction was instinctive. I felt the push at my back, immediately flung out my arms, and *pushed* myself off against the side of the bus."

He rummaged in the bag once more. "Unfortunately, I then was catapulted backward, and landed on my . . . Where's my cap?" He grabbed the bag and looked inside it. "My hat. It's gone. Bloody hell."

"Your Mets cap?" Maggie sifted through the rumpled clothing, except for the white cotton briefs Saint Just grabbed and stuck under the blanket. "It must have come off when you hit your head. You did hit your head, right? The concussion Dr. Thompson talked about? I'm sorry about that. We'll get you a new one. Now get dressed, and let's get out of here. Sterling's waiting in chairs. He's so worried about you."

"Sterling is a true friend," Saint Just said, then looked at her, waiting. "Well?"

"Well, what? Get dressed, and let's go."

"Maggie," Saint Just said quietly, "isn't it enough that you invite all of the world and his wife into my bed with me, to titter over my romantic exploits? Do you now believe you should be here while I don my clothes? I think not. There are limits, you know."

"Oh, right." Maggie made a face. "How

do you feel about that, Alex? That I write about your . . . your seductions."

"I'm delighted, straight down to my toes," Saint Just said facetiously. "How do you think I feel?"

"Oops, dumb question. But I have to put sex in the books, Alex. I hate it as much as you do, you know. It's difficult to create characters you really like, and then have to strip them down to insert Tab A into Slot B."

"How wonderful. You've reduced my expertise in the boudoir down to Tab A and Slot B. I'm so gratified. Now, and yet again, if you would please remove yourself? Sterling, remember? We don't want to keep the poor fellow waiting."

"You know," Maggie said, wagging a finger at him. "I'm *NYT* now. Five books out, one more in the can. Sex sells, but now the series sells. I could probably get away with pretty much closing the bedroom door from now on, and nobody would care all that much. I can think of a lot of other writers who began their series with some pretty graphic sex scenes, but they don't have them in the books anymore. Especially now that you're here, you know? I mean, it's sort of weird, thinking about writing a love scene with you in it, when you're here. Yeah, I think I might be able to get that past Bernie. Plenty of sexual tension, some innuendo, but no more Tab A and Slot B. I think I'll —"

"Leave this area immediately?" Saint Just concluded for her. "I don't know which is worse. Having that leech poke around at my hindquarters, or listening to you constantly saying Tab A and Slot B."

"Oops, sorry," Maggie said, unable to hold back a smile. "I'll be outside with Sterling. Hurry up."

"Hurry up? Hurry up, you say, after delaying me for no good reason. Now *I'm* to hurry up? Woman, you're impossible. No wonder my head aches."

"Hey, at last, a reason to like you, Miss Kelly," Dr. Thompson said, poking his head around the edge of the curtain yet again. "Here," he said, holding out a white paper. "A prescription for some industrial-strength ibuprofen. He's going to need it."

Maggie took the paper as she breezed out of the cubicle, her chin high, for she was pretty sure she'd been insulted. Twice. At the minimum.

Dr. Thompson pressed the wall switch opening the double doors, and Maggie was once more in the waiting area. She looked around for Sterling, but didn't see him in chairs.

"Sterling?" she said, not that loudly, but he heard her, as he was standing in front of the reception desk.

"Here I am, Maggie," he said, and she walked over to him. "Allow me to please introduce to you Miss Martha Kovacs. Miss Kovacs, Miss Maggie Kelly, better known to you as Cleo Dooley. Miss Kovacs and I were passing the time in a most delightful discussion about your books."

Miss Martha Kovacs was a plump woman in her midforties. Her blond hair was overdyed and overpermed, her makeup overly bright. She stood up and came around to the front of the desk to shake Maggie's hand. Maggie saw that she was wearing an off-the-shoulder peasant blouse and a garishly flowered, ankle-length full skirt. She looked like *Heidi Goes to Wal-Mart*. "Oh, yes, Miss Dooley. I'm a huge fan. *The Case of the Misplaced Earl?* My favorite. I must have read it at least a dozen times."

"My first," Maggie said, with a weak smile. Nothing like hearing you've been going downhill with every book since the launch of the series. Her day was just getting better and better. "And you like that one best?"

"Oh, yeah," Miss Kovacs said, blushing slightly. "When the viscount did that thing — you know, that *thing* — with Lady who-ever it was? In the grass behind the green-house thingie? When she wrapped her legs around his — well," Miss Kovacs broke off, fanning herself. "It's my favorite."

"Not the mystery?"

Miss Kovacs gave a small wave of her hand. "Oh, oh, yes, that, too. But that Saint Just? To *die* for. He could park his shoes under my bed anytime, let me tell you."

"Well, thank you. Nice meeting you, really," Maggie said, then motioned for Sterling to follow her. "Who am I writing for, Sterling?" she asked him as they headed toward the doors to the street. "Please don't tell me I'm writing for *her*. It's too depressing. Wait till I tell Alex. Looks like he's got a lot more Tab A into Slot B in his future, poor guy, because if Martha Kovacs likes to see him in bed, so will Bernie."

"Maggie? I'm sure you understand exactly what you're saying, but if I could inquire as to Saint Just? How is he? Is he badly injured? Miss Kovacs said he wasn't."

"Oh, Sterling, I'm so sorry. I do tend to go off on tangents when I don't want to think about something else, like Alex under the wheels of a bus," she said, giving him a quick hug. "Alex is fine. He has a headache, some bruises, but he's just fine. He'll be going home with us as soon as he gets dressed."

Sterling visibly sagged. "How I had hoped I was right," he said, then smiled at her. "As long as you don't kill us off, Maggie, I don't think we can die. Isn't that splendid? It certainly does wonders for my worries about too many potato chips."

Any lingering thoughts about Tab A and Slot B flew from Maggie's mind as she goggled at Sterling. "I . . . I never thought about that. Could you be right? I mean, the man was hit by a bus. Or hit a bus. Same difference. He can bruise, he can bend, but maybe he can't break. Wow."

"Wow, indeed," Saint Just said from directly behind her, and she whirled around to face him. He had come up quietly and was standing there, leaning a bit on his cane. "Wow, and ludicrous. If I can bend, I can break. I gave the matter some thought myself while I was lying on that torture rack in there, and that is my conclusion. I'm sure I'm correct, and mortal. Sterling?

How good of you to come along, worry about me."

"You're all right, then? I must say, it gave me quite a turn to hear what happened. The police phoned us, you know."

"This city seems to be chockful of helpful police officers, ambulance attendants, leeches. They had wanted to transport me to another hospital, but when I refused to go anywhere but this particular den of torture, they were fairly amenable. Now, perhaps we may adjourn to the apartment and put our heads together as to who pushed me into the path of that bus."

Maggie frowned. "What? They didn't get the guy? I figured it was just another nutcase, going around pushing people. Push people onto subway tracks, stick people with needles, you name it. Sort of our version of welcome to the big city."

"No, my dear, no one was apprehended. No one saw anything. In fact, there is no word save mine that I didn't trip, or jump at the bus. Dr. Thompson seemed determined to make me say that I'd deliberately jumped. I think the man has problems, don't you?"

"Yeah, but you're leaving, so he'll be all right now," Maggie said quietly. "Come on, we'll hail a cab."

"No need," said a voice behind Maggie. She whirled around — getting dizzy, with all these people sneaking up behind her — to see Steve Wendell standing there. "Hello all. Big Apple door-to-door delivery, at your service. I've got a cab waiting outside." He smiled at Maggie. "Socks let me know where you were. I came to take you to dinner, remember?"

Maggie looked at her watch. "Oh, wow, I'm sorry. I should have called you."

"Don't worry about it. Blakely? You look like you've had a bad day. Look at me, I'm all broken up about this. Really." Then he winked at Maggie.

"It wanted only this. *Left*-tenant," Saint Just said, bowing rather stiffly, obviously attempting to maintain his dignity in very undignified circumstances, poor thing. "How wonderful. Here you are again, in your usual happy imbecility. Far be it from me to depress you when you're obviously so pleased with yourself, but it may be pertinent to the Toland case to tell you that someone has tried to kill me."

Wendell shifted his gaze to Maggie, who nodded. "Wow," he said.

"Yes, wow," Saint Just said, in some disgust as he turned to the door, doing his best to make a dramatic exit with typical Saint Just panache. "There's a lot of *wow* going around here today. Too much, frankly. Shall we go?"

"Yo, Blakely," Steve Wendell called after him. "Do you know your slacks are ripped? Right on the backside."

All the tension Maggie had felt wrapped up inside her shattered in a heartbeat, and she leaned against Sterling, laughing until she cried.

CHAPTER 18

"I'll assume this is in some way punishment for my sins," Saint Just commented, looking at the bowl of broth Tabitha Leighton had set on the coffee table before returning to the kitchen in a flurry of domestic efficiency. "Along with everything else which, not to put too fine a point on things, includes having the place stuffed with females intent on driving even the strongest man into a sad decline with their nervous flutterings. Sterling, some wine, if you please."

"Maggie says no to wine, Saint Just," Sterling said, hovering over the back of the couch like a hen with one chick. "It's not good for your head."

"Having everyone staring at me as if I might suddenly start foaming at the mouth is not good for my head," Saint Just pointed out, still eyeing the insipid broth. "Wine is medicinal."

"Yes, yes. Still, wouldn't you rather some sal volatile? A bit of hartshorn? Oh, I have it — burnt feathers. Marvelous restorative powers if you feel faint and all of that."

"I *feel*, Sterling," Saint Just said, carefully easing himself to a sitting position and throwing off the afghan Bernice Toland-James had tucked around him, "as if I have been ridden hard and put away wet. That does not, however, mean I'm in imminent danger of expiring. Unless, if I may offer a caveat, I am not provided with a glass of wine in the next ten seconds."

"Oh, stay there, I'll get it." Sterling breathed the sigh of the sorely oppressed and walked over to the liquor cabinet. "Just as well, I suppose, as I haven't the faintest notion where to get feathers. Could slice open a pillow, I suppose. Maggie probably wouldn't like that above half."

Saint Just accepted the glass of wine, easing himself back against the mountain of cushions Maggie had provided him with, and took a deep swallow. "Ah, much better. Sterling, if you whisper it to a soul I shall have to punish you, but I must tell you that I ache in places I didn't know I owned. Now, tell me again. Why are Bernice and Mrs. Leighton here?"

Sterling walked over to the facing couch and sat down. "Socks. It would seem that Bernice has him on retainer, and has since Mr. Toland expired. Anything untoward happens, he is to alert her immediately. We, of course, told him where we were going when we rushed out to the hospital.

He phoned Bernice, Bernice phoned Mrs. Leighton, and there you have it. I think it wonderful that everyone is showing such concern, don't you?"

"I'd think it wonderful, Sterling, if they'd all toddle off to their own homes and mind their own business, particularly the *left*-tenant."

"You can be very ungrateful at times, Saint Just," Sterling said, frowning. "And don't forget, the *left*-tenant had plans to escort Maggie to dinner this evening. You've ruined his plans, as Maggie says you can't be left alone tonight. In case your head explodes."

Saint Just took another sip of wine as he looked toward the kitchen. "Ah, yes, the famous dinner. I wonder, Sterling. Do you think it's time I asked the *left*-tenant the precise nature of his intentions?"

"Setting yourself up as her guardian, are you?"

Saint Just picked up the rumpled afghan and tossed it on the back of the couch. "We do have an interest, Sterling. Our own disposition if the two of them were to wed, for instance. I am still not enamored of this YMCA you spoke about, you understand."

"Oh," Sterling said, frowning. "I hadn't thought of that." Then he brightened. "But it's early days yet, and you might still be in the running. You are interested, aren't you, Saint Just?"

"Mildly, yes. Perhaps," Saint Just said, slowly turning the wineglass in his fingers, his thoughts his own. "Here you go, my friend. Hide this away, won't you, so that Maggie doesn't bring a lecture down on my aching head on the evils of wine and cranial injuries, and then please have everyone assemble here in the living room. I believe we have a quorum, and I would like to discuss Toland's murder again. Never let it be said I failed to take advantage of every opportunity."

In one of his flashes of insight that kept him a favorite with Maggie's readers, Sterling said as he plucked the empty glass from his friend's hand, "Every opportunity to discuss the murder, or every opportunity to come between Maggie and the *left*-tenant? There are times, you know, Saint Just, when you really do bear off the palm."

Saint Just watched his friend go, heading for the kitchen, and said to himself, thoughtfully, "I must consider myself reprimanded, I suppose. Yes, definitely reprimanded. Rather like being attacked by a fluffy bunny."

Then he watched as, one by one, everyone entered the living room, either finding seats or remaining standing — the *left*-tenant taking up Saint Just's favored position of authority, in front of the fireplace. Maggie curled up on the window-seat beside her desk, her legs bent, her arms wrapped around her knees. Another fluffy bunny, but with sharper teeth.

Sterling hovered behind Saint Just's couch, and the two ladies sat on the facing couch, Tabitha Leighton looking at him for outward signs of injury, Bernice Toland-James lounging at her ease, liberally oiled by what was probably her third scotch of the evening . . . and the evening was still young.

"Are we going to play Charlie Chan gathering the suspects again?" Bernice asked, grinning at Saint Just. "Can I be Number One Son? I love those old movies."

"I have absolutely no idea what you're prattling on about, Bernice," Saint Just told her, "but if you wish to contribute something to the discussion, you might want to forgo any further liquid libations. Just a suggestion."

Bernie laughed, not at all insulted. "You're just jealous because Tabby fed you that broth. You want me to put an olive in it? One of those little umbrellas?"

"Bernie, let him alone. He was hit by a bus, for God's sake," Tabitha Leighton scolded, looking at Saint Just. "Are you sure you're all right?"

"Never better, thank you," Saint Just told her, and even went so far as to take a spoonful of broth, manfully swallow the tasteless, lukewarm swill. "Although I must admit that being taken in like the rawest of greenhorns gives me more discomfort than my bruises."

"What's he talking about?" Wendell asked Maggie.

"I haven't a clue," she said. "Alex? What are you talking about?"

Now that he had everyone's attention, as planned, Saint Just shifted in his seat, looking to each occupant of the room in turn. "I'm saying that I had departed Nelson Trigg's office today completely convinced he was not the killer, and still with no idea of the killer's identity."

The moments after his announcement went something like this:

Tabitha Leighton: "You suspect *Nelson?*"

Saint Just: "I didn't say that."

Sterling: "No. You said you were going to take the air, and I could stay in the apartment. Oh, for shame, Saint Just."

Steve Wendell: "When are you going to learn to keep your damn English nose out of police business?"

Maggie: "Oh, shit, Alex, I knew I should have gone with you. What did you do?"

And, lastly, Bernie: "Sterling, sweetheart, is there any more ice?"

"If the outbursts are concluded? Good," Saint Just said, resisting the impulse to rub at his throbbing temples. "Yes, it's true, I paid our Mr. Trigg a short visit late this afternoon, at the offices of Toland Books. He did say he'd be working there today, although, when I saw him, he was busily trying to give himself an apoplexy."

"Doing his workout," Bernie translated, nodding. "I've always wondered who paid for all that equipment. Guess now I have the chance to find out. Sorry," she said, wincing, "didn't mean to interrupt. Go on, Alex."

"Thank you, I fully intend to. I had gone to Trigg's office in the hope of satisfying myself once and for all on the subject of his guilt or innocence. The man proved to be as wishy-washy as I'd already believed him, and I left again, mentally crossing him off my list of suspects for all time. A few blocks later, as I walked back here, I was pushed in front of a bus."

"Trigg followed you, pushed you?" Wendell offered, nodding. "He's that stupid? I don't know, Blakely. Kind of obvious, don't you think?"

"What a cowardly act. The fellow's revolting," Sterling said, shaking his head.

Maggie waved her arms from her perch on the windowseat. "Whoa, whoa. You're saying that Trigg followed you, pushed you? I thought you said he was working out in his office. Are you telling me that nobody noticed a sweaty man in shorts and a tank top come racing hell-for-leather down the street, push you in front of the bus, then run away again? Even in New York, that's pushing it. Not far, granted, but it's still pushing it."

"He can do that, you know, exercise in his office, because he's got a shower in there. A whole damn bathroom. I'm lucky to have one damn window." Bernie took another sip of scotch. "I wonder who paid for that, too. Maggie, don't interrupt with logic, sweetie. Go on, Alex. I'm starting to like the idea of Nelson as the murderer. Except you're confusing me. I thought you said he isn't on your suspect list anymore. Or did that change when you hit the bus?"

Wendell left the spot in front of the fireplace, pulled out one of the armless chairs at the game table, and straddled it. "This goes back to the gambling, right? Toland as victim because he discovered Trigg cooking the books. Can anyone prove he's been stealing from the company, or is this all rumor, conjecture? And how did he do it? Remember, I'm from the just-the-facts-ma'am bunch. I can't get subpoenas or search warrants on a hunch."

"Bernice?" Maggie prompted.

Her friend shrugged her shoulders, encased at the moment in navy Armani. "I don't know. I hear what I hear. You have to admit Nelson went a little nuts when we talked to him about his trips to Atlantic City. I guess we won't know until the auditors go over the books."

"Can't you arrest him?" Tabitha asked, looking at Wendell. "Take him in for questioning, at least?"

"Only if he volunteers," Wendell told her. "He'd lawyer up in a heartbeat, and we'd get nothing. On top of that, he'd know we're looking at him, and could even destroy evidence. I sure don't have enough for a warrant."

"So that's it?" Maggie got up from the windowseat and sat down beside Saint Just. "We've decided on Trigg? I don't know, Alex, it doesn't feel right."

"Too bad. Lieutenant?" Bernice said brightly. "If we're taking a vote, mine's on Nelson Trigg. Anything to get myself out of the hot seat."

"Clarice will be devastated," Tabitha said quietly. "Poor thing, she worships the ground he walks on."

Bernie tossed back the remainder of her drink. "I don't know why. He's lousy in bed."

Maggie pounced. "Bernice Toland-James! Are you saying you slept with The Trigger? Yuk, and double yuk."

"Oh, grow up, people. We had mutual interests," Bernie explained to Saint Just, who looked at her in some amusement. "Fitness, for one. Vitamins, supplements. And the man had a fanny lift last year, if you can believe that." She pulled a face. "Not that it helped. He should have lost the B-12 and picked up some Viagra, let me tell you."

"Is there anyone in all of Manhattan you *haven't* slept with, Bernie?" Maggie asked, heading for the liquor cabinet, and not pulling out a can of lemonade, either.

"We're getting off the track here," Wendell pointed out from his chair. "Let's take a count. We eliminated Maggie; we're pretty sure we're eliminating Ms. Toland-James. . . ."

"Bernie. Call me Bernie," she interrupted. "And, yes, I'm eliminated. Definitely."

"Bernie," he said, nodding. "We've also eliminated your husband, Mrs. Leighton — Tabby," he added as the agent opened her mouth to correct him. "I'd rather not tell you how we did that, but we did."

"Shacked up with some babe for the weekend while Tabby was in Great Neck, right?" Bernie said, a twinkle in her eye.

"I didn't say that," Wendell pointed out as Tabby blanched.

"Didn't have to," Bernie countered. "Go on. We're eliminating suspects."

"Allow me," Saint Just said, slowly getting to his feet. He headed for the fireplace, and his quizzing glass, which he'd earlier laid on the mantel. He thought better when he could hold it, twist the riband in his hands. "Sterling and I have never been suspects as, being merely visitors to this country, we have no motive to kill Kirk Toland, or anyone else, for that matter. All you ladies have been eliminated. Mr. Leighton has now been eliminated — thank you, *Left*-tenant. I would have gotten around to questioning him more thoroughly, but he was, in fact, very low on my list of possible culprits. We can likewise eliminate Argyle, also a guest at the party before the fatal dinner, as he, too, has no motive."

"Which brings us back to Trigg," Maggie said. "Okay. But what about the rest of the world? Why concentrate only on people who were here at the party?"

Saint Just began ticking off the reasons on his fingers. "You want to go over this again? All right. One, everyone here heard that Toland would be your guest for dinner that Monday night. Two, everyone at the dinner also could have seen the note Clarice Simon wrote about the menu, or overheard her speak about it at the office. Except you, Tabby, but a flying visit to your office by Sterling and me — you were taking a nap, Maggie, and never missed us, in case you're about to ask — proved that you had a luncheon meeting with Kirk Toland that last day. You never mentioned that, did you, Tabby?"

The agent fisted her hands in her lap. "Nobody asked," she said, looking at Wendell. "We were talking about Maggie's new contract. I told him I was still shopping her, and he'd better find a way to come up with some more money. I didn't poison the man. We ate at the Plaza, for crying out loud."

"I know you didn't kill him, Tabby," Saint Just said. "Not with the contract negotiations going so well."

"How do you know how they were — Miranda, right? You got all of this from Miranda. I have to get that girl a muzzle."

"Not until I talk to her," Maggie interjected. "The talks are going well? Why didn't I hear this? I do have some small interest, you know, Tabby."

"Nothing's definite yet, Maggie, with Kirk just dead. I was going to tell you as soon as I had some harder numbers. Bernie and I are going to talk more, next week, but until then, everything at Toland Books is sort of on hold. Right, Bernie?"

"True enough," Bernie said, smiling at Maggie. "Oh, and in case you're wondering, yes, I'm open to bribes. We'll start with some of those pretzels you're guarding with your life, if you don't mind. Ah, thank you."

Wendell rubbed at his face, looking at Saint Just. "You know, I'm beginning to feel like I should be back on traffic control in the Bronx. You went to Mrs. Leighton's office, found out she was with Toland that day? How?"

"Miranda, Lieutenant, remember? My so-called assistant is crazy for anything in pants," Tabby fairly spat. "That idiot girl took one look at that face of yours, Alex, and told you anything you wanted to know, right?"

"Your assistant was happy to cooperate, yes," Saint Just agreed, tongue in cheek. "However, you're not a suspect at the moment because you really had no reason to murder the man. I'm of the school that believes there has to be a reason, you understand, even if I rely more on intuition than facts. Facts, as it would seem, have not gotten the *left*-tenant very far."

"It's kind of hard to look for trace evidence when the garbage man beats you to it. But you're wrong," Wendell pointed out. "There also are people who see murder as a sort of intellectual exercise, and getting away with the perfect crime is a game they play. There could be no bigger motive than that somebody just didn't like Kirk Toland, and figured he'd make a good victim. God knows I haven't found many friends of the guy's. Who better to kill than somebody everybody disliked."

"It's what I do," Maggie said, sucking on a pretzel stick while turning her Bic lighter over and over in her hands.

"Excuse me?" Wendell said, walking over to sit beside her in the seat Saint Just had vacated. "You want to run that one by me one more time?"

"Hmmm? Oh. Oh, no. In my books. I mean in my books. I only murder bad people in my books, never good ones."

"Because . . . ?" the lieutenant prompted.

"Because then nobody cares that he's dead, and the reader can concentrate on watching Saint Just romance the ladies and solve the crime. Not a formula, or anything like that, but just something I do. I just can't get into children or woman-in-jeopardy plots. So I only kill bad guys. It's like . . . well, it's like when I get stuck while writing the book. Sagging middles, that sort of thing. You know, when I've gone just so far and need something else to carry the interest along until the end, but I'm not ready to be at the end yet. Best way to fix it is to just kill somebody else. I mean it. When in doubt, kill somebody. Works every time."

"As long as it's fiction, I guess that's okay," Wendell said, grabbing a handful of pretzels from the bag on the coffee table. "I mean, just what I don't need — any upping of the body count. I've already got my captain breathing down my neck on this one."

Maggie watched him taking pretzels, making sure he left some for her. He was cute and all, but that didn't mean he could have all her pretzels. "Poor Kirk. So, Alex, process of elimination, you came up with The Trigger — or at least maybe you did. I'm still not sure if you think he's the killer or not. But it could have been anyone, right? I mean, like it could even have been Felicity Boobs Simmons, right?"

"Don't be vulgar, Maggie. Felicity Boothe Simmons? Your nemesis? She didn't like Toland?" Saint Just asked, unhappy to have another suspect enter the ranks, not now, now that he'd figured it all out so neatly.

Maggie bit off the end of the pretzel. "I don't know if Felicity liked him or not. I just know *I* don't like her. I don't like Nelson, either, but I really can't see him feeding Kirk poison mushrooms."

At last. Saint Just smiled, happy to see that Maggie agreed with him. Clever girl, Maggie, full of plots and scenarios and usually quite good judgment — her lapse with *Left*-tenant Wendell to one side, of course.

"Precisely. And that brings us up to today, doesn't it? I visit Trigg, and shortly thereafter, I'm pushed into the street, straight at a bus. For the past several hours, I've been mulling the idea that Trigg is more devious and less cautious than I had thought, and that he did indeed rush out of his office, follow me, push me in front of that bus. But then I realized something else, and that's why I feel like the rawest of — oh, damn and blast. Somebody pick up the phone, if you please."

Sterling grabbed the portable phone, spoke into it for a moment, then held it out toward Wendell. "*Left*-er-Lieutenant? Someone wishes to speak to you."

Saint Just sighed. Of course it would be the *left*-tenant who found a way to interrupt him just as he was about to make his grand announcement. The man was trouble, much more trouble than he was worth.

Now the drama was gone, burst like a bubble, and he would probably have to start over from the beginning.

"That was my chief," Wendell said as he pushed the Off button on the phone and handed it back to Sterling. "I don't know squat about spicing up sagging middles, but I think someone must have decided we've been having one, because I've got some bad news, I'm afraid. Building security just found Nelson Trigg's body in his office at Toland Books. It's only preliminary, but the gal from the medical examiner's office thinks he's been dead for about three or four hours. Somebody smashed in his skull with one of his hand weights. Blakely, is there anything you want to tell me?"

"Wait," Maggie said, taking hold of his arm. "Trigg's dead? Are they sure it's him?"

"Pretty sure. His office, right? Blakely?"

"I assure you, *Left*-tenant, the man was very much alive when I left him."

"And got pushed into the path of a bus by someone nobody saw. And barely hurt, too. Nice work, setting yourself up as a victim, then following it all up with this business about eliminating suspects. I notice you were quick to eliminate yourself."

"Oh, don't be ridiculous," Maggie said, ripping off her nicotine patch. "Damn, the whole world's out to keep me smoking. Lieutenant — Steve — you know damn well Alex didn't kill The Trigger. Don't you?"

"I don't know much of anything right now, Maggie," Wendell said, heading for the door. He stopped and pointed at Saint Just. "I never thought I'd say this, Blakely, especially to a guy who torks me off as

481

much as you do, but *don't leave town.*"

Saint Just struck a pose. "*Left*-tenant, I believe it is time you fortified yourself to the likelihood that I shall not be departing this vicinity anytime soon. Perhaps never."

"Gee, that made my day," Wendell said, and slammed the door behind him.

The living room was utterly quiet for some moments after Wendell's hasty departure, then erupted all at once.

"Nelson, dead? Murdered? Oh, Christ, the fighting that's going to go on over getting his corner office. I don't want to think about it."

"And the *left*-tenant suspects you, Saint Just? This isn't anything like what you said would happen when we came here."

"I'll make us some coffee."

"Alex, are you thinking what I'm thinking? Now that Nelson's dead? Maybe even before we heard about Nelson?"

Saint Just smiled at Maggie. "That would depend, my dear. What are you thinking?"

She grabbed his arm and walked him to a corner of the room. "Clarice. You're thinking Clarice, aren't you? The one person everybody forgets, including me, a couple of minutes ago. You eliminated everyone who was at the party, except Clarice. Why?"

Saint Just absently twirled his quizzing glass by the ribbon as he smiled at her. "You will notice, Maggie, that the *left*-tenant also didn't mention the fact that I'd neglected to include Clarice Simon? That should tell you something about the man, shouldn't it?"

Maggie wrinkled her nose. "Yeah. It tells me you love that he forgot. This isn't a pissing contest, Alex, it's a murder investigation. Two murder investigations. My God. I can't take it in. The Trigger's dead?"

Saint Just allowed a twinkle to enter his eye. "I warned him, exercise could kill him," then rubbed at his upper arm, because Maggie had punched him. "Might I remind you, madam, that I am an injured man?"

"Oh, yeah? And might I remind you, this isn't one of our books. This is real, damn it, and Kirk and Nelson are both dead."

"Yes, and now we know who killed at least one of them," Saint Just told her. "Now, if you could please find some way to shovel Bernice and Tabby out of here, perhaps we can finish this?"

Maggie turned her cheek for Tabby's obligatory air kiss, then shut the door, leaving her agent with the responsibility of pouring Bernie into a cab. She threw the deadbolts, the chain, then turned to look at Saint Just.

"Okay, they're gone, and Sterling's cleaning up in the kitchen. Now, tell me what the hell you meant. We figured out one of the murderers? Are you saying there's two?"

"Possibly," Saint Just said with such maddening calm that she longed to give him another shot in the arm. "You do realize that we have much the same cast of characters — suspects — knowing that Toland would have dinner with you that fateful night, *and* knowing that Trigg planned to work at his office today? I'm sure that fact hasn't been lost on you, yes? I don't know about you, but I feel very good about that. I've definitely been correct to believe someone from the party is our murderer. Still, I've yet to be certain if our so recently departed Mr. Trigg had a falling-out with a coconspirator, or if he is just one more victim of the same murderer."

"Who you think is Clarice," Maggie said, rolling her eyes. "Now I know you've got a concussion. Clarice? She couldn't kill a bug if it was biting her, for God's sake.

And Trigg? She certainly couldn't kill him. She worshipped him. I mean, I don't know if she's in love with him or sees — saw — him as a sort of father figure. Maybe a little of both. Oh, yuk, I don't even want to go there."

Saint Just, who had poured himself a brandy, sat down on one of the couches, elegantly crossing one leg over the other. "Thank you, Maggie. It's a trip I also would rather not take. Now, to get back to motive."

"Okay, that's good," Maggie said, grabbing her cigarettes and lighter and sitting down on the opposite couch. "Let's talk motive. Why would Clarice want to kill Kirk?" Then she held out her hands, a cigarette in one, the Bic in the other. "No! Wait. First I want to know what you meant about being taken in like a greenhorn today."

"I exist to be at your service, my dear," Saint Just said, and Maggie wanted to fatten his smugly smiling Val Kilmer lips. She'd never before realized how damn annoying he could be when he was solving a case.

"As I said, I visited Trigg today, his last day, at the offices of Toland Books."

"Yeah, and probably made him real

happy," Maggie interjected, blowing out a stream of smoke.

"He wasn't best pleased, no," Saint Just drawled. "As I said, I went there hoping for enlightenment, a reason to accuse or dismiss him, and left convinced he was not our killer, only to be pushed into a bus."

"Okay, the bus. And Trigg didn't push you? You're sure of that?"

"Trigg showed me his arms," Saint Just said, closing his eyes at the memory. "Very muscular, actually. He seemed quite proud of them. If he had pushed me, I might have suffered a more serious injury. No, the person who pushed me was not nearly so strong. A woman, Maggie. The more I think about it, the more convinced I am that I'm correct."

"A woman. Okay. Were you followed to his office? Somebody followed you there, then tried to kill you on the way back to the apartment? Is that what you think?"

"No, I think someone followed me *from* Trigg's office and tried to kill me. A rash act, an impetuous act, and one that does not bode well when we consider that our murderer is still out there. Poison takes planning. A shove in the back, a bang on the head? Those are crimes of passion, of improvisation. Or of desperation."

"Clarice," Maggie said, getting a mind's-eye picture of the woman who, as she had declared only a few days ago, "wouldn't say boo to a goose." It just didn't compute. "You want me to believe that Clarice is capable of cold-blooded, premeditated murder. *And* crimes of passion? Nope. Can't do that. Sorry. Can you at least give me a reason why you suspect her?"

"In a moment. First, we will continue our discussion as to why I believe Clarice pushed me into that bus, and not any of the other women involved in this case. One, Tabitha would not have been able to withstand the urge to then pick me up, dust me off, and offer me a bowl of insipid broth. Two, Bernice is too memorable — that mane of bright red hair. Conclusion, it had to be a person no one remembered seeing, a nearly invisible person who could push me, then walk away, with no one noticing her."

"Clarice. Okay, I'm beginning to buy this. But just a little. Go on."

Saint Just lit his cheroot, held it between his even white teeth, clearly the Saint Just of her books, the man about to dazzle everyone with his rather off-the-wall brilliance. "I drank freshly made coffee in Trigg's office," he said. "I don't know why

I didn't realize it at once, why it took until I was lying on my rack of pain in that hospital to see the obvious. Nelson Trigg would never stoop to preparing his own coffee. People prepare coffee for him."

Maggie waited, but it appeared that Saint Just had finished. "That's it?" she asked, shaking her head. "That's your big reason to suspect Clarice? Because you decided that The Trigger wasn't the type who made his own coffee?" Then she shrugged. "Oh, hell, you oughta recognize the type, shouldn't you? You don't make your own coffee, either."

"Try to concentrate your mind, Maggie. If Trigg didn't prepare his own coffee, that would mean that someone else was in the offices of Toland Books while I was there, putting forth my suspicions about him, letting him know that I knew about his problems with the dice. He even admitted them to me, rather frankly, although he said that if I repeated what he said he would deny everything. The standard response of the guilty, and one they believe will actually work, when everyone knows it won't. I'm already convinced that the *left*-tenant is investigating Trigg's finances, so the truth will out, one way or another."

Maggie raised her eyebrows and looked

at him with growing respect. "You got Trigg to admit he was cooking the books? You're kidding."

"You have my word on it. You can't have Trigg's, unfortunately, as he has shuffled off this mortal coil. He all but swore he returned every penny, but did say there were still some problems with the books, something he was going to be working on — I'm afraid the intricacies of bookkeeping elude me."

"That's because I can barely balance my checkbook. I'd never built a plot around something like embezzling, because I don't know a debit from a credit. I guess I could do something in the next book, make you a whiz with numbers? I write it, you become it, right?"

"It does seem to be how it works, yes. But to get back to the point at hand — who else would have been in the offices late on a Saturday afternoon, other than Trigg, trying to, um, *uncook* the books? Who else, Maggie? Who would have prepared the coffee?"

"His loyal companion, Lassie," Maggie mumbled under her breath. "Clarice," she said then, pushing her hands through her hair. "Loyal, hard-working, do-anything-to-be-close-to-The Trigger Clarice. Oh,

brother. So you think she was there somewhere, heard the two of you, then followed
you, figuring that killing you, or at least in-
juring you, scaring you, would protect
Trigg? Is that what you're saying?"

"Not precisely. Ah, Sterling, thank you,"
he said as Sterling handed him a small
bowl of cheese balls, a new favorite of
Saint Just's. "Sit down, join us. We're
solving the murders."

"Yes, I heard as I came into the room.
Clarice Simon pushed you into the bus?
Can we prove it?"

Maggie stubbed out her cigarette. "Sure
we can, Sterling. All we have to do is tell
Steve Wendell that The Trigger wouldn't
ever make his own coffee at the office.
Damning evidence. Man, he'll have her
locked up so fast, our heads will spin.
Yeah," she said, falling back against the
cushions. "R-i-i-ght."

"Sarcasm does not become you,
Maggie," Saint Just told her, puffing on his
cheroot. "So what we have is that either
Trigg and Clarice were working together to
kill Toland, or that either Trigg *or* Clarice
took the initiative to eliminate Toland so
that he either wouldn't find out about the
cooked books or, if he already knew,
couldn't do anything about it. Understand

now? Either they were coconspirators, in other words, or — since Trigg is obviously no longer a suspect — Clarice Simon is and has always been a woman on her own mission. What still puzzles me is why she would now kill Trigg, if she had tried to murder me in order to protect him."

"Yeah, that does punch a pretty big hole in your theory, doesn't it?" Maggie said, rising from the couch. "And, until you can figure that one out, Sherlock, I'm going to keep on thinking that Clarice Simon is just who she seems to be. A very sweet, timid girl. Sorry, Alex. You're selling, but I'm not buying."

"She all but attacked you at Toland's memorial soiree, if you'll recall," Saint Just reminded her.

Maggie considered this for a few moments. "True. But that's because she thought I murdered Kirk. Are you trying to say that she was just putting on a show, pretending to think I killed him in order to take suspicion away from herself? And why would she do that, if no one suspected her? Hell, no one even remembers her, poor kid."

"Maggie may be right, Saint Just," Sterling said, reaching into the bowl for a handful of cheese balls. "I think you'll need more than you usually have. The coffee isn't enough. Especially now that Mr. Trigg is dead."

"Right again," Maggie said, picking up her purse as she looked at her watch and saw it was only ten o'clock. "And now I'm going over to see Clarice, as soon as I look up her address." She walked to the desk and began flipping through her address book. "I should have it, for my Christmas card list . . . ah, here it is. She shouldn't hear about The Trigger on the news, or in tomorrow's newspaper."

"Splendid," Saint Just said, also getting to his feet. "We'll go with you."

"In a pig's eye you will," Maggie said, heading for the door. "You ran into a bus, remember? You're staying here, and Sterling is going to make sure you stay here. Right, Sterling?"

"Absolutely," Sterling said with a sharp look at Saint Just, a look that sort of melted as Saint Just stared back at him. "Well, I shall be valiant in the attempt."

"Do more than try, Sterling," Maggie said, going back over to her desk, picking up her address book, and tucking it in her purse. "I'll be back in about an hour or so. Clarice as the murderer," she muttered, shaking her head as she left the apartment.

"Boy, now I've heard it all."

"You will be prudent, won't you, Maggie?" Saint Just asked her. "Just tell her Trigg is dead, and let her turn into a watering pot?"

"I know how to handle this, Alex," Maggie said. "The last damn thing I'd do is tell Clarice you think she's the murderer. Especially since I think it's a screwy idea."

"Oddly, I trust you to be discreet. But we will keep a candle in the window for you, so please don't be too long."

She hailed a cab herself when the weekend doorman didn't show up, and rode toward the Village, turning over Saint Just's words in her head.

Ridiculous. Clarice had no reason to kill Kirk. Unless she did it out of some crazy notion that she would be protecting The Trigger, because Kirk was going to blow the whistle on his embezzling, maybe even implicate Clarice in the crime. If The Trigger was cooking the books, Clarice, as his personal assistant, probably had to know it.

Okay, that would work. But then why kill The Trigger? That was the part that didn't work, would never work, no matter how much Saint Just tried to make it work. Clarice loved Nelson Trigg, was absolutely sappy over him. She'd never kill him.

And how would she have killed Kirk? The poison mushrooms, right. Clarice knew about the mushrooms, because she was the one who called to get the menu. Kirk's very favorite meal, steak smothered in mushrooms and onions, baked potato and salad. Okay, maybe not his favorite dinner, but the one Maggie always prepared for him when he came over for dinner because it was about all she knew how to cook.

And everybody knew that, too. It wasn't exactly a state secret that Maggie was a meat-and-potatoes kind of cook, and that the most exotic she could be was to slop some onions and mushrooms on top of a hunk of cow.

Which meant that whoever called her that day — okay, everybody knew it was Clarice — would have already known, as Kirk himself had already known, what she'd serve that night. So why would Kirk have anyone call her, ask her the menu? He already knew the menu; he'd certainly complained enough about the lack of variety in the dinners.

Yes, the whole phone call was suspicious, wasn't it?

So maybe Clarice, who also had to know the menu, had called on her own, just nervously double-checking, so that when the deadly mushrooms were found in Kirk's system, it would also be learned that he'd eaten mushrooms that night for dinner.

"Yes," Maggie said out loud, "but she couldn't know that I wouldn't have extra mushrooms in the fridge that I didn't use up, or the leftover stuff in the fridge, proving that they weren't poison mushrooms. If I was supposed to be the main suspect, a quick check of the mushrooms in the fridge would have cleared me. So why bother? Why wait for the chance to implicate me? Why bother with mushrooms in the first place? Why have him get sick at my place?"

Maggie reached in her purse for her cigarettes, then glared at the large No Smoking sign on the back of the front seat of the cab. "Shit," she said, knowing she'd think better with a cigarette in her hand. Seven seconds, that's what it took for the first hit to the brain after she lit up. Imagination and inspiration mainlined via nicotine. She needed some of both.

The cab stopped in front of a rather run-down apartment building and Maggie paid the fare, then stood on the pavement, wondering if this had been the smartest move she'd ever made.

What if Alex was right? Yeah, sure. Alex was her creation. His imagination was actually her imagination. On his own, could he deduce himself out of a paper bag?

But if he could . . .

Maggie looked up at the third floor of the narrow converted house and saw lights in the windows. Clarice's apartment was on the third floor, probably one of only two on each floor. Was this one hers? Was she awake? Should she bother her, ruin her evening?

Maggie paced the pavement, smoking, hoping for inspiration. "Oh, this is ridiculous. Unless . . ." She stopped dead, so that a passerby bumped into her, cursed her, and moved on.

"Unless the poison was in the wine, and Clarice wanted to know whether or not I was going to drink the wine? Red wine for Kirk, zinfandel for me. I told her that, told her I don't drink the red, just the zinfandel. Is that how she did it? She needed a way to get the mushrooms to him and, after I told her about the zinfandel, she spiked the red wine Kirk brought with him?"

"You okay, lady?"

Maggie blinked and looked at the uniformed cop who had appeared out of nowhere. "Me? Oh, sure. I'm fine."

"Then move along," he said, moving along himself.

"Gotta stop talking to myself," Maggie said, then grinned as she realized that she was, yet again, talking to herself. "And I've got to stop thinking of Clarice as a murderer . . . murderess . . . killer. And another thing. The same goes for the wine bottle as it does for the mushrooms. The police could have tested the bottle if it had still been in the apartment."

Then it hit her.

"Sonofabitch," she said, hailing another cab. She headed back uptown, to Toland Books.

CHAPTER 19

Steve Wendell met her in the lobby of the building after being called down from the murder scene. Maggie watched as he walked toward her, his badge hung over his shirt pocket, his hair rather adorably mussed, his expression grim.

"Maggie? Is something wrong?"

She shook her head. "No, not wrong. Well, not really." She looked around at the uniformed cops that were milling in the lobby, then grabbed Wendell's arm as two men in blue jumpsuits wheeled in a gurney and headed for the elevators. "They're bringing him down?"

"Pretty soon, yeah. Is that why you came? To make sure it's Nelson Trigg? It is. Somebody did a damn good job of bashing in his skull."

"With one of his hand weights, right?"

"One is missing from the stand holding his weights, so we're assuming that's our weapon, but we won't be sure for a while yet. Maggie? What's the matter?"

She took a deep breath and looked up at him. "Why aren't I a suspect anymore? Just because the garbage man took away what could have been the evidence? Is that the only reason?"

"Damn," Wendell said, scratching at that spot behind his left ear. "I was hoping you wouldn't figure that one out."

"Figure out that the lack of evidence was pretty convenient? Figure out that maybe I'd hit Kirk on purpose, either to knock him out or at least stun him, so that he'd stick around, get sick in my apartment, let me play the role of hysterical girlfriend who couldn't possibly have poisoned dear, darling Kirk? Figure out that Sterling may have cleaned up some stuff, but that I had hours and hours to clean up other stuff before Kirk woke up, sick? Figure out that I could have bought mushrooms from Mario to cover my ass, and also collected some of my own in Central Park or someplace? I should still be a suspect, shouldn't I? Steve? Why aren't I still a suspect?"

He took hold of her arm at the elbow and led her to one of the couches in the lobby. "Now why do I think you're about to tell me that, too?" he said once they were both seated.

Maggie pulled out her cigarettes and lighter, and a rent-a-cop immediately barked out, "Can't smoke in here, lady."

"I have to give this up, I swear it. Either

499

that, or become a hermit," she said, stuffing everything back into her purse. "Okay, I'll do this solo, no nicotine crutch. I'm not a suspect, Steve, because you think I was meant to be the second victim."

"Oh, boy," Wendell said quietly. "How did you figure it out?"

Maggie felt her stomach do a small flip, but not in fear. In excitement, just as it did when she got a new idea, knew it would work. "Then I'm right? Let me see if I've got this right, okay? You figure that someone learned about the menu, then spiked the wine while it sat in Kirk's office, before he showed up at my place — injected it with a syringe, something like that, right through the cork. At least, that's how I'd do it, if I wanted to put poison into a closed bottle of wine."

"Remind me to always provide my own liquid refreshment when I'm with you," Wendell said, smiling.

"Wait, there's more. Back to the wine, okay? The fact that I served mushrooms means nothing, because the poison was most probably in the wine, and when you found the bottle and our bodies, you'd know. Using those poison mushrooms was just a little extra added red herring, to slow you guys down, confuse things. Our killer likes to confuse things, keep you guys on your toes."

"So far, he's doing a pretty good job of it, too."

"Please don't interrupt, Steve. This is hard enough, doing it off the top of my head, without taking notes. But that's it, isn't it? Hell, it could even have been serendipity — mushrooms were the poison, and I just happened to be cooking mushrooms. Coincidence. No matter how it was, I wasn't supposed to be a suspect, not seriously, unless either Kirk or I pulled a murder-suicide thingie, which could work as a plot, but it's stretching it, don't you think? Seriously — bottom-line time — you think I was supposed to be *dead*. As dead as Kirk."

"If we believed you about where you bought the mushrooms, yes," he said, taking hold of her hands, which had begun to shake.

"Alex never figured that out. He just knew I hadn't killed Kirk, and left it at that, went looking for anyone who might have wanted Kirk dead. Oh, he'll go ballistic when I tell him."

"Yeah, well, Secret Squirrel and his injured ego to one side, how are you feeling about all of this, Maggie?"

She shook her head. "I'm not sure, except about the dead part, because you're wrong on that." She looked at him evenly and asked her most important question. "Is that why you've been hanging around the apartment, around me? Because you thought I could be in some danger?"

"It may have started out that way," Wendell admitted, squeezing her hands again before pulling her to her feet. "It sure wasn't so I could listen to Blakely's pearls of wisdom about the case. But our date for tonight? That was on my time, Maggie."

"So maybe I'm at least semi-irresistible? Good for me." She didn't know where to look, and unfortunately, she chose to look toward the elevator, just in time to see Trigg being wheeled out in a body bag. "Oh, God," she said, her knees sagging, so that Wendell quickly grabbed her and held her close.

"We're going to solve this, Maggie, I promise," he said into her hair. "And then you and I are going out to dinner. Okay?"

Maggie felt good in his arms, safe, protected. Another woman would milk the moment for all it was worth. But not Maggie. A person had to have priorities, and right now murder was tops on her list.

She pushed herself out of his arms, dropped the hammer, and hit him with her conclusions. "Steve? This is important. Did I tell you that I don't drink red wine? I said something at the hospital, I'm pretty sure of it, to the doctor, but did I ever tell you? I don't think so, I really don't. I just told you what Kirk had for dinner."

"That's all I asked," Wendell said, wincing as he realized what Maggie had just said. "Man, I really screwed up. Sorry."

"That's okay. I should have volunteered, and I didn't. I was too busy trying to make everyone understand that I wasn't the killer. Now, let's see if this makes sense. I told Clarice, when she phoned me that day. I don't drink red wine, I drink zinfandel. That wasn't something she'd write in a note to Kirk, who knew I only drink zinfandel — she would have just written the menu for him so he could choose the wine — so the only person who knew for sure I wouldn't be drinking the red wine was Clarice. Not you, because I didn't tell you, not anyone else, because Clarice's note supposedly only contained the menu for dinner — it was up to Kirk to choose the wine. Are you with me so far?"

"Catching up," Wendell said with a small

smile. "Keep going."

"Good. Kirk brought a bottle of red, and zinfandel for me, just as he always did. In fact, Clarice's entire telephone call was a waste of time — Kirk knew we'd have steak, knew he'd want red wine, knew I'd want the zinfandel. I never cooked him anything but red meat. Red meat, red wine. He knew that. I doubt he ever asked her to call me. Nobody tried to kill me, Steve. Someone tried to make doubly sure I *wouldn't* die. Just Kirk. That one mistake all killers make. The phone call was that one mistake. The kind of mistake a woman would make, because even as a killer, she still had a conscience, and I was a friend."

Wendell looked at her for long moments, then said, "Well, shit."

"You took the words right out of my mouth. You've been looking for someone who wanted both Kirk and me dead, right? But the killer only wanted Kirk dead. And now The Trigger," she said as she looked through the large window to the street, where the doors were just closing on the back of the coroner's wagon. "Alex also thinks it's Clarice."

"I thought you said he didn't know about the two wines?"

"No, he has another reason. He remembered that there was fresh coffee in The Trigger's office when he was there today. He's convinced that The Trigger wouldn't lift a hand to make his own coffee, and that Clarice was also there somewhere, being the good assistant. He thinks she overheard their conversation, which included The Trigger admitting he was embezzling from Toland Books, and then followed Alex, pushed him into the bus. To protect The Trigger."

Wendell walked a few feet away, then turned back to face her as he stabbed his fingers through his hair. "So. You think it's Clarice because she called and learned that you don't drink red wine. What if you did?"

Maggie shrugged again. "I don't know. Maybe I would have just been collateral damage, if I did. Or maybe it wasn't about the wine at all, and she just needed to make doubly sure I was serving mushrooms, which I always did when Kirk came to dinner, and that even if I had *good* mushrooms in my fridge, it would still be such a mixup that you guys would be looking everywhere, and finding nothing but a puzzle. You have to admit it, Steve, using mushrooms as the poison the same night I served mushrooms is a damn good red herring. You've been looking everywhere but where you should look. Maybe she even got the poison into him earlier, before he came to dinner. The wine is only one possibility, and seems logical. But you'll never be sure, unless Clarice confesses. Man, and she even threw that phone call in my face the day of the memorial lunch. Why didn't I figure this out sooner? It was like she was laughing at me, laughing at us all, saying 'catch me if you can, jerks'."

"Uh-huh. And your cousin also thinks it's Clarice Simon — because Trigg wouldn't make his own coffee?"

"Not just that," Maggie corrected, feeling the need to defend Alex, who was, after all, a figment of her imagination, so that, in a way, his ideas were her ideas. So she added a hopefully logical conclusion to Alex's assumptions. "He thinks that maybe The Trigger was in on killing Kirk, and then somehow he and Clarice had a falling-out tonight, which is when she killed him. After running after Alex and pushing him into the path of the bus, that is."

"Busy girl. And us without a shred of proof, even if I could wrap my mind around the idea of that little mouse murdering anyone."

"That's what I was trying to do. Wrap my mind around Clarice as the killer as I rode down to her apartment, to tell her about The Trigger."

"Jesus, you went to her apartment?"

"Not all the way. I stopped on the pavement, smoked on it a little, and figured out that maybe I was about to pick up a candle and go down that dark passage everyone told me not to go down. You know, the Gothic heroine syndrome? The dummy with the candle, going where she has no business being, while the reader is screaming 'No, no, not there, you idiot!' Anyway, when I finally figured it out, all I wanted to do was see you, ask you if I was right to think what I was thinking."

"Good. Because if you're right, if Blakely is right, Clarice could be on a pretty short chain right now. Damn, and me with no real evidence. I mean, we'll find evidence of Clarice all over Trigg's office, but that means nothing, because she worked with him. This is going to be a tough one, but I have a judge who owes me a favor, so I think I'll get my act together, give him a call tomorrow. If I can get this past one of the assistant DAs, that is."

He turned as someone called his name. "I've got to go. Look, Maggie, about my not telling you that I thought you could have also been the killer's target? I want you to know that —"

"It's okay, I think," Maggie interrupted. "It was an either-or kind of thing for you. Either I was the killer, or I was another potential victim, so you decided to stick real close to me. You were still sorting everything out."

"Only the cop part of me," he said quietly, his green eyes looking at her in a way that would have made her forgive him almost anything. "Well . . . gotta go. Shall I have one of the uniforms take you home?"

No thanks, I'll float there, Maggie thought, then quickly told him not to worry, she'd catch a cab.

"You're sulking."

"Gentlemen do *not* sulk. They brood, darkly and dangerously, which I also am not doing," Saint Just told Maggie, then went back to staring into the middle distance. "You did tell me that the *left*-tenant still has no real proof. I'm merely thinking of some way to get Clarice Simon to admit what she's done."

"No, you're not," Maggie said, sitting at her desk, starting a new game of Snood. She aimed the Snood tosser at two purple triangles, and shot them down. "You're wondering how the hell you missed it, how you didn't figure out that I could have been a victim. How you could have missed something that important. Admit it, Alex, you've been sulking — brooding — about it ever since breakfast."

"Oh, very well, if it makes you happy, satisfies you in some way. Yes, I'm extremely disappointed in myself for not considering the possibility."

"Because you were too worried that Maggie might be hauled off to the guardhouse, leaving us to fend for ourselves," Sterling put in as he folded the scattered sections of the Sunday newspaper. "You're a cold man at times, Saint Just."

Maggie turned on her swivel chair and looked at Sterling. "Really? Do you really think Alex is cold? I would have called him arrogant, toplofty, unbearably smug and sure of himself at times. But not cold, not unfeeling. You don't think he shows enough emotion, Sterling?"

"He's protecting himself," Sterling said with a small nod of his head. "His sad childhood and all of that. The distant mother, the ineffectual father, that initial disappointment in love. Everything you wrote in his character description. I read it the other day, found it on your desk while I was straightening up. Mine, too. Mine was shorter. Lovable, sweet, helpful, not too bright, but sometimes wonderfully insightful. And an orphan, thankfully. No, perhaps Saint Just's not cold. Perhaps he just protects himself."

Saint Just stood up, his spine stiff. "If you're quite done?" he asked Sterling, who seemed to suddenly remember something to do in the kitchen. "Yes, I thought so," he said to his friend's departing back, then turned on Maggie. "This is all your fault, you know. If I hide my true feelings, I do it because of how you made me."

"My fault?" Maggie put her computer to sleep and headed for one of the couches. "Why do I get all the blame?"

"I would think that is self-explanatory. You created me, gave me a history. Gave me some of *your* history, Maggie, although I can see by the stunned expression on your face that you had not as yet figured that out for yourself. You made me a man who thinks with his head, not with his heart. A man who protects his heart at all times, protects himself at all times. If I'm cold, I have reason. Just as you do. Do you consider yourself cold, unfeeling? Or just careful?"

Maggie looked at him for long moments, moments during which he saw many emotions coming and going on her very expressive face. "I never realized . . ." She shot off the couch and began to pace. "Do you know how many times I've told people they're full of crap, that I do *not* use personal experiences to create my characters?"

Saint Just watched her for a few moments, a slight smile on his face. "We are not entirely alike, you know," he told her kindly. "For instance, I had absolutely no problem in speaking to Doctor Bob's woman of affairs or whatever she is, canceling your appointment for tomorrow morning."

"Yippee," Maggie said sourly, circling one index finger in the air. "I gave the lion a heart for courage." She stopped, looked at him, blinked back tears. "That's me, you know. Oz. The little pip-squeak behind the curtain, pretending to be bigger than I am. Or the ventriloquist. Yeah, the ventriloquist, that's even better. I've read about them. Shy, introverted people who can only say what they really want to say while they have their hand stuck up some doll's back, moving his mouth for him."

"I don't understand," Saint Just said,

wishing Sterling had kept his mouth shut. Maggie had enough on her plate without this.

"You," she said, pointing at him. "You're my ventriloquist's dummy. I hide behind you, speak through you, give you the courage I don't have. You don't just have my failings, you also do everything I can't do. Ride, shoot, fence. Tell everyone to go to hell and get away with it. You name it. Anything I'm afraid to do, you do." She laughed, hollowly. "Of course, I didn't expect you to turn into *Chuckie*, come to life, start making me crazy. Crazier," she amended, wiping at her eyes.

"And another thing," she said before Saint Just could do more than stand up and head for the liquor cabinet to pour her some brandy that would hopefully calm her. "This is wrong. This is all wrong, and has been wrong since the day you and Sterling showed up. Do you know what would happen if I put all of this in one of my books?"

"No, I don't," he said, handing her the small snifter.

"Well, let me tell you what would happen. The reviewers would crucify me, that's what would happen. Imaginary characters come to life, murders all over the place, two love interests, stupid psychological stuff cluttering up the place. Pick a subject, Ms. Dooley, that's what they'd write. You're trying to do too much, Ms. Dooley, and you haven't the talent for it. I can't have *real* talent, you know, because I write books with happy endings, because I once wrote romance. Ergo, anything I do has to stink, except when it works, which is when they say I'm *lucky,* or that *my fans* will like it. But the hell with that; I can live with that. But the rest of it? God, Alex, my life's a zoo, and I've taken the worst parts of it and handed them to you. Screwed-up parents, fear of commitment, all that crap. I'm so sorry, Alex."

"Two love interests?" he asked, just because he had to. He really had to.

"*Oooooh!* Why do I bother?" She pushed the snifter back at him, stood up, and ran down the hall to her bedroom.

Sterling shortened his steps, falling slightly behind Saint Just as the two of them headed for the light spilling onto the pavement through the plate glass window of Styles Cafe. "Are you sure Maggie doesn't suspect anything?"

Saint Just tucked his cane under his arm and stopped, waiting for Sterling to catch up with him. "I told you, Sterling, she's still too busy sulking to notice a dead horse in the living room, let alone believe we have some ulterior motive for stepping out this evening."

"Brooding. This afternoon, you said brooding."

"I was brooding, Sterling. Maggie is sulking. A man broods by sitting quietly, staring, sipping brandy, looking profound. Very dignified. A woman sulks by turning herself into a watering pot, throwing things, and eating all the ice cream we'd planned for dessert. Which, in a way, is a good thing, because our excuse that we needed to go find ourselves some food was then believable. Still not quite as simple as having Maggie out of the house, holding Bernice's hand, but since Bernice is no longer a suspect, that point is moot, isn't it. Sterling? The time, if you please? I believe our friends may be late."

Sterling pulled out his pocket watch and held it up to the faint light from a passing car. "A few minutes past ten. You're right, they're late. Perhaps they're not coming. Ah, well, a pity and a shame. Shall we go?"

"Oh, ye of faint heart," Saint Just said, shaking his head. Then he turned toward a slight noise coming from the alleyway.

"Sterling, I believe it's a *go,* if I'm using the vernacular correctly."

"If we were launching a rocket," Sterling grumbled as Snake, Killer, and Mare stepped out of the shadows. "You really should watch more television with me, Saint Just, if we live long enough, that is."

"Madam, gentlemen," Saint Just said, bowing slightly to each of them in turn, "how good to see you again. Shall I assume that you have the papers?"

"That would depend," Mare told him, keeping close to the alley, staying in the shadows. "You have the money?"

"Oh, dear, now here's a dilemma," Saint Just said, watching as Killer moved to his left, Snake to his right. "I sense a marked lack of trust. On your side, my dear. And, to be quite frank, on mine as well. Snake? You will oblige me by standing very still."

"I ain't doin' nuthin'," Snake protested, raising his hands to show that they were empty. "I just thought I saw somethin', that's all."

"Sterling? Look behind us, if you will. Do you see anything?"

Always obedient, Sterling turned around. Looked. "Um . . . Saint Just?"

"Yes, Sterling?" he answered, still watching Snake and Killer, who appeared to wish to be anywhere but where they were at the moment.

"It's . . . well, it's Maggie," Sterling said quietly, turning around once more, this time looking at Saint Just. "She doesn't look very happy."

"Hi, everybody," Maggie said, walking up on Saint Just's left, her hands in the pockets of a light cotton jacket. "Having a meeting, are you? What's the name of your club? Idiots' Delight?"

"Not now, Maggie, if you please. I am conducting a piece of business."

"Sure you are. With them? What are they doing, selling cookies? Send this punk to camp? What?"

"Hey," Mare said, stepping into the weak light from the street, "who's the smart mouth? Nobody said anything about an audience. Come on, guys, we're outta here."

"I have your money," Saint Just said quickly, as Mare turned her back to him.

She stopped and looked over her shoulder. "Stuff your money. I don't know what you're talking about. I never saw you before in my life. Right, guys? We never saw these two before in our lives. Probably perverts. Go fuck a duck, buddy, because we don't do that stuff."

"Saint Just? They're leaving."

"Yes, Sterling, I had noticed that. Thank you, Maggie. Now, if you'll excuse me?"

He left Maggie and Sterling standing on the street, Maggie glaring at Sterling, Sterling trying to appear invisible, and followed the spooked trio into the alleyway.

He'd taken only three or four steps into the darkness when Mare moved in front of him, her knife drawn. "Who is she?"

"A thorn in my side, the bane of my existence, the nosiest woman this side of Perdition," Saint Just drawled, using his index finger to push against the blade, turning it away from his belly. "And, lastly, not a part of this. Now, let me see that you have the papers, and I will hand over your payment. Or do you really believe I would go to all of this trouble only to walk away? Have *you* gone to all this trouble, only to walk away? From this?" he ended, reaching into his pocket and pulling out a thick wad of bills.

Mare reached out to grab the money, but Saint Just had already moved to his left, putting the safety of a building wall at his back, his sword cane stripped and ready for business.

"Jesus, would you look at that?" Snake crept closer, his eyes on the money. "Come on, Mare, give him the stuff, and let's get out of here."

"Yeah, Mare. Take the money," Killer prompted, doing a small dance in the alley. "She can't be a cop. No cop would be stupid enough to step into the middle of a deal. She would have waited until we'd handed over the papers, taken the cash. She wouldn't show up so soon, not if she was a cop."

"My felicitations, Killer," Saint Just said, holding the wad of bills aloft once more. "You seem to have quite a good head on your shoulders. Of course the woman is not a cop. Now, come along, Mare. We've been rubbing along so well, let's not balk at the first small obstacle. Here. Take it. I'm showing you how much I trust you. Go on, take it."

Mare seemed to be chewing on something, her jaw moving as she looked at the money, looked up at Saint Just, looked at the money again. "The paper's good. Really good. Don't you want to see it first?"

"That's not necessary. I fully believe in your expertise."

She gave her head a small jerk to one side, then handed over a large brown envelope. "Okay. But I couldn't get a gun. I tried, really. Not my thing, you know? I'm sort of nonviolent, you know?"

Saint Just sheathed his sword, smiling as he heard Snake's relieved sigh. Children. He was dealing with naughty children . . . and very poor liars. "That is depressing, my dear. I suppose I'll just have to buy yours?"

Mare whirled on the two boys. "Who told him? Which one of you *idiots* told him?"

Killer shook his head in denial while Snake goggled at her. "You've got a gun? Jeez. Can I see it?"

"Oh, for Christ's sakes," Mare said, stuffing the money into the pocket of her sweatshirt. Then she reached behind her, to the waistband of her jeans, and pulled out a small silver revolver that looked almost toy-like. "Here. It's loaded, so be careful. A guy I know sold it to me for you, said it's clean. I never really wanted to keep it for myself anyway."

Saint Just carefully removed the gun from Mare's hand, hefting it, liking the feel of its weight. "Never play cards, my dear," he said, tucking the gun into his pocket. "Either that, or learn to tell when an opponent is bluffing. You see, I had no idea if any of you had a gun in your possession.

Now, how much do I owe you for the weapon?"

"It's a gift," Mare said quickly, motioning for the boys to follow her, and the three quickly melted away down the alley as Maggie and Sterling appeared at the end of it.

"Saint Just? I tried to stop her, but —"

"Never mind, Sterling. Maggie? I imagine you have a few questions for me?"

She advanced on him, each footfall louder and more determined than the next. "Sterling told me. You bought ID, right? From those *kids?* What are you, nuts? How much did this cost me? And let me see this stuff," she ended, grabbing the envelope from his hand. "Come on, back to the apartment. Let's all look at how you just cost me another pile of money."

"Better follow her," Sterling suggested as Maggie stomped off, expecting them to heel, like obedient hounds. "She says we probably got skunked, whatever that is. I just know she's not happy."

"Oh, and one more thing," Maggie said, heading back toward them, her right hand held out, palm up. "I'll take the gun, thank you."

Saint Just looked at his friend. "Sterling, you didn't. Yes, of course you did."

"*Now*, Alex," Maggie said, making a come-here motion with her fingers. "I'm not kidding, give me the gun."

"Very well, Maggie," Saint Just said, pulling the weapon from his pocket and holding it out to her, smiling slightly as she reflexively stepped back a few paces, her face pale in the dim light.

"Shit, you really have a gun, don't you?" She stepped forward again, looked at the weapon as if deciding how to pick it up, finally deciding to gingerly grasp the handle between thumb and forefinger. "It's kind of cute, for a gun. Okay, now what do I do with it?"

"I don't suggest dropping it," Saint Just drawled, almost amused, but not quite. He knew he would find the gun later, however, in the locked drawer in Maggie's room, so he could afford to be amenable. "I likewise don't recommend walking down the street like that, holding it in front of you at arm's length. Passersby might be offended."

"Oh, shut up," Maggie said as she fumbled with the unsealed envelope, at last opening it enough to slide the gun into it. "There. Now let's go home, where I can yell at you better. And hurry up. Steve will be here in about a half hour, and I need to hide this stuff. He says he's got a plan."

Saint Just neatly tucked his cane under his arm as he bowed to Sterling, urging him to precede him down the sidewalk. "The *left*-tenant has a plan," he said to no one in particular, his tone devoid of humor. "The mind boggles."

CHAPTER 20

"Remind me again why I said yes to this," Maggie said into the V of her blouse, then smiled at a woman who looked at her as if wondering if, gee, was she seeing one of those New York wackos everyone in Bakersfield talked about? *You betchum, lady, I'm talking to my own boobs. Don't you?*

She smiled at the woman, who quickly turned away, then pressed a hand to her ear, tapping on her earpiece at the same time she patted at the center clasp of her bra. "Hey, Steve? Are you hearing me? I can't hear you."

"We hear you, Maggie," Steve said, his voice tickling her ear. "You aren't hearing me because I'm trying to maintain radio silence. But stop patting at the mike, or I may never hear anything else, ever again. Those mikes are supersensitive."

"Okay, sorry," Maggie said, nearly tapping at the mike again in apology before quickly lowering her hand. "This is kind of cool, you know," she said, trying to talk without moving her lips. "Unless you can hear my stomach growl. Could you hear my stomach if it growled? I'm so hungry, it might just do that."

"It already did," Steve told her. "About five minutes ago. You should have eaten lunch."

"I was too nervous," Maggie said, putting a hand over her mouth, as if covering up a cough. "Is Alex still with you? For God's sake, Steve, don't let him out of your sight."

"He and Sterling are right here, Maggie. We're deep in a corner of the main dining room, far enough away not to be noticed, close enough to get to you quickly if we need to. Remember, the reservation is in your name. The hostess already knows where to seat you."

Maggie nodded, then remembered Steve couldn't see her. "Ten-four," she said, feeling more than a little silly. "I guess I'd better shut up now, in case Clarice is on her way."

"Good plan," Steve said. "We'll all go silent now, but your mike stays live. Be careful, Maggie. Just keep it light until the two of you are seated in the restaurant. Then you can start asking questions."

"Uh-hmm," she said, and continued pacing the wide walkway in front of Tavern on the Green, on the lookout for Clarice Simon.

She adjusted her purse strap on her shoulder, her "feedbag," as Alex called it, heavier than usual, thanks to the small silver gun she'd slipped into it at the last minute. Not that Alex knew that, or Steve. Could she fire it if she felt the need? How many years would carrying an unlicensed weapon, concealed yet, get her in prison? Not as many years as getting dead would get her in a grave, that was for sure.

She could shoot a gun, to protect herself. She felt certain she could; she'd never written a wimpy heroine in her life. And she could hit a target, too. She played Snood, didn't she? She knew how to aim.

Okay, getting a little too weird here, a little too nervous. She had to calm down.

And not that she didn't trust Steve to come to the rescue if things got sticky. He'd explained it all to her last night, and then twice more to Alex, who had been very much against the idea.

It was all so strange. They all believed that Clarice was their murderer, and they all disagreed on their reasons for suspecting her.

Alex's reason got Maggie's vote for Most Lame, the fact that there had been fresh coffee in the pot in The Trigger's office. Although his notion that a woman had pushed him sounded a little less feeble.

She liked her own reason: the telephone call that Kirk really wouldn't have asked Clarice to make. It made sense; it was logical. And it was her conclusion, and that made it a smart conclusion, damn it.

But, she had to admit — even Alex had to admit — Steve's reason was the best one:

"Clarice Simon was born and raised in Rochester, and she still owns a house up there."

That had been his reason, and when he'd explained why this was important, Alex had nodded his head, seeming to take some of the credit for himself.

"See," Steve had told them last night, when they were all sitting around the game table, eating pizza and planning strategy, "I can't arrest somebody because she might have made coffee, or because she made that phone call to you, Maggie. Even if I believe you two might be on to something. I need proof, something to take to one of the assistant DAs, get a search warrant, bring her in for questioning instead of just asking her if she'll volunteer to come in on her own. So I spent the day looking around, mostly thanks to you, Blakely, something you said the other day."

"Indeed," Saint Just had said, eying him levelly. "And what did I say?"

"Well, two things. One you said, and one you didn't. Let me explain," he said, propping his elbows on the table. "The thing you didn't say was Clarice Simon's name, during our recent Stump the Cop session. You mentioned everyone's name *but* Clarice Simon's, as a matter of fact. The call from my chief, telling me about Nelson Trigg's murder, interrupted you right at the punch line, didn't it?"

"Punch line?" Saint Just repeated, looking at Maggie.

"The denouement," she told him, smiling. "And Steve's right. The phone call came just as you were about to tell us all that Clarice murdered Kirk."

"Actually," Wendell said, scratching that spot behind his left ear, "I'm kind of glad I missed that. If I'd known your reason was a pot of fresh coffee, I might not have taken your earlier advice."

"And this advice would be . . . ?" Saint Just prompted. "Really, *Left*-tenant, you could try to organize your conversation more. Truly."

"Yeah, well, I get where I'm going, and that's all that matters. So, the thing you said. Maybe you'll remember. It was the day we were looking up Destroying Angel mushrooms on the Internet. I didn't know the poison could take up to ten days to act, and you said —"

"A prudent man does his own investigating," Saint Just finished for him. "Am I correct?"

"Absolutely. So, I did my own investigating of Clarice Simon, and some more digging about those damn mushrooms. And you know what I found out?"

"Perceive me sitting here, breathless with anticipation," Saint Just said, earning himself a quick kick under the table from Maggie.

"I discovered that the information I had from the doc at the hospital, and from the Internet, was pretty vague. North America. That's what I got out of it — Destroying Angel mushrooms grow all over North America."

"Yes, I remember," Maggie had agreed. "So the mushrooms could have come from anywhere. Even Central Park, right?"

"Not really," Wendell said, and now he looked a little smug, reminding Maggie that her character didn't have a corner on the smug market. All men could be smug, from time to time. "You see, when you look deeper — when I looked deeper — I found out that North America was a pretty broad term. When you get right down to it, there are lots of these mushrooms in Nova Scotia, that part of North America, and small pockets of them in some other areas."

"Like Rochester, New York?" Maggie asked, finally getting it. "You're kidding."

"Not kidding at all. They also grow in the San Francisco Bay area and someplace in Oregon, in the southern part of the state, I think. But they're not really native to North America, not our part of it anyway. They got to Rochester by way of being transplanted there along with some Norway Spruce trees that were planted in a park in the Irondequoit area north of Rochester — Durand Eastman Park, to be specific, in the nineteen-seventies sometime. I mean it, I'm a real fountain of information on Destroying Angel mushrooms now."

"My felicitations, *Left*-tenant," Saint Just said, lifting his glass to him, "you may at last have found your true calling. King of the encroaching mushrooms."

That earned him another kick.

"Cute, Blakely, but there's more. The mushrooms got their start in the park, under the spruce trees, but now they're even more widespread, living under oak trees, places like that. Residents in the Rochester area have to have been hearing about these mushrooms for years, how dangerous they are, all of that. And here's the kicker. These mushrooms are found there from late September through the end of October."

He sat back, smiling at Maggie.

"But it's May," she said. "Where did she get these mushrooms in May?"

Wendell shook his head. "No, no, you're not getting this, Maggie. Yes, it's May. And that means that Clarice Simon — we still don't know if Trigg was in on it, too — has been planning this for a long time. At least since last fall. Premeditated, cold-blooded murder. I think I've got enough for a search warrant for her house in Rochester. An ADA is checking on that now, dealing with the red tape because we're out of the city with this one. And, although we couldn't use it in court, having Clarice admit to what she did, on tape, would go a long way toward shutting the jail door on her, even if we get the warrant, because who knows how well she covered her tracks. This is not a stupid woman. We might get the warrants, and come up with bupkus."

"I agree with most everything you've said, *Left*-tenant," Saint Just interrupted. "Save one thing. Clarice Simon, although not a stupid person, has passed beyond her original intent, that of ridding the world of Kirk Toland, and gone on to impulsively dispatch a man Maggie assures me Clarice loved, adored. Something happened, *Left*-tenant, something unforeseen, and our Miss Simon is now desperate, uncontrolled, and definitely more dangerous."

"On tape," Maggie repeated, trying not to look at Saint Just, who would be figuring out what "on tape" meant any moment now — then go ballistic. "And this is where I come in? A little payback to Clarice for putting me through hoops — the wringer. Okay, let's do it."

And now she was doing it, and Saint Just had only agreed to the plan if he and Sterling were allowed to come along, be part of the action, protect Maggie if necessary.

She'd phoned Clarice early that morning, invited her to dinner at Tavern on the Green at six o'clock, to talk about funeral arrangements for Nelson Trigg, a small memorial scholarship Maggie wanted to set up in both his and Kirk Toland's names. She couldn't believe Clarice had swallowed that one, but she had, and the date was set.

Maggie had been wired for sound and given an earpiece so she could hear Steve. The lieutenant, Alex, and Sterling were already inside the restaurant, ready to grab Clarice if the plan went south (that was how Steve had phrased it).

And here was Maggie, pacing outside the restaurant, waiting for Clarice to show up. She looked at her watch, saw that it was almost six, and walked to the nearby park entrance to watch for Clarice's arrival.

There were quite a few horse-drawn carriages in the area, both a little way down the path from the restaurant, and lined up on the street, where they probably weren't supposed to be. Crowds of tourists loaded down with cameras and maps were coming and going, a few of them stopping to listen to some idiot with a bullhorn who was standing on a box, yelling about the end of the world.

New York City. You had to love it. Stand in one spot long enough, and you saw everything. Heard everything.

The man yelled through the bullhorn. "Heed me, people, for it's true, the End Is Near. Yes! Within the year! The Four Horsemen will ride out — Death, Famine,

War . . . um . . . um . . ."

"Pestilence," Maggie said as she smiled and shook her head, looked for Clarice. Then she saw her approaching from the direction of Columbus Circle.

The woman looked terrible, dressed once more in that heavy black suit, that same white blouse with the slightly worn collar. She'd pulled her hair back in a bun, which seemed somehow to sink her eyes deeper into her head.

"Clarice, sweetheart," Maggie said, opening her arms to the woman, sure she would burst into tears at any moment.

Clarice walked into her arms, held her close, patted at her, actually. "Oh, Maggie, Maggie, thank you for asking me here today. But I can't. I really can't. I was here with Nelson, you know, last Christmas, for the Toland Books holiday party. I . . . I can't be here today."

Maggie stepped back and tried to pull her hair back over her ear — the one with the audio plug in it. "But . . . but I have reservations. Are you sure?"

The woman's eyes narrowed slightly, if that was possible. "Oh, yes, Maggie, I'm sure. I tried calling you, but you were already gone. I bought some cold cuts and things, have them back at my apartment. I really can't be in public right now, I look terrible. And I wanted to show you my photo album. I have so many wonderful pictures of Nel— Mr. Trigg."

"Yeah, well . . . pictures, huh . . ." Maggie began to agree, then mentally slapped herself. "But no, no. Going all the way down to the Village, in this traffic? Why don't we just go somewhere closer, leave the album for another day? Clarice? Wait — don't flag down that . . . oh, shit."

"*Break it off, Maggie,*" Steve's voice said into her ear. "*She might smell a trap. Break it off; come inside to us.*"

"Damn, we were so close. Okay, I'm no hero; I'm breaking it off." Maggie headed into the street, where Clarice stood, one arm raised, to flag down a cab. "Clarice? I really don't have the time right now. I'm sorry I chose the wrong restaurant, but we can reschedule, okay?"

Clarice turned to her, those deep-set eyes mere slits. "I *said* we're going to my apartment, Maggie. You really should listen to me."

"*Maggie, now! Screw polite. Get out of there, damn it! Blakely, stay here. Just stay the fuck here. I'm on the move, Maggie, coming at you.*"

Maggie looked down, at the way Clarice's

right hand was jammed into the pocket of her suit jacket, the way the jacket pocket bulged.

"You're kidding, right? You don't have a gun in there. You don't really think I believe that."

"Oh, but I do, Maggie; I do expect you to believe it. My caretaker called me, you know. Just as I was leaving my apartment to meet you. He called me from my house in Rochester. The police were there, with a warrant. If I'm going down, first I'm going to get rid of you, you nosy bitch, because I'll bet you had something to do with it. A memorial scholarship for that pig Nelson? Give me a break."

"Shit. First time an ADA got off his ass this fast. She's got a gun? Maggie, stall her; I'm on my way. You! Get the hell out of my way — police business." Maggie heard crashing, as if Steve had run full-tilt into a waiter carrying a dozen plates, heard Alex asking questions, heard Steve's heavy breathing, more than a few curses.

Maggie got the sinking feeling that, at least for the next sixty seconds, she was on her own. She started backing up, ready to run like a rabbit. It was harder to hit a moving target, right?

A cab pulled to the curb and Clarice

backed up two paces herself, opened the back door with her left hand, her right hand still in her pocket.

"You want me to get into a cab, Clarice? This cab? Cab ten-forty-seven? Big yellow —"

"Would you just shut the hell *up!*" Clarice pulled the gun from her pocket. "I'm not kidding, Maggie. Get in the cab, or I'll do you here. I've got nothing to lose."

"Do me? *Do* me? Man, you do read a lot of murder mysteries, don't you? Oh, okay, okay, don't get nervous. I'm going."

"First pull that earplug out of your ear and hand it over. Or did you think I didn't notice it when I was patting you down? You're probably wearing a wire, too, but at least you won't be able to hear them, and I'll get rid of the wire soon enough."

Maggie gave Clarice the earplug, then got in the cab, surreptitiously reaching into her purse, her fingers closing around the silver gun. It was nuts, sure, but if Clarice could have a gun, then so could she, damn it. Fair was fair. Besides, she missed her earplug.

Clarice slid in beside her, gave the driver an address Maggie couldn't hear, then sat back, looked at Maggie, the gun once more in Clarice's pocket, but definitely aimed at her.

"I've got one, too, Clarice," Maggie said, feeling as if she were in the middle of a dream where anything could happen, and everything would work out just fine — just like in novels. Only, this time, she was going to be the hero. She sure wasn't going to lie down and play the wimpy victim. "No, really. Honest. I've got one, too. See?"

Maggie yanked the weapon from her purse, and pulled the trigger just as if she'd been doing it for years.

The top of the gun clicked, opened, a flame appeared, and Clarice Simon laughed rather maniacally as the cab pulled away from the curb. . . .

"Get up," Saint Just said, pulling on Wendell's arm as the cop slipped and slid on a floor covered in linguine in slippery, buttery clam sauce. "Come on, come on."

"I'm on it," Wendell said, pushing away the waiter who seemed to want to tackle him, pulling linguine from his hair. "Maggie says she's got a gun. She's got a gun? Maggie's got a gun?"

Saint Just was already moving again, quickly threading his way through the ridiculously overcrowded restaurant, around occupied tables jammed in closely together, past waiters loaded down with heavy trays. "She's got a cigarette lighter," he called back over his shoulder. "It was a small joke a very good cardplayer foisted on me, I'm afraid. She may have thought it was a real weapon. Sterling, do try to keep up."

Sterling, momentarily distracted by a waiter carrying the largest lobster he'd ever seen, quickly brought himself back to the moment and jogged after his friend.

Saint Just silently cursed himself for not removing the gun from Maggie's locked drawer once he'd discovered that Mare had tricked him, badly. But if he'd done that, Maggie would know he had access to her small hiding place, so he'd left it there, right beside her bag of Good & Plentys.

Saint Just felt panic rising in his chest and beat it down. Maggie probably had just tried to shoot Clarice Simon with a cigarette lighter. It was the outside of enough, it was ridiculous in the extreme — it was a chance taken that could have ended with Maggie very dead.

Saint Just, Wendell, and Sterling pushed their way through the throng of tourists awaiting their chance to pay way too much for chopped sirloin, and burst through the doors, into the fading sunshine.

"The cab. Where's the cab?" Wendell called out. "Cab ten-forty-seven? Shit! It's gone. Come on, we'll have to flag down a car, commandeer it. Damn chief, refusing to give me backup. Wait — Maggie's talking again."

Wendell stopped to listen, one hand cupped over his ear.

"I need to know something, Clarice. How did you do it? Better yet, why did you do it? And why The Trigger?"

"Why don't you do yourself a favor, Maggie, and sit there with your mouth shut. The wire, remember? Once I get that off you, then we'll talk. And keep smiling, so the cabbie doesn't suspect anything, or I'll shoot you right here."

"Clarice still has the gun on her, and knows she's wearing a wire," Wendell yelled, causing several heads to turn in his direction, then began running again, this time following in Saint Just's wake. "Hey, wait — what are you doing?"

Saint Just ignored him. He already had the bullhorn in his hand — and a pissed-off doomsayer on his heels — as he and Sterling bounded toward the first carriage waiting in line in the street outside the park.

Without breaking stride, he leapt up to

the box, grabbing the reins as the driver, who'd been drinking a Yoo-Hoo as he lounged on the seat of the large, two-seated open carriage, started yelling.

"Oh, do be quiet," Sterling said, huffing and puffing as he climbed in beside the driver. "It's not to worry, I assure you. Saint Just is at home to a peg with the ribbons, a capital fellow, and all of that. Saint Just? What about the *left*-tenant?"

"He's coming. Sterling, I need you up here, with me. Come along," he said, already kicking his foot against the brake to release it.

Sterling clambered onto the seat beside Saint Just and was handed the bullhorn. "What is this?"

The carriage moved away from the curb, just as Wendell flung himself into it, landing on the driver, the two of them falling onto the narrow floor of the carriage in a tangled heap.

"So happy you could join us, *Left*-tenant," Saint Just said as Wendell rummaged in his pocket to pull out his badge, which did very little to shut up the driver, who was, at the least, highly indignant.

"You again!" the driver yelled at Saint Just as he tried to pull himself back up on the seat.

"Yes, my good man, me again. How pleasant to see you. Sterling? Push the large button on the side of that instrument, if you please, and call through it, warning everyone out of our way."

"Call through it?" Sterling said, trying to inspect the bullhorn at the same time he attempted to hold onto the seat and not tumble into the street. "What should I say?"

"Say anything you like," Saint Just said, neatly cutting around a city bus, giving himself a clearer vision of the lanes of traffic in front of him. "Just do it."

Sterling sighed. "Oh, very well." He pushed the button, lifted the bullhorn to his mouth, and yelled: *"Ooo-ga, ooo-ga!"*

"Splendid, Sterling," Saint Just said, just as Wendell managed to finally right himself, climb the rear-facing seat, and stick his head between Saint Just and Sterling.

"Do you see it? Do you see the cab?"

"I see quite a number of cabs, *Left-*tenant, the roadway is thick with them," Saint Just yelled. He had to yell, because Sterling was becoming quite enamored of the bullhorn and kept shouting *Ooo-ga, ooo-ga!* for all he was worth. Argyle had been correct; the sound had an immediate effect on all who heard it, and then quickly got out of the way, pedestrians and vehicles both.

"Hey! Watch those wheels," the driver warned from the rear seat. "I just had those mothers painted! I'm *so* gonna sue your asses — the city, too. Just you wait."

"Hey, Bozo. How'd you like me to toss you out here?" Wendell asked the driver, who prudently shut up. "There!" he said a moment later, pointing toward the intersection at Seventy-seventh Street, just at the American Museum of Natural History. "Ten-forty-seven. See it? Stopped at the light. Oh, good girl, Maggie. Hold on, we're coming!"

Saint Just saw a sea of yellow vehicles, but followed Wendell's gesture, finally made out the number ten-forty-seven on one of the cabs. "I trust you have your pistol, *Left*-tenant? Once I'm past these few vehicles, I should be able to cut them off and stop the cab, but I'll be busy with the ribbons, leaving you to do the pretty, rescue the fair maiden you've put in jeopardy."

"Even when I'm liking you, you find a way to get a dig in. Okay, cowboy, I'm ready. Get past that limo and pull the horse to the left. Hurry up, before the light changes. Sterling — hit it!"

"*Ooo-ga, ooo-ga!*"

★ ★ ★

It was a good plan, and might have worked like the proverbial charm, if Clarice hadn't turned around and seen Saint Just and company bearing down on the cab in a horse and carriage.

She pulled the gun from her pocket and pointed it at the cabbie. "Go!" she shouted. "Come on, screw the light. *Go!*"

Some rather hysterical Arabic followed, and the cabbie stepped on the gas, shooting across Seventy-seventh Street.

Maggie looked through the rear window, saw the carriage, saw Saint Just up on the box, Sterling beside him. She *heard* Sterling. And then, her eyes widening, she watched as Saint Just — magnificent Saint Just — neatly slipped the carriage between a limo and a UPS truck with only the slightest feathering of the off-wheel, then urged the horse into a near gallop, so that the carriage was soon side-by-side with the cab.

That was when Maggie saw Steve Wendell, trying to stand up on the rear-facing seat, balancing himself against Saint Just's shoulders. He finally got himself steady, his gun drawn and held in his right hand, and *launched* himself onto the roof of the cab.

"Jesus," Maggie said, looking up. "I couldn't have written this one in a million years."

The cabbie, either frightened into it, or at last remembering that, praise Allah, he did have bulletproof glass between himself and his gun-toting passengers, slammed on his brakes just as the carriage pulled in front of him and cut him off. Two womanly screams, one imaginative Arabic curse, and two seconds later, the cab slammed into a hot-dog cart smack in front of the museum, scattering a crowd watching some street performers.

Maggie, who hadn't put on her seatbelt, was flung forward, hitting her head on the bulletproof glass, and lost consciousness, so that she didn't get to see Steve rip open the back door, grab the gun from Clarice's limp hand (people really, *really* should wear seatbelts), then drag the woman's semi-conscious body out of the cab.

In fact, when Maggie did open her eyes, it was to see a mime, face starkly white, eyes and lips painted, white gloves in front of him, pretending to lean on the glass, and making faces at her through the side window.

That was when she finally screamed, then promptly fainted.

★ ★ ★

"I knew I'd get her sooner or later. Karma, or something like that," Dr. Thompson said as he stepped from behind the privacy curtain in the Lenox Hill ER, looked at the trio who had been waiting for him. "Hey, she's fine, really. She's got quite an egg on her head, but she's fine. Now, is somebody going to tell me what's happening? I'm thinking about writing a book."

"Isn't everybody?" Maggie called out from behind the curtain, proving that she was, indeed, all right.

"I want chocolate. Why do I want chocolate? I can actually smell it. And garlic. Man, do I smell garlic."

"Those would probably both be me," Steve Wendell said, pulling at his knit shirt, the one covered in dried Yoo-Hoo and clam sauce. "I'm going to have to start keeping a change of clothes at the station house. Are you sure you're up to hearing this now? It's pretty late. Man, can that woman talk."

Maggie snuggled back against the couch cushions, fingering the soft afghan Sterling had covered her with when she'd first returned from the hospital. "Oh, no, I won't sleep at all until I hear what Clarice told you."

"I agree," Bernice said, pouring herself a second cup of coffee, apparently having taken some sort of pledge, for no good reason except that the pot was on the coffee table, handy. "What did she tell you?"

"Told me, told the female officer who strip-searched her, told the tech who took her fingerprints, told everyone within ten miles. She just won't shut up," Wendell said, shaking his head. "I really think she's proud of herself. Either that, or she's trying to get around the Miranda, which isn't going to work, because I've got that one on tape, twice. And remember, you're not hearing any of this from me, okay?"

"I rarely hear anything you say, *Left*-tenant," Saint Just said as he strolled into the room from the kitchen. He sat down on the facing couch beside Sterling, who had already begun making inroads on the take-out chicken Wendell had brought with him. "But I do believe I'll make a small exception in this case, as I find myself fairly agog with curiosity. So, which one of us was right?"

"All of us," Wendell said, pulling out a chair from the game table and straddling it. "And none of us. Maggie, you were right and wrong about the phone call. Clarice called, not to hear about the menu, but only to make double-sure Toland was still coming to dinner, because she wanted him to get sick here, in your apartment, and she couldn't chance asking him directly, since the two rarely talked about anything."

"That's true enough," Bernie said. "I don't think Kirk even remembered her name, and she's worked for Toland Books for nearly ten years. Or five. With Clarice, who remembers? But why was it so necessary for her to know Kirk was coming here?"

"Why? Because, according to Clarice, Maggie writes a pretty good murder mystery, and she wanted to have her so involved that she'd have to try to solve this one. Match wits with her. Then she could sit back, watch, and know she was smarter than the great Cleo Dooley. As long as she was killing somebody, and this is nearly a direct quote, she might as well have some fun with it. The woman's a little twisted. Make that a lot twisted."

"Gee, that makes me feel all warm and cozy," Maggie said, adjusting the ice bag she held pressed to the mouse on her forehead. "The bad part is that she did have me fooled, but for all the wrong reasons, apparently."

"And the coffee? The bus?"

Wendell gave a small nod of his head. "You were closer, Blakely. Clarice did push you into the street, into the side of the bus, because she overheard Trigg hinting to you about something she didn't want you to know."

"Ah, did he? I suppose you mean his mention of some *problems* with the books? I had no idea. Although I would have, eventually. Still, I did come to the correct conclusion, didn't I? Clarice Simon is our killer, and I knew it first."

"That's you, Saint Just," Sterling said, beaming with pride. "Sharp as needles."

Wendell shook his head. "Yeah, sure. Anyway, she didn't make the coffee. Not that day, anyway. She did make it the day Toland came to dinner here, got sick here."

"Ah, at last we know when the poison was administered. Good."

"Glad to make you happy, Blakely. Anyway, she made the coffee and laced the raw honey with dried and, it would appear, highly concentrated Destroying Angel mushrooms. We'll know just how concentrated when we get the stuff to the lab. She served the poisoned honey to Toland when he came to Trigg's office, to talk about your new contract, Maggie, how Toland had talked to Mrs. Leighton about it over lunch, about how he was going to get you back in the sack, keep you in line. Sorry. That's Clarice quoting Toland here, not me. The wine, the mushrooms you served, Maggie, were all just little bonuses meant to confuse us for a while, because you're right. Clarice knew you always served steak and mushrooms. Kirk Toland was a dead man the moment he accepted that cup of coffee."

Saint Just crossed one leg over the other and fingered the riband of his quizzing glass. "And the mushrooms? She had them dried — as you call it — and ready to go? Why?"

Wendell smiled. "Okay, here's the neat part. Well, not for everybody. One, Clarice didn't just have mushrooms. I've only got a partial listing faxed to me so far, but that house of hers in Rochester? It's stuffed with poisons, illegal weapons, books on poisons and weapons, and enough murder mysteries to start her own library, to hear the ADA up there tell it. It would seem your quiet little mouse is more than just fascinated with murder. She's got her own murder *shop*."

"Everyone should have a hobby; that's what I always say," Sterling said, obviously not quite getting everything that was going on at the moment.

Wendell laughed. "Good one, Sterling. Oh, and in case you're wondering, the house in Rochester doesn't belong to her dead parents, and it's no little duplex. It's a freaking mansion, on about twenty-five acres, and it's all hers, bought about three years ago."

"But how did she —"

Wendell held out his hands, so that Maggie let her question hang. After all, it definitely did seem to be his turn to talk. She sneaked a look at Saint Just and saw that he, too, was more than a little interested.

"Here's what we've got, Maggie, everybody. Trigg used to take a couple of bucks here, a couple of bucks there, and always replaced every penny. Criminal, but not a full-scale embezzler. He just sort of *borrowed*. But Clarice? Oh, no, not Clarice. She's been robbing the place blind for years."

"Whoa, time out. How blind?" Bernie asked, sitting up very straight.

"Damn," Maggie said, lowering the ice bag. "You'd think she'd dress better, live better."

"And she does, in Rochester. But she was smart. Hey, just ask her, she'll tell you. If she started throwing money around here, in the city, everyone would notice. In Rochester, everyone thought she'd inherited a fortune from some dead aunt. The cops who searched the place found passbook accounts for several off-shore banks, jewelry, clothes out the wazoo, antiques, you name it — along with her branch office of Murder Incorporated and a boy toy named Lance they discovered relaxing in a tanning bed, who is still swearing he doesn't know what the cops up there are talking about. Your little mouse was leading a doozy of a double life. But she made one mistake. Two, actually."

"They all do," Saint Just said, flicking a bit of lint from the knee of his khakis.

"Hey, over here," Bernie said, waving her hands at Wendell. "Screw the boy toy. How blind? We're talking about my money here, you know."

Maggie patted Bernie's hand. "Shhh, let him finish. Steve? What was her biggest mistake?"

"That's easy. Once started, she couldn't quit." Wendell reached behind him to grab a handful of pretzels from the bowl on the table. "If she quit, the discrepancies would show up, and she'd be busted. So, she decided that the place in Rochester had to go. All of it had to go, most of it overseas, with her. She was already on the move, the mansion up for sale, and the Rochester police found a box full of fake passports, other ID. That's becoming more and more of a bitch for us. It's getting so that every guy with a home computer can fake that stuff."

"How interesting," Saint Just said, looking at Maggie, who had reluctantly agreed that Mare's forged ID's were pretty damn good. Nearly good enough to have Saint Just forgive the little pink-haired minx for that small joke she'd played on him.

"Interesting, but not perfect. See, she made another mistake. She got too greedy. She let the five million dollar life insurance policy on Toland lapse last month, pocketing the yearly premium as a sort of going-away present to herself. I take it the premium on a five million dollar policy is pretty hefty. You remember that policy? Ms. Toland-James mentioned it. Toland got a call from the insurance company and went ballistic, asked Trigg what the hell happened. That was the Friday before the murder. Toland's murder."

"Oh, shit." Bernie collapsed against the couch cushions. "Oh — *shit!*"

"Okay, I think I've got it now." Maggie sat up, feeling the tingle of excitement she always felt when a plot finally came together for her. "So, with Kirk asking about the lapsed policy, The Trigger starts digging into the books he let Clarice handle while he did his hamster routine on his treadmill. Clarice reads the writing on the wall, knows she's going to be caught just as she was about to get out, takes a quick trip to Rochester to see the boy toy, and pulls one of her handy-dandy poisons off the shelf — which just happens to be Destroying Angel mushrooms — and kills Kirk? Why? That would only delay things for what — a week or so?"

"Right. Which was how long she figured she needed to go back through the books, make it look like Trigg had been the one who took all the money. She was his assistant, but she really ran the place. Trigg, according to Clarice, only worked on his exercise routine. All she needed was a little time, and when the books were checked, and Trigg's personal accounts were checked, she'd be free and clear, and Trigg would be up a creek, for embezzlement, for murder. She even replaced the insurance company premium out of her own pocket that same Friday afternoon — that's a little joke, I guess — and the insurance company bought her story that the check must have gotten lost in the mail."

Bernie's sigh was deep and heartfelt. "Friday afternoon. Friday afternoon *before* the murder? Okay, okay, so the policy was still in effect when Kirk died. Thank God. Jesus, I was getting a little worried there. Phew. I need a drink. Sterling, be a doll and get me some scotch. I don't think my knees are strong enough to get me from here to the bottle."

Wendell took a bite of pretzel. "You have to hand it to the woman. The container of raw honey and Destroying Angel mushroom? The raw honey Trigg used because he was a health nut? Only fingerprints on it belong to Trigg. We know that, because she told us so. It's sitting in the back of one of his file cabinets, for us to find. I've got someone over at Toland Books right now, picking it up. She wasn't very nice about that one, saying we're a little slow on the uptake."

Maggie couldn't sit still anymore. "But there's still the real stumper. I thought — we all thought — Clarice was nuts for Trigg. But she sure didn't sound nuts about him today, in the cab. And now you're saying that she was setting him up to take the fall for Kirk's murder right from the get-go?"

"Only to end by killing Trigg herself," Saint Just said as Sterling shook his head, *tsk-tsked.* "As William Congreve said so well, 'Heaven has no rage like love to hatred turned, nor hell a fury like a woman scorned.' "

Wendell looked at him and nodded. "Yeah, all of that. She may have loved him once, but she loved money more, loved being smarter than everyone else even more than that. Clarice had put the life insurance premium back, set up Trigg to take the fall for Toland's murder, thought she was home free, and went back to planning her exodus to parts unknown. She even enjoyed herself watching you, Maggie, try to talk yourself out of being a suspect. And that's where you guys come in, screw up the works for her."

"Of course," Saint Just said, lifting his chin. "How?"

"With your little parlor sleuthing, or whatever you want to call it. Trigg panicked when you guys started asking him about his gambling problem, the chance of an audit. He started going back over the books, making doubly sure he'd put everything back that he'd taken, and began finding places where Clarice had been playing. She was sticking close as glue to him, watching him check the books, ready to pounce if he got too smart too fast."

"You know for sure that he ever found the discrepancies?" Saint Just asked him. "He didn't seem overly concerned about the books when I visited him, and he was dead shortly after that."

Wendell looked to Maggie. "True. But when Clarice came back from her little run down the block — to push Blakely into the bus — Trigg confronted her about the lapsed insurance policy, how she could have said the check had been lost in the mail when the records he'd just checked showed that it was supposed to have been an automatic withdrawal from one of the Toland Books accounts. It was definitely the wrong question to ask her. Trigg turned his back, and she nailed him with one of the hand weights. Several times. I mean, he was a mess."

"She spun out of control," Saint Just told Maggie, "just as I had predicted. One murder is seldom enough and, as is the way with a lie, only leads to another. But that was not what brought her down, was it? It was her desire to confound you, which meant also confounding me — a vain gesture at best — that caused her inevitable downfall."

"Hey," Wendell said, getting up from his chair. "We would have solved this on our own."

"Would you have, *Left*-tenant? I wonder."

"Hey, who gives a flying — sorry, Maggie." Bernie threw back the rest of her scotch and put the heavy tumbler down on the coffee table. "What I want to know is — how much money did Clarice steal? A mansion, you said, right? Clothes, jewelry, the boy toy? What kind of numbers are we talking here?"

"Ms. Toland-James — Bernie?" Wendell said, picking up the empty glass and heading toward the liquor cabinet. "That was scotch you were drinking, right? How about I fix you another one, maybe make it a double?"

EPILOGUE

Hello, again.

We're doing rather well, rubbing along nicely, having survived those first, always awkward weeks in any new association, although Saint Just is pushing rather hard to have Clarence become a more important character, so that he might be coaxed to appear here in the apartment, clutching both his favorite pressing iron and his boot blacking to his breast.

Bernice, bless her, is coming to grips with her new situation. The house in the Hamptons is on the market, along with the plane and the yacht, although she swears she'd eat dirt before she'll sell the limo. A strong woman, Bernice.

Mrs. Leighton, Tabby, is quite pleased with Maggie's new contract, which actually made headlines in something called *Publishers Weekly*, thrilling the woman no end. Mrs. Leighton, Saint Just has commented, is easily amused.

Argyle, poor boy, is back to opening doors and carrying packages, as his high hopes were dashed when Mr. David Leighton and Mr. Frank Fortune had a falling-out over whether Argyle's most impressive appendage should be wrapped in something called neon, and the show was abandoned. But Argyle, always looking on the bright side of things, and all of that, is unfazed, and about to audition for yet another part. Saint Just, of course, is acting as his mentor.

The lieutenant is still numbered among our visitors, which appears to cheer Maggie, while Saint Just for the most part ignores him. Poor Saint Just, he has no idea what's going on inside him, having spent all his years until now totally heart free.

Maggie and Saint Just have begun work on another book, which at times causes a marked friction between them, so that I've taken to riding out on my scooter most days, exploring the city.

I'm still waiting for Alice to answer my letter, but am assured she will, in time.